DAWNLANDS

By the same author

History
The Women of the
Cousins' War:
The Duchess, the Queen
and the King's Mother

The Plantagenet and Tudor Novels
The Lady of the Rivers
The White Queen
The Red Queen
The Kingmaker's Daughter
The White Princess
The Constant Princess
The King's Curse
Three Sisters, Three Queens
The Other Boleyn Girl
The Boleyn Inheritance
The Taming of the Queen
The Queen's Fool
The Virgin's Lover
The Last Tudor
The Other Queen

Order of Darkness Series
Changeling
Stormbringers
Fools' Gold
Dark Tracks

The Wideacre Trilogy
Wideacre
The Favoured Child
Meridon

The Tradescants
Earthly Joys
Virgin Earth

Modern Novels
Alice Hartley's Happiness
Perfectly Correct
The Little House
Zelda's Cut

Short Stories
Bread and Chocolate

Other Historical Novels
The Wise Woman
Fallen Skies
A Respectable Trade

The Fairmile Series
Tidelands
Dark Tides

Children's Books
The Princess Rules
It's a Prince Thing
The Mammoth Adventure

PHILIPPA GREGORY
DAWNLANDS

**SIMON &
SCHUSTER**

London · New York · Sydney · Toronto · New Delhi

First published in Great Britain by Simon & Schuster UK Ltd, 2022

Copyright © Vivat Publishing Ltd, 2022

The right of Philippa Gregory to be identified as author
of this work has been asserted in accordance with the
Copyright, Designs and Patents Act, 1988.

1 3 5 7 9 10 8 6 4 2

Simon & Schuster UK Ltd
1st Floor
222 Gray's Inn Road
London WC1X 8HB

Simon & Schuster Australia, Sydney
Simon & Schuster India, New Delhi

www.simonandschuster.co.uk
www.simonandschuster.com.au
www.simonandschuster.co.in

A CIP catalogue record for this book
is available from the British Library

Hardback ISBN: 978-1-4711-7289-2
Trade Paperback ISBN: 978-1-4711-7290-8
eBook ISBN: 978-1-4711-7291-5
Audio ISBN: 978-1-3985-1279-5

Family tree designed by Jill Tytherleigh

Typeset in Plantin by M Rules
Printed and bound by CPI Group (UK) Ltd, Croydon, CR0 4YY

DAWNLANDS

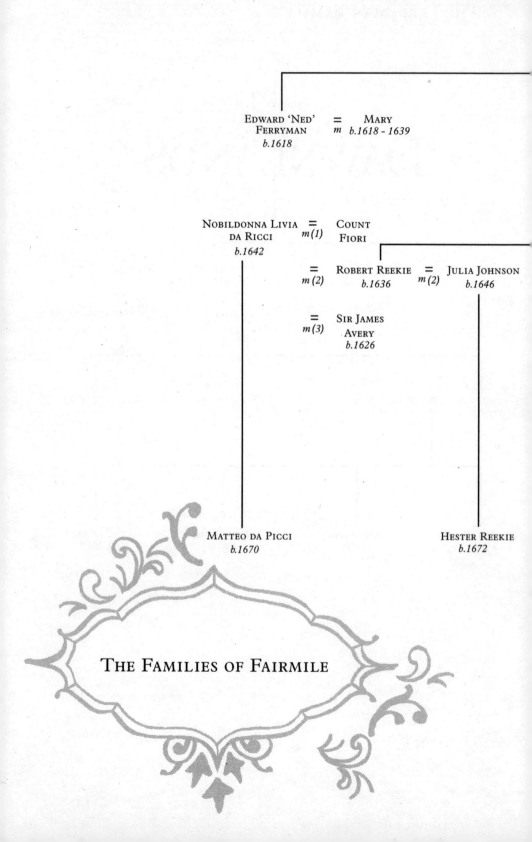

EDWARD 'NED'
FERRYMAN
b.1618

=   MARY
m   *b.1618 - 1639*

NOBILDONNA LIVIA
DA RICCI
b.1642

=   COUNT
m(1)   FIORI

=   ROBERT REEKIE   =   JULIA JOHNSON
m (2)   *b.1636*   *m (2)*   *b.1646*

=   SIR JAMES
m(3)   AVERY
b.1626

MATTEO DA PICCI
b.1670

HESTER REEKIE
b.1672

THE FAMILIES OF FAIRMILE

The Ferryman Family

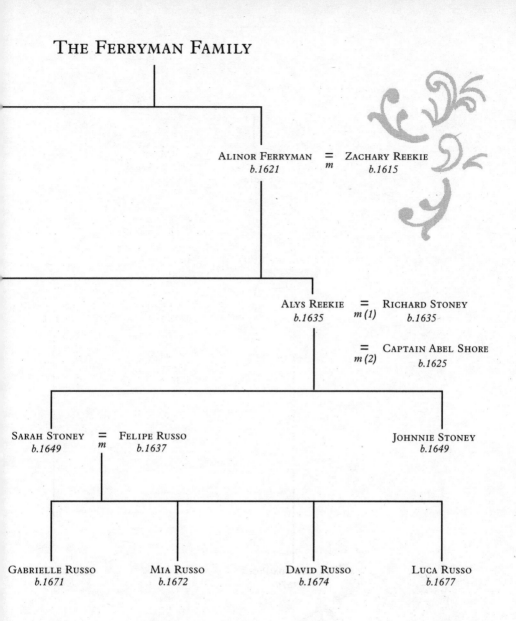

Alinor Ferryman
b.1621
= *m*
Zachary Reekie
b.1615

Alys Reekie
b.1635
= *m (1)*
Richard Stoney
b.1635

= *m (2)*
Captain Abel Shore
b.1625

Sarah Stoney
b.1649
= *m*
Felipe Russo
b.1637

Johnnie Stoney
b.1649

Gabrielle Russo
b.1671

Mia Russo
b.1672

David Russo
b.1674

Luca Russo
b.1677

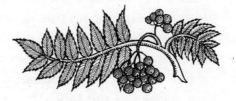

NORTHSIDE MANOR,
YORKSHIRE, SPRING 1685

Livia Avery came down the grand staircase of Northside Manor in a tailored black velvet riding habit, her gloved hand lightly on the bannister, the heels of her riding boots clicking on the polished wood. Her husband Sir James, crossing the stone-floored hall, looked up and noted the letter in her hand and the flush in her cheeks.

'So, you finally get your wish,' he said levelly. 'You've waited most patiently. It's been five years since you met the duchess, and now she is queen. I thought you had given up.'

She took a little breath. 'I never give up.' She showed him the royal seal.

'Is it a royal summons?'

'We can't speak here!' she ruled and led the way into the library. Large logs smouldered in the hearth; she undid the mother of pearl buttons on her dark riding jacket and pulled at the cascade of fine lace at her throat. He observed her beauty with nothing but weariness. She was like the classical statues she had dotted around his house and gardens – lovely to look at, but meaningless to him.

She sat in the great chair before the fire, leaning slightly forward, her face glowing in the firelight as if posing for a portrait. Her hair was still glossy black, the creamy skin smooth on her cheeks, a few light lines around her dark-lashed eyes. She waited for him to take his seat opposite her before she would speak.

'I'm all ears,' he said ironically.

'I am summoned to court,' she breathed. 'James, Duke of York is to be crowned king, his wife is queen. There is no support for the late king's bastard. James the Second will inherit without challenge and my dearest friend Mary of Modena will be queen.' She was as exultant as if she had herself persuaded the people of England to crown the unpopular roman catholic brother to the king, instead of the adored protestant bastard son. 'She writes that she needs me, she is unwell. I will, of course, obey.'

Still he said nothing.

'You could come with me? I am to be a lady-in-waiting, we could open Avery House? I could get a place at court for you. This could be a fresh start for us.'

He cleared his throat. 'I'm not sure that I want a fresh start. I doubt that I'd want anything you can give me.'

Her dark eyes flashed with irritation. 'You cannot expect me to refuse a royal invitation; it's practically a command.'

He turned his face from her show of temper. 'Really? I imagine that you could very well refuse. But I am absolutely certain you have courted her – writing every week, sending little gifts, all your engaging tricks – I imagine you have begged her to invite you. And now: she does.'

'You should be grateful to me . . .'

'You can go.' He had no interest in what she might say. 'I will send you in the carriage. I imagine you will live at St James' Palace while they rebuild Whitehall. I assume you will return here when they go to Windsor in the summer?'

'You agree?' she demanded.

He shrugged. 'You may do as you wish. As always. You are aware that the court is famously—' He broke off, searching for the right word. 'Extravagant,' he said. 'Corrupt,' he added. 'Lascivious. But you will not mind that.'

She raised her eyebrows as if in disdain; but her face was pale. 'You can hardly think that I—'

'No, I believe that you are quite above weakness. I am quite sure you will lock your bedroom door in London as you do here. Perhaps there, you will have reason.'

'Of course, my reputation will be without stain.'

'And you should be discreet in the practice of your faith.'

She tossed her head. 'Her Grace – I should say Her Majesty – and I are proud of our shared faith,' she said. 'She will open the royal chapel in St James' Palace. She is appointing the Benedictine order—'

'London will not tolerate roman catholics practising religion in public,' he told her. 'You may attend the queen's oratory inside the palace, but I advise you not to show off in chapels outside the palace walls. There's bound to be trouble, perhaps even worse than we've had already. Their Majesties should be as discreet as the late King Charles.'

'We're not all turncoats!' she flashed.

'I renounced my roman catholic faith to live my life as an English gentleman,' he said steadily. 'The Church of England is my faith; not a failing.'

She thought his whole life was a failure: he had changed his faith, he had betrayed his first love, Livia herself had played him for a fool, and trapped him into marriage for his name and fortune.

'I am roman catholic,' she told him proudly. 'More so now, than ever. All of England will return to the true faith, and it is you who will be in the wrong.'

He smiled. 'I do admire how your devotion increases with the fashion. But you had far better be discreet.'

She looked at the fire, the heavy wooden carving of his coat of arms on the mantelpiece, and then to him, her dark eyes melting, a little smile on her lips. 'James, I want to talk to you about my son.'

He settled himself a little deeper into his chair as if he would dig his heels into the Turkey rug.

'Once again, I ask you to adopt him and make him your heir.'

'And once again, I tell you I will not.'

'Now that I am bidden to court—' she began.

'He is no more my son than he was before. And I doubt you were bidden.'

'He has been educated at the best schools in London, he will eat his dinners at the Inns of Court, he is being raised as an English gentleman by the family that you chose for him. You can have nothing against him.'

'I have nothing against him,' he agreed. 'I am sure he is being raised well. You left him with a family of high morals and open hearts. He can visit you in London if you wish – but you may not go to the warehouse and see them, his foster family. You may not disturb them or distress them. That was agreed.'

She folded her lips on an angry retort. 'I've no wish to see them. Why would I go downriver to a dirty wharf? I don't wish to speak about them, I never even think about them! It is Matteo! We are talking about my son Matteo ...' She put her hand to her heart.

Unmoved, he watched her dark eyes glisten with tears.

'I have sworn that unless you make him your adopted son and heir, I will conceive no other,' she reminded him. 'My door will stay locked as we grow old, childless. I will never disinherit my boy. You will never have a legitimate son if you do not first give my son your name. You will die without a legitimate son and heir!'

He barely stirred in his chair, though she had raised her voice to him. 'You do know that I have rights to your body by law?' he confirmed. 'But – as it happens – I do not assert my rights. There was never any need for you to lock your bedroom door. I don't want to come in.'

'If you want to live like a priest!' she flamed out at him.

'Rather a priest than a fool,' he replied calmly.

She put her hand to the back of her neck, pinning back one of the dark ringlets that fell over her collar. She made her voice warm and silky. 'Some would say you are a fool not to desire me ...'

He looked at the flames of the fire, blind to the seductive gesture. 'I was led down that road once,' he said gently. 'Not again. And you're what? Forty-five? I doubt you could give me a son.'

4

'I'm forty-two,' she snapped. 'I could still have a child!'

He shrugged. 'If I die without an heir then so be it. I will not give my honourable name to another man's son. An unknown man at that.'

She gritted her teeth, and he watched her fight her temper. She managed to smile. 'Whatever you wish, Husband. But Matteo has to have a place of his own. If he cannot be an Avery of Northside Manor then he has to be da Picci of Somewhere.'

'He can be da Picci of Anywhere; but not here. I have nothing against the boy, and nothing against you, Livia. I acknowledge you as my wife and him as your son. You won my good name when you deceived and married me, but that was my own folly and I have paid for it. Your son will not enter into my estate, but he is free to make his own fortune if he can, or batten off you if he cannot.'

'If you're still thinking of her and her child . . .'

His face showed no emotion. 'I have asked you not to speak of her.'

'But you think of her! Your great love!'

'Every day,' he conceded with a smile as if it made him happy. 'I never pray without naming her. I shall think of her until I die. But I promised her that I would not trouble her. And neither will you.'

BOSTON, NEW ENGLAND, SPRING 1685

Ned Ferryman stood on the jumble of quays and piers and wharves of Boston harbour, his collar turned against the cold wind, watching his barrels of herbs – dried sassafras, black cohosh roots and ginseng leaves – roll down the stone quay and up the gangplank to the moored ship. Six barrels were already stowed below decks and Ned squinted through the hatch to make sure that they were lashed tight and covered with an oilskin.

Beside him on the quayside the master of the ship laughed shortly. 'Not to worry, Mr Ferryman, they're safely aboard.' He glanced down at Ned's worn leather satchel and the small sack of his goods. 'Is this all you have for your cabin? No trunks?'

'That's all.'

The cabin boy from the ship came running down the gang-plank and scooped up the sack. Ned slung the satchel around his shoulder.

'You'll have heard the king's dead?' the captain asked. 'I was the first ship to bring the news. I shouted it the moment we threw a line to shore. Who'd have thought a king that lived so wild would die in his own bed? God bless King Charles, lived a rogue and died a papist. His brother James will have nipped on the throne by the time we get home.'

'Only if they crown him,' Ned remarked sceptically. 'James the papist? And that papist wife alongside him?'

'Eh – I don't care for him myself – but what choice is there?'

'The Duke of Monmouth, the king's own son, a man who promises liberty, and freedom to choose your own religion.'

'Born a bastard. And we can't send a Stuart king on his travels again. We've only just got them back.'

A rare smile crossed Ned's stern face. 'I don't see why they can't go again,' he said. 'What has any Stuart ever done for a working man?'

'We'll know when we get there,' the captain summed up. 'We sail with the tide, just after midday. There's a noon gun.'

'Aye, I know Boston,' Ned said shortly.

'You've been here a while?' The captain was curious about his quiet passenger, his deeply tanned skin and his shock of grey hair. 'It's a great city for making a fortune, isn't it?'

Ned shook his head. 'I don't care for a fortune, stolen from natives who gave all they had at first. I make a small living, gathering herbs. But now it's time for me to go home. I'll be aboard before noon.'

He turned from the quayside to go back to the inn to settle his slate. Coming from the opposite direction, tied in a line with tarry ropes, were a score of prisoners trailing their way to a ship for the plantations. Ned could tell at once that they were the people of several different Indian nations: the high top-knots and shaven heads of some and others had a sleek bob. Each face showed different tattoos: some high on the cheekbones or some marked straight across the forehead. There were even one or two wearing the proud all-black stain of 'warpaint': the sign that a man was sworn to fight to the death. They were roped in a line, dressed in a muddle of ragged English clothes, shivering in the cold wind, alike in their shuffling pace – hobbled by tight ropes – and in the defeated stoop of their shoulders.

'*Netop*,' Ned whispered in Pokanoket, as they went past him. '*Netop*.'

Those who were closest heard the greeting – 'Friend' in their forbidden language – but they did not look up.

'Where they going?' Ned asked the red-faced man who was herding them, his hands in his pockets, a finely carved pipe clamped in the corner of his mouth.

'Sugar Islands.' He turned his head and barked: 'Wait!'

Obediently, the line shuddered to a halt.

'God help them,' Ned said.

'He won't. They're all pagans.'

Dourly, Ned turned away, spitting out the bitter taste in his mouth, when he half-heard a whisper, as quiet as a leaf falling in the forest:

'*Nippe Sannup!*'

He turned at the familiar sound of his name in Pokanoket: 'Waterman'.

'Who calls me?'

'*Webe, pohquotwussinnan wutch matchitut.*' A steady black gaze met Ned's. A youth, beardless and slight. There was no pleading in his face but his lips formed the words: '*Nippe Sannup.*'

'I need a boy, a servant,' Ned lied. 'I'm going to England. I need a lad to serve me on the ship.'

'You don't have to buy one of these,' the man advised him. 'Just shout in the inn yard and half a dozen little white rats will pop up their heads, desperate to get home.'

'No, I want a savage,' Ned improvised rapidly. 'I collect Indian herbs, and pagan carvings. Things like your pipe – that's savage work, isn't it? My goods'll sell better with a savage lad to carry them around. I'll buy one of 'em off you now,' Ned said. He pointed to the youth. 'That one.'

'Oh, I couldn't let that one go,' the man said at once. 'He's going to grow like a weed that one: thicken up, broaden out, going to be strong. I'll get good money for him.'

'He won't last three seconds in the fields,' Ned contradicted. 'The voyage alone'll kill him. There's nowt on him and he's got that look in his eyes.'

'They die just to disoblige me!' the jailor said irritably. 'They don't take to slavery. Nobody'd buy one, if you could get an African. But a slave's a slave. You've got it for life – however long it lasts. What'll you give me?'

'Fifty dollars, Spanish dollars,' Ned said, naming a price at random.

'Done,' the man said so quickly that Ned knew it was too much. 'Sure you want that one? Another pound buys you this one, he's bigger.'

'No,' Ned said. 'I want a young one, easier to train.'

'You hold the pistol while I untie him,' the jailor said, pulling a pistol from his belt, showing it to the prisoners who turned their heads away as if in disdain. He pressed it into Ned's hands. 'If anyone moves, shoot them in the foot: right?'

'Right,' Ned said, taking the heavy firearm in his hand and pointing it at the huddled crowd.

The jailor took a knife out of his boot and slashed through the ropes on either side of the youth, pushing him, still tied and hobbled, towards Ned. He made the trailing ropes into two rough but serviceable loops and handed them to Ned, like the long reins for a young horse, as he took back his pistol.

Ned opened his satchel and counted out the coins. 'Does he have any papers?'

The man laughed. 'Do cows have papers?' he demanded. 'Do pigs? Of course he don't. But we can take him to the blacksmith and brand him with your initial on his cheek.'

Ned felt the cords in his hand tighten, as the slim youth braced himself against terror.

'No need,' he said. 'We sail in an hour. I'll load him on board now and lock him in my cabin.'

'Mind he don't drown himself,' the jailor said. 'They do it the moment they get the chance. Someone told me they think they will rise out of the waves on a muskrat.' He laughed loudly, showing his yellow stumps of teeth, rotted by sugar and rum.

'Yes, they do think that . . .' Ned remembered his friend telling him the Pequot legend of the making of the world: a muskrat bringing earth from the sea bed as a gift of life from the animal to the first woman in the world.

'Take a brace?' the jailor gestured. 'You can have another for the same price?'

'Nay.' Ned tugged gently on the rope that trailed from the lad's tied wrists and led the way to the ship. The boy followed with his shuffling walk. Ned did not look back, no white man looks for his slave, and the boy hobbled behind him.

Ned did not speak to the lad, not even when they were on board. He locked him in the windowless cabin and found the loadmaster and paid for another passage, a quarter price as it was a slave. He refused the offer to chain the boy in the cargo hold and pay for him as if he were baggage. He went back to the inn and bought a few shirts and a pair of breeches for the lad, and then he stayed on deck until the captain shouted, the gangway was drawn in, the ropes cast off and the bell towers and roofs of the city got smaller and smaller until the new city of Boston was just a smudge on the horizon, the sun sinking behind it. Ned stretched his aching back and went through the hatch and down the ladder to the tiny cabins below the deck.

The lad was seated on the floor, his head resting on his knees, as if he did not dare to touch the narrow bunk. When the door opened on Ned, carrying a gimballed candlestick in one hand, the bundle of clothes in the other, he rose to his feet, alert as a cornered deer. His breath came a little quicker but he showed no sign of fear. Ned, knowing the extraordinary courage of the Pokanoket, was not surprised. He put down the candle, the counterweight base moving gently with the ship to hold the candle upright.

'You know me,' Ned fumbled to remember the words of the banned language of Pokanoket. 'You called me *Nippe Sannup*.'

The youth nodded stiffly.

'Have you seen me in the wilderness? Have I traded with your people?'

The boy said nothing.

'Have your people traded furs with me? Or gathered herbs for me?'

Still there was no answer.

'What language do you speak?' Ned asked in the forbidden language of the Pokanoket, then he tried again in Mohawk.

'I can speak English,' the youth said slowly.

'What is your people?' Ned demanded.

The boy's face was expressionless but one tear rose up and rolled down his face. He did not brush it aside, as if the name that might never be spoken was Sorrow. 'We are forbidden to say our name,' he said quietly. 'I knew you when I was a child. You were *Nippe Sannup*, the ferryman at Hadley. My people took your ferry when the Quinnehtukqut was in flood.'

Ned felt the familiar sense of longing for that lost time. 'Fifteen years ago? When I kept the ferry at Hadley?'

The youth nodded.

'That was a lifetime. You must've been a child.'

'Are we at sea? Is the boat at sea?' he suddenly demanded.

'Aye.'

'You will not throw me over the side?'

'Why would I do that, fool? I just rescued you! And paid a fortune!'

'You have saved me from the plantations?'

'Aye, we're going to London.'

The youth gritted his teeth on the terror of another unknown destination. 'I thank you.'

Ned grinned. 'You don't look too thankful.'

'I am. You knew my grandmother, her name was Quiet Squirrel. D'you remember her? She made your snowshoes. D'you remember them? And my mother?'

'Quiet Squirrel!' Ned exclaimed. 'She did! She did make my snowshoes. And she taught me ... She taught me every—' He broke off. 'Is she ...'

'She's gone to the dawn,' the boy said simply. 'All my people are gone. All my family are dead. Just a few of us were captured alive. The village is gone. You can't even see the post holes. They burned us out and they ploughed our ground. They have made us ...' he sought for the word, '... invisible.'

Ned sat down heavily on the side of the bunk. 'Invisible? How can a people become invisible?' He had a sudden, vivid memory of the village of Norwottuck: the houses around the central fire, the children playing, the women grinding corn, the men dragging in a shot deer, the girls carrying long spears loaded with fresh fish. Impossible to think it was all gone, yet he knew it was impossible that it had survived the three years of bitter warfare. 'And you ...' He looked at the youth. 'Were you one of the little lads?'

The youth pressed his lips together as if he would hold in dangerous words, but he forced himself to speak. 'I met you when I was a child of six summers. You used to make me laugh when we crossed the river on your ferry. Back then, I was called Red Berries in Rain.'

Ned's eyes widened; he got to his feet, put his hand under the youth's chin, turned his face to the light of the candle. 'Red Berries in Rain?' he whispered.

There was a day in his mind, long ago, more than fifteen years ago, when the women had been on his ferry and they had been laughing at the little girl who had hidden behind her grandmother and peeped up at him with huge dark eyes. 'You're a lass?' he asked disbelieving. 'You're that little lass?'

She nodded. 'Please ... Please don't give me to the sailors,' she whispered.

'God's blood! D'you think I am a beast?'

She flinched from his outrage. 'The jailor gave my sister to the sailors.'

'I'd never do such a thing!' he swore. 'I'd never – well, you're not to know. But I have a sister in England! I have a niece! God knows, I'd never ...'

'I said I was a boy and they gave me a shirt and breeches.'

'Aye, it's best.' Ned gestured to the patched breeches and old shirts on the bunk. 'You'd better stay as a lad till we get to England. We'll say you're my serving boy.'

'Thank you,' she said. 'I don't want to be a girl until I am a girl of the Dawnlands again.'

'What'll we call you?' he asked. 'I can't call you Red Berries in Rain.'

'It was a mosmezi tree,' she offered. 'You had one growing by your gate. A slight tree with white flowers in spring, and in autumn: red berries? We use the bark for healing?'

'I remember,' he said. But he did not want the pain of remembering the tree at his gate, and the ferry across the river, and the women who had been his friends, and who had walked with him into the New England village, sure of their welcome, with baskets of food and fish on strings. 'It's a rowan tree,' he told her. 'We can call you Rowan. And here ...' He pushed the clothes towards her. 'You'd better get out of those rags, they're probably lousy. I'll get the galley to boil them.'

'Can I wash?' she asked.

He hesitated, knowing that at every dawn, her people would wash and pray, facing the rising sun. They were the People of the Dawnlands, they were the people of the long dark coast that was the first to see the sun every day. Of all the unknown peoples in all the great forests that stretched to the west far away behind them, they were the first to see the first light.

'Not like you do at dawn,' he told her. 'But I can get you a jug of water and some soap.' He put his hand on the latch of the door.

'Shouldn't I get it?' she asked him. 'As I am your slave? You're not mine.'

She surprised him into a laugh. 'Aye, I'm not. Come then, I'll show you the way to the galley and the stores, and around the ship. You should really sleep in the hold, but you'll be safer in my cabin. You can have the bunk, I'll take the floor.'

'No! No!' she refused at once. 'I sleep on the floor.' She looked up at him to see if he would smile again. 'I am your slave. You're not mine.'

'I'd never have a slave,' he told her. 'All my life I have believed that men – even women – should be free. I'm going back to England now to help set my countrymen free.'

She nodded, following the rapid words and watching his lips, so she saw his smile when it came. 'But you can sleep on the floor.'

'Because you have a niece?' she asked him with a gleam in her dark eyes.

'Because I am old enough to be your grandfather,' he said dourly. 'And as stiff in the morning as frozen laundry on a washing line.'

Ned had guessed she would wake before dawn and he was instantly aware of her, awake but silent. 'You'll want to see sunrise,' he said quietly into the pitch darkness.

'Can I?'

Outside Ned's door a ladder led upwards to a battened-down hatch. Ned went first, lifted the hatch and breathed the cold saltiness of the sea air. He put the cover aside, climbed out and turned to help her but she was already up on deck gulping in the clean breeze, her arms thrown wide as if she would have the wind blow through her clothes, blow defeat out of her soul.

The sky was lightening all around them, but the sun was not yet up. Ned raised his hand in acknowledgement to the steersman and led the way fore so that they were facing east, facing England. There was a clean bucket on a frosty rope for sluicing down the deck. Ned lowered it into the sea and felt it tug in his hands. He hauled it back in and put it at her feet. 'Best I can do,' he said, and stepped back.

Rowan looked out along the bowsprit to where the horizon gleamed with a cold pale light. She loosened the shirt at her neck; she did not dare stand naked as the ritual demanded, but she splayed her bare toes on the deck and stood tall, swaying slightly at the roll and dip of the ship through the waters. She took a cupped handful of icy water and poured it over her head, over her neck, another full into the face. She tasted the salt and opened her eyes. She whispered: 'Great Spirit, Mother Earth, Grandmother Moon, Grandfather Sun, I thank you. I pray to the four directions ...'

Carefully she turned to the four points of the compass, looking out over grey rolling waves east then north, south and west until she was facing the brighter horizon once more. 'I thank you for all my relations: the winged nation, the creeping and crawling nation, the four-legged nation, the green and growing nation, and all things living in the water. Honouring the clans: the deer – *ahtuk*, the bear – *mosq*, the wolf – *mukquoshim*, the turtle – *tunnuppasog*, the snipe – *sasasō. Keihtanit taubot neanawayean.*'

The head of a silvery sun was rising from the grey faraway waters as she murmured the prayer. She bowed her head and poured more water over her head, her face, her neck, her breast, as the sun rose. She looked towards it, as if it might tell her how she should survive this extraordinary transition in her life, from one world to another, from one life to another, from one country to another. She had no fear. She felt the strength in her feet on the scrubbed wooden deck, the powerful beating of her heart, and the limitless confidence of youth.

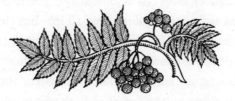

ST JAMES' PALACE, LONDON, SPRING 1685

If Livia was nervous, as the Avery carriage drove through the rolling deer park and turned into the great arched doorway, she showed no sign. As the coach rattled through the imposing north gatehouse, the wheels echoing loudly on the cobbles, guardsmen saluting the Avery crest on the carriage door, Livia settled her cape around her, tied the silk ribbons on her hat and straightened the ribbon bows over her shoulders. All she could see were the tall walls of red brick relieved with white pillars and mullioned windows. The carriage halted and the steps were let down. Livia's grip was firm on the footman's arm, her step light on the pavement. The lace edging on her hat did not tremble, the smile on her beautiful face was steady. Her tight bodice hid her breathlessness; the thick silk of her gown and her billowing petticoats swished around her as she followed the new queen's chief secretary into the first court, across the rigidly formal garden, through inner doors and up the stairs. Finally, the chief secretary nodded to two men at arms to throw open the double doors of the queen's presence chamber and announced: 'Lady Livia Avery, Your Majesty.'

The dark-haired queen was seated at the window, looking far younger than her twenty-six years, some fine embroidery in an ivory frame beside her, two maids of honour sorting embroidery silks on low stools beside her and two ladies-in-waiting opposite her. In the corner of the room a lutist and a singer created a gentle warble, enough to mask indiscreet conversations from the hearing of the servants who stood at the buffet of silver-ware. Queen Mary Beatrice was wearing a deep-red silk gown trimmed with silver lace, cut very low over her breasts and across her arms to show her white shoulders. Her slim neck was loaded with jewelled necklaces, she had diamonds in her ears and chains of diamonds wrapped around her arms. Her dark hair was piled on her head falling in ringlets to her shoulders. She turned a pale face to the door but as she saw Livia she lit up. 'Oh! Livia! My dearest Livia!' she exclaimed at once in Italian. 'You have come! In this terrible weather! You have come to bring the spring!'

Livia sank into a deep curtsey and kept her head down, but the queen raised her at once and fell into her arms. She was slight – beneath the flowing embroidered silks Livia could feel a body as slim as a girl. Over her shoulder Livia could see the grim faces of the other attendants as they noted the arrival of a new favourite.

'*Carissima*,' the queen whispered. 'I have longed for you. I will be grateful for all my life that you have come to me.' She turned. 'Are Lady Avery's rooms prepared for her?' she asked. 'The best rooms, near mine.'

Lady Isabella Wentworth rose up and dropped a small curtsey to Livia. 'Shall I show Lady Avery to her rooms?'

'No!' The queen turned impulsively. 'I'll come myself.' She paused for a moment, shaken by a cough. 'You all stay here,' she said, catching her breath. Defying protocol, she took Livia's hand and the two of them followed Lady Wentworth from the presence chamber, through the privy chamber, through the queen's bedchamber to a gallery of doors for the ladies-in-waiting. One was already painted with the Avery crest. Livia's dark eyelashes hid the gleam in her eyes at the triumph, but she said nothing and waited for the footman to dart forward and swing open the door. Lady Wentworth stepped back to allow her queen and Livia to enter first.

Livia's drawing room had a warm fire in the grate, a pair of silk upholstered chairs before it, an expensive rug on the floor. There was a grand mahogany table with six dining chairs under the window so that she could dine with friends and enjoy the view of the privy gardens and beyond them the rolling lawns of the deer park. There were portraits on the walls and a tapestry depicting a white hart being brought down by huntsmen. There were sconces with candles and candelabra on the tables holding pure white wax candles. Livia crossed the room and looked out of the window. She allowed herself to imagine the south bank of the river, far away, due east. The poor wharf, the cargo ships bobbing in dirty water, the little home where she had gladly left her son so that she could rise, unhampered to this greatness. She was pleased she could not see it – it was too far away – around the broad loop in the river, beyond London Bridge, beyond the Tower, far from the wealth and elegance of the royal palaces, far away from her new life.

'Is it all right?' the queen asked humbly.

Livia turned. 'It's quite all right,' she said smiling. 'It's perfect for me.'

REEKIE WHARF, LONDON, SPRING 1685

Beyond Livia's horizon, three and a half miles downriver, on the south bank, Ned stood for a moment to look at the Thames in flow, the waters rushing past the quay, the boats riding high, unladen, in the centre of the stream.

On the distant opposite bank Ned could see the river wall was being extended, the mud and pebbles of the foreshore enclosed by great beams packed with stone. The green weeds and water had dried out, the wading birds had deserted it. New buildings, streets, slums, hovels were being built on a tumble of stone and rubble. The city was spreading downriver, making more and more wharves for more and more ships as if trade itself were a new king that could demand selfish changes to England.

Rowan, close behind him, was dressed as a manservant: shoes and woollen stockings on her feet, wool breeches and a linen shirt and wool jacket under a warm travelling cape. A cap pulled low over her cropped dark hair completed the disguise. Ned led the way down the alley that ran between the warehouse and its neighbour, until he came to a lantern door set into the big wagon gates which were bolted and closed for the night. Inside the yard, he could hear someone bedding down horses, the splash of water being pumped into a bucket, and the bang of the stable door. He put his hand on the iron ring to open the little door, but she saw him hesitate.

'I can hardly go in. I've not seen my sister for twenty-five years. I never thought I'd come back.'

He turned the handle, opened the door and stepped through. It was a prosperous yard, swept clean around raised beds of herbs. There were four big horses nodding over the stable doors, and two carts stored in the cart shed. The double doors that led to the warehouse were safely locked, but the door to the kitchen was half-open. Ned could see the cook bending over a new cast iron stove. She turned as she heard the lantern gate and came to look over the bolted lower door, wiping her hands on her apron.

'Is it a load?'

'No,' said Ned. 'I've come to see Mrs Reekie.'

'If you want the herbs I can sell them.'

'I'm her brother, come home from New England. I'm Ned Ferryman.'

'Oh, my Lord!' she exclaimed and then clapped her hand to her mouth to stifle the oath. 'Oh, my word! Well! You're very welcome, Sir. Come in! Come in! You should have come to the front door, not in the yard like a carter. Come in, and I'll tell them you're here.'

She swung open the bottom half of the door and shouted to

the kitchen maid to come and take their bags. She went surging into the hall, to the parlour at the front of the house which overlooked the quay and the river. 'You'll never guess who's in the yard!' she exclaimed to the middle-aged couple in the room. 'You'll never guess.'

The woman rose to her feet. 'Of course I won't guess,' she said, a tolerant smile on her face. 'Who's come at this time of night to the yard gate, Tabs?'

'Your uncle Ned!' the cook exclaimed triumphantly. 'Who would ever've guessed that! Your uncle Ned from the Americas. Large as life and his lad at his side.'

Alys went swiftly past her to the kitchen and then checked as she saw the broad grey-haired man, swinging his satchel to the floor, and behind him, the most beautiful boy she had ever seen, dark haired, dark eyed, head up, light on his feet as a deer.

'Uncle Ned?' Alys asked uncertainly. 'Tabs said you were my uncle Ned?' and when he looked up and smiled at her, she said with sudden certainty: 'It *is* you!'

Alys' husband Captain Shore filled the doorway to the hall. 'Ned Ferryman?' he queried.

Alys was in Ned's arms, hugging him, patting him, pulling back to look into his worn grooved face. 'Uncle Ned, God bless you! We never thought to see you again!'

'I know. I never thought I'd come back. But here I am!'

'Praise God you're safe, after such travels!'

'Amen, amen. My sister Alinor is well?' He looked around for her.

'Yes – speaking of you only last night. And you know there's a new king on the throne? Crowned and anointed just last week? King James. Does that mean you're safe to come home now? And the troubles are all forgotten?'

'They're not all forgotten,' he said steadily.

'You've not come back to rise up again? You're not for the protestant duke?' she demanded anxiously, interrogating his face with a frowning gaze.

'Hush,' Captain Shore intervened. 'Come into the parlour,

Sir. I take it you're my uncle-in-law, and I am your nephew Abel Shore.'

'Congratulations, and I'm glad to meet you at last!' Ned said. 'I sent you some buckskins for your marriage bed.'

'I sleep under them every night,' the Captain said. 'Cosiest bedding I've ever had. Much needed this winter gone. We're grateful. And who's this?'

'My lad. This is my serving boy: Rowan.'

'Well, come in, both of you,' Captain Shore said. 'Have you dined?'

'There's enough for us all,' Alys assured him. 'The maid can run out to the bakehouse and get a chicken pie. Uncle Ned, I must take you upstairs to Ma at once. You know, she was speaking of you only last night. She dreamed of you, at sea on dark tides.'

'Aye, I wondered if she'd know I was on deep waters,' he said. 'But you'd better prepare her.'

'We'll wait for you down here,' Captain Shore said, waving Rowan back to the kitchen. 'You get warm in the kitchen, lad. And, Uncle Ned, if Mrs Reekie wants you to dine upstairs with her, Sir, you just say the word. Sometimes she comes down for dinner, sometimes she don't. It's always her wish, just as she wants.'

Ned followed his niece up the wooden stairs to the next floor. To his right was the door to his sister's room, and to his left the bedroom that Alys shared with her husband, and another door to the smaller spare room. The narrow stairs for the servants' rooms went up into the eaves of the roof.

Alys tapped on the door and went in, leaving it half-open. 'Ma,' Ned heard her say. 'Be steady, Ma. I have some news.'

'I can tell it's good news from your face,' he heard his sister reply.

At the sound of her voice he could not make himself wait any longer. He pushed open the door. 'It's me, Alinor. I'm come home.'

Alinor rose up from the sofa, her pale face flushed with joy, her hands outstretched to him. 'Ah, Ned! You've come home at last.' And in a moment, she was folded in his arms.

Later that night, after a bustle of preparation and dinner and drinking of healths and exchanging news, Ned went to Alinor's room to say goodnight and sat on the end of the sofa. 'I daren't keep you late,' he said. 'Alys gave me such a scowl. Are you tired?'

She put her hand to her chest where her breath came short. 'I'm too happy to be tired. I always thought I'd see you in this life again, Ned. But I never dreamed you'd come home like a merman out of water, without a word of warning.'

'I never thought I'd sit at a table with my family again. I've been solitary for so long.'

'But now you've got Rowan for company?'

'He's just with me for the voyage,' he said. 'I can't bear to keep a servant, Sister. You know my feelings. I paid for his passage over, but he's free.'

She slid a sideways look at him. 'Rowan? Named for a tree? Neither girl nor boy but a being from the forest?'

He smiled ruefully. 'Of course, you saw her at once. Aye, she's a lass. The grand-daughter of a woman who was kind to me when I was first in New England. They call themselves the Pokanoket, the People of the Dawnlands.' He corrected himself. 'No. Not any more. They did. They were the ones killed in the wars, and now their name is forbidden.'

'Have you escaped one war to wage another?' she asked him acutely.

He glanced to her closed bedroom door, as if even in her own house, he was wary of eavesdroppers. 'Aye, I got a message,' he said shortly. 'Old comrades tell me that the new king is a papist and a French spy. They say that no-one will stand for it, the people will rise again and put the Duke of Monmouth in as a new Lord Protector. Another Cromwell. So I came at once. Like an old horse at the sound of the trumpets! To see it happen – the freeing of the people. Once again.'

She nodded. 'It's true,' she said. 'Captain Shore keeps his own counsel, and we're far away from St James' palace, but even the merchants' coffee houses say that the new king prays like a papist in a foreign tongue, kneels for Mass with his foreign wife, and the court is bought and sold by France. There's not an honest man among them. And the young Duke of Monmouth is said to be in the Low Countries, building a fleet. They say he'll come to save us and the Church of England. The country'll be divided again into royalist against roundhead.'

'There'll be a war?' he confirmed. 'Another civil war?'

'Not for you,' she urged. 'Not for you who left England rather than be subject to a king. You've done enough, Brother. Come to watch if you must. But don't you risk a beating. You can't bear that grief again.'

His slow smile told her that he regretted nothing. 'Nay,' he said. 'All my life I've thought that God made man and woman, not kings and servants. I was proud to serve under Cromwell to set the men of England free. I was glad we won our freedom. I was sorry we gave it away again. I'd be proud to fight for the men of England once again.'

'We can't,' she told him. 'The family can't. We've taken years to build the warehouse trade, and now we have our own ship: Captain Shore's ship. We've bought the wharf next door, we trade in fine things from Sarah in Venice. Johnnie is a writer at the East India Company and Rob is a doctor, he's put up his door knocker in the City – our Rob! A proper doctor! We can't throw that away for the king's bastard. We can't do it, Ned. You can't ask it of us – not of the young ones when they're doing so well. Not of Captain Shore and Alys now they're settled.'

'No, no,' Ned said quickly, clasping her hand. 'Not any one of you. I'll go to Monmouth as a single man, without ties, without family. This is my battle – not theirs. If the Duke of Monmouth takes me into his service, I'll be Ned Ferryman come from New England to serve my countrymen – and nothing to link the Reekie wharf to me.'

'You'll think me chicken-hearted,' she said ruefully.

He shook his head. 'I wouldn't have you lose your home again. Once was enough.'

'It's not home,' she said quietly, thinking of their house beside their ferry on the tidelands. 'But it's a good living.'

''Course,' he agreed. 'And maybe I'll come out of this so well that I'll buy you a house at Foulmire, and you and I will end our days there, watching the waters rise and fall in the harbour, with no lord ruling over us and no king over England, and it'll be a new dawn.'

ST JAMES' PALACE, LONDON, SPRING 1685

The newly crowned queen was sick: bleached by the pain in her chest, in her back, cold despite the heaped lambswool covers on her bed. No doctor had been able to cure the cough which came and went with the seasons; the hard-hearted courtiers said it was a weakness of her family, and that she would die before she was thirty. She would see no-one but Livia who lay with her in the bed, as close as a lover, warming her with the heat of her body.

Mary Beatrice could not rest. She spoke feverishly of the conversion of England, of the winning of all the souls to the true faith, with fire if need be. She coughed and said that she must have a son, a son baptised into the roman catholic church to cement the conversion, that her life would be wasted if she died of this cough, of weakness, before giving the Holy Father a papist prince of Wales, an heir of the true faith for England.

Livia, too much of a courtier to argue, thought the country had been protestant for too long to change back again, the church lands sucked into private estates, the abbeys rebuilt as private houses, the nuns married off, the priests vanished. Not even the stones stood where the monks had set them, the relics of the saints were missing from honoured tombs, the pilgrim ways growing grass. The lands dedicated to holiness were growing wheat at a profit. English lords had exchanged God for great wealth and it would be hard to change them back again.

'My son will be crowned by the Pope,' the queen predicted. 'Not like us, in secret.'

'You were crowned by the Archbishop of Canterbury in Westminster Abbey, before everyone?' Livia corrected her gently, thinking she must be delirious.

'Of course, we had to go to Westminster Abbey, as the protestants wanted, but it was an empty show. We were first crowned and anointed in secret, in the roman catholic chapel at Whitehall, by the king's confessor.'

Livia was aghast. 'My dear, you must never repeat that! People would go mad if they found out. They would tear down the palace.'

'Of course, it is secret,' the queen said more calmly. 'But think of the glory! I am the first queen crowned in the true church since England turned heretic. Think of that! I am the first queen crowned by a priest since the sainted Catherine of Aragon, since Queen Mary.'

'Because the church changed! England has changed.'

'I will change it back . . .' Her voice trailed off as she fell asleep, but Livia did not close her eyes. She gazed up at the rich canopy, half-dreaming half-planning, as if she could see the future in the golden embroidered sunburst, the circling stars of silver thread, trying to imagine if this queen and king could dominate the country, could re-make England. Mary Beatrice stirred in her sleep and Livia turned to her like a lover and kissed the line of her neck from her ear to her collarbone, pressing herself gently, tightening her hold.

REEKIE WHARF, LONDON, SPRING 1685

Ned, flushed and awkward, waiting for his nephew Rob, and the family's foster son Matthew to arrive for dinner, felt too big for the parlour at the front of the warehouse, ungainly at the window overlooking the river, awkward at the dining table. In the kitchen, Rowan, equally out of place, was clumsily loading a tray with a bottle of wine and glasses and an earthenware pitcher of small ale.

'Take it! Take it!' Tabs commanded, sweating over the stove. 'You're his serving lad, ain't you? Serve it!'

Rowan abandoned the attempt to claim that she was a serving lad who did not serve, and carried the heavy tray into the parlour.

'Here, lad! Put it down before you drop it,' Ned said, helping her with the heavy tray as the glasses clinked dangerously together. 'Neither of us is at ease here.'

Alinor, seated at the fireside, smiled at Rowan. 'I hope you'll feel at home soon.'

There was a knock at the front door.

'That'll be Matthew, home from college,' Alys said, emerging from the counting house at the back of the hall, her husband Captain Shore behind her. 'Or maybe my brother Rob come early.'

Ned nodded to Rowan. 'Answer it, lad.'

'How?' she said very low.

'Just open the door and stand back and bow. Don't be a gowk.'

Rowan threw him an exasperated look, but went to the door

and opened it to a tall slim man aged about fifty years. He handed her his fringed hat and cape without remark and went past her into the parlour. Rowan went to shut the front door when she heard a shout from the quayside – 'Hold up!'

She hesitated, as a long-legged youth of about fifteen came bounding towards the open door, light-footed over the cobbles.

'Here – you're new!' he exclaimed. 'Did you come with my great-uncle Ned? From America?'

She nodded as he slipped past her and into the parlour of his home. The door closed on them and she scowled at her pang of self-pity. It was strange to think that a man that had always appeared so solitary, in his lonely house, beside a cold river in the Dawnlands, should have had all this behind him: family, house, business, on the side of the great river of London; and that she – a girl embedded in her family, born of ancestors from the dawn of time, whose seat was the cliffs of Montaup – should find herself all alone in a strange flat land that faced north.

In the parlour, Ned was greeting Rob after a gap of twenty-five years. 'A doctor's knocker on your door, half of London coming to you for physic, and a wife and child! I'm so glad for you. It's more than we dreamed of, that first day when we sent you to be apprenticed at Chichester. And your Ma in tears at losing her little boy!'

'I remember you giving me money for dinner, in case they underfed me! You got me started, Uncle Ned, and then I was lucky in Padua at my university and then in my practice in Venice,' Rob told his uncle.

'Thank God you got out of there safely.'

'Ah, it was a long time ago, and we don't speak of it.' Rob glanced towards the fostered boy, Matthew. 'Better for the lad that we don't.'

'Secrets?' Ned's grizzled brows twitched together in a frown.

'Some things are better left unsaid,' Rob said firmly.

'A lad should know his father's name.'

'Only his mother knows that!' Rob said low with a half smile. 'Livia Avery left us far behind when she married Sir James. She left her son for my Ma and sister to raise as their own, without a backward glance. We don't speak of her, and he never asks. But I should say – my wife Julia sends her apologies. She hopes to visit tomorrow.'

'For sure,' Ned said easily. He glanced back at Matthew, who was watching the two of them. 'But what name does the lad go by? Not yours?'

'Not mine! Before she married for name and a title, Livia called herself Picci, sometimes da Picci, and Matthew uses that.' He glanced over at Matthew. 'I'm telling my uncle Ned you're doing well in your studies.'

'I'm working hard, whatever Ma Alys suspects!' the youth assured them. 'I'm lucky to have a place at Lincoln's Inn.'

Alys offered him a glass of wine and water. 'He had to do a speech in Latin! Can you imagine?'

'Good for you, lad.' Ned offered a callused hand. 'Think of us having a lawyer in the family!'

Susie the maid put her head in the room. 'Am I to serve dinner now?'

'Yes,' Captain Shore told her. 'We won't wait for Johnnie.'

Everyone drew up their chairs to the table as the cook Tabs, the maid Susie, and Rowan brought dish after dish, some of them bought from the bakehouse, some of them cooked at the stove, the butter cold from the larder, the small ale brewed in the malt-house across the yard.

They heard the front door, and Alys' son Johnnie came into the parlour, his hat in his hand, his brown hair ruffled by the wind from crossing the river from the City. 'Grandmother Alinor, Ma, I'm sorry I'm late. I had a ship come in with mail and I couldn't leave before I read it.' His brown gaze fell on his great-uncle. 'And you must be my uncle Ned! Sir! Welcome home!'

Ned stood and hugged the handsome young man. 'Look at you! I left a lad of eleven years, and now you're a man of business.'

Johnnie thrust his thumbs in his waistcoat and spun around to show his great-uncle his fine embroidered jacket and his deep crimson breeches. He had his mother's golden brown hair and

PHILIPPA GREGORY

square honest face. Ned laughed at his vanity and clapped him on the shoulder as he sat down at the dinner table.

'He always wanted to work for the East India Company,' Alys said proudly, passing her son Johnnie a plate. 'And he trades on his own account.'

'Do you?' asked Ned. 'What sort of goods?'

'Mostly silk and dry goods,' Johnnie said, helping himself to a slice of pie. 'I get opium for Uncle Rob, spices for Ma to sell to grocers. And I send silk from India: overland – to my sister Sarah in Venice – and by sea – to here.' He looked up, as Rowan awkwardly held a dish. 'Hello, who's this?'

She did not bow and lower her eyes as a trained servant would have done. She did not wait for her owner to answer for her like a slave. She met his gaze like an equal. 'I am Rowan. I came with your uncle Ned.'

'A slave?' He turned to Ned.

'Certainly not.'

'I choose to serve him,' Rowan told Johnnie.

'You make it sound like he's honoured!' he smiled at her.

'He is not honoured,' Rowan corrected gravely. 'And I am no slave. We have an agreement.'

'A native Leveller,' Rob observed quietly to his mother Alinor. 'I think Uncle Ned has met his match.'

'And are we equals?' Johnnie asked Rowan, smiling. 'All equals? My great-uncle Ned whom you agree to serve, my uncle Rob a physician, and my Ma and Grandmother who own this wharf, and Captain Shore who owns the ship at the quay outside? Do you have no betters?'

Rowan glanced at Alinor to see if she might answer, and at her nod, she quietly replied: 'Sir, I am very sure you are a great family. But I was born one of the People. And we are the first to see the sun in the morning.'

'How very Copernican!' Rob was amused by this exchange.

'D'you even know where the sun rises?' Rowan challenged Johnnie.

He hesitated. 'There, isn't it?' Johnnie pointed to his right.

'Isn't that north?' Rob asked.

'It's downriver,' Alys told her son. 'Fancy you not knowing!'

Captain Shore laughed. 'Just as well for you all that I know!'

Alinor pointed due east.

'It is that way,' Rowan agreed.

'But it doesn't matter to us,' Johnnie pointed out. 'We go by addresses in London, the names of streets, we don't navigate by the sky.'

'I don't know your streets,' she admitted. 'But I know where I am under the sky. And if your streets tumble down . . .'

'Some of them were burned to nothing,' Alinor pointed out.

'Then there is only the sky. And you will not know where you are. But I always will.' She took the empty dish from Johnnie and went back to the kitchen as Ned gave a little crow of laughter.

'You think you're having an ordinary talk and suddenly you're on to the stars, or the words of the wind.'

'What're you going to do with him, though?' Rob asked, as Susie followed Rowan out of the room. 'Clearly, he can't serve.'

Alinor and Ned, brother and sister, exchanged a hidden smile at her son. 'Ah Rob, how can you be such a great physician and yet blind?' Alinor asked him. 'D'you not see that's a girl?'

'A girl? A native girl?' Alys exclaimed. 'I didn't know!'

'Bless me!' Captain Shore said.

'But why's she dressed like that?' Johnnie demanded.

'It was easier that she pass as a boy while we were travelling,' Ned said. 'And now I have to find somewhere that she can be safe as a girl, and work that she can do as a maid. I can't take a girl where I am going.'

'Where are you going, Uncle Ned?' Rob asked.

'Better that I don't speak of it here.'

Johnnie was alert to the danger. 'You're not expecting trouble, Sir?'

Ned shook his head and said nothing. Rob spoke into the silence: 'Uncle, you've been away too long. It's not the same cause, it's not the same Stuart. Your man Cromwell is dead and buried. The Charles they invited back is dead too, and when his royal brother James took the crown they shouted Vivat Rex for him! Nobody likes the king's religion, not many like him. But the country has chosen him. There'll not be another civil war.'

'Maybe not,' Ned said briefly.

Matthew looked curiously from one determined face to another.

'I promise you,' Rob told his uncle, 'the war you fought is over, there will not be another.'

'Better that I don't speak of it.'

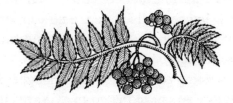

ST JAMES' PALACE, LONDON, SPRING 1685

Mary Beatrice was half-carried home from the state opening of parliament. Livia received her in her arms at the doorway of her privy chamber, helped her into her chair, taking the crown from her head and passing it aside as if it were nothing in her haste to get the heavy robes off the queen's shoulders.

'It was too much for you,' she scolded. 'I said you should not have gone.'

Mary Beatrice shook her head, sipping wine and water. 'It wasn't the weight of the crown – that was nothing – it was what they said!' she exclaimed. 'What he said!'

'Why? What did they say? What did they dare to say?'

Mary Beatrice pulled Livia close so she could whisper. 'It was the king himself! He said the most dreadful thing. He told them – we are going to be invaded!'

Livia was stunned. 'Invaded?'

'The Earl of Argyll – a most desperate rebel – has ships and men, allied with the Duke of Monmouth, the late king's son, and they have sworn to overthrow us!'

Livia gave a little gasp. 'What?'

'So the king told the parliament. Argyll can call up every Scot in the land. He's the chief of the Campbells, and there are thousands of them. He's a bitter presbyterian – so all the heretics will follow him. And everyone in England loves Monmouth, they wanted the late king to make him legitimate, name him heir instead of us. And now, he and the earl have joined together and landed somewhere in Scotland. They'll march on London. They'll muster thousands.'

'But why would the king announce it?' Livia demanded. 'Why tell everyone? Won't they all run to them?'

'He thought he was being clever,' she said uncertainly. 'He thought to outwit parliament into giving him everything he wants: the money to raise an army, the right to call out the militia. Parliament are so wicked as to not trust kings: they never allow royal troops. But my husband has triumphed. He has frightened them into giving him new powers. More money to raise his own army. He says it's a victory for us? He says it's a victory for all kings.' She looked doubtfully at Livia.

'Well, yes, if his new army can beat the earl and the Duke of Monmouth.'

'Not together! No-one could beat them together!' The queen turned from the watching court, whispered that she would go to her bedroom. Livia nodded to the footman to open the doors, carry the queen into her bedroom, and close the door on the anxious faces.

'You must be calm,' Livia urged, kneeling before the queen to chafe her hands, heavy with rings. 'You have to be as still as a field for sowing. A son will make us all safe.'

'It's too late for my baby if Argyll and James of Monmouth march on London. Nothing will save us if the people flock to Monmouth! He was commander of the English army, and they all loved him ... even I loved him, we all did ... He was the most handsome young man, the most charming, the king's most beloved son ...'

'No, no ...'

'And he has a son of his own – a son to be heir to our throne. He has two, he has three! God has blessed him with ... I don't know how many heirs! Protestant heirs. Perhaps God will give him the throne as well!'

'No! No!' Livia felt more and more helpless against the rising distress of the young queen, overwhelmed by her rapid speech, catching her sense of panic. 'No! You know you are chosen by God to bring the faith to England. The Pope himself sent you. You've only been queen for a month! God would not—'

'Maybe that's all I'll ever be! Queen of four weeks! Only four weeks and already there's an army marching on us. They don't want us! They hate me!'

'No they don't,' Livia said staunchly, completely out of her depth. 'And anyway, who cares what the people want?'

REEKIE WHARF, LONDON, SPRING 1685

Rob reluctantly brought his wife to meet his uncle Ned, knowing that she would dislike him on sight as a working man, and an exiled Cromwell soldier, and that Ned would dismiss her as an idle woman of fashion.

Alinor watched from her high bedroom window as the wherry carrying Rob and Julia bobbed at the Horsleydown water stairs, and then she crossed her room and called down the stairs. 'Susie, open the front door. The doctor and Mrs Reekie are here.'

Instead of Susie, she saw Rowan's dark crown and then her smile as she looked upwards through the well of the stairs.

'Susie's out in the yard. Shall I open the door?'

'Lord no,' Alinor laughed. 'Mrs Julia would take a fit. Send Tabs, and you keep out of her way.'

Rowan nodded and called Tabs, who surged out, wiping her hands on her apron.

'Hello, Tabs,' Rob said, as his wife flinched at the cook opening the front door. 'We've come to see my Ma.'

'Upstairs,' Tabs said shortly, heading back to the kitchen. 'And Mrs Shore is in the counting house,' she called over her shoulder.

'Oh, I want to see Alys,' Rob remarked and turned into the warehouse, ignoring his wife's touch on his arm.

Julia mounted the stairs slowly, braced herself before the closed door to Alinor's bedroom, tapped on the panel with one gloved hand and entered. 'Mother Alinor,' she said faintly, brushing a kiss on Alinor's cheek and sinking down on the sofa.

'Dear Julia,' Alinor replied. 'How are you today? I'm sorry you weren't well enough to come yesterday.'

'It's my head.' Julia loosened the ribbons and took off her hat as if the weight of feathers was too much for her.

'I should give you a tisane.' Alinor gestured at the muslin bags that were spread over the table before her chair, as she sewed them for herbs for tea.

'Rob gives me laudanum.' Julia averted her eyes from evidence of Alinor's work. 'It's the only thing that helps me.'

'Surely not every day?'

'Without it, I can do nothing.' She smiled, as if it were an achievement.

'I have to be doing something.'

'I wasn't raised to it,' Julia said flatly.

Alinor nodded, gritting her teeth on a retort. 'I know that, my dear,' she said. 'How is Hester? I am sorry you didn't bring her. I haven't seen her for a long time.'

'If only Rob would set up a proper carriage ...' Julia's soft complaint died away. Her daughter Hester wore a metal brace on her left leg to straighten her club foot and Julia had established early on that she could not allow the child to cross the river on a wherry boat. She had asked Rob to set up a carriage on her wedding day, and plaintively repeated her request every month of every one of the fourteen years, ever since.

'Well, I shall have to visit you,' Alinor said cheerfully, avoiding the perennial question of the carriage.

'Surely it's too far for you? If we had a carriage, I could send it to fetch you.'

With a sense of relief, Alinor heard a heavy footstep on the stair. 'That you, Ned?'

Ned's first thought on coming in was that Julia Reekie must be quarrelling with her mother-in-law, her face was so sulky. She did not rise to greet him but leaned back on the arm of the sofa as if exhausted. Then he saw the pallor of her powdered skin and the rich sheen of her silk dress and realised that she was copying the languor of the ladies of the court, and his nephew Rob had escaped a false marriage with the adventuress Livia Avery who never stopped scheming, for the safety of a woman who did nothing.

He took her gloved fingertips. 'Honoured.'

'Do sit down, Ned,' Alinor urged.

He took a chair opposite her at the worktable. 'Did Rob come with you, Mrs Reekie?'

'He went to the warehouse to see his sister Mrs Shore,' she said. 'I can't bear the noise.'

Ned took care not to exchange a glance with Alinor. 'Can't you?'

'Will you take a hot chocolate, Ned?' Alinor asked.

He rose from his seat. 'Nay, I'll have a small ale with Rob in the counting house. But I'll send up my lad with your cups.'

Julia gave a little cry of alarm and sat up. 'Not the native!' she exclaimed. 'I beg that he doesn't come in here—'

'Send Susie,' Alinor interrupted with a warning look at Ned. 'Julia, dear, don't be ...'

'What's supposed to be wrong with my lad?' Ned asked quietly.

'I would be so afraid,' Julia said. 'The things we've heard of them. The way they have gone wild!' She turned to Alinor.

'Do you keep him in the house at night? Aren't you afraid he might . . . ? I mean, they can never be trusted.'

'Ned!' Alinor cut across his angry retort. To Julia she said gently: 'My dear, you shouldn't believe all that you read in the news-sheets. Rowan is our guest, and we are glad to have her.'

'Her?' Julia repeated on a rising note. 'Never tell me it's a girl?' She shot a horrified glance at Ned. 'You brought a native woman into your home?'

Ned folded his arms and watched his sister try to recover.

'Him,' Alinor corrected herself. 'Well anyway. You know what I mean! Anyway – Ned, send Susie up with the drinks.'

Ned, Alys and Rob, drinking a cup of small ale in the counting house, heard the front door open. 'That'll be Johnnie,' Alys said. 'He comes to do the books every week.'

In the narrow hall, Johnnie took off his thick jacket and hat and handed them to Rowan. 'Here you are again,' he said. 'Are you finding your way around London? Do you know the name of this street?'

She nodded. 'It's Shad Thames Street.'

'Very good,' he said. 'And I remember due east.' He pointed. 'Have you been out to see other streets? Have you been over the river to the City?'

'I've been to the market with Tabs.'

'The market? What did you think of it? Very busy?'

'It smells of dead food,' she said bluntly and made him laugh.

'You should see London Bridge, you should see the Tower of London.' He paused. 'Shall I—' He broke off. 'I could—'

Alys called from the warehouse. 'Is that you, Son?'

'I have to go,' he said.

Rowan stepped to one side. Still Johnnie did not go down the hall.

'Do you get a day off?'

'Off?' she repeated. 'Off what?'

He realised she did not understand what he meant, and the gulf between their worlds was unbridgeable. 'Nothing,' he said, and he smiled and left her in the hall.

'Ah, our Company man! Are you rushed off your feet with business?' Rob joked, as Johnnie kissed his mother and shook hands with his great-uncle Ned.

'I'm waiting on a shipment of tea,' Johnnie said equably. 'I've got nothing to do till it arrives. But I'll take no aspersions from a doctor, whose patients only labour every nine months.'

'Did you visit the Gregsons?' Alys asked him.

Johnnie exchanged a glance with Rob. His mother's hopes that he would marry a young woman with a profitable business were well known to everyone. 'Not yet. I am to go to dinner next week. But more important than that – I have a letter for you, Ma. From my sister.'

Alys exclaimed with pleasure, broke the seal and read aloud:

Dear Ma and dearest Grandmother,

I am sorry not to have written for so long, we've been busier than usual as a church nearby is changing their hangings and we are chosen to sell their old silks when they buy new, so now I have a warehouse full of dusty old silk altar cloths and beautiful vestments, hangings, curtains for statues and drapes for tombs that will indeed be worth a fortune when they are cleaned and darned. Felipe is selling, in their place, most of the consignment of silks that Johnnie had shipped to us from his Dutch trader in Japan. I suppose the new king and queen need vestments and altar cloths for the new royal chapels? We hear that they are turning the whole country papist!

Alys broke off. 'The rest is about the silks ... Oh!' she said in quite a different tone. 'She says:

I also will send a rather precious consignment – to wit – two beautiful grand-daughters for you! If you agree, I should like

36

Mia and Gabrielle to come to you for a long visit. It is very hard for me to give them the girlhood I would like them to have in this city. Girls of good family are kept very strictly at home, and there is no society for young people at all. It is hard for me to find tutors and quite impossible to find anyone to teach Science and Philosophy to girls. There is almost no education for girls outside the convents. They are both very scholarly girls which is not easy in Venice, where women are mostly encouraged to religious studies. Gabrielle in particular shows a great interest in herbs and plants – just like my dearest Grandmother. Felipe says if they are Venetian girls then they should be betrothed in two years, married in three, and that would solve the problem with a cradleful of babies by the time they are eighteen – but I say, they are English girls and I don't want them married young and their life in the keeping of a husband.

We have talked of this with the girls, and they are eager to come. I always thought that this visit would happen – I did not think it would be so soon!

I will, of course, pay for their keep with you and pay their fees for what tutors you can find for them. Please deduct it from our trade balance with you. They are truly dear girls and no trouble, their only flaw is this terrible cleverness. I think they must have it from you, Ma, with your head for business and from you, dearest Grandmother, and your love of herbs. For sure, I have never been interested in anything but hats and making money so there should be no blame attached to me for raising girls who want to study things and think about them.

Felipe tells me to warn you what you do, for if you are successful in ridding us of our two girls, we have two boys coming along behind them that he will send to you as well. David should join the navy for sure, and Luca is very talented in music, at least I think so. But Felipe is just teasing me for he knows I cannot bear to be parted with any of them. It's such a relief to know that Captain Shore sails regularly between us, it feels as if I am never far from you. And if anything were to go wrong – for a moment – you must send them home to me, whatever it is.

And Ma – do say no if it is too much for you? Please ask Johnnie what he thinks and ask him to send me a note with his opinion. Tell him one of the silks he sent is very lovely. I can sell it very well here, or to let me know if he wants it sent on with Capt. Shore? Yellow with gold thread, and an ell wide and ten long.

I write in haste as a Dutch ship will sail this morning for London and I can send this to you if I get it to the Capt. now – I send you all my love as always, dearest Ma and dearest Grandmama, hoping you are well and the family too, as we are . . . Sarah'

'What a riot her brain is,' Johnnie said. 'And how can you even read it? The last paragraph is scrawled sideways through the rest.'

'I like hearing the scramble of her thoughts,' his mother said smiling. 'Wouldn't it be wonderful to have her girls to stay here?'

'Julia would be glad to have them in Hatton Garden,' Rob put in.

Both Alys and Johnnie ignored the polite lie.

'Can you manage two girls here, Ma?'

'Oh yes, now that we have the second warehouse. Tabs and Susie can sleep over that side and the girls could go in the eaves.'

'They'll be used to something a bit grander than servants' rooms,' Rob pointed out.

'I won't be in your way for long,' Ned offered.

'I think the rooms are the least of your worries. What does she say?' Johnnie consulted the letter. 'Philosophy and Science? And one of them interested in herbs and plants?'

'What about St Saviour's?' Rob suggested. 'The school is for boys only, of course, but the new Master's wife has set up a class for girls in their parlour. They say that she's teaching the same subjects as the boys are learning! And the girls can take lessons with Hester's governess until they start.'

'What a good idea!' Alys said, her eyes shining. 'They can come on Captain Shore's return voyage. He sails in mid-June. And if you leave Rowan with us, Uncle Ned, she can serve as their maid. She can come out of her boy's clothes and look after the two of them.'

'Would she want to do that?' Rob asked doubtfully. 'Is she at all trained?'

'She'll do as she pleases,' Ned replied stiffly. 'She's not to be trained like a dog.'

'No, of course . . . I meant no disrespect. Just whether it would suit her? Will you ask her?'

'Alys can ask her, if she wants to,' Ned said unhelpfully.

'I'll ask,' Johnnie interrupted. 'She might feel obliged if it came from Ma.'

Alys gathered up the scrawled pages of the letter. 'I'll go and read this to Ma and Julia.'

'Come and have a look at this barrel of herbs of mine,' Ned invited Rob. 'I've got a sort of moss that might interest you. The native peoples use it for wounds, it stops bleeding.' Ned led Rob through the door into the warehouse as Johnnie crossed the hall and stepped over the stone sill into the kitchen.

Rowan was at the table, an apron around her breeches, her boy's shirt sleeves rolled up, floured to the elbows, inexpertly kneading dough. Tabs was seated at the head of the table.

'Gently! Gently!' she insisted. 'You're kneading it, not beating it to death!' She rose to her feet when Johnnie came in. 'Master Johnnie,' she said with pleasure. 'Good to see you. Will you take a glass of small ale? And an apple puff when it comes out the oven? If it isn't crushed flat?'

He smiled at her. 'Hello, Tabs. I've just come for a word with young Rowan here.'

'Brush the flour off your hands and take off your apron and go with the master into the parlour,' Tabs told her.

Rowan followed Johnnie into the front room. It was cool as the room faced north over the river, the greenish lights dancing on the ceiling as the early summer light reflected off the high tide.

Rowan pulled down her shirt sleeves. He thought how unlike an English woman she was: the way she stood in alert silence.

'Mrs Shore is going to invite her grand-daughters from Venice,' he told her. At the narrowing of her eyes, he guessed that she did not know of this side of the family and had never even heard of Venice. 'Mrs Shore, my mother Alys, has a daughter: my sister Sarah – very dear to me. She lives with her husband and children in Venice, far away from here – more than thirty days' sailing. They have four children and the two oldest, two girls, are coming on a visit.

'If you wish, you could be their maid. If you wish. You're not obliged. But it would give you a trade, and a safe place.' He was surprised at himself, taking any trouble over her.

'What would I do?'

'You would take them their breakfasts in the morning and help them wash and dress. You would clean their rooms and wash their linen. You would walk out with them when they wanted to go out, you would carry things for them and run errands. You would help them change their clothes in the evening and put them to bed at night. I suppose you would mend their clothes and arrange their hair.'

'They are babies? Little girls, who need help to dress and eat?'

'No, they are young ladies,' he said. 'They are . . .' He thought for a moment. 'Thirteen and twelve years old.'

She looked at him with the straight gaze of a young man, as if breeches made her honest in a way that a young lady in a sea of silk and lace and petticoats could never be. 'No, I won't do that.'

'You would be paid,' he told her, more hesitantly. 'If you do well, you could go into service, and work your way up.'

'Up where?'

He laughed, but then realised it was a genuine question. 'Up to another position. With a young lady of higher rank. And then up again. While you worked hard and pleased people you would rise.'

'No,' she said simply.

'But what else can you do?' he asked her.

'I am one of the People,' she told him again. 'We are not born to be servants; nor slaves.'

'They're not the same thing at all—' he began.

'Would you serve a young lady?' she demanded.

He laughed awkwardly. 'Well, really, I could not.'

'A young gentleman? Fetch and carry for him, get him dressed, put him to bed? Spend your life in making him comfortable, as if he did not have hands and feet to fetch and carry for himself?'

'No!' he said. 'I would not. But I am—' He broke off.

'You're an Englishman,' she named him. 'You have pride in your milk skin. You have pride in your wealth. You have pride in the things that you know, and no interest in the things that you don't. You would serve nobody, because in your heart you think that nobody is above you.'

He could not disagree.

'I'm not saying you're wrong,' she said gently. 'But you must know that I am proud – just like you. I am proud of my brown skin and my hair as black and straight as an icicle. I too think that nobody is above me. You are an Englishman – and that seems a very great thing to you; but I am a child of the Dawnlands. To me, that is better.'

'The English are the greatest nation in the world …' he started. He could not explain to her the thousands of ships at sea, shipping cargo all around the world, guns to Africa, slaves to the New World, cotton and sugar on the homeward leg, goods to the Americas. His own hugely profitable trades in India: cotton, tea, silk. 'You know nothing about my people.'

'You know nothing about mine.'

'But what will you do?' he demanded as anxious as if he was the one alone in a strange country. 'This is a hard city for young women. My uncle says you can't go back to your home, that your tribe are all dead. How will you live if you don't make money?'

She flinched as he called them a tribe, a dead tribe. 'It's not a hard city for me. Nowhere is hard for me but winter.'

'What if someone attacks you?'

She hid a smile. 'No man puts a hand on me.'

'Oho? You can fight?' He meant to tease her; but the grave look she gave him told him that she could fight to the death.

'It is true, there is no home for me to go back to,' she conceded. 'I shall have to find a way to live in this old world, this world of sunsets.' She paused for a moment as if she realised what she had said. 'Ah . . . it is an old world of sunsets.'

'All this about the dawn means nothing!' he exclaimed.

'It means nothing to you.'

ST JAMES' PALACE, LONDON, SPRING 1685

The king was closeted with the queen in her privy chamber over-looking the gardens, only Father Mansuet, his confessor, and two ladies-in-waiting in attendance. Livia, striking in a gown of dark blue silk cut low across her creamy shoulders, stood behind the queen, her dark eyes on the king's excited face.

'I shall be master,' he gabbled, his face flushed, his wig pushed slightly askew. 'I shall be master in my household and father to the nation. Parliament have given me all I need to dominate this rebellious kingdom.'

'Have they agreed that men of our faith shall be army officers and MPs and justices of the peace?' Father Mansuet prompted, his eyes on his own hands, clasped as if in prayer, before him. 'Men of our faith must take power, so we can bring England to God without opposition.'

'Not yet! Not yet! I can't get our people into the law or into parliament yet. But I have won my own army officered by true believers. Right now, I've got only ten thousand men scattered all around the country, in no state to fight.' He laughed excitedly. 'But I shall raise an army of true believers and march on Scotland and the presbyterians myself.'

'No!' The queen spoke for the first time, raising herself from her chair. 'You can't go.'

'Who should lead my army of true believers, but me?'

She compressed her lips on the answer. Everyone knew that the king could not risk his life when he had no heir but girls: first his daughter Mary – ruled by her husband William of Orange: a dyed-in-the-wool protestant – and then the protestant Anne. No catholic would see the sacred Mass ever again if they took the throne. 'What about me?' she demanded. 'I was called by God . . . by God . . .' She lost her voice. Livia put an arm around her waist, and James looked at the two beautiful dark-haired women entwined like lovers.

'You shall fulfil His will,' he promised.

'Her Majesty will bear a son,' Father Mansuet predicted. 'A roman catholic Prince of Wales.'

'But how many ships have landed?' Livia asked. 'Argyll's ships?'

The angry glance from the king told her that he had no idea how many ships had invaded, nor how many men they carried, nor how many men had rushed to join the rebellion when they landed.

'And is James, Duke of Monmouth with Argyll?' the queen demanded.

'I don't know. I know they've got turncoats and traitors. I ordered that William dismiss Englishmen from his army. I don't want Englishmen marching against France.'

'But if they had done nothing wrong . . . ?' she queried.

'Anyway, William did as I ordered. He dismissed them – and now they've gone straight to Monmouth!'

'You ordered that Englishmen should be dismissed from the Dutch army – and they've all gone to Monmouth?' she repeated, disbelievingly.

'I had to! I couldn't have English soldiers fighting the French!' James shouted, covering his mistake with bluster. 'King Louis is our only friend in this damned protestant world! He's the only one I can count on. He is of the true faith, he has promised me funds to restore the faith to England. We are as one: he and I! We are brother monarchs! We are brother catholics!'

'But everyone in England hates him!' the queen exclaimed. 'And to please him, you've given Monmouth an army of experienced English soldiers.'

'I didn't know they would go to him! I thought they would just come home.'

'They may indeed come home!' she said furiously. 'With Monmouth at their head!'

'I'll be ready for them,' the king swore. 'I'll raise the militia in Scotland, I'll go to the privy council and order them out, right now. I'll call on the north to arm.' He turned to Livia. 'How many men can your husband muster for my cause in Yorkshire?'

'Hundreds,' Livia said firmly.

'I'll come with you to the council.' Father Mansuet went to follow him.

'Wait!' Livia said to the priest. 'Won't it look as if you are advising the king?'

'Of course I advise him,' he said proudly. 'We care nothing that they see it!'

The queen watched them leave and waved the ladies-in-waiting away. She turned to Livia. 'Only now is he calling out the militia? Though he has known Argyll was sailing for weeks?'

Livia had no answer.

'And anyway – who will the militia fight for: the king or the duke? Where is the loyalty in Yorkshire?'

'Probably for the protestant duke,' Livia reluctantly spoke the truth. 'All of the Yorkshire spinners and weavers are protestant, many of them fought before for Cromwell. They've faced a royal army before. They have no fear of it, they have no respect. They're independent men, their own masters, they all follow their own consciences, they obey no-one.'

'So, when you told the king that your husband could raise hundreds . . . ?'

'I didn't know what to say . . .'

'Everyone does that!' the queen exclaimed. 'No-one tells him anything that he will not like! Just like his father, King Charles. He thought he was safe, they put him on trial and he expected to speak – in the very hall where we went to open parliament! I probably stood in his footprints! I probably stood in his blood-stained footprints! He did not know, until it was too late, that people hated him!'

Her terror was infectious. 'It will never happen again!' Livia promised.

'You heard the king. He doesn't know. They've hated me since I came here, they burned an effigy the day I arrived! My wedding was held in secret for fear of the mob. They hate catholic queens. They fired on Queen Henrietta! They would have killed her. She had to flee for her life!'

'She ran away?'

'She had to! I will have to! If Argyll and Monmouth are on the march, then I'll have to go to France like she did. Her husband could not protect her and neither can mine!'

REEKIE WHARF, LONDON, SPRING 1685

Johnnie, surprised at himself, was drawn back to the warehouse within the week, and found his uncle Ned on the quayside with a cargo manifest in his hand.

'Has my Ma set you to work?' Johnnie asked, crossing the cobbles.

'No-one's idle in this house. But actually, I am doing nothing more than holding this while your Ma goes to find a missing barrel. I am the equivalent of a book stand.'

'It was you I wanted to see,' Johnnie said awkwardly.

'Here I am,' Ned said, and when the younger man hesitated, he said: 'Still here.'

'Yes, I know. It's ... it's about your lad ... about Rowan, I mean. Your er ...'

'About Rowan,' Ned prompted.

'I keep thinking about her!' Johnnie exclaimed, and then flushed. 'Not like that! I mean, I have been thinking about her position. Here. And I've found her a place if she wants it.'

'That's good of you,' Ned said carefully, looking at the younger man. 'Good of you to take the trouble.'

'It's no trouble. I've found her a place at a school, a dame school. She'd be a pupil in lessons and earn her keep by helping with the housework. I thought she should learn to read and write there. If she showed aptitude she could perhaps become a pupil teacher. She obviously doesn't want to be a servant.'

'Why are you so interested in Rowan?' Ned asked.

The younger man flushed. 'It's not anything ...' He trailed off. 'I just think she should have a chance,' he said. 'Coming as she does from ... over there. And everything must be so strange for her here. She's got such courage ... Anyway, what do you plan for her? And what happens when you leave?'

'I don't have any plans,' Ned admitted. 'I bought her out of slavery on the dockside with no plan but to save her life. I thought she'd find her own way. Perhaps she'd take to your idea. You'd have to ask her.'

'You'd let her go?'

'I don't own her. She'll do as she pleases.'

'But she needs a protector,' Johnnie suggested.

'I doubt that. Anyway – tell her about the place.' Ned hesitated. 'Be warned: she may not be grateful – her people don't tally up favours like we do.'

'But I can speak to her?' the younger man confirmed.

Ned waved towards the warehouse. 'She's in the yard.'

Johnnie nodded and went down the alley at the side of the house to enter the yard through the open gates.

Rowan was squatting on her haunches, carefully picking the yellow buds off a bed of herbs and putting them in a basket. The sweet scent was all around her, her fingernails stained green. She heard footsteps on the cobbles and rose up in one supple movement to confront the intruder. He saw her relax as she recognised him.

'I've come to see you,' he said.

She did not curtsey as a young woman should, nor did she bow as a servant should. She just stood waiting to hear why he had come. Now he was before her, he did not know what to say. Her dark gaze was fixed on his face and – unlike an English girl – she did not smile or help him speak. She waited as if the silence was not awkward.

'I've found a place that might suit you,' he said. 'You'd be attached to a school for young girls. You would have to do some cleaning and perhaps . . .' He looked down at her basket of flower heads. 'Perhaps garden work? But you would be taught to read and write and you might learn a trade.'

'In London?' she asked.

'Yes. In this parish. St Olave's church has a school for boys, and girls are taught by the clergyman's wife. They need a pupil teacher who would help with lessons and with running the vicarage.'

'Why?' she inquired.

'It would give you a way to earn a living. It would protect you from strangers and . . . You would be chaperoned by a good woman and live in her house. You would dress in proper clothes and attend church.'

'No,' she corrected him. 'Why have you found this place for me?'

'I'd like to help you.' He could hardly believe that she was so composed while he was stumbling over his words and shifting from foot to foot as if the favour would be her gift to him. She was in his mother's yard and in his great-uncle's service, but she seemed blind to her dependency. Johnnie, a businessman and the son of a wharfinger, realised she could not be bought or sold; and he had thought everything had a price.

'Do you want me as your woman?' she asked bluntly.

He blushed at her bawdiness. 'No! Don't say that!' he said hastily. 'You can't speak like that. In our world, you can't say something like that.'

She looked puzzled. 'Then how does a woman tell her man she wants him?'

He shook his head, loosened his collar against a sudden heat. 'She doesn't. She doesn't speak of such things. A young lady waits for her father ... to tell her ...that a marriage is arranged. She cannot speak for herself.'

Rowan shook her head, quite baffled. 'We just say. A woman makes her choice and tells him.'

'You're not in your country now!' Johnnie snatched off his hat and ran his hand through his hair. 'You're under the protection of my great-uncle. He will answer for you.'

'I am not his woman,' she pointed out.

Johnnie cast an anxious look at the open kitchen door for fear that Tabs or Susie was listening. 'No! I know that!'

'Oh – you don't want me?' she asked as if she were merely trying to get something clear.

'I do – I would – but I must not—' He was choking on his words. 'I may not say ... I have no intentions towards ... this was an offer of charity ... not a proposition. I would not insult you or my uncle by suggesting ...I would never ... in my mother's house!'

They stood in silence; he was burning with embarrassment and she was perfectly calm.

She shrugged her shoulders as if she gave up the puzzle. 'I don't understand you people,' she said flatly. 'But I am not free.'

'You're betrothed to someone?' He swallowed his dismay. 'You're married?'

'Ned Ferryman saved my life. Until I repay the debt to him, I owe him my life. I am not free to leave him nor go to any man. It is a blood-debt.'

He nearly laughed with relief. 'Oh, that doesn't matter. He wouldn't think that ...'

She was completely serious. 'It does not matter what he thinks, or what you think. He saved my life – until the debt is repaid, I am his.'

'He won't have a slave,' Johnnie reminded her.

'I am not enslaved, I am indebted.'

'If you were not indebted, would you like me?' he asked, struggling to find words. 'As a friend? I cannot offer any ... as a friend?'

'I have not seen enough white men to know one of you from another. And most of you are savages.' She picked up her basket and patted the calendula flowers.

'Savages!' He repeated the word which was used for her people, not his.

'Killers. Rapists. Men with power but without law.'

Johnnie realised that she had survived events that he had never even heard of. 'I like you, Rowan,' he said carefully. 'And I will be your friend. I will help you in any way that I can.'

She nodded gravely. 'When I know what I want, I will tell you,' she promised. 'Until then, I will go where Ned Ferryman goes, until my debt is paid.'

'He might lead you into danger,' Johnnie warned. 'You don't understand. He is not a good guide for you. He doesn't believe in kings, he doesn't believe in masters—'

He broke off when he saw her mischievous smile. 'But neither do I. My Massasoit – my king – is dead. I will never serve a master, I shall go with your uncle Ned until I am free and I know what I want to do.'

'And what then?' he demanded. 'What – when you know what you want to do?' He was dazzled by her easy confidence:

'Then I will do that.'

AMSTERDAM, HOLLAND, SPRING 1685

It was not hard for Ned, with Rowan like a silent shadow at his heels, to track down James, Duke of Monmouth to his inn on the Martelaarsgracht of Amsterdam.

'What kind of land is this with no rivers but all the water between banks of stone?' Rowan demanded, horrified. 'Is it like Johnnie said – all street and no sky?'

'They're great ones for building, the Hollanders,' Ned said. 'All of this here will once have been tidelands, waterland. But they build a wall against the sea, and then pump the land behind it dry. Every street is a quayside in this town.' It was impossible to explain to one of the People, who lived on an unending continent, that there was not enough land to be had.

'They live all the time in these ...?' She had no word for the row of low-browed houses that scowled over the narrow stinking canal.

'Aye,' Ned said.

'They have no woods? They have no fields? They are so very poor, they don't even have forests?'

'No! This is the wealthiest trading country in the world. They used to own all the wealth of the East until we set up our own East India Company – the one my nephew Johnnie works for. Even now, they still hold more than half of the trade.'

'They choose this?' she asked incredulously, gesturing to the narrow door that fronted the canal and the glazed window beside it that gave them a glimpse of a low-ceilinged wood-panelled room, and a closed stove with a blue and white tiled surround, a table before the window dressed with a Turkey rug. Ned thought it a fine stone-built house. He stepped back to admire the gables and the upper windows and the painted sign of the merchant householder.

'To an Amsterdammer that's a grand house,' Ned told her. 'Now, hold your tongue, we're going into an ale house to meet a lord and his council.'

He gestured her to follow him down the half dozen stone steps to a narrow wooden door into the wood-floored, wood-panelled public room of the Karpershoek inn. She hesitated at the head of the stairs, peering into the darkness.

'It's below the water?'

'Follow me,' Ned said over his shoulder.

A man was sitting at the great table at the back of the room, half a dozen men around him. A beam of sunlight, crossing the gloomy room from the high windows, illuminated the shine on his dark brown ringlets over the white lace collar. Ned recognised, without pleasure, the Stuart family charm and the Stuart good looks. 'Wait here,' he said to Rowan. 'Better that you hear nothing.'

Rowan stood still beside the stubby newel post of the stairs. Ned glancing back saw that she melted into the gloom of the room, just as she would have disappeared into trees when hunting at her home. Ned doffed his hat and approached the table.

The duke looked up, a slight smile on his face. 'Come in,' he said, as if he were in his private house.

'I'm Ned Ferryman,' Ned said with a little bow. 'From New England. Come to enter your service, if your cause is just and you'll have me.'

'I've no money to pay you,' the duke said honestly.

'I'd serve for the cause alone; if it's a good one.'

'It seems good to me, but I won't command any man's conscience.'

'You would keep England in the reformed faith?'

'I'm the protestant prince, everyone knows that.' He nodded

at the tap boy who was standing with a cloth over his arm and a jug of beer. 'Pour this good man a drink.'

The boy set a mug before Ned and went out, closing the door behind him.

'I'll serve you if you wear the green ribbon,' Ned said. Green was the colour of the Levellers, the radicals of the old Cromwell army. These days it was worn by the men who drank at the King's Head in London, talking of freedom and of the rights of men. To every Englishman it meant the right to his own religion, to his family, to his own land, and legal limits on the power of the king.

'We're all of that mind. D'you know anyone here that can vouch for you?' The duke gestured around the table. He smiled at a fresh-faced young man of nineteen. 'Not William Hewling here. But anyone else?'

'I've been away from England for many years. Half my comrades are dead of old age! Anyone who was in my company at Naseby might remember me,' Ned hesitated. 'I don't know that's a recommendation to you, Sir: I was fighting your grandfather Charles I.' Ned glimpsed the Stuart mournful smile.

'A civil war is always a family matter. I'll be taking up arms against my uncle, an ordained king. I shall be the first Stuart to deny the power of the king. I shall be a Leveller Stuart.'

'My father was a major in the New Model Army,' a man of about twenty years spoke up from the foot of the table. 'Major Wade? D'you know him? A one-armed man, but he could ride a horse as well as any other.'

Ned grinned at the trap that had been laid for him. 'The Major Wade I knew had two arms,' he said. 'A godly man, name of John. Family were great men in Bristol. Cursed like a stevedore when he was angry.'

'That's him,' Nathaniel Wade nodded. He glanced at Monmouth. 'Probably is who he says he is,' he said grudgingly.

'I've made covenants with these men already,' the duke replied. 'I've said that if I succeed in England and the throne is offered me, I'll take it, only if the people of England want a king.

If they want a Lord Protector, I'll offer to serve. But it shall be for the people to decide.'

'You'll hold parliaments every year?' Ned persisted. 'And not when it suits you?'

The duke nodded and waited for more.

'And give every landholder a vote?'

'If the parliament requests it.'

'And impose no religion or belief on any man or woman, but let each consult his own conscience? No imprisonment without just cause. No picking of judges to suit yourself. No new taxation?'

The duke nodded again.

'Then I offer you my service,' Ned said. 'Such as it is.'

'I accept your service,' the duke said. He gestured for Ned to sit at the table. 'Did you train men for the New England militia?'

'Aye,' Ned said. 'And in England, in the first civil war. I can drill foot soldiers and teach the use of a musket.'

'D'you have any funds?' a handsome man demanded from the end of the table. 'For all this talk of kings – and some of us would have no kings ever again – we need a royal fortune to kit out a ship.' He hesitated. 'I'm Thomas Dare, from Devon.'

'I've no more than I stand up in, and a few coins in my pocket. I can pay my way and buy my weapons.'

'D'you have family? Tenants? Servants?'

'I'm a single man.'

'You've got a slave,' another man observed in a rolling west country drawl, glancing at Rowan who stood still and silent by the stairs at the door. 'Can you sell him?'

'He's free,' Ned said. 'He travels with me until he wishes to leave.'

'We're desperate short of funds,' Thomas Dare explained. 'I'm Paymaster – but I've nothing to save or spend. And we have to hire ships and buy arms, and pay for munitions, banners and favours, and we're taking a printing press to print the muster...'

The duke gave a little grimace and plunged his hand into the deep pocket of his richly embroidered jacket. He brought out a fat purse and slid it across the table.

'My honour is in this purse,' he said. 'Make sure you get full value for it.'

Thomas Dare, who had been a goldsmith in his home of Taunton, untied the purse and peeped inside. He let out a quiet whistle and tied the purse again and put it in his own pocket. 'Her ladyship's jewels?' he asked the duke.

Monmouth nodded. 'She has given up everything for me,' he said quietly. 'And now the very rings from her fingers, and from her own mother's neck.'

'I should get enough from this and from the sale of your goods to pay the rest of the fee for the ships and buy arms,' Dare said, rising to his feet.

'Take Mr Ferryman with you,' Monmouth said. 'He can check the guns. And I'll write to my friends again, someone must lend us more money. I'll pawn the rest of my goods.' He frowned. 'I'll clear the house, even the linen from the beds.'

'And quickly! We're promised to sail within days,' another man reminded him. 'Argyll is counting on support; we can't fail him.'

'I'll pawn the jewels,' Dare promised, nodding to Ned to follow him. 'And we'll buy the arms. I'll meet you at the quayside at Texel tomorrow afternoon, Sire.'

REEKIE WHARF, LONDON, SPRING 1685

Matthew was eating his breakfast at the scrubbed table in the kitchen warehouse. Alys poured him a mug of small ale and took her seat opposite him. For a moment she admired his profile, as straight and beautiful as any of the Greek statues they sold, a handsome youth on the edge of manhood. 'D'you get enough to eat? Do they give you a good dinner at the Inns of Court?' she asked.

'You can see, I'm not fading away,' Matthew replied.

She smiled; he was fifteen years old but already the top of his head was level with her own neat white cap.

'You're all legs,' she said fondly. 'There's nowt on you. Will you come home on Friday evening?'

'Course,' he said, his mouth filled with bread and beef.

She hesitated. 'Have you heard from your mother?'

He took a long draught of small ale. 'Not since she wrote to me that she was coming to the queen's court, weeks ago. Have you?'

'I don't expect to hear from her,' Alys said flatly. 'If she invites you to visit, will you go?'

'I'm curious. I've not seen her since she visited us when I was ten and she was come and gone in an hour. I can only remember her carriage, and the cake she gave me. I wouldn't know her if I passed her in the street.'

'Oh, you'd know her soon enough,' Alys said wryly.

He looked up at the woman who had been his foster mother since infancy. 'She's so beautiful?'

'Not even that. She has . . .'

'Style? Italian style?'

'She takes your attention,' Alys said. 'If you passed her in the street, she'd take your attention.'

'She smiles at you?'

'She's more likely to look down her nose at you for having the nerve to glance at her.'

'She's proud?'

'Very.'

'Well, she's not likely to condescend to visit me – a little "puny" at Lincoln's Inn.' He smiled at the nickname for the junior scholars. 'And even less to come here. So I'll have to wait for an invitation to court, if I hope to see her.' He took one last gulp of small ale and rose from the table.

'I'll come with you to the water stairs,' Alys folded her lips on a warning that his mother might disappoint him.

He left the dishes as they were and went into the hall. His jacket was on the chair, his hat beside it, and a satchel of papers – his legal studies – on the floor. He shrugged into his jacket and placed his hat at a rakish angle on his long curly hair. Alys put her hands on his shoulders and he bent his head like a boy, for her to kiss his forehead.

'God bless you, Son,' she said. 'Work hard and keep out of trouble.' She hesitated; the students of the Inns of Court were notoriously rowdy and hard drinking. 'You are learning?'

'Ma!' he protested. 'We can't all be like Johnnie and live for nothing but work!'

'At least don't be a spendthrift!' she replied.

'D'you think I have folly in my veins?'

She feared worse; but she shook her head. 'I know you're going to be a good man. You're our boy before you are anyone else's.'

He tapped his hat more firmly on his head and took up his satchel. 'I'll be home late Friday. Don't wait up for me.'

'You be home late, and you'll find the door bolted against you,' she threatened, smiling. 'I'll have no wild young men hammering on the door at midnight.'

He laughed, knowing she would never lock him out. 'Come on, then. I can't be late now. I am to listen to a pleading in the law from one of the senior scholars, and at a crucial moment I have an important task: I am to hand him a pen.'

'That's your only work for the day?'

'That's my greatest moment,' he corrected her. 'All eyes will be on me.'

They walked arm in arm upriver along the quay past their own ship, to where the Horsleydown Stairs ran from the quay to the lapping water below.

'But you are learning?' Alys confirmed.

'I am, but everyone says, it's not what it was. Some scholars do nothing but dine there, never open a book. Some of the qualified men don't even use their chambers but let them out to visitors to

London like an inn. But some of us read in the library, and I am learning. I eat my dinners and I listen to the discourse, I'll serve my terms and maybe catch someone's eye and get a pupillage. I will come out of this a lawyer, Ma. I'll be able to defend you, whatever you do.'

'I'm a hardened criminal,' Alys confessed. 'We need a lawyer in the family.' She hugged him goodbye at the top of the stairs and stood on the quay as he went down the wet steps to signal to a passing wherry. The boatman pulled alongside and Matthew climbed aboard, settled himself in the stern and raised his hand to her. She watched him go, the wherryman pulling against the ebbing tide, upstream to the wealth of the City where Johnnie worked, to the Inns of Court where Matthew studied, and beyond them, to the palace where his mother had lived for weeks and never sent for him.

Alys turned and went back to the warehouse. Her husband's ship, *Sweet Hope*, was at the quayside and she could see him on board, checking the loading. She waved to him, as she stepped over the stone sill which kept high-tide floodwater from the front door, and climbed the steep wooden stairs to her mother's bedroom which overlooked the quay at the front and the River Neckinger at the side. Alinor was seated at the round table, windows wide open, herbs and muslin purses spread around the table.

'Has he gone?' she asked, glancing up from her work as Alys came into the room.

Alys sniffed at the fresh smell of dried mint and another perfume, more exotic.

'Sassafras, mint and scurvy grass,' Alinor told her. 'Slavers' tea.'

Alys took a handful of the mixture and buried her nose in it. 'Delicious,' she said. She put down the herbs and sat opposite her mother, took up a purse and tipped in a measure of the dried leaves as Alinor went on working, her thin hands deft from long practice. 'He told me he'd be late Friday night as he's dining with friends.'

'Cut his allowance,' Alinor joked with a warm smile at her daughter. 'If he can treat his friends, you're giving him too much.'

'I don't want him to look poor beside them. If he's to go among gentlemen scholars I don't want him behindhand.'

'Don't you spoil him,' Alinor advised. 'You and Rob didn't turn out badly and neither of you ever had more than a ha'penny in your pocket.'

Alys flushed. 'We turned out all right in the end,' she emphasised. 'There's no comparison, Ma – not between the tidelands and the wharf: now that we've got the ship and my Abel in partnership with us – Johnnie trading in the East India Company and Sarah sending us such goods from Venice!'

'I'm grateful for our blessings.'

'Don't forget what it was really like,' Alys reminded her. 'We never ate meat unless I'd poached it from the Peachey lands. We ate fish when you caught it. We ate butter and cheese when you were given it instead of wages. White bread was a rare treat at harvest time, cream was something you skimmed for others. It wasn't that you chose not to spoil us – you could barely feed us! I've sworn that I'll never be poor again, and we never will.' She rapped on the wooden table for luck. 'It's worse than ill health,' she said. 'It ruins everything.'

'It's just—' Alinor broke off. 'The sky over the harbour,' she said, her voice full of longing. 'The seeping of the water over the shore at high tide. My own parents buried in the churchyard, their names over their resting place. The stile into the churchyard where the roses grow. The oak tree that bends over the mire and the green of the water under the green leaves.'

'It'd be all changed,' Alys pointed out. 'The Peachey family have all died out and the manor gone to the crown. We don't even know who's got our ferry now. We'll have been forgotten.'

Alinor smiled. 'Someone will have made up stories about us,' she said. 'As if we were never real at all. As if we just washed in and away again with the tide.'

'What d'you think they say?' Alys asked smiling.

'Oh – a woman who danced with fairies and ran away with a merman? A wise woman who paid her debt in faerie gold? A woman swam as a witch and could not drown?'

Alys shivered as if she was cold though the sunshine still shone through the window into the little room. 'Let's not think of it. When's Uncle Ned coming back?' she turned the talk. 'Has he really gone to join Argyll in Scotland?'

'Monmouth,' Alinor said shortly. 'He's gone to the duke.'

Alys looked down at her husband's ship below. Lumpers were tossing hessian sacks of woollen cloth, one to another, across the quay for stowing in the deep hold. Alys could calculate to the nearest shilling the value of the boat, the value of the load, the likely profit from a good sale in Venice, the value of the art works and luxury goods that her daughter Sarah would send on the return voyage. Her constant calculation of value was not driven by greed but the dread of ruin. 'If Uncle Ned is taken for treason we would lose everything,' she said very quietly.

'He won't name us,' Alinor said gently. 'He's promised.'

'He'd have done better to promise to have nothing to do with it at all!' Alys exclaimed.

'Aye. So you say. But all his life Ned has been a parliament man. Before you were even born, Alys. He's always been for the Church of England and the people of England. He's bound to fight against a king who's lived in foreign parts for most of his life, is a declared papist and has a foreign papist wife.'

'Still crowned King of England,' Alys said stubbornly.

'So was his father,' Alinor said cheerfully. 'And your uncle Ned saw him beheaded and came home and told us all about it: and we were glad.'

'Hush,' Alys said, turning from the window. 'I won't have a word of it in this house. It's nothing to us! Trade is good, the country is quiet, they're still rebuilding after the fire, and everyone wants our stonework and statues for their houses and gardens, our art for their galleries and our silk for their walls. Even your tea sells faster than you can make it for the slaving ships. We've got nothing against this king. He can pray as he likes, and as long as he doesn't tax like a papist, I won't hear a word against him.'

'You won't hear a word against him from me,' Alinor pointed out mildly. 'I'm not the ranting sort.'

Alys was forced to laugh at her mother, sitting so quietly behind her table with her pile of sweet-smelling herbs and her muslin purses. 'You!' she said. 'You've got a wild streak in you, Ma – and I see it in my uncle Ned, and in our Sarah when it took her to Venice, and I pray to God that I never see it in Johnnie or Matthew.'

Alinor did not deny the wildness. 'It was a long time ago –men questioning their king, women questioning their husbands, and everyone questioning their God. Everyone thought that anything could happen. Everyone was drunk with questions.'

'Those times are gone,' Alys told her severely. 'We all want peace now and a sober life.'

'Not all of us,' Alinor warned her with a gleam of a smile. 'Some of us would be glad to be drunk with questions all over again.'

AMSTERDAM, HOLLAND, SPRING 1685

Ned and Thomas Dare, followed by Rowan, turned into a dark doorway and went down a short flight of stairs into a metalwork shop. The forge was blazing bright in the yard outside and the workshop was ringing like a belfry with the noise of men hammering hot iron. The acrid smell of charcoal smoke drifted into the low-ceilinged room.

'Take a good look at the muskets before I pay,' Thomas Dare told him. 'Put aside anything faulty. We only want the very best.'

Ned had seen colonial-made muskets blow off a rifleman's hand. 'The lad knows good workmanship,' he remarked.

'I thought they weren't allowed weapons?'

'We only sell them faulty ones,' Ned said with grim humour. 'That's how he knows.'

The owner of the shop greeted Thomas, nodded to Ned and waved them to a pile of muskets ready to be wrapped in sacking and packed into boxes. There were more than a thousand, piled in the corner of the room. Ned made a soundless whistle with his lips and Rowan glanced at him.

'Check one in every ten,' he told her.

'You'll find they're good,' the forgemaster said as he came over, his leather apron stained with scorch marks and his hands rough with old burns. 'I sell my muskets to the Dutch East India Company – they don't pay me to fail!'

'They better be,' Thomas Dare replied. 'I'll leave you here, Ned, while I get this purse pawned.'

'Very well.' Ned and Rowan pulled weapons from the stack, checking the sighting, peering down the powder pan and moving the trigger. They tried the ramrod down the barrels to ensure they were straight. They worked their way through the weapons, and as they passed them to one side, one of the smiths came in and wrapped them in sacking and packed them into wooden crates and nailed them shut.

Ned's head was half-deafened by the noise of the yard by the time they had checked the whole pile, and Rowan was pale under the bronze of her skin.

'All good?' Thomas Dare demanded, darkening the room as he came in the doorway.

'All but those.' Ned indicated the handful of weapons that had faults.

Thomas Dare handed over a heavy purse; the forgemaster tipped the coins into his scales and weighed them, pulling one or two out to bite in his teeth to see that they had the softness of true gold. Then he and Dare shook hands, and he promised that the weapons should be delivered to the quay at Texel at once.

Dare, Ned and Rowan emerged with relief into the sunlight of the street.

'What now?' Ned asked.

'Leather jackets,' Dare replied. 'We need a thousand; they're being made at the tanners' canal, at Jordaan. Shop in the name of Jan Muis – sign outside is a mouse. You can get them, pay for them and get them delivered to the ship. And powder horns, get as many as you can for the money.'

He reached into his pocket, took out a purse, hefted it in his hand and passed it over to Ned. 'See if you can get the price down, for the Lord's sake. Check everything, only pay for good work.'

Ned nodded.

'And there's a special leather jacket for his lordship on order. Make sure they deliver them together to the *Helderenberg*, on the dock at the Island of Texel. You'd better go with them. I'll meet you there.'

LINCOLN'S INN, LONDON, SPRING 1685

The usher brought a note to Matthew when he was studying in his room, the window thrown open for air, the sultry stink of the City drifting in.

'Lady sent this,' he said shortly.

Matthew lifted his head from his books. 'A lady?' He dropped his pen where it splattered black ink on the case that he was preparing to argue – Soledad v Timmings – and took the note. It was addressed to him as Matteo da Picci, and as soon as he saw the name, in the beautiful script, he knew it was from her.

Son,

I would be obliged to you if you would meet me at the coffee house at Serle Court. I will wait only half an hour.

Your mother – Nobildonna Livia Avery

Matthew pushed back his chair and snatched up his jacket, thrusting his arms into the sleeves. A glance in the looking glass over his bed showed a handsome young face, half-man, half-boy. He crammed his pupil's hat on his long curling hair and crossed the little room in one stride.

'When did you get this?' he threw over his shoulder to the usher who waited on the stair.

'Just five minutes ago, Sir,' the man said. 'A lady, with her maid behind her.'

Matthew clattered down the winding stone stair, his hand dropping from one worn wooden peg to another on the central stone pillar, and ducked his head under the narrow stone doorway.

Matthew's rooms were in Gatehouse Court, a tall red-brick building trimmed with pale sandstone that had seemed over-whelmingly grand to him when he first took his room as a student to the Inn. Now he did not notice the buildings set in the huge well-kept gardens, as he pulled his jacket straight on his shoulders and strode, long-legged, across the paved courtyard, through the deep arch into Serle Court, where the stone masons were carving blocks for the new buildings in one corner and builders were tying wooden poles of scaffolding together nearby. Even from the court-yard Matthew could smell the roasting coffee beans and the rich smell of yeast from brewing ale. He pulled off his hat as he ducked his head under the doorway and opened the door on his right.

The place was quiet; Mr Hart the owner looked up but did not stir from his stool for a mere puny. Only a couple of clerks were seated at the big central table, spread with pamphlets and newspapers. A lawyer and his client were in one corner discuss-ing their case in low tones.

'Good day, Mr Hart,' Matthew said politely, looking past him to the interior.

A veiled lady was seated at a table at the back of the room, her maid standing behind her like a guard. Before her stood a tiny cup of strong coffee. Matthew skidded to a halt and watched her put back her veil, lift the cup, take a sip of coffee, and release her veil to hide her face again. He had seen nothing but rouged lips. His heart thudded at the realisation that his mother, his beautiful mysterious mother, had finally come for him.

'The lady is here for you?' Mr Hart rapidly modified his view of Matthew's unimportance.

'Yes.' He walked across the wooden floor, conscious of the creak of his shoes, and stood before her table, her letter in his hand. He thought he must look like a child, summoned to stand before his schoolmaster.

'My lady, you sent for me?' His voice sounded unsteady in his own ears. He flushed. 'I am Matthew,' he said, and now he was too loud, bellowing like a fool.

She swept back her veil and pinned it on her hat with one swift gesture, as if she were ready to reveal herself to him. Matthew stared into a face that he felt that he knew, that he had somehow always known. She was unforgettable. Thick dark hair was piled off her unlined forehead to tumble in curls to her shoulders, dark eyebrows were arched in interrogation, dark eyes raked him up and down. Her red lips curved into a conspiratorial smile, as if the two of them shared some kind of secret. Dimly, he supposed that they did.

He scanned her face for similarities to his own and found them. Her eyebrows slanted up a little at the end, as his did. Her eyes were as dark as his, the two of them – mother and son – had the same classically beautiful profile, but his smile was wide and frank, his face was open; hers was veiled even when the lace was put aside.

'Ah, so you are my son,' she said. He heard the lilt of her Italian accent, carefully preserved after fifteen years in England. 'I would have known you anywhere.'

He made an awkward bow and she rose from the table and put her hands lightly on his shoulders and drew him towards her, kissed his forehead like a blessing and then – like an Italian – kissed him on both cheeks. Her perfume, a light scent of roses, brushed his memory.

She stepped back to inspect him, as if calculating how best she should treat him. She saw the flush in his cheeks and realised that he was still a boy, a youth, sheltered by a loving foster family, kept from the temptations of the City and the dangers of the world. He might be smartly dressed and handsome, he might be studying law; but he was no match for a woman of her sharp acquisitive wits.

'So . . .' She was reassured. She took her chair and gestured that he should sit opposite her. 'So, we meet again. Do you remember me at all?'

'Very slightly,' he stumbled.

'Of course, it was a long time ago. You may sit down, my dear boy, my dearest son. *Caro figlio.* You speak Italian?'

At his downcast face she laughed. 'Of course you do not. How should you learn? But you are educated? I pay the fees, you know? You read Latin at least? And speak French, I suppose?'

He nodded. 'I didn't know you paid . . .'

'Well, yes! The good women of the warehouse could never afford it and would not have known what school you should attend, or how a gentleman should be raised. I took care of all of that. You have to have guarantors to enter the Inns – they're called "manucaptors" – I provided them too.'

'They never said . . . I didn't know.' He flushed, angry at himself for blindly assuming that his foster mothers had provided for him in a world they had never known.

'I doubt they speak of me at all! Do they? And never of what they owe me!' Her musical laugh made Mr Hart look up, and at her gesture, he came over with a fresh pot of coffee and a cup for Matthew.

'They don't,' Matthew admitted. 'But I thought that was your wish? I thought you told them to raise me and never trouble you?'

'*Allora!*' she exclaimed. 'I see you are a lawyer in the making indeed. *Caro*, I was in no case to issue instructions. I was trapped between the wishes of my new husband and the will of the stubborn old lady. They would have nothing to do with each other, and I had to find a safe haven for my beloved only child, while I made my new marriage.'

'For fourteen years?' he queried.

She shot a quick look at him as if assessing his tone. 'You feel that I should have sent for you earlier? Would you not have been torn between the women of the warehouse and me? Between two worlds and secure in neither? Was it not better to let them give you a childhood – an English childhood – of great safety and peace?'

'Yes . . .' he said uncertainly.

'And so that is what I did. You lived with them under their name – Reekie – only I cannot say it! So I call you Picci, da Picci for my title. And only now that you are a young man, a proper young man, and I am free of the demands of my husband and the manor and Yorkshire, can I visit you and see that my son has grown, and what we might be to each other.'

He felt slow and stupid. 'What we might be?'

'Yes of course, I want to help you to make your way in the world, and I am sure that you would want to see me rise.'

'I thought you . . .' Under her bright gaze he found his mouth was dry and took a gulp of coffee. It was scalding hot. He swallowed, feeling the burn go down his gullet. He flushed scarlet at the pain and blinked tears from his eyes.

'You thought I had risen?' Livia guessed, ignoring his discomfort. 'Toll-loll! You must know I was a great lady in Venice, of the Fiori family, and then I came to England and married Sir James and became a great lady in Yorkshire, and now I am a great lady in London – a friend to the Queen of England! So, yes! I have risen. And I continue to rise—' She broke off and snatched a quick look at him. 'But these are troubled times and I need to know that you are with me. As I work for our good.'

'You are working for our good?' he queried.

'Always,' she assured him. 'When my dearest friend your foster mother and her mother agreed to take you in, I knew you would be safe with them. But I knew too that the day would come when I would come back for you and make you my own again.'

She was unstoppable. He felt his head spinning and his throat hurt.

'I won't leave them.'

'Of course not! It would be most churlish. They have been as my nursery-maids, they have been as rockers for you. But I am your mother – that was never forgotten. And I will open doors for you that would otherwise be distant dreams. I will take you to court, you shall meet the king and queen.' She assessed the impact she was having on him. 'You want to be a lawyer?' she asked abruptly.

'Yes . . .' he said. 'Or at any rate some post—'

'There you are then!' she said triumphantly. 'I shall find you a post. None of them at the wharf could do so! But now tell me – does the wharf have its own ship now? Alys married Captain Shore, did she not? He still has his ship?'

'Yes,' he said.

'Very good, very good. And this ship – it is in London now?'

'Yes.'

'For how long?'

'I don't know. They're loading.'

'And if I wanted to take passage I could go?'

'I suppose so. They often take passengers.'

She smiled at him. 'You will be puzzled by all this, I know, Matteo. But I need you to trust me.'

The Italian version of his name, spoken lovingly in her accent, startled him. He felt that he had heard her say his name in that caressing voice, through his dreams, for all of the fourteen years that he had answered to Matthew.

'You cannot trust me yet,' she said understandingly. 'But you will. It may be that I need your help in a matter of life and death. You may be able to save me, your own mother, and . . .' she leaned forward and lowered her voice so that he had to lean towards her to hear her whisper, 'the Queen of England herself!'

He could feel her breath on his cheek, he could smell the sweet dark scent of coffee.

'The queen needs a ship?'

She sat back and smiled at his stunned face.

'Because of the invasion?'

'Of course, I cannot say! But you speak to Alys and to Captain Shore and tell them we may need two cabins, perhaps at once, perhaps in some weeks' time, and I will send to you if I need you.'

'I may tell them why?'

'As much as you think safe. As little as you can.'

'Won't the king provide for her safety? What about the navy?'

She shrugged. 'Oh, perhaps! But if he is away fighting with his army? And who should provide for me if not my own boy?' She rose from the table and pulled down her veil from her hat, so her face was hidden.

'Your husband?' he suggested weakly. 'Shouldn't he ...'

She laughed. 'He doesn't have a ship and – *allora!* – you do!'

Her maid, who had been standing behind her, came forward and offered her arm. Livia turned to Matthew who stood, quite stunned, before her.

'I shall come again in a few days,' she promised, as if he had asked for her. 'We shall meet here.'

He made a little bow. 'As you wish, your ladyship,' he said.

She gave him her gloved hand to kiss. He put his lips to the warm silk.

'You may call me Lady Mother,' she told him. '*Signora Madre.*'

TEXEL ISLAND, HOLLAND, SPRING 1685

The *Helderenberg* rocked in the strong onshore wind, with two smaller ships moored nearby, loaded with weapons, armour and uniforms for officers who were waiting in England, banners for the crowds, a printing press to publish the duke's manifesto, a printer to set the type, barrels of the rusty brown water of the island, famous for good-keeping on long voyages, barrels of wine, small ale, crates of fresh food and two brace of hens to lay eggs for the duke's breakfast.

Eighty-three men were mustered to sail in the invasion, some dismissed from William of Orange's army to follow the beloved duke, exiles from King James' England, his lordship's own servants who would die for him, and only one other nobleman: Lord Grey of Werke, who had been set on overturning the monarchy for all his life.

'But never heard a shot fired in anger,' Ned said quietly to Samuel Venner, a veteran who had served under Monmouth against the French in the Dutch War.

'He's gentry,' Venner replied. 'So he can ride a horse, can't he? Cavalry officer? They don't have to do more than gallop in the right direction. And he'll bring out all of Sussex for us.'

'Are we landing in Sussex?' Ned asked.

'I don't know where,' Venner said. 'And I don't care where, just as long as the wind changes and we can get out of port.'

'A papist wind,' Ned said sourly.

Every day the danger increased that King James' urgent

demands to his son-in-law William of Orange would stir the Dutch authorities into arresting the rebels and impounding the three ships. Every day that they bobbed at the quayside increased their visibility.

'Surely they'll turn a blind eye to us,' Venner suggested. 'We've had nothing but good will from the people of Amsterdam. They're praying for our success in the chapels. They've fought papists for years.'

Rowan appeared at his side, so soft-footed that Venner started and cursed her. She said nothing but touched Ned on the sleeve and pointed down to the twilit quay beside them. He could just make out two figures, city fathers by their rich clothes, broad beamed as barges, waddling towards them, papers in hand.

'Trouble?' she whispered.

Ned went without a word to the bridge, found the young recruit William Hewling on anchor watch and ordered the gangplank to be drawn in and the duke and his officers informed.

'They're onshore, dining,' Hewling said, looking anxiously over the side of the ship at the approaching officials. 'I don't even know which inn.'

Ned turned to Rowan. 'Go and find the duke,' he whispered. 'Make sure you're not seen. Tell him not to come back to the ship until we know who these men are. Tell him he might have to get away.' He caught her hand as she turned for the gangplank. 'Not that way, they'll see you. Can you get down the mooring rope?'

She nodded and disappeared before his eyes. It was as if she had melted into air. One moment he held her warm hand and saw her confident smile under the shadow of her hat, and the next there were just shadows, not even the outline of her shadow, not even the whisper of her cape. He looked aft where the rocking ship was pulling the line taut and saw her for just a moment, silhouetted against the grey horizon as she slung a leg over the rail, then she was gone. The men holloaing from the quayside had their backs to her as she wormed down the rope, going hand over hand with her legs wrapped around it, and jumped soundlessly onto the shore. She dropped into a low crouch and froze as Ned leaned over the side doffing his hat. 'Good evening, *Mijn Heren*,' he bellowed.

On the bridge behind him he heard the quiet click of Venner arming a musket. William Hewling behind him was white as a sail.

One of the men looked up. 'Are you captain of this vessel?' he demanded.

'The captain is off watch, Sir,' Ned replied. 'May I serve you?'

'What's its name and where is it bound?'

Out of the corner of his eye Ned saw a shadow – nothing more than the torchlight flickering – and knew that Rowan was on her way.

'It is the *Helderenberg*, bound for Bilbao.'

'We have information that this ship has been commissioned by the Duke of Monmouth for an invasion of England.'

Ned shook his head, the image of doltishness. 'Nay, I don't know anything about that,' he said slowly. 'We're laden with *baccalà* – salted codfish – and sailing for Spain as soon as the wind drops.'

'Where is the duke?'

'What duke?'

'Monmouth! Where is Monmouth?'

'Near Wales, I believe,' Ned said earnestly.

Hewling, caught off guard, snorted with laughter.

'We can do nothing without the facts!'

'No, Sir. No more can I. What facts?'

The men spoke among themselves. Ned could not understand their language, but he could see the world-wide unwillingness of small-town officials to exert themselves in uncertain times.

'I cannot admit you on board unless you have papers,' Ned said apologetically. 'Do you have papers?'

From the exclamation of irritation from one of the gentlemen Ned guessed that the necessary papers – in this most bureaucratic of countries – had not been provided.

'We will come back when we have the right papers,' the senior man said. He brandished a handful of documents. 'The English envoy failed to make the correct request.'

'The English envoy tried to stop us selling codfish to Bilbao?' Ned asked, deeply shocked at the interference in trade.

'A mistake,' one of the men said irritably. 'And us looking like fools.'

'Not at all! Not at all! Come back when you are fully certified. If you would be so gracious as to let us know when, I can make sure the captain is here to receive you.'

The Amsterdam official consulted his timepiece, a handsome large silver watch chained over his broad belly. 'When the envoy makes the correct application we will return,' he said. 'And you are?'

'Let me give you a note of my name,' Ned said. He found a piece of paper and dipped a pen in the ink-standish. 'Sir James Avery, Northside Manor, Northallerton,' Ned wrote with mischievous joy, scattered it with sand to dry, tied it in the plumb line and tossed it down to the officials.

The Amsterdammer untied the note and read the aristocratic scrawl. 'Sir James?'

'At your service, Sir,' Ned said, reeling the line in. 'Sir James Avery. Trader in codfish.'

Rowan led Ned at a loping run to the quayside inn where the duke was dining.

'I told him,' she said shortly.

Ned patted her shoulder. 'You did well,' he said. 'You went down that rope as quick as a rat.' He left her at the door of the private parlour, knocked and put his head inside the room. The duke was dining with his senior officers, Lord Grey at one end of the table, Colonel Foulness, Lieutenant Tallier and Captain Kidd between them.

'Your pardon, Sire, reporting from the ship,' Ned said.

'Come in,' Monmouth said. 'We've been waiting. You did well to send your lad to warn us. What's happened?'

'Amsterdam officials, inquiring about our business,' Ned said. 'I told them we were bound for Bilbao with freight but they've been set on us by the English envoy and they'll be back. They have to get a proper warrant before they can impound the ship – I couldn't understand it all, Sire, they spoke in their own language among themselves. But I did get – loud and clear – that they'll be back. My advice is that we sail, whatever the weather.'

'You've done me a service,' Monmouth nodded. 'Ned Ferryman, isn't it?'

'We could go on the ebbing tide, at night,' one of the men said.

'The wind's still against us,' someone else answered. 'We'll struggle to get out of port.'

Monmouth shook his head: 'We can't wait a moment longer.' He glanced at one of the men. 'Hire barges, extra barges, to tow us out. Once we're out the harbour we can run before the wind wherever it takes us. But we leave in the first lull.' He rose, and everyone leapt to their feet, calling for the reckoning and going to their rooms for their belongings. Ned, an old campaigner, quietly pocketed two bread rolls from the table and turned to the door.

REEKIE WHARF, LONDON, SPRING 1685

Matthew was not late on Friday, as he had threatened to be. He came home early, oddly subdued, hung his coat on the hook in the warehouse and kissed his foster mother.

'I thought you were out roistering,' Alys said.

'No, I wanted to come home. Is the *Sweet Hope* sailing soon?'

'Next month. Why?'

'Someone asked me.'

'Is everything all right, Matthew?'

He did not look at her. He thought how the other woman had called him 'Matteo', as if he were someone else. 'Yes.'

'You've not lost money gambling?' She went straight to her greatest fear.

'No, Ma. How often do I have to say!' He checked himself at her stricken face. 'No. But I'd like to talk to you and to Mother Alinor. Is she well enough to see me?'

'She's well, she's in her room.'

He led the way upstairs so that she should not hurry in front of him and warn her mother that he was in trouble. Alys followed the polished heels of his smart shoes and felt her heart sinking with dread.

Matthew tapped on Alinor's door and heard her take a breath enough to say 'Come in!' and stepped inside the room. He stood before her, hands at his sides, his face as blank as the beautiful statues that he resembled. Alinor raised her silver head and took him in, from the velvet bows on his shoes to the crown of his dark curling hair, noting his grave expression and the hurt in his eyes.

'Oh, you've seen your mother,' she said at once.

Alys dropped into a chair as if she had been winded. 'Oh,' she said. 'Oh! Is that it?'

Matthew nodded. 'She sent for me to meet her in a coffee house,' he said.

Alinor held out her hand. 'Come, my son, sit here.'

He crossed the room and sank onto a stool at the side of her sofa. He leaned back and she stroked the dark curling locks of hair from his forehead. Suddenly, he looked very young, and Alinor was reminded of the little boy he had been, the baby who had been left in their care because his mother did not want him. She laid her hand on his forehead as if she would test the heat of his skin for fever. 'Go on,' she said gently. He was steadied by the coolness of her hand and the faint scent of herbs in the room.

'This is my home,' he said.

'It is,' Alinor confirmed quietly. 'No doubt of that. You've got nothing to fear, and neither does Alys. Nothing can untie the love you two have for each other. You don't have to be born a son to a mother, to be a mother and son. You two have a bond that nothing will break.'

He nodded. 'It's true,' he said. He looked across at Alys who was frozen in her chair. 'It's true,' he repeated. 'Don't look like that, Ma.'

'How do I look?' she demanded.

'Like I was threatening you with a knife.'

'Aye,' she said bitterly. 'She's a sharp blade. What did she want?'

'I don't know what to tell you . . .' he began.

'Better say it all,' Alinor counselled. 'There's enough secrets already.'

'She wants a passage on Captain Shore's next sailing. She wants two berths. I said he took passengers and that he was due to go out next month as soon as she was loaded.' He turned to look up at Alinor. 'Was that all right to say?'

'Aye,' she said shortly. 'Go on.'

'She told me who the berths are for – but I don't know if I should repeat it.'

'For herself,' Alys said harshly. 'She never does anything for anyone.'

'It's for herself and for the queen,' he said, his voice low. 'In case Argyll and Monmouth invade.'

'The king's going to surrender?' Alys demanded incredu-lously. 'He'll go like his father? Give himself up to them?'

The youth shook his head. 'I don't know. That's all she told me.'

'And what did you say?' Alinor prompted gently.

'I said I would ask. I made no promise.' He shifted uneasily and Alinor's hand tightened comfortingly on his shoulder. 'She said some other things . . .'

'Did she?'

'She said that she would serve me, take me to court, that we should help each other rise in the world.'

'I daresay she will serve you,' Alinor spoke before her daughter could reply. 'Why shouldn't she? She's your Ma by birth, she'll be ambitious for you. Of course, she'll want you to do tasks for her. She's a woman accustomed to service.' She felt the rapid pulse at his collarbone. 'Did you like her, Matthew?'

'She called me *caro figlio*,' he said. 'It means dear son.'

'She said she would never take you from us!' Alys burst out.

'She hasn't done so,' Alinor said steadily. 'She's given him some errands to run. She can't take him, Alys. He spent his childhood with us, he's had our love poured on him. Nobody can take that from him.' She smiled at Matthew whose colour had risen. 'Nobody can take him anywhere – nor can we keep him. He's old enough to choose where he wants to live and what sort of man he wants to be.'

'Here?' Alys turned to the boy she had raised as her own son, her blue eyes imploring in her square face. 'You'll live here, in your home? As we raised you.'

He rose to his feet. 'Ma – this will always be my home and you're my mother.'

She waited.

'But of course I want to rise in the world!'

There was a silence in the sunlit room. Outside, the gulls cried over the flowing tide, wheeled on silver wings.

'We have risen,' Alys said defensively. 'You've no idea what it was like here when we first came. We've risen. Through hard work. Slow but steady. Trading, little profits, well earned. Hard earned. We never sold underweight. We never borrowed, we always paid on the nail. We never issued a note of credit without money behind it.'

'You didn't send me to Lincoln's Inn to come home to be a wharfinger.'

'It was her who sent you,' Alys said resentfully. 'To turn you into a gentleman. I always feared she would spoil you—'

'I am a gentleman!' he exclaimed. 'I was born a gentleman! I am descended from the Fiori family!'

'Are you?' Alinor asked.

'Yes, of course. I am stepson to Sir James Avery!'

'Was he there?'

'No. Just her. I don't know what she wants. Only what she tells me.' He looked at Alys. 'What am I to tell her?' he asked.

They both turned to Alinor, as if her foresight could keep them safe.

'You can tell her that she can have passage in Captain Shore's ship, if he agrees to it,' she said gently. 'You'll have to ask him yourself. Make sure he knows who he'll be carrying. And you can tell her when he'll sail. I doubt he'll wait for her and you shouldn't ask it of him. If we're no use to her, she can find someone else.'

He nodded. 'Is that all right with you, Ma?'

Alys' face was shut and resentful. 'She comes to us whenever she wants something and then she goes again. Sir James is just the same. They just turn up when they want something, and they break our hearts and go . . .'

Alinor's smile at her daughter was filled with compassion. 'Yes,' she said. 'They have to come to us, because they have so little of their own. They have to come to us, they are so poor themselves.'

'I think she's very rich . . .' Matthew said tentatively.

Alinor smiled at him. 'They are poor in heart.'

TEXEL ISLAND, HOLLAND, SPRING 1685

Monmouth was on the bridge of his ship, checking that men and stores were aboard before the gangplank was run in and the lines cast off from the shore. Extra barges surrounded the ship, lines attached, preparing to tow the *Helderenberg* out of the harbour into an onshore wind that was wheeling at last to the east, the stocky bargees spitting into their work-worn palms and predicting that it would be a hard pull. The little ships were readying themselves to follow. The Dutch pilot was beside the steersman, pointing a route through the sandbars and mudbanks, warning of the wrecks in the shallows. Tentatively, the ship rocked and then started to glide away from the dark shore studded with flickering lights from lanterns. The waves slapped loudly against the keel as the wind blew them back onshore and the barges, with their crews straining to keep the pace, fought to tow the ship out of the harbour. Ned had a familiar feeling in the pit of his belly, a mixture of excitement and dread, and knew that he was headed into battle again, surely the last battle of his life, for the freedoms of the men and women of England.

He turned to Rowan, at his side as always. 'When we land, I'll give you money and you must make your way to London, to my sister's warehouse. She'll give you a bed and your keep until this is over.'

He could not see her expression, her face was hidden by her hat, but her voice was clear. 'I'll stay with you.'

'I'll be going into battle if the king's army comes against us,' Ned said. 'And if it doesn't, I'll be training men. I don't even know where we'll land, but we've got to take the capital. If we land up north, up the east coast, it could be many days' march, south to London.'

'Then you'll be going to London as you say I must,' she pointed out. 'I'll go with you.'

'Not with an army of raw recruits!' he exclaimed.

'Don't you want me with you?'

He checked his sudden denial and measured his words, conscious of her trusting gaze on his face. 'Rowan, this is my mistake. I never thought we'd sail at once. I should've left you in London.'

She stepped a little closer. 'But as your servant . . .'

'We both know that you're not my servant. I bought you out of slavery to set you free.'

'Then as a free woman, I will stay with you until the danger is past,' she said.

'There's danger now,' he said, looking out into the darkness where the wind was whipping up the dark sea into rolling waves with white caps.

'I'm not afraid of the sea,' she said – a woman of the ocean who had shot the breakers of the Atlantic shore in her own canoe since childhood.

He had to stop himself reaching out to cup her defiant face in his rough palms. He wanted to draw her closer, hold her, wrap her in his old cape, keep her safe. He wondered at himself that he should have become so fond of a stranger young enough to be his grand-daughter.

'I should order you to safety.'

'After we land,' she bargained with him. 'When we see what danger there is. Order me then.' She nearly trapped him into agreement.

'And you'll obey me then?'

She laughed like the Pokanoket child he remembered. 'Yes! If I think you're right!'

'Very well,' he said, hiding his tenderness. 'You can stay with me as we march on London, unless it looks like there's danger, and then you'll go to Alinor.'

'Agreed,' she said cheerfully.

ST JAMES' PALACE, LONDON, SPRING 1685

To Lady James Avery,

Madam,
I have been commanded to muster the militia and prepare
for an invasion by Argyll and Monmouth. I doubt that local
forces will be able to hold the rebels from marching on London.
Accordingly, I am sending my carriage with outriders
today, to bring you home to safety. I order you, Madam, to
make your excuses to their Majesties, and come home.
Your obdt. servant and husband
James Avery

Livia refolded the letter and tapped it, thoughtfully, against
her rouged lips. Disobeying her husband would be a great risk;
he had an undeniable legal right to order her home, but if she
defied him and stayed, and the third civil war broke out and
the royalists lost – as they had done twice before – then Livia
would be on the losing side, in a royal household at the time
of its fall.

Whether she should take the Avery carriage and run home
to safety, or gamble everything on a royal victory, was something she could not decide, though she walked up and down the
queen's gallery, tapping the letter against her lips until it looked
as if it were bloodstained in her hand.

The double doors opened and the queen came in, ladies

around her, courtiers behind them. Her pale face was set in a rigid smile, as if she would deny her fears. She called for the card tables to be set up, and for a glass of wine; gaily she challenged her courtiers to a game of ombre, and the musicians started to play. Livia was not deceived; she drew the queen into a window-seat.

'Your Majesty – is there bad news?'

Queen Mary held up her fan to hide her words. 'Our commander Lord Dumbarton is marching to Scotland with our army.'

'He's just set out north, in the hopes of finding the invasion?' Livia asked incredulously.

'What else can he do? Better to march north than do nothing.'

The two women looked blankly at each other. 'I know nothing about warfare,' Livia said.

'And now the king tells me that there are uprisings in the south also.'

'What sort of uprisings?' Livia cried. 'Why are they not put down? They wouldn't allow any uprising in Venice. You're not allowed to even think against the Doge in Venice. Why does the king allow it?'

'Have you heard of a town by the name of "Taun-ton"?'

Livia shook her head, her sense of the huge strangeness of England all around them.

'It's beyond Bath,' the queen said as if she were describing New England far away in the Americas, over the ocean. 'Further west even than Bath. They have called out the militia against rebels there, in Somerset.'

'Is the militia loyal to us there?'

'I don't think so. They sound frightened. They write to the king that there have been births of monstrous girls, and an earthquake, and three suns in the sky. They say this foretells the fall of the throne.'

'I don't believe that there were three suns in the sky. How could there be?'

'It's what they're saying!' the queen repeated unhappily.

In the room before them someone threw down their cards and laughed at their bad luck. Livia cast an irritated glance before she remembered that she was supposed to be carefree. She smiled as if the queen had said something amusing. She put her hand to her throat as if she were overwhelmed, and she laughed and laughed, flicking out her fan.

The queen caught sight of the stained letter in Livia's hand. 'Oh! What have you there? Is it news of our ship?'

'Yes,' Livia lied smoothly. 'As I promised, I have a ship for you. We need not be afraid of suns and monsters. We will be safe whatever happens.'

'We can sail away? We can go to Rome? The ship will take me to my Mama, Duchess Laura at Rome? I can tell her I am coming home?'

'Yes,' Livia said boldly. 'And my carriage is coming from Yorkshire. At the first bad news we will get safely away, either by road in my carriage or by sea in my ship.'

AT SEA, SPRING 1685

Monmouth set a watch and turned in to his cabin for the night; the senior men had bunks in shared cabins and the rest slept in corners of the hold, curled up in spaces between the cargo or wrapped themselves in their new jackets against the onshore wind and slept on the deck. Ned and Rowan found a corner on a folded sail and made a comfortable nest. Rowan lay on her back and looked up at the night sky, the sail sometimes billowing out to hide the stars from her, sometimes dropping back when the wind eased. Ned folded his arms behind his head and watched her profile as he fell asleep.

Suddenly there was a shout from the lookout, and the sound of a cannon firing, the whistle of a cannonball and the great splash as it landed in the sea just astern. The ship rolled as the steersmen dragged on the wheel to change direction.

Ned was on his feet in a moment, Rowan beside him. The watch clanged the bell to muster the soldiers, and the look-out on the mast pointed to a yacht that had suddenly loomed out of the darkness behind them. Ned, glancing back at the quarterdeck, saw Monmouth, bare-headed, wearing nothing but a white shirt and his breeches, dashing up the compan-ionway. Ned jumped up and ran after him, Rowan beside him. 'Get down!' he threw at her over his shoulder. 'Get behind the mast!'

'Ferryman!' Monmouth yelled down from the quarterdeck. 'Is that the Amsterdam magistrates?'

Ned raced up to the quarterdeck and took the telescope that Monmouth offered him. He could see the pale outline of a yacht with no lights, broadside to them, ready to fire again, grappling hooks at the ready and the crew preparing to board. He focused on the flag of the States General. 'Aye. Looks like they've got their warrant. That was a warning shot. They're signalling us to hove to. They're preparing to board.'

'We'll run for it,' Monmouth decided. 'Captain, cram on sail, get us away. Ferryman – tell them a round of cannon, to keep them back, but make sure to miss. We can't sink them!'

'Yes, Sire,' Ned said and jumped down to the deck and slid down the ladder to the gun deck. The crew were ready, each standing by their guns, the hatches open, the guns rolled for-ward, each gunner waiting the command, the gun commander halfway up the companionway ready for his orders.

'Fire to miss,' Ned told him. 'Fore and aft the ship. Make sure you're wide. Don't hit it.'

'Aye, aye,' the man said steadily. He turned and raised his voice to his crew. 'Fore and aft. Wide. Everyone wide. On my word—'

He glanced down the waist of the ship to see that they were all poised ready. 'Fire at will!' he yelled.

There was a roar of explosions and a rumble as each cannon spat out flame and rolled back into the ship, each gunner leaping aside to avoid being crushed by the recoil. At once they swarmed over the guns, ramming down gunpowder, wadding and another cannonball and readied the pan for another round. Above them on deck they heard the crackle of musket fire. Ned prayed briefly that Rowan was hidden.

'Hold your fire!' Ned yelled. He peered out through a gun port.

'Hold fire!' the gun commander confirmed.

'They've dropped sail, they're not pursuing,' Ned said. 'Stand by.'

He waited a moment longer, and then Rowan's head appeared, leaning down into the hatchway. 'The ship's turning,' she told him. She was pushed aside by a tall man who scrambled down the companionway.

'And who the hell're you?' the man demanded in a strong Scots accent.

'Well done, lads!' Ned said to the gun crew. 'Stand down, stand easy.'

They gave a ragged cheer, rolled back their weapons and closed the gun ports. Each man cleaned his cannon, tidied his station and closed the store of gunpowder. Ned tipped his cap to the man, obviously a gentleman, one of Monmouth's officers. 'Ned Ferryman, Sir.'

'An' who gave you the order to fire?'

'Monmouth.'

He was thrown. Ned looked around to see that everything was safe, especially that lights were out, and moved towards the ladder.

'I am in command of the gun deck,' the man insisted. 'I should have given the order. I am Andrew, Lord Fletcher. Commander of the cavalry.'

'I must report to the duke.'

'I shall report to the duke,' Andrew Fletcher insisted.

Ned stood back to let him lead the way up the ladder and up the companionway to where Monmouth was waiting on the bridge.

'Cannons discharged and rolled back, Sire,' Andrew Fletcher said.

'Thank you,' Monmouth said briefly. He turned to Ned. 'Will you stay up here on the bridge now, Ferryman? Take a watch. You've been of great service to me today. I won't forget it.' To the steersman he said: 'Set a course. South-west coast of England. Devon.'

'Aye, aye, Sir.'

Monmouth went below and Andrew Fletcher followed him without another word as Rowan appeared out of the darkness.

'You go and sleep,' Ned said. 'I'll come and find you at dawn.' Obediently, she turned to go. 'Were you afraid?' he asked her curiously. 'When the cannons fired?'

She gave a little shrug of indifference. 'The worst has already happened to me,' she said simply. 'Anything now is just finishing Misery Swamp.'

'When your king was killed?'

'Killed by a traitor when we were already defeated. Killed before us, and his wife and son captured, and me taken with them,' she said. 'We'd rather have died than lose them. But we didn't die. I saw him go down, and then they took her and his son: our boy.'

He reached for her and turned up the collar of her cloak as if to keep her warm. 'There will be a dawn,' he told her. 'You're a child of the Dawnlands. It seems like very dark night now for you, but you're young, you'll see a lot of dawns – and they'll be happier than this one, I promise you.'

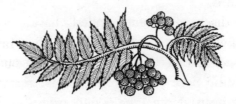

THE COFFEE HOUSE, SERLE COURT, LONDON, SPRING 1685

Matthew, first to arrive at the coffee house, chose a bench seat with a high back, tucked away in the corner. Most of the customers were seated around the large central table, newspapers of the day and pamphlets scattered before them, discussing the implications of a recent judgment, and prices for legal services, vacancies for clerks and the delay at the courts. Serle's patrons were mostly lawyers, juniors, clerks and students seeking work. Clerks for rival chambers were seated at one end of the table, assigning cases for their lawyers; one or two clients hovered anxiously, hoping to meet their lawyers, some with sheafs of old papers hoping for free advice.

A stunned silence fell when Livia walked in and paused, savouring the attention. She looked around her as if she might buy the place outright. Mr Hart bustled up to her, bowed and offered to seat her; but she caught sight of Matthew rising from his corner table, and walked past the owner without a word. Her maid followed and drew out the chair as Livia put back her veil, kissed Matthew on both cheeks and then seated herself. Her maid stood silently behind her.

Mr Hart placed a small cup of coffee before her with a heaped bowl of sugar. Livia nodded, took a sip and then regarded her son.

'You have spoken to the women of the warehouse?'

'To my foster mothers, yes,' he said, nettled.

She smiled at his pride. 'They agree?'

'I had to speak to Captain Shore, he sails in the middle of June. He will reserve two berths for you. I had to tell him who would be aboard.'

'He will be discreet?' she demanded.

'He doesn't want to be mixed up in it at all,' Matthew told her bluntly. 'He won't speak of it, and he hopes you will not have need of his ship.'

'They are royalists now?' she asked curiously.

'They take no interest in it,' Matthew said. 'They are loyal and law-abiding, and they don't want trouble.'

'But the brother in New England . . .' She waved a hand as if to show that she could not recall his name. 'He was an old Cromwell soldier, was he not? Fled abroad after his defeat? He was on the other side, the wrong side?'

'I don't know,' Matthew said cautiously. 'It was a long time ago.'

'Long before you were born, *caro figlio*,' she said, suddenly turning her attention to him. 'You have done very well for me. Your mother is grateful to her clever boy. You will be rewarded. You will see the benefit of serving me. Do I have to pay before we sail?'

'You do, and if you don't sail you lose your money,' Matthew said awkwardly. 'I am sorry, but those are the usual terms.'

She shrugged her shoulders; her dark cape fell slightly open and Matthew could see the gleam of jewels on her breasts in the low-cut gown. 'It is of no matter,' she said. She nodded to her maid, who handed a heavy purse to Matthew. 'This is enough?'

He untied the string and looked inside. 'It is more than enough. About half would be—'

'Take it! Take it! It may be that you have to buy some things that we need, or pay a wherryman, or who knows what? But pay Captain Shore with it, and reserve our berths.'

Matthew nodded and pocketed the purse.

'And if we do not sail – if all this has been a fuss about nothing, as the English do – then I will introduce you at court,' she promised him. 'I shall see you are rewarded whatever happens.'

'I don't need a reward,' he said.

'We do,' she corrected him. 'We who serve for love, should be rewarded for our love.'

'I just want to finish my studies and become a lawyer,' Matthew protested.

'You shall be an ambassador,' she decided. 'And you will need a seat, a country seat.' She gestured to the communal table where the men were talking and exchanging papers. 'You don't want to spend your life here, arguing with fools about details. You shall have a post in one of the foreign courts, or you shall become a judge, or advise the privy council. So you will need a name, a title and land.'

Matthew gaped at her. 'I wouldn't know how to begin!'

'Not at once,' she agreed. 'But it was always my intention that you should be a great man. I had hoped to get you Northside Manor; but Sir James is stubborn. The place is entailed on the next male heir, and he will not adopt you. Anyway – he will not die soon. Probably not for years.'

'I wouldn't want Sir James' place,' he exclaimed. 'I couldn't accept it. I wouldn't be his heir even if he . . . At the warehouse . . . we don't speak of him. There was some offence . . .'

She made a dismissive wave of her hand. 'Old quarrels,' she said vaguely. 'He and Alys are old enemies. From long ago. He injured her mother and they stole from him or something.'

'My grandmother Alinor would not steal,' he said flatly. 'Nor my mother Alys. There must be a mistake.'

'Oh! He adores Alinor!' she said airily. 'And she forgave him. It's all long ago. It matters nothing to us.'

He blinked, observing that now there was a shared view of what mattered to them – that now they were a couple. 'Well anyway,' he said uncertainly. 'I don't look for Sir James' estate, and I know of no other.'

'They do, though,' she said as a thought struck her. 'The women. They are continually speaking of the place where they lived. In the tidelands, what do they call it, Foulmire? I always thought it sounded completely vile.'

'Could I get a house there?' he asked, startled.

She shrugged. 'If you wanted it, I could discover if there was a royal manor that we might get.'

'It's the only place I would want! Mother Alinor could live there! She has always wanted to return, she's never even gone back for a visit. It's her home, her childhood home.'

She raised her eyebrows. 'I offer you the chance of any royal manor in England and you want a house in a sea of mud so an old lady can live there?'

He did not hear the sarcasm in her voice. 'Yes! Yes! It would be to repay their kindness to me. She's been like a mother to me, she and Ma. If I could get a house for them there, and they could live in comfort, restored to their home, and if it was the big house that they speak of, Mother Alinor could have her own still room and a herb garden!'

'Toll-loll!' she said, smiling at him. 'I can ask; if that's what you really want, and if it is good enough for us, rents and so on. But it shall be in our name, not theirs. And you shall be the lord of the manor, not them. They will have no rights there, they will be your guests.'

'It would be such a wonderful thing!' He was filled with enthusiasm. 'I would be so happy.'

She smiled. 'See? You do want a reward for service! Everyone has a price, Son. Remember it. But I hope you learn more ambition. This place sounds like a lonely muddy little strand. But I will ask: if it is your choice. If the house has an estate of a decent size, and if there is a church with the living attached, and a parliamentary seat, then I shall try for it. What's it called again?'

'Foulmire!' he exclaimed. 'Foulmire, near Sealsea Island, south of Chichester.'

'Dismal name!'

A bell rang the hour, and then distantly, others joined in; the clock on the wall of the coffee house rang a silvery note, and some of the clerks gathered their papers and went out, the black sleeves of their gowns billowing. Livia rose to her feet and stood still as her maid arranged her cloak around her shoulders. 'You must come to the palace when I send for you,' she told him. 'Come by boat and keep it waiting at Whitehall Stairs. You won't speak of this to anyone else. And you won't fail.'

'I won't!' he promised her.

Her rouged lips parted over little white teeth. 'And I shall see what I can get us,' she smiled. 'The Picci family seat.'

REEKIE WHARF, LONDON, SPRING 1685

The Reekie family were going to dinner on Saturday evening. Johnnie laid a gentle hand on his grandmother Alinor's arm, and held her back to ask her: 'Grandma, have you heard anything from my uncle Ned?'

'I don't expect to hear from him,' she told him. 'He won't write until it's over.'

'Is she with him?' he asked quietly.

She looked at him with interest. 'Rowan? You care for Rowan?'

Though he was a man of thirty-five, he looked bashful, like a boy. 'Of course not! I hardly know her. And she is . . . perhaps . . . unknowable! But I don't like to think of her in danger.'

'I expect he'll send her back here if there's danger,' Alinor predicted.

'He should have left her here!'

Alinor looked at the troubled face of her handsome grandson. 'I think it was her choice,' she told him gently. 'If you care for her, you will have to learn that she thinks that no man is her master.'

'I found her a place of work,' he said. 'I said I would befriend her.'

'Did she ask you to?'

He looked rueful. 'I meant to help her.'

Her smile was knowing. 'Some people only want to find their own way.'

'Did she tell you?'

'No; but I was once a woman who wanted to find her own way.' She paused. 'I expect we will see her again.'

'Can't you foresee?' he asked her, trying to laugh it off. 'Can you foresee her coming back here?'

'No,' she said thoughtfully. 'I've only dreamed of her once, just once. A strange dream of a bluer sea than I have ever seen in this world, and she was in a little boat, with a boy. In my dream, she was going home.'

'She can never do that!' he told her.

'Come and sit,' Alys called them to the dinner table. Alinor smiled at Johnnie and took her seat between Rob and Captain Shore, as Johnnie sat down beside his mother. Alinor gave thanks for the food and blessed those who were absent that evening – 'Our daughter Sarah and her family in Venice, and my brother Ned, wherever he is tonight, and his companion Rowan, our dear son Matthew. Keep them safe, Lord, and bring them safely home. Amen.'

'No Matthew tonight?' Captain Shore asked his wife.

'His mother invited him to dine in her rooms at court.'

He raised his sandy eyebrows at Rob. 'He's dining with her now?'

'Why not?' Alinor asked generally. 'She's his own mother, in London. It makes no difference to us.'

Captain Shore served himself with a generous slice of roast chicken and glanced at Rob. 'Does it make no difference to you, Doctor?'

Rob shrugged. 'No difference at all. The false contract between us was declared invalid and she married Sir James, good luck to him. I've a wife and child of my own; I never think of her, and my wife doesn't even know of her existence.'

'You never mentioned her?'

'I told Julia's father, the Alderman, when we were negotiating the marriage contract. I would've told Julia, but he advised me to say nothing, and forget about it myself. It's more for you, Sister – you raised Matthew. And for you, Ma – you've kept him here and treated him like your own child. You can't welcome her back into his life. Let alone yours?'

'She's not in our lives,' Alys said stoutly. 'We'll never see her here – that's for sure. But a child should know his mother. I never pretended he was mine. I've loved him as much as a mother does, the Lord knows – but he's always known her name. Ma said: "better that he meets her, than imagines an angel" and I think she's right.'

'No chance of him mistaking her for an angel!' Rob said shortly.

Alinor smiled at her daughter. 'Livia Avery did one good thing in her life when she left him with us.'

'She's taken a berth on my ship to Rome,' Captain Shore told Rob. 'I didn't think to ask you . . .'

'No need to ask me,' Rob confirmed. 'And no need to tell me either. I'd rather know nothing. But make sure that you leave her at Rome! We don't want her disturbing Sarah's happiness with her husband Felipe and their family in Venice.'

'Aren't you even curious?' Alys questioned her brother.

He shook his head. 'I promised myself I'd never look back. I advised you to do the same. She's like laudanum: at first it's wholly beneficial, then you can't imagine your health without it's support, and you want more and more.' He looked at his sister. 'D'you know what I mean?'

She scowled at him and shook her head. 'I forget.'

'Have you said nothing at all to Julia of your past?' Alinor asked him quietly.

'I told her that I'd been wrongly arrested in Venice, and that Sarah came and got me out of the Doge's prison. I've never said more; and she has no curiosity.'

His mother and his sister exchanged a quick glance at the thought of a woman with no curiosity, but neither of them challenged him.

'I'll take a fee for the passage, and I'll deliver her and her mistress to Rome and gladly never see her again.' Captain Shore promised him. 'She won't come here, she can board at Greenwich.'

Alinor nodded. 'And in any case, Captain Shore has far more interesting passengers for the return voyage. Sarah is sending her girls to us for a visit.'

'Ah, they're coming!' Rob said warmly. 'They must come to my house and meet their little cousin, they can share Hester's lessons. I owe my life to Sarah – her girls can count on my home as their own.'

'Better check with your wife first,' Alys said with a sly smile to her mother, knowing that Julia welcomed no-one from the wharf at the elegant house in Hatton Garden.

Rob flushed. 'Julia will be pleased to meet her nieces,' he said flatly. 'You must all come and dine with us when they arrive.'

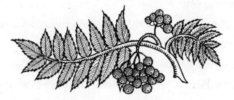

ST JAMES' PALACE GARDENS, LONDON, SPRING 1685

The king and his gentlemen were walking with the queen and her ladies in a show of royal confidence that fooled no-one. Queen Mary, exhausted by sleepless nights of worry, could have been carried in a sedan chair; but she would not show weakness before the residents whose windows overlooked the royal gardens. The king's notorious mistress Catherine Sedley had built a little hill at the end of her garden, with a winding path and a banqueting hall at the top, so that she could overlook the royal gardens and be seen by her royal lover. Now, as the royal party went past, they saw a swirl of bright silk as Catherine Sedley dashed to the top of the hill and waved joyously at the king.

'Halloo!' she bellowed like a huntsman sighting a fox, and when he looked up, she swept a deep curtsey to him.

The king was in no mood for Catherine Sedley today, nor was he moderating his pace to suit his wife. He strode ahead of her, stopping only with a grunt of impatience when he remembered that they were supposed to be walking arm in arm. He looked as if he wished he were back on a quarterdeck facing his enemies, instead of idling in a garden while they mustered against him in the north of his country, rioted in the west country, and whispered in the streets of his own capital.

'You seem troubled, my lord?' the queen asked breathlessly, trying to keep up with him.

'Halloo! Halloo!' went Catherine Sedley, until the king turned and bowed to her, as she kissed her hand to him.

'I've had a letter from my daughter's husband, William of Orange,' the king said irritably.

Livia, walking close enough to hear, noted that William was no longer described as a son-in-law.

'Beautiful weather!' bawled Catherine Sedley from her garden.

'Indeed,' the king said, with a distracted smile to his favourite. 'William tells me – now he tells me! That he has learned that the Duke of Monmouth remained in Amsterdam after Argyll sailed. So James Monmouth is not with Argyll in Scotland as I thought.'

'But that's good, isn't it?' the queen asked. 'You said that they would be impossible to defeat together?'

'I never said that.'

Behind them, Catherine Sedley was curtseying to the retreating court. The queen compressed her lips and turned her head away.

'And anyway, it's not good!' the king told his wife. 'It's bad news. The worst I could get. William tells me that Monmouth has sailed, but he has no idea where!'

She was aghast. 'Then where is he?'

'He could be sailing up the Thames right now! How would I know? He could have gone further up the coast to the north, where they're all protestants and dissenters. Or west where they're practically heathen. But since I had no warning of him sailing, I could not put ships in his way. Thanks to William, he can land where he will!'

'I have to go inside,' she whispered. 'I cannot walk and pretend that everything is well with us.'

'Go! Go!' James waved her away, furious at his own impotence.

She hesitated. 'Husband, should we not leave London?' she asked, her voice a thread. 'Is it safe to stay here? And with your daughter Princess Anne about to go into her confinement any day?'

'There's no safe haven for us Stuarts!' he said bitterly. 'Don't you hear me? The west is all for Monmouth, and the north. The Scots are all for Argyll! If we're not safe in our own capital city, where we can fall back into the Tower if we come under siege, then we're not safe anywhere!'

'Siege?' She managed a curtsey to him with shaking legs, and Livia sank down beside her, their silks skirts billowing together; but James had already turned and was stalking across the grass, towards the open door to Catherine Sedley's garden, his gentlemen following him in stricken silence.

'Did he say we were not safe anywhere?'

Livia helped her up. 'Remember, I have a passage in a ship for you,' she whispered. 'I will keep you safe.'

REEKIE WHARF, LONDON, SPRING 1685

Captain Shore came to the back door of the warehouse for his midday dinner and seated himself at the kitchen table as Alys came in from the counting house.

'You can have your dinner in the parlour, Abel,' she said, seeing he was slicing his own loaf of bread and spreading it with butter. 'Susie will bring it to you.'

'I'm in my working clothes,' he said. 'I'll just take a quick bite.'

She smiled at him. 'It's your own dining room,' she said. 'You can eat in your working clothes in your own room if you want.'

He smiled up at her. 'I know you keep it nice for your Ma,' he told her. 'And I've been loading wool, I stink of lanolin.'

She sniffed at the warm animal scent in the room. 'Reminds me of home,' she said. 'Ma used to roll the fleeces for the shearing gang. I'll seethe you some ale.'

The pot of ale hissed as the red hot poker went in, and she spooned in sugar, then they sat in companionable silence while he finished his meal and drank the hot ale. When he had finished, he wiped his mouth on his sleeve. 'Heard from your uncle Ned?'

'No,' she said. 'I don't expect to. Not till it's all over, one way or another.'

'That coaster from the west country that came in this morning – captain told me that all of the west is expecting the duke any day. Every chapel and ale house thinks he's coming; there was a riot at Wellington fair and another at Taunton.' He smiled at her anxious face. 'Don't you worry! Looks like your uncle picked the winning side! Captain said they're calling out the militia, but nobody's volunteering. There's no love for this king as there was for his brother. And even King Charles played us false and was a papist all along. God knows, they're not a trustworthy family.'

'But what about us?' she asked. 'What about the business?'

He rose to his feet. 'Duke or king, people still want trade,' he reassured her. 'As long as there's no privateering, and no warships coming upriver, we trade as usual.'

'Did the captain say when?'

'Soon,' Abel Shore told her. 'Before June is out. God bless him, he could be landing in Plymouth right now.'

'Maybe Livia Avery will need that berth in your ship,' Alys said with rare spite. 'Her and her papist queen.'

'So there's another one that thinks the Stuarts will be on their travels again. And she should know.'

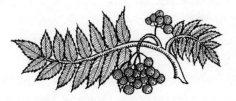

AT SEA, SUMMER 1685

The little flotilla sailed slowly, against a contrary wind, past the Isle of Wight and onward to the west. Monmouth ordered the two accompanying ships to drop back, in case of any English naval patrols coming from Portsmouth harbour, or lookouts from the cliffs of the island. But no warning guns were fired, and no beacons lit up the evening sky. It was as if they slipped by on invisible tides.

'Where's the king's navy?' Monmouth demanded of Ned Ferryman. They were both scanning the darkening horizon. 'I felt sure he'd have lookouts.'

'Happen he can't trust the navy,' Ned offered. 'Half of them signed on under Cromwell, they've no love of a papist king and his officers.'

'Lord!' Monmouth said happily. 'I knew the army was half mine, but I didn't hope for the navy too! But it looks like they won't trouble us. We're safely past Portsmouth and we'll go ashore before Dartmouth. Mr Ferryman, I know you're off watch – go and get your share of dinner before it's all gone.'

'My lad saves mine,' Ned said, climbing down the companionway to the deck to find Rowan seated on a coil of rope before the mast with a bowl of stew, a heel of new-baked bread, and a cup of rum and water.

'Thanks,' he said. 'Have you eaten?'

Rowan nodded. 'It's good,' she said. 'I killed the chicken for the cook and plucked it for him.'

Ned smiled. 'Why're you helping in the galley?'

'He was going at it with a cleaver. He would have hammered it to death and ruined the meat.'

'And you wrung its neck?'

'I said farewell and thanked it, and wrung its neck,' she confirmed. 'It was quick.'

Ned sat beside Rowan and took the food. 'It's good,' he agreed. 'Would you like to learn to cook, Rowan? You could make a good living as a cook?'

She shook her head with a little smile. 'No.'

Ned ate his stew in silence and then wiped out the bowl with the bread and ate that too.

'Is there nowhere in England that I can live in the forest and hunt?' she asked. 'Somewhere in the east that faces the dawn?'

He felt his heart ache for her homesickness. 'There's wasteland and commonland especially in the north of the country. But even there, people live in small cottages and shanties, and I doubt they'd welcome an incomer. There are no long strands and forests that run for hundreds of miles in this country.'

'Deer?'

He shook his head, silenced by his remorse that he had brought her to such a strange land. 'They all belong to the king, and he hunts them for sport in the royal parks. They hang people for poaching.'

She was silent for a moment. 'Killing is a sport?'

'For the king.'

She nodded, taking it in. 'In a park? Fenced in? So the deer are not free? The king has slaved them?'

'Yes – in a way.' He glanced at her downcast face. 'Would you go back to America, if I bought you a passage? Could you join another People?'

'I couldn't join my enemies.'

'What about the People you don't know? If you were to go south of the Dawnlands? Somewhere safe? I've read of them that live in Virginia ...' He hesitated. King Philip's war that had destroyed the Pokanoket was only one of many savage wars that the English colonists had waged. The Powhatan people had been driven from their homes, beyond the English borders, forced to walk, starving, into exile. The Pequot people had been all-but destroyed when settlers burned them out. A thousand Narragansett had died in the Great Swamp Massacre; the colonials turned on their allies the Occaneechi, killing them without warning. At Turner Falls the English militia had killed women and children while they were fishing in the river, clubbed them to death among their fishing nets.

'I don't know where's safe,' he admitted. 'These are troubled times. Maybe go further west?'

'No,' she said. 'The people are not my people. We don't speak the same language. You look at us with your blind eyes, and you think with your empty heads that we are all the same. But one nation is as different from another, as you are from us. But you don't like to think that. You like to look at a stranger and think all strangers are the same; that it is only you who are special.'

'But where will you live? You have to go somewhere!' The thought of her in a strange country, trapped between two armies, made him nauseous with anxiety.

'You shouldn't have bought me if you didn't want me,' she said reasonably. 'You saved my life. I'd be dead by now if you hadn't bought me. You saved my life – it is yours.'

'I don't want it,' he said meanly. 'I don't want your life. I don't want you. I can't . . .'

She looked at him, saying nothing for a moment.

Ned clamped his hands on his knees to stop him reaching for her. 'I can't keep you with me.'

'But I am yours,' she said simply. 'It is a debt.'

ST JAMES' PALACE, LONDON, SUMMER 1685

The queen was composing a letter of congratulation to her step-daughter Princess Anne, on her safe delivery of a healthy child. Livia was at the table, her pen poised, waiting to write. Mary Beatrice, opposite her, rested her heavily coiffed head in both hands as if the weight of the hair pieces and the jewellery was too much for her.

'Oh, write whatever it is I should say!' she exclaimed. 'You're absolutely sure it's a girl?'

'It's a girl. God be praised for His favour to you: she's not had a Stuart boy.'

'But even so . . .'

Livia waited in case the queen would say any more, then she put the quill down and went to stand behind the younger woman, bending over her, wrapping her arms around her shoulders. Mary Beatrice leaned back, her head pillowed on Livia's breasts, giving herself up to the gentle rocking, as if she were a hurt child.

'There would still be no reason to grieve, even if Princess

Anne had a dozen boys,' Livia told her softly. 'You will live long and conceive many children of your own and they will come before any child she has. Princess Anne will be thrust down to third place, her child to fourth, and she will not matter anymore.'

Mary Beatrice turned her tragic face up to her friend. 'But what if I don't?' she demanded simply. 'What if I don't conceive a son? Then there is the protestant heir Mary and her husband William, and after her, there is Anne. Two protestant queens, one after another: and I will have failed in my duty to my husband and to my God.'

'But why should you not have a son?' Livia regretted the question the moment she had asked it. She had been in court long enough to know the whispered gossip that French pox had left the king infertile and would bring him madness in his old age, and his wife would break out in chancres all over her body and die in agony from his disease.

'The king goes . . . elsewhere,' Mary Beatrice said quietly, her head drooping as if she were ashamed. 'He always has done. And he has bastard sons, so everyone knows he can make a boy.'

'Bastards don't count,' Livia said staunchly.

'Half of England wants to put the last king's bastard on the throne,' Mary Beatrice argued. 'He's coming over the seas towards us right now!'

There was a bleak silence. 'My son is coming to day,' Livia said encouragingly. 'He'll take our bags for safekeeping, ready to load on the ship. We could set sail next week. You can disembark at Rome. You can write to your Mama, tell Her Grace Duchess Laura that you are coming soon. We have a plan, we are ready, if the king loses.'

'If he loses?' the queen said flatly. 'With two protestant armies coming against him from either end of the country, how can he possibly win?'

There was a tap on the bedroom door. Livia went to answer it, opening it a crack to look out.

'A visitor for you, Lady Avery,' the lady-in-waiting said

resentfully. 'A young man. I did not know if I should interrupt you or no?'

Livia turned back to the room, to find Mary Beatrice drying her eyes. 'There!' she said. 'Did I not promise that Matteo would come?'

The queen led the way through the privy chamber, where everyone rose and curtsied, to the small antechamber beyond. Matthew was standing nervously by the table. He bowed very low when the queen entered, and Livia raised him with a gesture and kissed both his cheeks.

'My son!' she said, proud of his youthful good looks in his smart dark suit.

'Ah! He is so like you!' the queen smiled at him. 'Such a handsome boy. If I had seen you before you were at college, I should have made you my page.'

'Look! He is blushing!' Livia cooed. 'We must not embarrass him. *Caro figlio* – is everything going well? The ship is loading? You can take our bags for safekeeping?'

'I'll store them at the warehouse,' he said. 'They'll be safe there. If there's anything of value I will lock it in our cash box.'

'And when will the ship sail?' the queen asked.

Matthew bowed again. 'On an ebb tide, next week,' he told her. 'When it is loaded. I will tell my . . . I will tell my mother, the Nobildonna when it is ready to sail.'

Mary Beatrice gave him her hand and Matthew kissed it. 'I am grateful,' she said. 'I will see that you are rewarded for your service. I am grateful to your mother – who I love very dearly – and to you.'

Livia gestured to the four bags at the door. 'This one has her jewels,' she said quietly. 'Keep it safe, for God's sake.'

'I will,' he said fervently. 'Do I go now?'

'You go now, discreetly.' She kissed him on both cheeks, watched him load himself with the bags, and opened the door for him. She closed it behind him with a triumphant smile and came to the queen and took her hands. 'Did I not say we would be safe with him?'

'Such a charming boy! So young to be so trustworthy?'

Livia shrugged. 'It's breeding, is it not?' she asked. 'Well bred, and well raised. The pity is that he does not have the place in the world that his breeding and his education deserve.'

'But why not?' the queen asked. 'I thought he was at Lincoln's Inn?'

'He has no inheritance,' Livia explained glibly. 'My husband's lands are entailed away from him. My poor boy is the son of my first husband, a Venetian prince, so he inherits no English land. He is studying to be a lawyer, but how will he advance in this world without his own property? My own fortune, of course, is all in my husband's hands.'

'He has no English lands?'

'No – as it happens. I would like him to have lands in Sussex – his foster family used to own a manor in the tidelands, near to Chichester, in Sussex.'

'Who owns it now?'

'Why, I believe they are royal lands!' Livia exclaimed in surprise. 'The last lord of the manor died without an heir – Sir William Peachey – and all his lands reverted to the crown.'

'Then surely I should be able to give them to you! I will ask—' The queen broke off. 'I cannot ask now. Everything is so difficult now.'

'But that's why you should reward Matteo,' Livia pointed out. 'Because he is loyal in difficult times. If the times were not dangerous, you would have no need of him.'

'That's true. I will ask my chamberlain.'

'Oh, don't ask him!' Livia objected. 'He will ask you why, and what Matteo has done for you, and how you met him, and our secret will be out. Ask the king for the manor and the lands, as if you wanted them for yourself, and then give me the deeds? The exchequer and your chamberlain will have nothing to say about it. They won't even know till it's done.'

The queen hesitated for a moment.

'After all, it's not much to ask for,' Livia remarked. 'His Majesty gave Catherine Sedley that great house in St James'

Square that overlooks your garden. And she flaunts herself in her stupid banqueting house every time you walk past.'

'Yes,' the queen said resentfully. 'I will ask for it as a country house for me. He cannot deny me that.'

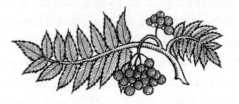

LYME REGIS COAST, SUMMER 1685

The evening sky was a cool pale blue, the sea colourless as a looking glass, reflecting the long tresses of grey clouds, as the waves moved the ships, rolling their deep backs under the wooden keels. Ned, like most of the men, was leaning on the rail, looking towards the dark grey blue cliffs, the colour of slate facing the sea in a forbidding wall, as the captain gave the order to drop anchor, outside the tiny fishing port.

Thomas Dare clapped Ned on the shoulder. 'I'll see you in London,' he said. 'I'll buy you a bottle of wine to drink to our victory.'

'You're going ashore?'

'Going to call out the west country men, going to my home town, Taunton. Andrew Fletcher's coming with me. I'm going to requisition some horses for his cavalry regiment, see if any of these fishermen can ride! I'm proud—' He broke off and grinned at his emotion. 'Proud to be the first ashore. God bless the duke and God speed.'

'God speed,' Ned replied. 'And good luck, Thomas Dare!'

The sailors lowered a dinghy into the water and Thomas went down the rope ladder followed awkwardly by Andrew Fletcher in his high leather riding boots. Rowan joined Ned at the ship's rail and watched as the little boat pulled away and rowed steadily into the bay.

'What do we do now?' she asked.

'We wait,' Ned replied. 'Most of soldiering is waiting around, then being terrified, and then waiting around again.'

She smiled at him. 'I'm not terrified,' she said.

'You're not soldiering. Nor ever going to.'

She ducked her head to avoid another argument. 'No.'

The dinghy reached shore; they could just see the distant figures jumping out of the boat, and a couple of fishermen approaching them. They all talked together then Thomas Dare and Andrew Fletcher waved goodbye and turned inland, while the dinghy came back to the ship.

The boatman, climbed the ladder and went straight to the bridge. Ned watched the duke's face and saw his growing smile. Monmouth turned from the boatman and addressed his men.

'Good news,' he said. 'The best news. Even the fishermen here in the west country know that we are on our way to victory. The Earl of Argyll has drawn the royal army north, they're lost in Scotland. James is calling out the militia in every county – he has no idea where to look for us. The south west is ready to rise for us, the fishermen are for us. We'll go on to Lyme Regis and land there!'

The busy port of Lyme Regis was only four miles away. The Cobb – a massive sea wall of tumbled stones – curved like a claw before the harbour, sheltering the trading ships from the sea. The *Helderenberg* sailed so close to the shore that Monmouth could see, through the captain's spyglass, the men playing bowls on the seaside green.

There was a shout from the lookout as a fishing boat approached. 'Man selling fish, Captain!'

Monmouth grinned. 'Tell him yes! We'll buy all he has!'

Slowly, the ship made way past the Cobb, behind the defensive cannon that pointed over the harbour mouth, to the beach beyond. Sailors bustled to reef the sails and tie up as the soldiers packed their kit and stood ready, divided into three regiments with their own colours, red, blue and white. Ned, in the red jacket of Monmouth's own division, turned to Rowan.

'You come ashore with me,' he told her. 'Stay at my side.'

She grinned at him, her belongings in a little sack slung over her shoulder. 'Yes, Sir!'

Ned tried to scowl at her. 'Then you'll go to London,' he told her.

'Perhaps we all will!'

ST JAMES' PALACE, LONDON, SUMMER 1685

Mary Beatrice, the queen, was standing alone in her privy chamber, looking out of the window over the gardens, when Livia came in.

'Your Majesty?' Livia dipped a curtsey, instantly alert to the frozen figure.

'We're lost,' Mary Beatrice said simply. Now, at the moment of defeat, she was calm. 'Argyll has landed and thousands of men have flocked to his standard. He is marching on Glasgow, and once he takes that town with our stores, and recruits the castle, they think he will march south, here, to London. He will march with our men and our arms against us.'

Livia thought briefly of her husband and his lands that lay before an army of violent highlanders, the certainty of his defending his home, the likelihood of his death. 'And what about Lord Dumbarton's army? Will he fall back and protect the north of England?'

'He hasn't even found the rebels! We don't know what he's doing. This isn't news from him, but from the local lords, sending desperate messengers, demanding help. They haven't even seen Dumbarton! He's probably wandering around lost while Argyll knows all the roads: he built them himself on his own lands!'

'What will the king do?'

'Nothing!' she burst out furiously. 'He has no plan. This is his terror. The terror of the Stuarts. It's what the late king always said to avoid, whatever the price. Never let the people see a flag or hear a drum, they'll just run after it like fools. He's sent his army to Scotland and lost them. The rebels are marching south and there is no-one to stop them. I've told the king, I told him that I dare not stay. My Mama, Duchess Laura, has written that I must go to her in Rome. I told him: I want to go to my Mama!'

'Will he send you?' Livia asked.

The younger woman's hands were clenched into fists. 'First he said he would send me to Portsmouth, and he has a coach and horses ready for me to go, and a ship to take me to Mama. But now he says he doesn't dare! Monmouth could be anywhere! He could have landed at Portsmouth. I could be going straight towards him. And if I set sail in a royal ship, I could run into him at sea! He'd recognise the royal yacht in a moment, he must have sailed on it a hundred times. What if he fired on me? What if he captured me?'

Livia took the queen's hands in a firm clasp, hiding her own fear. 'Be calm, my dear,' was all she could say. 'Be calm. We're in danger; but we're not lost yet. If the king cannot send you to Portsmouth, if you can't take the royal yacht then we can take our berths on the little ship. Nobody will know you are aboard. Nobody would look for you on a little trading ship. It's due to sail this week, it's worked out for us perfectly . . . we can go.'

Mary Beatrice gripped Livia's hands as if she would be hauled from danger. 'You will come with me?' she demanded.

'Of course.' Livia realised that she was speaking the truth.

'I couldn't bear to leave you.' She bent her head and kissed the queen's trembling hands. 'I will never leave you,' she promised. 'Exile or victory, I will be at your side.'

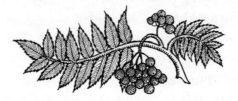

LYME REGIS, SUMMER 1685

Ned stood behind a table in Lyme town hall registering a long queue of volunteers. The line stretched out into the street, men joining the back as fast as men were sworn in at the front. All the west country wanted to serve the protestant Protector. The only man to speak against the duke – the town mayor – had scrambled for his horse and ridden to London when he failed to persuade the townsmen to turn the cannons on the ships and open fire. No-one else had a word against the duke and his army that flew the green banner: 'Fear Nothing But God'.

A clatter of hooves outside was so loud that Ned paused in his work and looked through the doorway to see a huge number of horses, glossy, fat and well-muscled, clattering up the street and, at the head of them, on a big high-stepping warhorse, Thomas Dare, tipping his hat at the cheers as he rode in with such a prize. Monmouth himself came out of the doorway of the George Inn to see the arrival of his new horses. Dare halted before him and jumped from the saddle. 'Your cavalry, Sire!' he said.

'Good God be praised!' Monmouth said exultantly. 'How many d'you have there, Mr Dare?'

'Forty horses!' he crowed. 'Forty! And more promised for when I go back tomorrow, and men following them on foot to join you.'

'Get them into the pound field,' Monmouth ordered the riders.

He turned to Dare. 'This is a triumph. Thank you, Thomas Dare. I will see you well rewarded for this.' He looked at the horse Dare was riding, a big dark bay, almost black in colour with a white star on its forehead and a single white sock. 'And he is a great beauty.'

'He's yours,' Dare said instantly. 'A gift from my friend Prideaux, of Ford Abbey.'

'No, no, you keep him,' Monmouth said. 'I've got my own horse and you've got many days in the saddle ahead of you. How many men have you?'

'I've got a hundred recruits from Taunton and many more waiting for you there, Sire. I brought these back now, so that Andrew Fletcher can set about training them. He came in ahead of me, said he'd make sure the pound was ready for the horses.'

'I haven't seen him,' Monmouth said.

'And I'll go out tomorrow to Bridport – they've taken up a subscription for you there and they're collecting stores. It's the same story all over. Men volunteering and people giving everything they can.'

'Any news of the king in Taunton?'

'I doubt he even knows we're here,' Thomas Dare crowed. 'His main army is lost in Scotland, all he has in the west is the militia and nobody's volunteering in Dorset! Same in Somerset. The road to London is wide open to you, Sire, and the king doesn't even know you're on the march.'

Monmouth laughed out loud and slapped Dare on the back. 'Get yourself dinner and drink, Dare. You've done a great service to me today.'

'The first of many days,' Thomas promised, and bowed as the duke went back into the inn.

'Well met,' Ned said, coming down the hill from the town hall. He patted the warm neck. 'Handsome horse. Was he really a gift?'

'His owner would have ridden with us if he could. How are things here?'

Ned gestured to the queue of men waiting. 'They're coming

in faster than we can sign them up. You get your horses to the pound, I'll get the men to their regiments and I'll meet you here for dinner when we've finished.'

Andrew Fletcher lurched out of the inn door, his face flushed with drink, Venner, the veteran soldier behind him.

'So you got here at last?' Fletcher demanded.

Dare tipped his hat. 'We came as fast as we could, riding and leading.'

'No point in you having a horse like that if you never get out of a trot,' Fletcher said rudely.

'Leave it,' Venner advised him. 'Come back to dinner.' He pulled at Fletcher's arm but the drunk man shrugged him off.

Ned looked from the cavalry commander's flushed face to the cool hostility of the Paymaster. 'Now, good Sires—' he started to say.

Fletcher put his hand on the reins of the horse. 'I'm having him,' he said, his speech slurred. 'He's a fine horse, wasted on you. I'm commander of the cavalry, he should be mine.'

Dare twitched the reins; the horse jerked his head up and sidled away at the sudden tug. 'Not so. The duke says I am to keep him. I'll ride him safely and return him to his owner, a good friend of mine.'

'I'm damned if you do,' Fletcher said, his voice rising. 'I'm commander of the cavalry, I need a good horse. He's too good for you, parading yourself before a bunch of yokels. Give him here.' He lurched forward to take the horse again.

'Easy there,' Ned said. 'No need for comrades to quarrel. Go inside and take another glass, my lord.'

Fletcher tightened his grip on the reins. 'I'm stabling my new horse,' he said with the stubbornness of an angry drunk.

'You step back,' Dare told him. 'You've done nothing to earn him. I've done more today for the cause than you've done in the months you've been with us. Unhand the reins!'

Fletcher grabbed the horse by the cheekpiece and was pulling it towards him, the big horse backing, showing the whites of its eyes.

Ned said: 'Come on, my lord, this is no way ...' and tried to get hold of Fletcher, who shoulder-barged him and shouted:

'This is mutiny! Mutiny! To me! To me!'

Men tumbled out of the inn and from the town hall to see the brawl. Venner returned to the doorway. 'Come on now, Fletcher!'

'It's theft! You let go my horse!' Dare shouted and raised his whip to strike down on Fletcher's shoulder. But the horse jerked, pulling Fletcher up, and Dare's whip missed his shoulder and lashed his face. The man screamed at the sudden pain of it, released the horse, tore himself out of Ned's grip and dived through the door of the inn.

In the sudden silence Thomas and Ned exchanged one shocked look. 'What the—' Ned started to say, then Rowan from the town hall door shouted a warning: '*Sannup!*'

Ned whirled around and saw Fletcher in the doorway, a red weal on his face and his primed pistol pointed at murderously close range.

'Stop!' Ned yelled. There was a tremendous explosion and at once the horse reared up, huge hooves high above their heads, then wheeled and clattered down the street reins trailing as Dare dropped, crumpled on the ground.

Ned gave one aghast look at Fletcher who had lowered the pistol, suddenly sober with shock.

'My God,' he said. 'It went off. I meant to just ...'

Ned dropped to his knees beside Thomas Dare and turned him over. He was completely limp, his face horribly smashed by the musket ball, blood pouring over the cobbles and running in scarlet streams between the stones, a grey mass of his brains pouring from the cavernous gap that had been his mouth and nose.

'He's dead,' Ned said coldly to Fletcher. He rose to his feet. 'You'd better go and tell the duke that you've fired the first shot in his war. And you've killed his Paymaster.'

Venner ordered the men to carry the body of Thomas Dare in a sailcloth to the square-towered church up the hill. William Hewling, fighting down vomit, walked alongside the men with the bloodstained burden, and saw that they laid it down on the chancel steps. Rowan caught the horse and led it to the pound. Ned found her sitting on the fence of the town field for straying animals, watching the horses grazing on the summer grass.

'Is he dead?' she asked him.

'Aye.'

'What happens to the savage?'

'Sent back to the ship under arrest.'

'Are you not allowed to kill each other?'

Ned remembered that she had seen English soldiers overrun her own people while they were sleeping, stabbing them and scalping them while they begged for mercy. 'No, you're not,' he said shortly. 'Not your own side.'

'We still go to war?'

'We do. But we've lost a good cavalry commander in Fletcher, and a brilliant recruiter in Thomas Dare. And it's a bad feeling ...' He shrugged off his sense of darkness. 'Tomorrow we march.'

'You don't listen to the bad feeling?' she asked him.

He hunched a shoulder and shook his head.

ST JAMES' PALACE, LONDON, SUMMER 1685

Once again, the king summoned his parliament, denouncing a rebellion, demanding more funds to defend against it; but this time the queen did not go with him. She and Livia walked together in the palace gardens followed by a quartet of musicians. The queen nodded her head in time, as if she were enjoying the music. The plumes in her hair bobbed, the diamonds at her neck sparkled. Only Livia knew she was listening for cannon fire from the city walls. 'The king has gone to parliament to demand that they change the law to allow roman catholics to be commanding officers,' Mary Beatrice told her quietly.

'But how does that help?' Livia asked.

'They will be faithful to us, if they are of our faith.'

'But to the soldiers, to their own men, they are heretics?'

'We can't trust protestants,' she said miserably. 'The king says we can trust none of them.' Her head jerked up. 'Was that cannon fire? Did you hear that?'

'No, no.'

A messenger came across the gravelled paths and proffered a letter to Livia.

'What?' she snapped.

'Just to say your carriage has arrived, my lady,' he stammered. 'And this letter for you.'

'Please excuse me – it is a letter from my husband,' Livia said and curtseyed to the queen.

'Has he been overrun? Has Argyll reached Yorkshire?'

Livia broke the seal and unfolded the single page. James Avery was even briefer than before:

Madam,
   Here is your carriage, I expect you to return to your
home at once.
   Your husband,
   James Avery

'Is Argyll there already?' the queen demanded? 'Is he coming south?'

'No, no.' Livia looked around; people were staring at them. 'Smile, Your Majesty,' she said. 'Sir James writes nothing that is of any interest.' Livia lowered her voice. 'But he has sent his carriage.'

'For us to run away?'

'Yes. If the ship fails us, we have the carriage.'

TAUNTON, SOMERSET, SUMMER 1685

The Lord Lieutenant of the county, Christopher Monck, Duke of Albemarle had his militia at full muster, at a safe distance outside Taunton, waiting for his chance to attack.

'Drunk Monck,' Monmouth said dismissively. 'He's not sober enough to ride a charge.'

Ned glanced at Nathaniel Wade and the young man winked.

'Did you know him from before, Sire?'

'We were roaring boys together,' Monmouth said. 'Difference is: I grew up and stopped drinking like a drain, and he married a madwoman and didn't.'

'I doubt he can hold his men,' Wade exclaimed. 'They're coming over to us, dozens at a time and bringing the weapons he bought for them.'

It was true. Monmouth's army on the march had become a joyous parade. The local militia declared for Monmouth as soon as they saw him high on his horse under his banner of liberty. At every stop from Lyme to Taunton, the county town of Somerset, Ned and the other sergeants signed up more and more men until he estimated that the rebel army was about four thousand strong.

'And the royal army is raw recruits,' Wade said. 'Many of them convicts, pulled out of the prisons. They'll run for their homes.'

Monmouth's men were farm workers or traders, weavers and brewers, and merchants, devout in their religion, radical in their politics. They came with weapons from the civil war when their fathers and grandfathers had marched for Cromwell. Farm workers brought their tools, scythes, sickles, axes, even spades. The armoury master had the blacksmiths hammer the blades and set them in long poles like pikes.

'Actually, these are far more deadly than a real pike,' Ned said, looking at the jagged length of the blade. He devised training exercises for the men, wheeling and going forward as a troop together. Every evening, after they had marched all day, he would have them charge hay bales and practise running together, holding the line, and attacking together.

'Going well,' Colonel Venner praised Ned in a meadow outside Taunton.

'As long as we meet with hay bales,' Ned said wryly.

'The royal army won't stand like hay bales – better than that – I think they'll run away. The mood is all for Monmouth. They just hailed him as a king in the town and asked him to take the throne.'

'King Monmouth? That wasn't supposed to happen?'

The camp watchman gave a warning shout and Ned's troop scrambled to their feet. Ned noted the men who had to pull on their boots and find their weapons, forgetting his coaching that they should always lie down ready to spring up and fight. 'Fall in!' he shouted.

'Holloah!' Venner yelled. 'Pretty maids by the look of it. Nothing to fear.' He took Ned by the arm. 'You'll remind your men: no looting, no raping, Sergeant.'

'Cromwell rules,' Ned confirmed as he and Venner watched Monmouth, wearing his beautiful jacket and followed by a procession of young women, flowers in their hair, garlands round their necks, banners streaming above their heads embroidered with Monmouth's slogan: 'Fear Nothing but God'. One banner, in lustrous green, read: 'King Monmouth'. The Taunton band marched behind them, tooting a triumphant jig; people were throwing flowers. The citizens and burghers of Taunton offered signed pledges of stores and money.

Monmouth's army rose to their feet and greeted their leader with cheers. More than twenty girls, led by their head teacher, processed with a drawn sword held up before them like a cross. They came to Monmouth and presented him with a Bible. One after another the girls lined up and each gave the duke a banner they had embroidered in their sewing lessons. As each girl, flushed with shyness and excitement, curtseyed to the duke he bowed and accepted their banners and handed them to his officers who unfurled them above his head.

Silently, Rowan appeared at Ned's shoulder.

'He's the new Massasoit?' she asked him.

'He is,' he agreed. 'Going to call himself king.'

'I thought you were better without a king?'

'I know I was,' he said. 'And God knows, an English king has never done anything for you.'

'Sergeant Ferryman?'

Ned turned to see the young volunteer from Amsterdam, William Hewling with a trumpeter. 'Hello, Hewling, d'you want me for something?'

'You're to escort us to Christopher Monck, Duke of Albemarle. I'm to take a letter, inviting him to come over to our side. He's at Wellington, waiting for orders from London.'

'Very well,' Ned said without enthusiasm. To Rowan he said: 'You wait here.'

'Can I follow without being seen?' she asked. 'Just in case.'

He was so certain that she could be invisible to any Englishman that he shrugged. 'As you wish,' he said, secretly glad to know that she would be within hailing distance.

They rode into the town under a white flag for a parley and were sent to Christopher Monck's headquarters in the local inn. Ned looked around for the back door and a side door as he bent his head to go through the narrow front entrance, but as soon as he saw the duke he lowered his guard. This was not a man who would spring to a sudden attack. The duke was seated behind a table, a full glass of red wine before him, two empty bottles on the floor. His round face was flushed, his mouth downturned.

'You think to insult me with this letter?' he demanded. 'You think I am not my father's son?'

Ned was very sure that he was not.

'His Majesty, King Monmouth, remembering your affection for him—' the trumpeter started his announcement.

'He's a traitor!' Monck shouted. 'And a rebel. No king! He's not even a duke now!'

'His father's son,' Ned remarked quietly from the doorway. 'A duke of the blood.'

'I'm damned if I'll say another word to you!' the duke said furiously. 'Wait outside and I'll write a reply.'

Ned bowed and left the room, the trumpeter hard on his heels. Outside, he said quietly to William Hewling: 'Take a look around, count the men and see the weapons.' To the guard he said: 'Your lord told me to wait by my horse.'

Ned walked slowly down the street to where the horses were waiting, looking all around him and calculating the numbers and the mood of the troop.

They were under-armed, many of them with nothing more than farming tools. And they were led by a man who – for all that he might be the son of a famous royalist general – was a drunk, and a fearful drunk at that. They looked as if they longed to ask Ned if they might be allowed to go home. By the time the guard came with Christopher Monck's scrawled reply, Ned was mounted on his horse with young William and the trumpeter at his side, confident that Drunk Monck would never get this militia to stand their ground against Monmouth.

ST JAMES' PALACE, LONDON, SUMMER 1685

Livia came into the queen's room and found her dressed for a journey, a dark modest gown high around her shoulders. She was stuffing her own nightgown into a little leather bag with her missal, her rosary, her Bible and her pearls.

'Let me do that!' Livia said swiftly.

'I didn't send for you to pack for me, but to see that you are ready. We have to go.'

'Now? But Matthew has not sent word they are sailing today?'

'We can't wait! We have to go at once. Monmouth has attacked – oh! I don't know the names of these towns! Bridport! He's marched out of Lyme, they couldn't hold him there, and defeated the Somerset militia – they just ran from him. They left their uniforms and weapons and goods so he has all their ammunition now, as well as everything he brought with him. He's marching here.'

'Does the king say you are to leave?'

'He says we shall die as martyrs on the steps of the altar in our own oratory.'

Livia checked her irritation. 'And what about Argyll?'

'He could be at Highgate village for all we know, and nobody sent a message because they are all welcoming him!'

'We take our ship now?' Livia was conscious of a cold dread in her belly.

'It is ready? It is waiting for us?'

'Yes.' Livia became aware that she was nodding, nodding and

nodding, without speaking. 'It is loading to leave, I expect we can make them go early.' She thought that in a life of great gambles this was the greatest stake she had ever put on the table, and by far the worst odds.

The queen turned to her little writing desk. 'The deeds,' she said, handing over a folded paper. 'I told the king that you were faithful to me, that you would see me safely to my mother, Duchess Laura, in Rome. I told him the manor was to be your reward. He has signed it over to your son. The deeds for Foulmire Priory, in the name of your son.'

Livia took the folded document, heavy with seals, into her hand and slid it into her capacious draped sleeve. She curtseyed. 'I thank you,' she said. 'My son thanks you for your favour to us.'

'If we are defeated and Monmouth is king, it will mean nothing,' the queen shrugged. 'Everything will be his, and the people will walk through my rooms, they will have bonfires in the garden and stable their horses in my oratory—' Her voice rose but she forced herself back into icy self-control. 'So when we are gone, someone will take it off you. This may be a scant reward for your service. But send a message to your son. I want to leave now.'

'Within the hour,' Livia said quietly, curtseyed and left the room.

She sent her maid running to Lincoln's Inn, and another to get a boatman to wait at the privy stairs at Whitehall. She did not dare use the Avery coach for such a secret journey but had a sedan chair wait for the queen at the garden door, and then she tapped again at the door to the privy chamber and went in. Mary Beatrice was on her knees with the royal confessor, Father Mansuet. When the queen kissed her rosary and rose to her feet, Livia mutely held her cape and wrapped her up.

'God protect you and guide you, my child,' the priest said.

'And you, Father,' she said. 'Will you go into hiding?'

'I will stay with the king,' he said. 'Till death.'

'I'm ready,' the queen said to Livia.

The chair was waiting at the gate; the queen, shrouded in a veil, stepped inside and the chairmen took up the poles. Livia pulled a veil over her own head and nodded to her maid to follow her. Livia walked beside the chair through the park. At every step she thought someone would recognise her and call out to her; but it was a hot sunny morning and those few people who were walking had taken seats in the shade of the trees or returned to the cool of the palace. Livia, sweating in her gown and travelling cape, kept pace with the chairmen through the park, through Whitehall Palace grounds, avoiding the builders, to Whitehall Stairs and the river.

Matthew was at the head of the water stairs, his pupil's hat crushed in his hand, pacing one way and then another, scanning the garden. When he saw the chair he froze. Livia was pleased that he did not bound forward; but waited until they came up to him.

'Don't bow!' she snapped, as the veiled queen stepped from the chair and took his hand.

He nodded his head and, without a word of greeting, helped the queen down the water stairs to the waiting wherry. The boatman steadied the boat as the two women got in, and Matthew followed them. Many veiled women had come and gone up and down the privy stairs since the Stuarts had been restored; the boatman had no curiosity. Matthew ordered him to set them down before London Bridge where the skeleton heads of earlier rebels grinned through the rotting flesh. The tide was rushing inland, the turbulent river was too strong, pouring between the wide piers of the bridge. Matthew helped the queen up Pepper Alley Stairs, over the road and guided her down Tooley Stairs, to call a new wherry on the other side.

'Horsleydown Stairs,' Matthew told him, and the man leaned forward and pulled hard against the incoming tide.

Livia helped the queen climb the stairs from the river and

Matthew carried their bags as they walked along the quay to Reekie Wharf. The three of them had to weave around goods, crates, sacks and barrels on the quayside, and avoid lumpers and porters.

'Is that the ship?' Livia whispered to Matthew, recognising the little warehouse and the familiar smell of the Neckinger drain.

He glanced at the *Sweet Hope* riding low in the water, fully loaded. 'Yes,' he said. 'That's her.'

At the front door, Matthew turned to his mother. 'Please will you wait here?'

'Of course not,' she said simply. 'We'll go straight inside.'

REEKIE WHARF, LONDON, SUMMER 1685

Livia walked in as if she owned the place, ushering the queen into the front parlour and seating her in the best chair. 'Tell Alys we are here,' she ordered her son. 'And find Captain Shore and tell him we wish to sail on the next tide.'

Matthew flushed, bowed to the queen and left the room. He found his foster mother in the counting house, seated on her high clerk's stool, her head bowed over the books. She looked up in surprise as he came in.

'Ma,' he said shortly.

'Matthew! I didn't hear the door?' She took in the sheen of sweat on his face and the grim look of his mouth. 'What's the matter? Here in the middle of the day? Are you sick? Are you in trouble? What is it?'

'It's the Queen of England. She's here, in our parlour. With the Nobildonna. I'm very sorry, Ma, but I didn't know what else to do.'

'She's here?' she asked, aghast. But it was not clear which of the women she dreaded the most: his mother or the fugitive queen.

'They want to sail now.'

'Monmouth's army is in London? Argyll?'

'He must be near, for them to want to get away.'

She nodded. 'Send the girl for Captain Shore. He's at Paton's coffee house,' she said. 'And tell Tabs to offer them wine and water.'

'Won't you come?' he asked her. 'They're sitting in the parlour. I don't think it should be Tabs . . .'

'I?'

'Please, Ma.'

'I swore I'd never see her again.'

'It's only for a moment . . . Ma. And she's rewarded me for this.'

He saw her summon her courage and square her shoulders. 'Very well,' she said. 'You go upstairs and tell your grandmother that the queen and the Nobildonna are here. Tell her she need not come down. Tell her they're not staying; and I will deal with them.'

He hesitated, his hand on the door knob. 'I'm so sorry, Ma,' he said.

She put her hand on his shoulder. 'It's not you. It's her. It's her who brings trouble to our door and she always has done.'

She went past him into the hall, and he heard her firm step on the stone floor and then the creak of the parlour door.

'May I present Goodwife Shore,' Livia said to the queen, her voice clear and steady, not a shadow of embarrassment at seeing the woman she had loved and betrayed.

The queen inclined her head but said nothing as Alys dropped a small curtsey. Behind her, Tabs came in, carrying a flagon of red wine and a jug of water on a tray with two glasses. They clinked in the silence as she put them down on the table and slowly withdrew. When the door was closed behind her, Alys said: 'I've sent the maid to fetch Captain Shore.'

'Thank you,' Livia said. She stepped to the table and mixed a small glass of wine and water for the queen.

Alys stared at Livia, trying to see that once-beloved face through the thick veil. As if she felt Alys' eyes upon her, Livia tossed the veil away from her face, over the brim of her hat, and once again Alys saw the dark arched eyebrows, the smiling dark eyes, and the perfect profile of the woman she had adored.

'You will think I am much changed,' Livia said, a caressing note in her voice.

She handed the queen the glass and stepped towards Alys. 'I have missed you, Alys. I did not want to leave you as I did, and it broke my heart that you would not see me when I visited Matteo. It was you I came to see, Beloved. It was you I was longing for.'

'Matthew,' Alys said curtly, resisting the enchantment of the lilting voice. 'We call him Matthew.'

'I understand, you still don't forgive me.'

They heard the back door to the yard bang and Captain Shore clattered down the stone-flagged hall. He opened the door to the parlour and recoiled at the sight of the three women, one veiled, one a great beauty, and his wife, her square face pale and her whole body as rigid as if their house were occupied by an enemy.

'What's this?' he asked of the room, and then turned to his wife. 'Girl said that I was to sail at once.'

Matthew followed him into the room. 'These are the ladies who have booked berths on your voyage, Sir. They have to leave today.'

'Going badly, is it?' the Captain asked cheerfully of no-one. 'Well, I'm agreeable. We're fully loaded and I pay no mooring charges at my own wharf.' He nodded to his wife but drew no answering smile from her. He was shocked by the cold bitterness in her face.

'When can we leave, Captain Shore?' Livia demanded.

'When the tide turns,' he said. 'On the ebb, in four hours. I'll send for my sailors now, they're ready. As long as no-one's been pressed for the navy.' He turned a baleful glance on the veiled queen. 'Someone should do something about the way they press good men into the king's navy,' he said ominously.

'Not now, Abel,' his wife said quietly.

'Aye. Very well. So, shall you ladies step down to the coffee house and order a dinner there and come aboard this afternoon at four?'

'We can't be seen,' Livia ruled. 'And better for you, Captain, if we're not known to be sailing with you.'

'That bad, is it?' he asked.

Livia smiled at him, her eyes warm on his weather-beaten face as if he were their only saviour and her particular friend. 'Just a temporary reverse,' she said, smooth as silk. 'But Sir, would you be so kind as to let us dine here, in your house, and go aboard when you are ready to sail?' she asked. 'It would be more comfortable, and discreet. You will be rewarded, when we come to our own again.'

'If you ever do,' he said bluntly.

He saw the warning narrowing of her eyes; but she turned to Alys. 'You will let us stay here, I know,' she said. 'You were always so good to me . . .'

Matthew saw his foster mother flush a painful red where she had been so pale. 'I didn't know what you were about then, and I don't know now,' she said shortly.

Livia took two steps across the little room and took her hands. 'Remember what we were to each other?' She lowered her voice. 'I never forget. You were everything to me.'

Captain Shore kept his eyes on his wife's face as Livia, still holding her hands, swayed slightly to her own words, as if she would dance her from her stubborn stance. Alys did not yield, but nor did she shrug off Livia's touch. She was frozen, as if the caressing tone were a spell that the beautiful younger woman was winding around her.

'You can dine here,' the Captain interrupted. 'My wife'll tell the cook to get something for you. Plain fare, since you gave us no notice. But good enough – since you've no choice.' He suddenly remembered that he was speaking to the queen and he pulled off his hat and bowed again. 'I'll come and fetch you on board when we're ready to sail, Ma'am.' He remembered that he should not turn his back on her and he reversed awkwardly, bumping the table, out of the room.

Livia released Alys with a teasing little smile. 'He is so kind,' she said. 'I do hope you are very happy? I think you are happier in your marriage than I in mine? I am sure you do not miss me, as I miss you?'

'I'll order your dinner,' was all Alys said, and she went out of the room.

Livia turned to the queen. 'Shall you take off your veil?' she asked gently. 'We are among friends. And your hat? Would you like to lie down before dinner? I can show you to a bedroom?'

The queen made a little gesture and Livia stood behind her, untied the ribbons of her hat and lifted it and the veil away. Matthew stood by the door, waiting to be dismissed, but his mother passed the hat to him and then stepped towards him to whisper: 'She's given us the manor of Foulmire! I have the deeds in my sleeve. I'll give them to you, here and now!'

With a rustle of silk she pulled them from her loose sleeve and unrolled them on the dining table and showed him where his name followed the royal seal, and before that was the earlier owner, Sir William Peachey.

'How lucky it is that the name is ours!' she exclaimed. 'Peachey – so you will be Matteo da Picci of Foulmire Manor, but you shall spell it the English way, Matthew Peachey, and everyone will think that we have owned it forever. And when this is all over and the queen comes to her own again you shall be knighted and then you can be Sir Matthew like Sir William our ancestor.'

'He wasn't our ancestor,' he pointed out. 'We cannot claim another man's name and family.'

'Oh, who knows? And who will ever care? When kings are coming and going, who is going to mind a mere Italian widow changing her son's name? And everyone is a son of God after all! As soon as we set sail, you must go there at once, move in, move the old lady in too, that was a good idea of yours. Do everything to make it look as if you have owned it for years, and if we are in exile for a while, for months even, then you at least will have your estate, and I will have somewhere to come home to.'

'If Monmouth comes . . .' he said very quietly, one eye on the queen who had leaned back in her chair and closed her eyes.

'If he comes from the west and Argyll from the north then you certainly should be in your manor in the south of England, and far from London,' she insisted. 'Take the old lady. Take Alys.'

'Sir James doesn't go with you?'

She shrugged her shoulders. 'I don't even know if he's still alive. He will have fought Argyll as he marched through Yorkshire, for sure. I've heard nothing from him. He said he would send his carriage for me, but it hasn't come. If you meet with him, tell him that I was beside myself with grief and not knowing what he would want me to do. When his carriage failed me, I had to get away by sea.'

'But Lady Mother – you always planned to go by sea . . .'

She put her silk-mittened hand over his mouth and he felt the warmth of her fingers like a kiss.

'It doesn't matter,' she told him softly.

BRIDGWATER, SOMERSET, SUMMER 1685

Ned, with Rowan at his side, marched his troop into Bridgwater between cheering crowds, people thrusting bread and whole hams and cheeses into the soldiers' hands as they went to their camp in Castlefield. The Somerset militia, armed and mustered to attack them, surged into the rebel camp, throwing their arms around men with the sprig of green in their hats, swearing that they too were for liberty, and were welcomed by the duke himself.

'This is a strange war,' Rowan observed to Ned. 'All dances and no fighting.'

'We've not yet met any who'll stand against us,' he said. 'But the king's regular troops must find us, sooner or later.' He paused for a moment. 'I've a mind to go down to the port and see if there's a coaster going to London that'd take you to Alinor.'

'No.'

'Better now, than we get taken by surprise.'

'Not today! I don't have to go today!'

He pulled her down to sit on his cape beside him. 'I won't be harsh with you, Rowan, but I can't keep you with me. Sooner or later there'll be a battle, and you should be in safety.'

She bit her lip. 'I'm safe with you.'

'Not if we come under fire. I couldn't protect you, and besides, I should be thinking of my troop.'

'But who will get your food, if not me?'

'I'll survive.'

'*Sannup*,' she whispered. 'Don't make me leave you.'

'Ah, for the Lord's sake, girl! Don't call me that!'

'Don't you call me girl,' she said resentfully, rubbing her face dry.

He choked on his laugh. 'What then? Young lady?'

'I am not your girl or your young lady,' she said angrily.

'I know well enough you're not mine,' he said, his voice very low. 'I know that well enough. And that's why you should go away. That's why I am trying to send you away.'

'If I were your wife, could I stay with you?'

Ned folded his mouth on the sudden pounding of his heart. After a few moments he spoke very quietly. 'I'm old enough to be your father. And I bought you to set you free, not to mew you up in marriage with an old man.'

For one long moment of silence he thought she might

contradict him; but she did not. 'If you order me, I will go,' she said unhappily.

'Very well then,' he said. 'It's an order. You'll have to go.'

REEKIE WHARF, LONDON, SUMMER 1685

Captain Shore jogged in his sea boots from the coffee house to the wharf where the *Sweet Hope*'s crew were stowing their own goods and rigging the sails ready for their departure. He went in the back yard gate and into the kitchen. 'Where's the missis?' he demanded.

'Sitting upstairs with Mrs Reekie,' Tabs told him. 'Those passengers are still in the parlour.'

'I have to speak with her. I'll go up,' he said. 'Tell Susie to send Matthew up too.'

Consumed with curiosity, Tabs watched him climb the wooden stairs from the narrow hall. 'Go on,' she said irritably to the maid. 'Go and find Master Matthew, he's standing out front looking at the quay as if he was a soldier on guard. Lord alone knows what's going on and what that Italian woman is doing here again. I thought we'd seen the back of her and her tricksy ways.'

Captain Shore tapped on Alinor's bedroom door and went into the room. His wife and her mother were seated either side of the table by the glazed balcony, both of them sewing tea bags for herbal tea as if today were the most ordinary of days. As soon as he saw them, busy as they always were, quiet as they always were, he felt his own alarm subside.

'There you are, God bless you,' he said.

'What's happened now?' Alys demanded.

Alinor gave him her steady smile and he waited for Matthew to come up the stairs and into the room before he replied. 'It's good news for the ladies. I was in the coffee house settling my slate before sailing, and Jim McDonald came in – he's a Scots trader – full of news. Said that the Earl of Argyll is run away and disappeared somewhere. He says the rebellion is all over for Argyll.'

Alinor looked towards the young man. 'You'd better tell your mother at once,' she said. 'It may make a difference to their plans.'

'I'd be glad not to be the man that ships them out,' Captain Shore confessed.

'Go with Matthew,' Alinor suggested. 'Tell Her Majesty directly, just as you told us.'

'Shouldn't the Nobildonna speak?' Captain Shore hesitated. 'She's the lady-in-waiting?'

'No, you tell her, Abel,' Alinor insisted.

'Why, Ma?' Alys asked.

'So that the queen knows everything that we know.'

'Because the Nobildonna might not say . . . ?'

'Who knows what she is doing? Who knows what she would say?'

'You're certain?' Matthew asked. 'The man could not be mistaken?'

''Course he could be!' Captain Shore said impatiently. 'But they can send to the palace, can't they? To be certain? Surely the king has spies and messengers of his own?'

Matthew nodded and clattered down the stairs to the parlour, followed at a more sober pace by Alys and her husband. Matthew tapped on the parlour door and entered, while Alys waited on the threshold, her husband behind her.

The queen was seated in her chair, leaning back with her eyes closed; Livia was at the window, looking out at the ship which would take them to safety. She turned with a little smile. 'Is it time?'

Matthew bowed. 'Captain Shore has some news from the coffee house,' he said. 'I believe he should tell you himself.'

'Her Majesty is resting,' Livia whispered. 'I'll come outside.'

Alys did not yield; as Livia came towards her, she deliberately blocked the doorway. 'Better that she hear this for herself.'

Livia glanced back at the queen, who opened her eyes and gestured that Captain Shore should come in. 'Leave this to me, Your Majesty,' she said.

Alys stepped into the room, as if she had no fear of Livia and no deference to the queen. 'I think you'd better hear for yourself, Ma'am.'

Livia laughed in her grave face. *'Allora!'* she said mockingly. 'Are you a royal herald now?'

Alys did not even look at her, and Livia fell back to stand behind the queen.

Captain Shore bowed, and told them the news from the coffee house.

'Just gossip,' Livia dismissed it.

'Could be true,' Alys warned.

'We shouldn't miss the tide.'

'You've got an hour before it turns,' the Captain pointed out.

'Why don't you send a message to the palace to find out?' Alys asked the queen directly.

'Please leave this to me.' Livia stepped in front of the queen and leaned over her, blocking the others from her view. 'What do you want to do, dearest? Shall we take ship, now we have got so far? Don't you want to go to your Mama?'

The queen sat up and gently put Livia to one side with a small gesture of her hand. She spoke directly to Captain Shore. 'Is the man who told you a trustworthy man?'

He shrugged. 'He's got no reason to lie, Ma'am.'

'Will you wait until I can get news?'

Livia stepped forward again. 'Of course he will. My son Matteo, who serves you so well, shall go to the palace and ask to speak to Father Mans—'

'Matthew can't speak with a priest!' Alys interrupted.

Livia's eyes flashed at her. 'His Majesty's trusted confessor,' she said. 'The safest person for us to consult.'

'Yes, go,' the queen ordered Matthew.

Matthew bowed and left the house. Both Livia and Alys followed him to the quayside.

'He can't be seen with a priest!' Alys raged at Livia. 'What if people take him for a papist spy? They'll tear him apart in the garden.'

'We have to know!' Livia returned fiercely. 'This is another civil war, like they had before. And I, and my son – and you – are on the side of the king and queen.'

Alys, terrified, shook her head. 'We don't take sides!' she said. 'We're just making a living here, we never take sides. And if we did . . . my own uncle—'

'It doesn't matter what you think, or what side you took in the past,' Livia ruled. 'It doesn't matter about the old Ironside brother in America! We are loyal subjects of King James and Queen Mary.'

'Of course, we are loyal—'

Livia turned and gave Matthew a little push along the quayside. 'Go! What are you even waiting for?'

'My Ma is under no obligation,' he said hesitantly. 'She shall not be—'

'Ah! It doesn't matter,' she gleamed at him. 'This is just a lovers' quarrel. And you have more important things to do. Go! Quickly! And tell me what Father Mansuet says. Come to me first.'

He glanced at Alys, and at her nod he walked to the river stairs and gave a shrill whistle to a wherryman, feathering his oars in mid-river drifting upstream on the flowing tide. Livia turned, her eyes blazing in triumph to Alys. 'I am going to put that boy into the greatest place in the kingdom, and I am going to be the first lady of the kingdom myself,' she said fiercely. 'Nobody can stand in my way. Nobody is going to stop me.'

'We won't take sides,' Alys insisted.

'You'll take the winning side fast enough,' Livia predicted. 'I'm telling you – I am on the winning side and so too is Matteo. If you don't want to lose him, you'll stand my friend. If you don't want to ruin his future, you'll do as I say.'

'I don't want to ruin him!' Alys exclaimed, her face flushed with tears. 'I'd lay down my life for him! I don't want any part of this! I don't understand it! I don't want the queen here! Why have you come and brought all this to my door?'

Livia gave a little sigh of deep satisfaction, slid her arm around the older woman's waist and walked with her back into the warehouse. 'Sometimes, I need you,' she explained. 'You are my first and my only true friend. And sometimes I will reward you.'

Matthew was back within two hours, soaking wet from shooting London Bridge on the turning tide. He walked towards the parlour as Alys took his cape and handed him a drying sheet. Livia blocked his entrance. 'You can't go in like that,' she said.

'I have to, Father Mansuet told me to tell her at once.' He stepped around his mother, avoided her detaining hand and bowed to the queen who had risen from her chair as soon as she heard his voice in the narrow hall.

'The news is true,' he told her. 'Father Mansuet knew it, the king himself told him. The rebellion in Scotland is all but over. Argyll is hiding out in the hills and no more than four score of men are holding out for him. They expect to hear at any moment that he's been captured.'

'God forgive him,' the queen said. She crossed herself and whispered a little prayer. Livia immediately copied her, and the three protestants in the room froze in horror at the illegal heresy. The queen opened her eyes. 'It's over?' she asked. 'The rising is over?'

'There's still Monmouth,' Livia pointed out.

'But now the royal army can march south, and they've only got one uprising to face,' Captain Shore reminded her.

'I shall go back to the palace,' the queen decided.

Only Alys saw Livia's anguished look towards the queen and guessed that she was thinking of the promised reward and wondering if the queen's gift would hold good if they did not sail.

'I won't need my berth in your ship, Captain Shore. I'm grateful for your patience.'

He gave an awkward bow. 'As you wish, Your Majesty,' he said. He turned to Alys: 'I'll go now then, Love.'

'Her Majesty and I are grateful for your service,' Livia delayed him. 'And especially grateful to my son Matteo, who has served the throne so loyally, and done so much at such risk to himself today.'

The queen nodded and gave Matthew her hand to kiss.

Matthew bowed. 'Shall I take you back to St James'?'

'It's best if we go back quietly,' Livia advised. 'Get us a wherry to Whitehall Stairs and we will take a chair from there.'

Alys and Captain Shore went out to the hall. She helped him into his oiled sailing cape. 'God speed,' she said to him quietly. 'Calm seas and steady winds bring you safe home to me, Abel Shore.'

'Amen,' he said and bent his head for her kiss, and then he went out to his ship.

In the parlour Livia dressed the queen in hat, veil and cape. It was not until they were on the quayside, and Matthew calling a wherry for them, that Livia took a quick step to Alys, who was watching her husband order the sailors to hoist the sails for his departure.

'I'll come back,' Livia promised.

'Don't. There's nothing for you here. And I don't want to see you.'

Alys could not see Livia's face through the thick veil, but she knew that she was smiling.

PHILIPSNORTON, SOMERSET, SUMMER 1685

Ned, warned by the Bridgwater harbourmaster that anyone embarking from the port while the rebel army held the town would be arrested in London as a spy, decided that Rowan would have to stay with the troops as far as Bath, where he could get her a passage on the stagecoach. He could not deny that she was in her element: fishing in the rivers, hunting in the woods and poaching in the fields as she followed the army, free at last, to run wild in the countryside where no-one questioned her, and all the normal rules of landlords and gamekeepers were set aside. She made friends with the women who were following their husbands and shared her catch with them. They treated her as a strange but helpful creature: some said that she was of the fairy folk – for how else could a lad stroll down to the river without even a rod and a line and come back with a string of river trout? Some said that the lad was a runaway slave, with all the skills of an unknown people. Some said that he was a witch and would overlook the royal army who would all fall asleep before him.

The army marched ahead of the camp followers during the day, but in the evening, when the officers requisitioned beds in the houses of sympathisers and the men camped in their fields, Rowan found Ned and the three sergeants who were his messmates and brought them dinner.

'Thank you.' The words were forced from him, as she skinned and boned a rabbit, caught in her snare, and stewed it in the kettle on the communal fire. She grinned at him, knowing that he was fighting to hide his hunger after a long day's march.

'You are welcome,' she said to him graciously. 'It was my people that fed your people, when you first came in the big ships.'

Ned nodded, knowing that she had made herself indispensable to his comfort, and that he was seeming as sulky as a boy. 'You can sleep here tonight and follow tomorrow.'

She nodded, as if she were not blazingly triumphant. 'Whatever you say, *Sannup*. I have made an agreement with one of the washerwomen and she will launder your shirts and dry them as we move, and I will get her and her husband their dinner.'

'Aye, you think you have bested me and got your way. The regular royal army has mustered and marched south and is so close that the city of Bath have closed their gates to us, so I can't leave you there as I planned. But truly, it's time I sent you away. The Earl of Argyll has failed, and we're on our own now.'

'He was defeated?' Rowan asked. 'Have they killed everyone? Did they take his scalp?'

Ned shook his head in dismay at her idea of warfare. 'No. He'll be executed, he's been captured, his army gave up without him. If we've heard it here, they'll know all about it in London. Monmouth is on his own.'

'Have we lost?' she asked calmly, as if victory or defeat were the same to her.

'We'll have to move fast. We have to win our victory before the northern army turns around and comes against us. The duke should be picking out his battlefield, and you should be somewhere safe.'

'We have to fight the battle at once?'

'We have to get to London before Dumbarton's army. We can hold London against them. Especially if we capture the king and queen. But some French lord is commanding a royal army and has come against us. We've got more to face than the militia. We're going to be in a battle against a royal army any day.'

'And then we've won?' she confirmed and made him smile.

'Oh, aye, you're a rebel now,' he said.

They were camped in fields either side of the George Inn where Monmouth had made his headquarters. The officers had beds in the inn, the troops rolled themselves up in their jackets and capes and slept on the ground. Ned lay on his back, his head resting on his pack, and Rowan lay beside him, her back against him for warmth. He folded his arms across his chest so that he did not wrap his arm around her and cushion her head on his shoulder. He looked up at the pale summer sky and the pinpricks of stars. He thought that he was in grave danger, in a world filled with uncertainty. He thought he had never known such joy and heartache at the same time.

In the dawn light, she was gone – down to the river for her prayers and washing. She came back as the troops were stirring and eating last night's bread for breakfast with a cup of mulled ale sent out from Monmouth's breakfast table when Ned heard the rattle of gunfire from further up the road.

'Stand to!' he shouted to his troop. 'Form up!'

He was pleased to see they had their weapons to hand; they were ready in moments. A scout came storming down the main street on his horse, flung himself out of the saddle and dived through the open door of the inn. Moments later the duke himself came running out.

'Á Monmouth!' he yelled and seized the reins of his horse, shouting orders to his officers.

'You go behind the inn and stay out of sight,' Ned snapped at Rowan as he led his troop out of the field to join the regiment. 'Disappear, Rowan!'

She nodded and he saw her loping run towards the ramshackle stables at the back of the inn, as he led his troops in a steady trot out of the field and up the road where he could hear the sound of a battle and the first roar of a cannon. In moments they had left the lane, filing through a gate that Monmouth ordered to be lifted from its hinges so it stood wide. Monmouth and his mounted officers led the way across two fields, tracking a path through the growing wheat, forcing their way through a hedge on the far side. Ned could hear the fighting at the crossroads, north of the town, at the rebel barricade. Somehow, the royal army had come upon them in the early hours for a surprise attack on this outpost.

In a fine piece of generalship, Monmouth resisted the temptation to charge down the main street to support the barricade. Cleverly, he led his troop around the skirmish. Ned's raw troops turned their heads to the sound of firing.

'March on,' Ned said quietly. 'Eyes front!'

Discipline was good, the order, passed in a low voice down the line. Ned nodded at his men and saw them grip the handles of their weapons – pikes, sickles, and in a few cases, nothing but pitchforks with sharpened tines.

'Ready,' Ned said, his voice low, and then as he heard the order come down the line, he told them: 'Forward!'

They ran as fast as they could down the road, the officers on horseback churning up the dust before them, and saw ahead of them the royalist army, pressing on the barricade, turn around white-faced at the sudden shock of a charge coming from behind them. There was a rattle of fire from their muskets; but the royalist cannon, facing towards the village, was useless against their charge. The barricade under attack set up a cheer of defiance. The rear of the rebel troops, coming up fast, broke through the hedge beside the royals and fell on them, who were now encircled but for the west. Then the Monmouth cannon roared out. Ned got his troop in the shelter of a hedge, commanded a fusillade of shots and advanced onto the lane. The royalists scrambled over the barricade they had been attacking, and tried to get behind it for shelter.

'Push on!' Ned told his men. 'Forward!' and brought them onward and onward until he heard the finest sound in the world – the bugle sounding the royalist retreat.

Incredulously, Ned, who had fought a royal army in three battles more than forty years before, watched the regular army under command of the French Earl of Feversham fall back from an attack by ploughboys and traders. The rebels yelled gleeful abuse, and Ned didn't stop them. William Hewling, the young volunteer, danced in the road with green handkerchiefs like a morrisman. Ned laughed, ordered his men into position, telling them to maintain fire, and went to find Monmouth for orders.

'They're retreating,' he grinned. 'We've won.'

Monmouth recognised Ned, though his face was blackened with soot and mud. A light rain was starting to fall and the summer dusk was cool.

'Ferryman! We'll go after them,' he said.

'No!' Colonel Venner dismounted from his horse and patted its heaving side. 'Let them go. We should march on London, not chase them around the west country. Half of them'll desert after this, anyway. This is the turning point for us.'

Monmouth looked undecided. 'A victory now . . .'

Ned agreed with the colonel. 'It's only the vanguard of the royal army. Not their full force. They'll draw back to reunite with the main army. It's a trap for us to go after them.'

The duke nodded. 'You're right. Beat the drums,' he ordered. 'Break camp. Prepare to march.'

'On London?'

'On London!'

REEKIE WHARF, LONDON, SUMMER 1685

Alys was having her breakfast with her mother at the little work-table, the glass door was open to the balcony and the sound of the gulls fishing in the flowing river came into the bright little room.

'I dreamed of Rowan last night,' Alinor remarked to her daughter.

Alys folded her lips and would not ask about the dream.

'I suppose she and Ned are still with the Duke of Monmouth,' Alinor went on. 'Do you pray for him, Alys?'

'Not as a rebel,' Alys said. 'And in the church when they pray for the king and the destruction of his enemies I say "Amen". There's always someone watching, you never know who might speak out against us. We're not so well established, even now, that we don't have enemies.'

'Will you ever feel safe?'

'Will you?'

Alinor took a moment to reply. 'A woman's never safe.' She glanced at her daughter. 'You know that, as well as me. And I suppose that's why I like Rowan so much. She's been close to death, like me, and survived it. You're no longer fearing the unknown. When they put me on the mill wheel to test me for a witch, I knew I was drowning. When I came back to life, and saw daylight through the water, I knew the worst was over. I'd faced death in the dark water. I'll never fear it again.'

Alys was bitter. 'It should never have happened. I should have spoken up. James Avery should have stopped it.'

'Perhaps – but it's left me without fear. Like Rowan.'

'Ah, her! Who knows what she thinks: she barely speaks! Who knows what Uncle Ned sees in her?'

Alinor smiled at her stubborn daughter. 'I think he loves her dearly.'

'Not him! He pitied her in slavery and then got himself stuck with her. She'll leave him as soon as she sees a better life. Probably with another man.'

'Johnnie was very taken with her, I thought?'

'Johnnie!' Alys was outraged. 'Johnnie has a better sense of what is due to him than to look twice at a girl out of the woods of the Americas with nothing but impertinence!'

'And courage,' her mother pointed out.

Alys nodded and took up her mug of small ale.

'And beauty.'

'You think she's beautiful?'

'Oh, very.'

Alys hunched a shoulder.

'Clever,' her mother pointed out. 'She speaks better than some country folk, and she had to learn it. And she knows herbs, and Ned says she can hunt and cook her own food.'

'What good is that to me in a daughter in law? She can't sew or cook or keep house,' Alys said. 'When my son Johnnie marries he'll need a woman who can run a good house, and the business as well. Johnnie wants a woman who can rise with him.'

'If he wanted a woman like that he would be married already,' Alinor said mildly. 'You've put enough in his way, God knows.'

'I want to see him happily married to a young woman of property—' Alys broke off as she heard a footstep on the stair and Matthew tapped on the door.

'Come in!' Alinor called and Matthew stepped into the room, knelt before Alinor for her blessing and then bowed his head for his mother to kiss him.

'What a surprise! Have a cup of small ale!' Alinor said, getting up from her place and fetching an extra cup from the sideboard.

'Is everything's all right?' his mother asked. 'Is there news?'

Matthew shook his head. 'I know nothing from court, I haven't seen my mother since I took her to the wherry. She's disappeared behind the palace walls as she always does. But in the coffee house they said that the Somerset militia dropped their weapons and tore off their uniforms rather than face the duke outside Chard. But I don't know where they are now.' He looked at the woman who had been a mother to him, and to her mother who had been his grandmother. 'I didn't come about Uncle Ned. I've got news for you about myself.'

He unrolled the Foulmire deeds on the breakfast table, clearing a little space and moving the plates. The two women looked at the vellum, the sealing wax and the wide ribbons.

'What's this?' Alys asked.

Alinor put a hand out and touched the document. 'Deeds?' she asked. 'For land?'

Matthew turned the document towards her and unfolded it

so that she could see the twirling gothic writing: *Deeds of the Manor and Parish of Foulmire in the Manhood of Sealsea Island, county of Sussex.*

'The queen gave it to my mother for me.'

Alys rose up from the table as if the document were a venomous snake which might lunge towards her. 'What d'you have to do for it?'

He smiled. 'No more than I've done already. I was loyal to the queen when she needed someone. I brought her here. You would have given her passage to Rome. This is our reward.'

'From the queen, perhaps,' Alys said, her hands on the back of the chair, staring at the document. 'But Livia'll want something more for it. This is not a gift but a bribe.'

'I'm not bribed!' Matthew said indignantly. 'This is a reward. We could've been the saving of the queen's life! She has rewarded us. And of course, my mother's prosperity is mine.'

'Her debts too, her crimes too,' Alys insisted.

'Ma Alinor!' he appealed to the older woman. 'I thought you would be pleased? I thought I'd take you to your home?'

Alinor was silent for a moment, her hand resting on the pages, then she drew them towards her and, carefully, her finger tracing under the long words, read the list of the property: the manor house and stables, barns and outbuildings, the equipment tools and beasts, the field near the seashore, the seashore itself. The settlement at East Beach, the ferryboat at the wadeway, the harbour known as Wandering Haven and the quay at Sidlesham. The woods, the shore, the fields and the summer pastures. The fishing rights and the church tithes, the living, and the sea wall, the game birds in the air and on the ground, salvage rights from the sea, the samphire on the beach and the minerals under the earth.

'It's all here,' she said wonderingly, as if she could see the landscape laid out before her, the old Priory house nestling in the meadows, the shingle beach beyond it, the church beside it and in the graveyard her own mother's stone and beyond that the ferryhouse where her brother and father and grandfather had worked the ferry between Sealsea Island and the mainland.

'It's all mine,' Matthew said simply. 'I've won it for you. For you both. Will you come and live there, Ma Alinor? Shall I take you home?'

BRIDGWATER, SOMERSET, SUMMER 1685

Monmouth called a meeting of his senior officers and trusted sergeants in St Mary's church. Ned leaned against a pillar at the back of the church listening, as the duke, looking years older than the arrogant aristocrat of Amsterdam, outlined an audacious plan. 'My lords, my comrades, this very day I have learned that the king's army is camped not three miles from here, all unprepared in the marshlands.'

There was a murmur of excitement. Monmouth threw up his hand. 'I know!' he said gladly. 'It's a chance, given to us by God. We outnumber them, and He is on our side. They outgun us; but they are sleeping tonight, with no idea that we are so close.'

'How is it they don't know we're here?' demanded Charles Speke, leader of 'Speke's Ragged Horse'.

Monmouth smiled. 'A good man, and a true churchman, saw them set up their camp, the officers commanding quarters in the houses at Westonzoyland, the men raiding the inns for ale and food and setting camp in the fields just outside. This man, Godfrey, came to tell me of them, and he's going to lead us through the wetlands.'

A shepherd holding a well-worn crook ducked his head and nodded at the company.

'We're going to circle the royal camp,' Monmouth promised. 'Just as we did at Philipsnorton. The infantry will engage them at the front and the cavalry will circle round and attack from their rear, like we did then. They're behind a drainage canal, called the Bussex Rhine; they're trapped in a bow of the water. The cavalry will drive them forward into the river, and the infantry will finish them as they struggle out on the bank. Your task . . .' his dark gaze raked the men sitting in the pews, leaning against the pillars at the back of the church, 'your task is to draw your men up to attack, in darkness, through wet and rough ground, in complete and total silence. Can you do it?'

'Aye.'

'Yes, Sire.'

'God bless you! Yes!'

The muted answers echoed round the church as if the officers were observing silence already.

Monmouth's face was bright with confidence. 'Very well then. Break camp at ten. You'll hear the bell. There's a moon but it's cloudy, and we should be invisible. March in silence! Complete silence! And may God be with us as we do His work!'

Some men said 'Amen', some said a muted hurrah. Ned bowed his head in prayer for a moment and went out to find Rowan.

She had lit a fire for him and his messmates, and was stewing a soup in the embers. A loaf of bread sat on a tin plate with a big wheel of cheese. She looked up as Ned came towards her, noted his grave face.

'*Sannup?*'

'I don't know the best thing to do,' he said bluntly. 'We're going on a night attack, you can't stay here. If we lose, the royals'll fall back on this village and God knows what they'll do in revenge.'

'Then I won't stay here,' she said simply.

'I don't know where you'll be safe,' he said.

'I'll go into the country,' she offered.

'It's not woods!' he exclaimed. 'There's barely any cover. It's as flat as the Hollands, if you get on a rise you can see for miles. And there are drainage ditches and canals and rivers all through it, hardly any hedges, just willows in the ditches and scrub. It's a marsh.'

'I can hide here,' she assured him. 'It's easy.'

He knew she could melt into a landscape. 'Keep hidden and follow the road to London.'

She poured soup into a bowl and handed it to him. Ned took his spoon from his boot, soldier-style, and started to eat. 'If we win, we'll march on London.' He gave a little smile. 'If we win, it'll be a triumphant march. You'll hear it from ten miles away. We'll have won the war, down here in the Somerset Levels. It'll be a parade.'

'And if you lose, will the enemy chase you back to the sea again?'

He grunted, cutting himself a hunk of bread and eating it with the cheese. 'Don't you come back,' he said. 'I don't want you coming back to the battlefield. Whatever you hear. You can wait by the London road, and if we're not marching up the road then it will have all gone wrong. You go up the road to London anyway. Go to my sister. And if our army is marching but I'm not with them, don't join. Go to my sister.' He looked up as she started to argue and all-but growled at her. 'Do as you're bid, Rowan.' He did not say that if he was not with the army then he was dead in a ditch and he did not want her to find him.

He pulled out a purse from his pocket. 'Take this. It's enough to get you food and lodging on the way. And if anyone asks: say that you've come off a ship that docked in Plymouth from the Americas, and you're making your way to London. Say you're Captain Shore's servant at Reekie Wharf.' He paused. 'Say that you're his slave so that people return you to him. God knows you shouldn't be here. God knows I should never have brought you. I pray to God, you get home safe.'

'Pray for us both,' she recommended, optimistic as ever. 'Why should you not win?'

He nodded. 'We might,' he said begrudgingly. 'It's a bold plan, against a half-hearted enemy. Better now than later, when they'll get reinforcements from the north. Best now, while they're drunk and sleeping. Go up the road to London, and if God wills it, we'll meet tomorrow night, and you can poach a rabbit for my dinner.'

'I will!' she promised him. 'I will obey you, Ned.' She dropped down to sit beside him and put her arm around his shoulders like a comrade. Ned froze. He sat like a block of wood as she kissed his stubbled cheek and laid her forehead against his broad-cloth shoulder.

'God keep you safe tonight and bring us together again,' she said.

He nodded in silence. She looked up at him. 'D'you not bless me?' she asked him.

He could barely speak for the love that was choking him. 'Bless you,' he said gruffly. 'God bless you and keep you safe.'

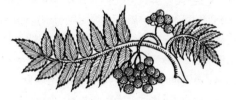

ST JAMES' PALACE, LONDON, SUMMER 1685

The queen and her ladies were at prayer in her oratory, as Father Mansuet, his back turned to them, prepared the Mass at the altar. Incense filled the air, a junior priest censed the room and sprinkled holy water. Livia watched as the queen lifted her face and closed her eyes to the smoke and the water, as if they were a blessing falling on her.

Livia watched the ladies pray, measuring the likelihood of any one of them being sincere. It was Livia's belief that few would be in the oratory if it were not the fashion of the royal court, the known route for royal favour. The whole country was determinedly protestant; but the court, following the king and queen, was almost wholly converted. Every appointment that the king made favoured his co-religionists, and every lady in the queen's room either converted to the Church of Rome or was ostracised as a heretic.

Even the army was now led by roman catholics. Parliament had granted the king the right to appoint roman catholic officers to the army and commanders to the navy and the roman catholic gentry were allowed to arm and lead their tenants. The king had put a sword in the hands of the enemies of the English church, and no-one knew where he would stop. The battle, which would come either in the west of England or on London Bridge, would decide whether the king was beheaded on the scaffold like his father, or triumphant as a tyrant: turning the Church of England into the Church of Rome.

They came out of the oratory into the blaze of sunshine streaming through the high glazed windows and walked down the long gallery towards the queen's dining room for breakfast. The usual crowd was waiting to see the royals go by, a murmur of alarm that the king was missing, a whisper of concern at the pallor of the queen. A few people stepped forward and bowed, petitions in their hands. Livia, as a senior lady-in-waiting, gathered them up with complete indifference to the whispered pleas for help. Then a man bowing to the queen stood erect and caught Livia by the hand. In the sudden shock of recognition, she saw her husband: James Avery.

'James!' she exclaimed. 'Oh God! It's you!'

'And good morning to you,' he said quietly. 'I believe that I ordered you to come home?'

Livia saw the queen glance back. 'Your Majesty, may I present my husband Sir James Avery.'

The queen extended her hand and Sir James bowed low. 'I am so pleased you have come to court. These are troubled times, we need our friends around us.'

'I was just telling Sir James that I may not leave,' Livia hinted.

'Oh no! I cannot spare her now. Not while . . .'

'I understand completely,' Sir James said urbanely.

'You may breakfast with us.' The queen led the way to her dining room where four great tables were laid for the principal officers of her household, the royal confessor and three Benedictine priests, her ladies and their companions.

Livia made sure that her husband was seated near her, as befitted his status, but not so close that he could speak privately, and she took her place near to the queen. Proudly, she did the work of the first lady, serving the queen with the ewer and towel for her fingertips, and folding back her long sleeves to dine.

James bowed his head for the lengthy Latin grace, ate heartily, chatted to neighbours at the table and rose respectfully when the queen went to her private rooms. Livia went to follow her, but the queen waved her away. 'Go and see your husband, I am sure he is eager to talk with you.'

Livia curtseyed, feeling no gratitude at all, and turned back to meet the steady brown gaze of the man she had trapped into marriage. 'Shall we walk in the gardens?' she asked.

'We'll go to your rooms,' he ruled. 'You will want to explain to me in private, without interruption.'

Nothing could be less true, Livia thought, as she led the way through the courtiers and up the stairs to her private rooms. A maid was on her knees sweeping out the fireplace. Livia snapped her fingers and waved her away, and seated herself at the table by the window, looking across the gardens.

Sir James stood opposite her, leaning on the back of the chair. 'I ordered you home and I sent my carriage,' he said quietly.

'You surely had my letter explaining why I could not come?'

'No, that must have miscarried.' His tone made it perfectly clear that he thought there was no letter.

She clasped her hands. 'Oh no! But I was advised by His Majesty himself that it was not safe to travel north until the Earl of Argyll was captured! I have been so anxious for you!'

'I am obliged to you,' he said icily. 'But my carriage will have arrived after his rebellion failed, and in any case, it has been days now, since his execution.'

'But then we heard of Monmouth's advance,' Livia said glibly. 'I assumed you would be raising a troop and coming to defend London? Have you not brought a troop with you now?'

He narrowed his eyes. 'I can't raise men in the middle of haymaking and shearing, as everyone knows. And they are militia – local troops. I am required to muster them to defend their homes; not to march them to Somerset.'

'But I thought you would want to?' Livia gleamed at him. 'I thought you would want to defend a king of the true faith, against a protestant rebel? You – who served his father against Cromwell?'

'My wife does not question my loyalty,' he said shortly.

'Then I pray you don't question mine,' Livia said sweetly.

'But why didn't you take the carriage?' he demanded. 'Why stay in London in danger? It's not like you.'

'My duty was with the queen,' she said smugly.

'You could do nothing for her! She's surrounded by guards and nobility.'

'I provided a ship for her!' she said triumphantly. 'No-one else did! I got her a passage on a ship to Rome to go to her mother. If Argyll had marched on London I would have got her safely away. The king himself was glad of it. He has rewarded me.'

He was astounded. 'But how did you get a ship?'

She widened her eyes at him as if he were a fool. 'Of course, you remember that I shipped my family treasures from Venice to London?'

'I remember you shipping stolen goods and fakes at a profit!'

She turned her head as if she cared nothing for his contempt and looked out of the window towards the river. 'I suppose that you remember the wharf?'

He was suddenly intent. 'Of course I remember them. But I said that neither of us would ever go there again.'

'I had to! I commissioned a passage on their ship. I took the queen to the wharf to wait for the tide. Then I got news that Argyll's army had deserted, and I brought her back to the palace.'

He was deeply troubled. 'Livia! We both of us gave our word that we would never trouble them again.'

'When the Queen of England's safety depended on it?'

He could think only of the woman whom he had loved and had last seen more than fourteen years ago. 'Were they ...? Is she ...?'

She let him flounder.

'Is she still alive?'

'*Allora!* You don't even know that?'

'I keep my word. I have not seen her or heard of her since I married you. I begged her pardon. I told her I loved her. And I walked away from her and have never seen her since.'

'An odd way to treat the love of your life!'

'The right thing to do. And it was what she wanted. She wanted me to leave her there – at the wharf – and never speak to her again. And so I have.'

She almost laughed at his discomfiture. 'Toll-loll! Well, I can tell you she is alive. And now, I have given her the one thing she wanted: her old home. She is very grateful to me. You – of course – she will never see again. But she will live for the rest of her life on my bounty, as a guest in my house. I am her greatest benefactor.'

He drew out a chair and sat down as if he could not stand.

'The queen gave me the manor of Foulmire.' Her voice was ringing with triumph. 'You never thought of that for her? Alinor's childhood home, that she loves so much? I got it for Matteo. The boy who had no inheritance from you. It will be his, and he can take her and take her daughter – take all of them for all I care – to live there.'

'She accepted?'

'With tears of joy.'

He doubted it; but he had no strength to argue with her. He rested his arms on the table and felt the old impotent rage shake his heart.

'She will live in the manor where she was nothing but a servant. And she will be buried in the graveyard though she was denounced as a witch,' Livia announced. 'I have restored her. Not you; just me. You ruined her but I have made all things well. They are grateful to me; I have been nothing but good for them.'

He put his bowed head on his arms as if he would sleep. 'They forgive you for all that you did? But they still do not even speak of me?'

'*Allora!*' Livia remarked as if this had just become apparent to her. 'As you say! It is just so. Quite unfair on you, is it not?'

WESTONZOYLAND, SOMERSET, SUMMER 1685

Ned, lit only by the moon, watching his footing on the rutted path, guided his troop along the wagon track called Marsh Lane that ran between the low-lying fields. Mist breathed from every ditch and stream that intersected the landscape, swirling around them so Ned, looking back, could hardly see his troop. As Monmouth's own regiment, the Red regiment, they led the way; ahead of them Godfrey the guide walked beside the mounted officers. The track was little more than beaten mud through wet fields. The deep wagon ruts made it impossible for more than two men to march abreast, so they went in double file, sometimes splashing through standing water, or dragging their feet out of deep mud, past Peasey Farm, which sat squat in the low-lying fields like a becalmed brig with no lights showing. They circled it in silence like a ghost army in the mist.

Past the farm, the way was even less used and harder going: a sheep track through a water meadow. In winter, all these fields would be drowned; in this damp summer the grass was sodden, the reeds as sharp as skewers poking through the puddles, the ditches overflowing. Only when the moon broke through the clouds could they see lakes of silver; when it went dark, the land

and water were an unrelenting black. They could have been creeping along a void with nothing all around them.

They were muffled by the mist – two miles of silently marching men – with officers riding up and down the train muttering 'Silence' and 'Not far now, lads!' A nightjar called, like an eerie creaking door, and one of Ned's troop started and fumbled for his pike. 'Hush,' Ned whispered to him. 'It's nowt.'

The moon shone on the silvery water of the Langmoor Rhine on their right-hand side, the only feature in the inky landscape that could guide them, and it took an uncertain path, arching away from the track, deep as a lake in parts, reedy in the shallows. The grey horizon, unbroken by trees, stretched all around them, rising up over one little hill, paler to the east but pitch-black overhead, the moon coming and going like an uncertain friend. Ditches and streams breathed out banks of mist that reared up like troops of waiting horsemen. Every now and then, there was a sudden bleat from a sheep, or the deep suspicious lowing of cattle marooned on the higher ground. Each time Ned felt his own grip on his weapon tighten, each time he said 'Steady, steady' to his men knowing that their nerves were as ragged as his own in the half-light of these waterlands.

He thought only once of Rowan and that perhaps her gods were with him, that they would recognise the quiet tread of men along old tracks. He glanced up and down his troop; their broken gait was quieter than the tramp of marching feet, and those who had muskets were holding them close, to prevent any chink of metal. The pikemen had their weapons slanted over their shoulders, except for those who were using the hafts as walking sticks to help them along the muddy track. Ned thought that if it was God's will that he died here, it would be very like the landscape of his childhood home. If his sister Alinor came to find his body, she would know that the last land he had seen was a watery marsh. She would be comforted by that, he knew, just as he was comforted now by the gleam of starlight on the Langmoor Rhine reminding him of the Broad Rife where he had manned his father's ferry all those years ago.

Ahead of them was another ditch, a deeper and darker tributary of the Langmoor Rhine that ran alongside their track, and the cavalry halted on the brink, their horses shifting warily, backing from the water which was silver in the moonlight and inky in the shadows. Godfrey the guide was whispering anxiously, going one way along the steep bank, peering downwards, and then turning on himself and going the other way. He knew there was a crossing point; but in the darkness, and with the future of England resting on him, he could not find it. At last, Ned heard him say:

'Here, my lords! Here! It's not too deep,' and he waded in himself, chest deep in the gurgling water.

Monmouth led on his horse, then the first of the men on foot struggled down into the water and then hauled each other up on the far side. One man lost his boot and one his pike. Ned whispered: 'Leave it! Come on! You'll pick one up.' When suddenly, there was a crack of a shot from a musket nearby, terribly close, the flame bright in the darkness, the report like a smack, and the scream of a wounded horse, and the sound of hooves coming at them out of the darkness.

Monmouth did not hesitate. 'Come on! Forward! Now!'

Ned urged his men. 'Quick. Leave the cavalry to this. We've got to get to the main camp! To the Bussex Rhine!'

He heard Nathaniel Wade repeat the order to his troop behind them. Together, they forced their men over the crossing point and onward at a struggling run, blinded by the ribbons of mist, deaf to the sound of fighting behind them. But Ned heard – just as the royalist sleeping camp certainly heard – a single horse from the royal patrol, galloping flat out, the rider screaming at the top of his voice: 'Beat the drums! The rebels are come! Beat the drums! For the Lord's sake! Beat the drums!'

'Shoot him down!' Monmouth yelled, aiming his pistol. Ned raised his gun, primed his weapon and shot, knowing the man was out of range already and their surprise was betrayed and half their cavalry engaged too soon.

Monmouth wheeled his horse towards the waking royalist camp: 'Onward! Follow me! Liberty!'

'Quick march!' Ned shouted to his troops. 'Forward!'

He glanced behind him; his men were heads down, running forward, in a race to get to the royalist camp before they were fully awake and armed. As fast as they could go, the men ran and stumbled, picked themselves up and forced themselves onward, half a mile to the Bussex Rhine that curved like a moat before the royalist camp, where they halted panting, fumbling to prime their guns. At that moment, with intense relief, Ned heard their own cavalry coming up behind them, shaken by their encounter, missing half their force, and saw Grey riding up and down the bank of the ditch looking for a crossing point. Ned could hear them shouting: 'Here! It's here!' and then: 'No! Over here!' as they tried to find a shallow point to break into the royal camp, cut down the troops as they woke, and drive them into the rhine and Monmouth's waiting army.

But now they heard drums on the far side of the ditch, and saw the flare of light as the royal soldiers kicked campfires into flame. They could see their enemies rising up from sleep, floundering in the darkness, looking for their weapons, unprepared, half of them still drunk, half of them sick. Ned called quietly to his men: 'Get ready lads. Ready for them to come.' Grey's cavalry were out of sight, but he imagined them, crossing the ditch and forming up to charge; the chaos they would cause when they tore through the waking camp, coming out of the darkness, driving them into the ditch, straight into the rebel fire.

'Steady now, steady,' Ned said. He could barely see his men on either side of him in the darkness, but he could hear them lining up as they had practised, the loading of the muskets. Behind them, he could hear the cannons being dragged into position, the gunners loading, and then the first roar that plunged the deadly cannonballs over their heads and into the royal camp.

'Hold your fire!' he ordered. 'Wait till you see them, they'll be forced into the water. Wait... wait...' But suddenly, there was a terrible rush in the darkness to his left, and the thunderous noise of horses: a cavalry charge, coming straight for them along their side of the bank. Ned looked, horrified to see the giant silhouettes of dozens of horsemen, riding them down. To his own men he shouted: 'Stand firm! Stand firm!'

Even as he spoke, he knew it was the wrong order. No untried infantry could stand against a cavalry charge, they could not bear it. The horses plunged among them, men went down under the hooves, knocked aside like children. Ned was bowled over and as he reached up to grab at the horse's reins he caught a glimpse, bright as a flash, of a green leaf in the bridle. He dropped into a crouch, his hands over his head, felt the blow on his side as the horse stumbled over him, realising, with sick horror, that it was their own cavalry, charging through their own men, on the wrong side of the river. They had failed to cross, they had been frightened into a bolt, they were unable to pull up, hopelessly out of control, mowing down their own musketeers and infantrymen in the rout. And – worst of all – now there could be no charge through the royalist camp. The rebel cavalry had ploughed through their own men and were gone. Then the royalist muskets sighted them and the fire crackled out.

'Stand firm!' Ned staggered to his feet, trying to rally his shattered troops. 'That's the worst of it gone! First rank kneel, second rank stand. Hold your fire till you see them ... Ready!' They could just see the royalist infantry on the other side of the ditch in the dawning light. 'Fire!' Ned shouted and there was a crack and a blaze of his men's guns and royalist soldiers went down. The second rank stepped forward and took aim. 'Fire!' Ned yelled. But now the royalist muskets had taken aim, and from either side of the ditch the troops exchanged fire.

'Advance! We've got to advance!' Nathaniel shouted at him.

Ned shook his head; he knew that if he could get his inexperienced troops to go forward against fire into the shelter of the ditch, he would never be able to get them out again. All the rebel army could do was stand their ground. But the sky was slowly lightening, and now Ned could see the royalist cavalry, horsed and armed, going up and down the bank on their side, looking for the crossing place, so that they could ford the ditch and charge down the rebel army.

'Withdraw to Langmoor Rhine!' Monmouth yelled. 'Beat the retreat!'

The drums started to rattle the rhythm for retreat. Ned glanced across to where Nathaniel Wade's troop were going backwards, those with muskets kneeling in front and firing to cover the pikemen, and then dropping back to kneel and fire again.

'Retreat!' Ned ordered, so that his troop went back, step by step alongside Wade's men, back along the road. He looked around; he could not see Monmouth; and Lord Grey and the cavalry must be halfway to Bridgport by now. He recognised William Hewling, keeping his men steady, his young face grim. Ned thought that if they could hold the crossing point and get their men out of these deadly levels, they could regroup on higher ground.

Monmouth had found and crossed some shallows. Now he called to the infantry to follow him. Nathaniel Wade and Ned halted their men before the crossing point and formed them up as a rearguard, as the army stumbled past them.

'Hurry!' Ned shouted at them. 'It's not over till we're all safe home! Hurry!'

They could see the royalist cavalry crossing the Bussex Rhine and forming up for a deadly charge, the Monmouth infantry scattering and running towards them, men dropping one after another under a rattle of musket fire. Ned glanced across to young Nathaniel. 'Steady!' he urged. 'Hold tight! We'll hold this till we've got the lads across.'

He did not hear the cannon at all. He had heard all the others, he had heard the first crackle of the muskets and the terrible thunder of his own cavalry bolting through his men. But the cannonball that struck him was silent until there was a crunch like a fist against his ear and then nothing at all.

REEKIE WHARF, LONDON, SUMMER 1685

Alinor jerked awake in the early morning, her hand to her ear as if she had been struck by lightning. 'Ned!' she cried out before she was even awake. 'Ned!'

Her scream woke Alys in the bedroom next door and she threw back the covers, jumped out of bed and ran into her mother's room. 'Ma? What is it?'

'It's Ned!' Alinor was white-faced, her hand to her ear, half out of bed. 'It's Ned. He's hurt, I know it.'

Alys guided her mother back to bed, leaned her back against the pillows. 'God save him! God bless us. Sit down, Ma, you'll make yourself ill.'

The older woman was fighting to get air into her weakened lungs. 'We've got to go to him.'

'Yes, yes, but hush now, Ma. Get your breath. Here.' Alys mixed some hartshorn and water that her brother Rob had left for their mother. 'Drink this.'

Alinor drank the glass with little sips, catching her breath, while Alys watched for the colour to come back into her cheeks.

'I've got to go to Ned,' Alinor whispered.

'Ma. You had a dream.'

'It was a Seeing. I'm not so old that I don't know the difference.'

'It was a dream. You were asleep. It was a nightmare, I'm sure. And no wonder. But we'll go to church this morning, as soon as we're dressed, and pray for my uncle Ned's safety. And then I'll go to the coffee house and see if there's news.'

A closed stubborn look crossed Alinor's face. 'Send for Johnnie,' was all she said.

'Ma, he'll be at work. I can't send for him.'

'He'll have news, and I want to see him. Send for him, Alys, or I'll go downstairs to the kitchen and send Susie myself.'

'I'll send a lad from the warehouse,' Alys bargained, 'if you'll rest now.'

'You'll send now?'

Alys nodded and her mother visibly relaxed. 'Eh – I'm sorry,' she said, suddenly obedient, allowing Alys to tuck the sheets in around her. 'I'm sorry, Alys. But you don't know what it's like. It's as if I felt the blow myself. It's not a dream. I do know.'

'Just rest, Ma, please rest. Go to sleep again, and I'll bring your breakfast up within an hour or so.'

'I can't sleep,' her mother said. 'Ned is in terrible danger, he needs me. I can't sleep, Alys. You have to send for Johnnie at once.'

Alys compressed her lips in a firm line to prevent any angry word escaping and went out of the room to her own bedroom. She pulled on her working clothes, a plain woollen skirt, a white linen shirt and a dark jacket. She glanced towards her husband's side of the empty bed, wishing that he was with her and not at sea. Then she went to the little table and drew the writing box towards her and took out a sheet of notepaper, dipped a pen in the inkwell and wrote to Johnnie.

Son,

Your grandmother has been troubled by a dream and won't be turned from seeing you. Please come as soon as you can without inconveniencing the Company. Whatever she tells you, Do Not undertake to find your uncle Ned – wherever he may be.

Your loving Mother

Johnnie, handed this note by one of the clerks in the huge hall of the East India Company's headquarters, read it quickly and went straight to his department head, got an indefinite leave of absence and left the building. He took a hackney coach back to his lodging, packed a bag, took a purse of money from the hiding place he kept under his chest of clothes, and set off at once to the water stairs to cross the river to the warehouse.

'Ma?' he said, coming through the front door and finding his mother at her desk in the counting office.

Absent-mindedly she kissed him. 'It's your grand-mother,' she said.

'Is she ill?'

'She's very disturbed.'

'Why didn't you call Rob?'

She hesitated and he knew that his mother, who rarely lied, was avoiding telling him something. 'She asked for you, and I didn't think . . .'

'You know that Rob would do anything for her,' he said, 'but you think that I will obey you and refuse her.'

She did not acknowledge that he was right. 'I can't bear for any of us to be mixed up in this folly of my uncle's,' she said fiercely. 'It was bad enough with Matthew bringing trouble to our door. But at least that was for the king, and nobody could blame us for being on his side. But Rob'll do whatever your grandma tells him. He thinks she's got the Sight. And you don't believe in such things any more than I do.' She looked up at him. 'You don't,' she told him, as if to persuade him. 'We don't. It's brought us nothing but trouble.'

Johnnie shrugged. 'More things in heaven and earth than are dreamt of . . .' he quoted cheerfully. 'I don't pretend to know, Ma. I know that Sarah and I could think the same thought and feel each other's pain. I know that Grandma sent her to Venice to find Rob because she knew he was in danger. I know she has dreams that can't be explained and foretells and foresees—'

His mother hushed him. 'She doesn't! She doesn't! And it's never brought us any good.'

'It was good for my uncle Rob. It was the saving of his life. Anyway, I'll go up and see her. Is she still in bed?'

'She's up. She's had breakfast, but she says she won't rest until she sees you.'

'Well, here I am!' Johnnie said matter-of-fact.

'She's going to ask you to go after your uncle Ned,' she burst out. 'It's to go straight towards danger. Johnnie, you've got to tell her "no".'

He put his arm around his mother and hugged her. 'I'll see what she says. Don't be upset, Ma. All old ladies get fancies. I'll see what she wants of me and put her mind at rest.'

She let him go alone, reassured that he would soothe his grandmother. But then she caught sight of his bag beside his travelling cloak hanging by the warehouse door, and she knew he had already decided to go.

ST JAMES' PALACE, LONDON, SUMMER 1685

'He has written to me.' Mary Beatrice held out a letter to show Livia. 'James, James Monmouth, that beautiful boy, has written to me, to ask me to plead mercy for him.'

'Will you?' Livia took the letter and scanned the urgent writing. Monmouth, captured in a ditch and imprisoned in the Tower, begged the queen's pardon, said that he had never meant to declare himself as king, that all he had wanted to do was to protect the Church of England – that he knew now that he had been wrong, that he begged her to save him from the scaffold.

'How can I?' Her pale face was twisted with strain. 'How can I save him? He says himself that he was opposing the true faith. How can I ask for mercy for a man who is an enemy of Rome? By rights he should be burned alive.'

Livia widened her eyes. 'I don't think a man can be burned for defending the Church of England.'

'No, of course not. Not here. Not until we change the law. He'll have to be hanged and drawn and quartered for treason. It's justice.'

Livia folded the anguished letter begging for mercy and put it away among the queen's papers. 'So, no reply?'

'What can I say?' the queen demanded. 'How can I write to him and tell him that he has to die?'

'Would the king spare him if he turned papis—' Livia nipped off the word. 'If he turned to the true faith? Our faith?'

Mary Beatrice nodded. 'Yes, he would. But he'd have to name his allies. The king would grant his life if he would name all of them.'

'Betray his friends to death?' Livia asked. 'To save his own skin?'

Mary Beatrice nodded. 'A full confession before God,' she said piously. 'Then we could execute them instead of him.'

Livia took a breath. 'D'you think he will betray his friends?' she asked.

Mary Beatrice's dark eyes were filled with tears. 'No,' she said desolately. 'I think he is lost to us. I think he is lost to us, and – even worse – he is lost to God.'

WEST COUNTRY, SUMMER 1685

Johnnie, in his hired carriage, jolting down the ill-maintained winding roads of the west country, learned he was approaching his destination not by the signposts, but because outside every village there was a fresh corpse on the gibbet. Outside the towns there were tarred and salted heads on spikes, their lips drawn back in a perpetual silent scream, the empty sockets of their eyes pecked out by crows, glaring down on the travellers who rode swiftly past burying their faces in their sleeves to shield them from the butcher-shop smell of freshly killed human flesh. Some villages had strange cages at their crossroads where the bodies of the village men were hanged forever. Their children ran under them when they were late for school.

Johnnie made himself look at every crow-pecked skull to see if he could recognise his uncle Ned. It might be the only way to find him. Only the people who left a flower at the foot of the scaffold, or wore a hidden black ribbon, knew who they had lost; the royalists had hanged hundreds of Monmouth's defeated army wherever they were captured, without trial, without bothering to record their names. A stranger from London would never be able to find a single man, whether he was imprisoned with hundreds of others starving for food and water, injured and dying in hiding, or beheaded and strung up as a warning to anyone who might defy the king.

The farther west Johnnie went the more he understood the impossibility of his task. After days on rutted and winding roads, held up for hours behind wagons bringing in the harvest, haggling at strange stables for a change of horses, delayed by a broken wheel spoke, he dismissed the carriage and hired a horse. He gave up asking for his uncle Ned Ferryman. It was treason to help an escaping rebel, punishable by death. It was treason to nurse a dying rebel. Nobody would admit to even seeing a soldier of Monmouth's army, or hearing their jaunty drums, or picking a green leaf for freedom. In any case, Johnnie might be asking for his uncle Ned; but all his hopes were on finding Rowan.

He did not know where to begin. He could not ask any of the country people if they had seen her – nobody would even speak to him, and when he bribed a ploughman, or a shepherd, walking down the drover road to market, they replied in accents so thick that he could not understand them, and he suspected that they were mocking him. Everyone stared with blank hostility as he rode by, on his hired horse. He thought that all he could do was to stay for a few nights as near to the battlefield as might be safe for him, perhaps Bridgwater, perhaps Taunton, and announce that he was looking for a native lad, a servant mislaid – and hope that she might hear of him, and come to him for help. The thought of rescuing her, made his head swim with desire. But as he travelled farther and farther west, through grieving towns that smelled of death, he became more and more certain that Uncle Ned was dead and rotting on a battlefield, in a ditch, or on a gibbet. And Rowan – innocent of everything – was dead beside him.

REEKIE WHARF, LONDON, AUTUMN 1685

Matthew attended church with his foster mother Alys. They gave thanks for the royal family and their miraculous preservation from rebellion. The vicar – normally a stout defender of the church against popish plots – had changed his tune at the threat of another civil war. Not even a protestant claimant to the throne could persuade the vicar of the parish of St Olave's that any cause was worth the disruption of trade. He spoke for God and for His English church, His trade, and His dominance of the high seas. Anything that disrupted business was against the will of God whose main ambition was – must always be – the prosperity of the English merchant and the victory of the English adventurers.

Alys heard the note of self-serving patriotism, and disregarded it. She followed to the letter the rising and kneeling, singing the hymns and reciting the English prayers from memory, following the readings in her own King James Bible. This was her faith, but also a show. Alys had learned from her mother, a wise woman, who had learned from hers, to follow the ritual of the service so precisely that no neighbour ever had an excuse to report them for any sort of suspicious behaviour that meant popery, or dissenting, or dark arts.

Matthew followed the service as he had been taught, seated in the family pew which had, over the years, moved closer and closer to the front of the church, as their business improved and their payment of the vicar's tithe increased. Now they were the third pew from the front, on the right, and only two wharfinger families took precedence over the family from Reekie Wharf. When Matthew put up his plate as a lawyer, or announced that he was lord of Foulmire, his foster mother would be able to claim a new place, at the very front of the church – as landed gentry and the undisputed leaders of the parish.

They walked home together, her hand on his arm, the household servants and some of the warehouse clerks demurely following, past the yard gate to enter at the front door.

Alinor was in the parlour waiting for their return from church.

'Are you ready to go to Foulmire this week?' Matthew asked.

'It's fit for us to live there? It's not been left empty?'

'It was a royal lodge, kept ready for a visit from the queen.'

Alinor gave a little laugh. 'Since I never went beyond the kitchen door, that should be good enough for me.'

'We'll take our own sheets . . .' Alys raised her head at a noise. 'Is that a wagon? There shouldn't be a delivery on a Sunday?'

It was a carriage, drawing up on the cobbled quay outside the front door, the Avery crest bold on the doorway, the driver and footmen in the Avery livery. One jumped down from his place at the back of the carriage and came to the front door, a letter in his hand.

'Oh no,' Alys said. 'Not her again.'

'I'll go,' Matthew said, not waiting for the knock. He opened the front door and the footman bowed to him and handed him the letter addressed to Mrs Shore.

'Wait here,' he said and took the letter into the parlour where his mother was looking out of the window at the imposing carriage.

'It's not the Nobildonna,' he told her. 'It's a letter for you.'

'For me?' Puzzled, she broke the seal and saw the signature. 'It's him,' she said, glancing towards her mother.

'And what does Sir James say?' Alinor asked steadily.

'He says: "I hope you will accept the loan of my carriage and servants to take you and your mother to Foulmire and home after your visit. I do not presume to hope for any future correspondence; but I would be glad to know if your mother is well. Please accept this as a small gesture of my respect for your mother, to whom I send my humblest service, as always. James Avery." Well!' She put down the letter and looked from her mother to her foster son. 'Well!'

'We may as well use it,' Alinor remarked prosaically. 'It'll be far more comfortable than a hired coach.'

'We don't want favours from either of them. Especially not from him,' Alys snapped.

Matthew knew there was no point in asking why. His foster mother had always regarded his birth mother with deep suspicion, and would not even speak of his stepfather.

'It was a long time ago. We can use their carriage,' Alinor overruled.

'Ma—'

'We can accept the Avery carriage to get there and back to the house the Nobildonna got for Matthew. It's no more than hiring one. Go and tell the coachman what time you want him tomorrow morning, Matthew. They can put up at the Holly Bush overnight.'

Matthew glanced at his mother.

'Very well,' Alys said. 'But we'll send them straight back to London as soon as we arrive. I don't want them at Foulmire, picking up gossip.'

Alinor smiled at her daughter. 'We'll be long forgotten,' she said gently. 'The name on the deeds is Peachey and we'll be known as Matthew's foster family. I doubt there's anyone left to recognise us. Half of them'll be dead of old age and buried in the churchyard. The king then, Charles the First, is dead, and his son, Charles the Second, dead too. And now they've killed his poor boy James Monmouth. It's all long long ago. And we'll never speak of it.'

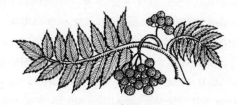

TAUNTON, SOMERSET, AUTUMN 1685

Johnnie rode into the little county town of Taunton a few days ahead of the judge from London. The entourage of judge, prosecutors, clerks and hangmen were working their way west, holding mass trials at all the market towns, leaving a trail of grief wherever they halted. Johnnie had to try three inns before he could find a bed for the night and stabling for his horse. The town was crowded with the families of the five hundred prisoners who were held in the town jail and in the cellars and dungeons of Taunton Castle. The London judge, George Jeffreys, the prosecutor Henry Pollexfen and scores of clerks, lawyers, reporters, the hangman and his assistant had requisitioned chambers in the castle and in the town and were expected any day.

It was as busy as an annual fair, but there was none of the cheerful jostling and clatter of setting up stalls, or hucksters calling in the streets. It was a surly crowd that milled around the castle, the town hall and jail, asking for news. There was a shanty town of anxious families camped in the grassy outer ward of the castle hoping for the chance to see their loved ones, praying that they would be freed.

It was impossible for Johnnie to make himself visible among so many people, all of them seeking information and losing hope; but as soon as he had secured his room and stabled his horse, he went out to walk the streets and ask people if they had seen a native, a servant, a slight dark boy by the name of Rowan. Half the people ignored him, turned away from any question, fearful that he was one of the many spies or ex-soldiers who were putting together evidence against a private enemy or to curry favour with the coming court. Other men seeking information were lawyers, appointed by desperate families, trying to show that a young man had joined Monmouth by mistake, or was not there at all. Nobody had any time for Johnnie though he showed the gleam of a silver coin in his hand.

They all knew that death was coming to Taunton. The judge, himself crippled by the spleen, had hanged men at every stop on his way to the west country, had left hundreds more in jails awaiting execution. His clerk told the accused men that there was no time to hear pleas of innocence; they had better own themselves guilty and hope for mercy. Jeffreys himself had sworn he would break the heart of the west country. The families who crowded around the jail, begging to have a moment – just one moment – with a beloved son, knew that it was only to say goodbye. In Winchester, Jeffreys had sentenced a seventy-year-old woman to be burned alive. In Dorchester, he condemned nearly three hundred men to death.

Johnnie scanned the long list of prisoners' names, looking for Ned Ferryman or any name that Ned might have adopted.

'That list is no good,' someone said at his shoulder.

'They don't bother to take everyone's name, and they're not true names either,' a woman told him.

'I'm looking for a young lad, a servant, from the Americas,' Johnnie said. 'Goes by the name of Rowan. He wasn't in the rebellion, he was on his way to London and I think he got lost.'

Her eyes were red as if she had been crying for days but her laugh was hard and bitter. 'You'll find that none was in the rebellion,' she told him. 'We was all on the way to London and got lost.'

'But have you seen him?' Johnnie asked in an undertone. A coin went from his hand to hers.

She took the coin for nothing. 'No,' she said. 'I haven't even seen my husband and the father of my children.'

'If you see him, or hear of him, I am Mr John Stoney at the New Inn,' he told her.

'Lawyer?' she asked, suddenly hopeful.

'No.'

She turned away and left him scanning the page. A clerk, dressed in a well-worn black suit, came up to him. 'Were you asking after a prisoner?'

Johnnie turned. 'No, a lost servant,' he said. 'A young lad, dark haired and slight, brown skin, from the Americas.'

'A savage?'

Johnnie grimaced. 'He's a Christian. But he's an Indian by birth.'

The man shrugged. 'If you need a lawyer, I can serve you. I am here buying prisoners.'

Johnnie frowned. 'Buying them?'

'The king gifts the guilty prisoners to his friends, to courtiers, or to the queen or her household,' the man explained, his eyes taking in the expensive cloth of Johnnie's suit and his good linen. 'They are selling them on. I can broker that for you.'

'Is it profitable?' Johnnie could not stop himself asking.

'Like all slaving – it's a fortune.'

'Unless they die on the way,' Johnnie interpolated.

'Yes,' the man smiled. 'But if you get a sturdy traitor you will make twenty per cent. Think of that over a hundred prisoners.'

'They're sold as slaves?'

'No! No!' the man corrected him. 'A ten-year indenture. And then they can come home.' He paused. 'If they're still alive,' he said fairly. 'Not many survive the sugar plantations.'

'I can buy a rebel?' Johnnie demanded.

'I can broker it, Sir,' the man said eagerly. 'How many would you want? Ten? Twenty? His Majesty owns them all, and he has already given many to Her Majesty, to her ladies, her secretary and to favourites. But there are hundreds and hundreds of men going spare. They can't all be executed – still, many hundreds must be shipped.'

'Can I buy a named man?' Johnnie asked.

He shook his head. 'No, this is not for the poor fools who hope to buy their brothers and fathers.' He made a contemptuous gesture at the crowd around the jail. 'It's not to free guilty men, nor ease their suffering. It's so that the king's court makes a profit from justice.'

'I'd like to buy perhaps ten,' Johnnie said, tempted by the profit. 'Come to my inn, the New Inn, at six o'clock tonight. And also watch out for my servant.'

'Is he a slave?' the man asked. 'If I see him, do I capture him?'

'No, no,' Johnnie said hastily. 'He's a free man, as free as you or I. But I fear he is lost. If you see him, tell him to come to me at the New Inn, and ask him where he is lodged so I can find him.'

The man shrugged, surprised at the effort Johnnie was investing in someone as unimportant as a brown-skinned servant while there were white-skinned prisoners to buy. 'Six o'clock, your honour,' he agreed.

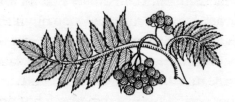

FOULMIRE, SUSSEX, AUTUMN 1685

The sun was setting on the right of the Avery carriage as it jolted down the Birdham Straight, the long straight lane, hedged on either side, that led due south on the Manhood peninsula. Alinor, who had been dozing for much of the journey, woke as if she knew that she was entering the landscape of her dreams. She opened her grey eyes and smiled at Matthew as she recognised the fields and hedgerows that they were passing through.

'Are we here?' Matthew asked, as impatient as a child.

'Nearly.' She leaned forward to look out of the window, as if to greet a friend.

Matthew, seeing the radiance of her face, followed her gaze and wondered at her joy in the low flat fields of stubble straw, and beyond them the rising slopes of dried-out meadowland. He was struck most by the wideness of the horizon and the lightness of the sky which arched above them like a great bowl.

'It goes on forever,' he said.

'I used to think I'd never get away,' Alys said grimly.

Matthew had been raised in a town, his view always blocked by buildings and walls and chimneys. This was a landscape with nothing higher than a twisted wind-bent tree: marshland, tidal land from sea to sea. Through the dusty window he could see for miles.

'Are we nearly here?' he asked. 'Is this it?'

Alinor's slate grey eyes flicked to his face. 'Not long now. Your lands start at Sidlesham. The next village down this road.'

'It's very flat,' he said. 'Not what I expected.' He tried to sound judicious, a landowner surveying his fields, but he could not keep the excitement from his voice. The road, now little more than a track, wound through a small village of old cottages, some with thatched roofs slipping down over the poky windows, some with gardens of vegetables and some late blooming flowers, some in a mess of mud and rubble.

'Nearly there.' Alinor took a little breath to steady herself. 'That is Mill Farm, and the tide mill.'

Matthew looked at the cluster of buildings and the tall granary behind them.

'We worked there,' Alys said, and her mouth shut tight as if she would never speak another word.

Matthew felt the carriage slow to a walk and then stop. 'Is something wrong?' He leaned forward to see out of the window.

'It's the Broad Rife,' Alinor said, as if she were naming a great stretch of water, instead of a sluggish river between muddy banks.

'There's a wadeway,' Alys told him. 'And a ferry for high tide. It was our ferry – my uncle Ned's ferry. But it's low tide now, the carriage can go through the water. The coachman's probably having a look at it.'

'If it's not washed away,' Alinor reminded her. 'It's been a long time since we crossed it.'

'At dawn,' Alys said with a sudden secretive smile. 'In a stolen wagon.'

'I'll get out,' Matthew said. He opened the carriage door and without waiting for the steps jumped the few feet down to the ground. The footmen swung down from the back of the carriage as soon as they saw him, and then paused, uncertain what to do in what was, to them, the middle of nowhere.

It was the middle of nowhere to Matthew too. The sweating coach horses had halted before a track which sloped gradually down to disappear into a river bed of oozing mud and puddles of briny water. Thick cobblestones marked the route, green with weed and half-covered with flotsam of stalks and straw. On both his right and his left, the water ran away into a sea of shoals, reed beds, lagoons and waterways, busy with little ducks and wading birds. A heron stood motionless looking at its own reflection in a deep pool. A constant babble of sound from the birds was overlaid with the loud crying of wheeling seagulls.

On the far side of the causeway was an old house with a lop-sided roof and an ancient plum tree bowed over the wall. The bee skep and the vegetable patch showed that someone was still living in the house, and a hanging bell showed that the ferry, nothing more than a raft with an overhead rope on a pulley, could be summoned when the tide was too high to splash across the wadeway. As Matthew stood, smelling the rich smell of warm mud, rotting seaweed and brine, feeling the heat of the setting sun on his cheek, the door to the ferryhouse opened and a man came out, pulling a hat off his head.

'Your honour!' he said on sight of Matthew. 'Welcome to – er – your lands, Sir. You're very welcome.' He spoke with the strong accent of Sussex, a low slow country drawl that Matthew – accustomed to the rapid patter of London speech – could hardly make out.

'Thank you,' said Matthew, painfully alive to the absurdity of being one side of a river of mud and his tenant bowing on the other.

'You're safe to cross, your honour. Just tell your driver to stay on the cobbles and he'll be over in no time. The horses'll come to no harm. They'll get used to it. I can lead them if he wants. We haven't had a coach cross for months, not for all this year. Not since the royal inspection when the king was crowned and they came all the way from London to see that we were here and not floated away—'

He broke off with a laugh at the folly of Londoners, and then turned it into a cough when the London servants and the London-bred Matthew looked at him, uncomprehendingly. 'The wagons go over every Saturday to Chichester market and back again, Sir, never fear. I'll come across to lead the horses if you like. We were glad to hear you were coming, Sir.'

Matthew nodded. He glanced up at the driver. 'Did you hear that?'

'Just about,' said the coach driver, disdainfully.

'Do you want him to lead them over?'

'No, Sir. I reckon I can drive my horses up and down a ditch, Sir.'

'Drive on then,' Matthew said and clambered back into the coach. The footmen closed the door and swung back into their places.

Alinor and Alys were silent as the coach eased forward, the iron-rimmed wheels sliding on the mud, the horses leaning back against the traces to keep the carriage steady on the downward slope, and then straining forward, their hooves slipping and grinding on the cobblestones, to mount the other side.

Matthew leaned forward and dropped the window as the fer-ryman came closer, his hat in his hand.

'All's well then, Sir,' he said. He stared into the carriage and bowed when he saw the two women who looked blankly back at him. There was no recognition on either side.

'And you are?' Matthew asked.

The man bowed. 'Tom Drydale, your honour. Tenant at Ferryhouse. Your tenant, Sir. And I work the ferry for you, Sir.'

Matthew found he had nothing to say to the first tenant he had met. He reached into his pocket for a coin and stopped when he saw his foster mother's tiny shake of her head. 'Thank you Drydale,' he said. He pulled the cord to tell the driver to go onwards, and the coach lurched forward, and the bowing tenant stepped back from the window.

'The lord doesn't pay a fee to cross,' Alys told him. 'It's your ferry. It's your wadeway. He pays you. Start as you mean to go on.'

'Leave the glass down,' Alinor said dreamily. 'I like the smell.'

'Mud?' Matthew asked.

'Why d'you think it's called Foulmire?' Alys asked.

Matthew shook his head. 'I thought it meant bird marsh. Fowl Mere?'

'It means stinking,' she told him. 'Foul Mire: Foul Mud.' She turned to her mother: 'You ever heard of the Drydales?'

Alinor dragged her eyes from the watery waste on the left of the carriage. 'Never,' she said to her daughter. 'Perhaps it's all new people under new names. And here we are, under a new name too. Here we are, anew.'

The carriage lurched past the ferryhouse.

'That was our house,' Alinor told Matthew. 'That was your uncle Ned's ferry, and our father's ferry before him. Our family were ferrymen here when the monks built the Priory. And we were ferrymen here when the monks were driven out.' She pointed to a ruined shanty on the bank of the harbour a little beyond the ferryhouse. 'And that was my—'

'That was our fishing hut,' Alys interrupted her mother. 'We had a fishing boat and we used to keep the nets and the lobster pots there. My father was a fisherman.'

Alinor regarded her daughter silently but did not contradict her, as the carriage jolted on, rocking in the ruts of the mud track. Both women were quiet, watching for the familiar landmarks that they had not seen for decades.

To the right of the carriage was a low flat plain intersected with draining ditches where the standing water shone in the setting sun which was sinking low on the rim of the flat land. To their left was a formless sea of unending mud, intersected with rivers and pools of water and reed beds, and now and then a shingle beach, thrown up by underwater currents. The sea, too far away even to be heard, seemed as if it would never return and the mud and shingle and scrub and the great broad rivers of still water would stretch to the horizon forever.

Suddenly, there was a roar like that of an enormous waterfall and a grinding noise of machinery and the coach lurched as the horses shied in fright and the coachman shouted at them and hauled on the reins.

'God's sake, what's that?' cried Matthew and hung onto the strap as the carriage bounded forward.

Alinor and Alys had tightened their grip on one another, but leaned back against the jolt of the carriage as the coachman hauled on the horses and the pace steadied.

Matthew turned to his mother: 'What in God's name was that?' He looked back the way they had come, and saw a gout of water spring from the bank behind them to gush, frothing and brown, into a deep channel in the middle of the harbour.

Alinor's face was as white as a drowned woman.

'It's safe!' Matthew said to her. 'It's all right. The horses are steady. But the noise! What is that? What on earth was that?'

'That was the tide mill,' Alys answered him and leaned slightly towards her mother so their shoulders rested together, as if to hold each other up. 'They open the sluice gates of the millpond and the water pours into the millrace and turns the mill wheel. The noise – that's the water rushing through the mill and turning the mill wheel for grinding and then the water pouring out into the harbour.' For the first time since the thunderous noise, she looked at her mother. 'Are you all right, Ma?'

'I'm all right.' The thread of her voice was almost drowned by the noise of the mill wheel and the tide race.

'It's a fearsome row!' Matthew exclaimed. 'I thought my end had come!'

His mother smiled thinly. 'It takes some getting used to.'

The carriage rocked down the rutted road going south through thick woodland, away from the harbour and the rushing water. Matthew could see occasional clearings and the heaped pile of wood of a charcoal burner.

'Now this is Sealsea Island,' Alys told Matthew. 'And everything either side of this road is yours.'

There was a low stone wall to the left of the road, beautifully built of knapped flints which gleamed a dull grey in the dying light of the day. Matthew looked backwards down the road at the receding countryside and saw a deer, poised on the track looking towards him, and then flirting its white tail and disappearing into the trees.

'A deer!' he exclaimed.

'Your deer,' his mother confirmed. 'All the game belongs to the manor too.'

'I own deer!' he laughed.

The coach turned through a high stone entrance, rattled down a long drive and then made a sweeping turn. The wheels crunched on shingle and the carriage stopped before a great wooden door.

'And here we are,' Alys said, glancing nervously at her mother. 'Here we are again.'

Alinor was leaning back against the silk squabs of the seats, her hand at her throat as if to steady the heaving of her lungs. The footmen jumped down, let down the steps and opened the carriage door. The double door of the house was flung open, and a man came out, a woman behind him, and behind them two maids and four house servants in a dark green livery, looking towards the carriage, waiting to meet their new masters.

Matthew got out first and tried to smile confidently at his servants, as if he were accustomed to this life, to the grand house, to the open door, to the rows of white-capped curtseys. He turned to help Alys and Alinor from the carriage and saw Alys supporting his grandmother and realised that she could barely stand. He stepped back to the carriage again and helped her down.

'Was the journey too much for her?' he asked Alys fearfully.

'It's not the journey; it's the returning.'

Alinor, her feet on the doorstep of the Priory, steadied herself to meet the steward. She had a sudden fear that he would be the same man who had forgiven her rent forty years ago, the man who knew of her terrible shame and public disgrace, the man who had seen her go into the stable loft to nurse a man with the plague and come down radiant, pregnant with his child.

But of course, it was not him. Mr Tudeley had been an old man then, he had died years ago, and the cook behind him was not her old friend. Alinor did not recognise any of the housemaids nor the stable boys nor the garden lads. She held tightly to Matthew's arm as he led her into the house and she heard the murmur of names as each servant ducked a bow or bobbed a curtsey, and all of them were unknown.

'The parlour,' the steward said, and Alinor forced herself to follow him, as if she had never before set foot on the polished wooden floor of the hall.

It was so much changed that she felt like the stranger she pretended to be. Wherever she turned was both familiar and hauntingly different. The stairs, where her son Rob had paused to show her his borrowed clothes, were just the same; but they descended into a hall which had been made-over, and the little boy with the bright face that she remembered was a grown man with a child of his own. The private chapel which had faced east, opposite the grand staircase, had been transformed into a dining room, its illegal vocation wiped clean; and where the altar had stood, there was now a tall cabinet for showy silverware. Sir William's gun room overlooking the garden was now the parlour. Alinor smelled rose petals, and missed the scent of cigars and gun oil. Sir William had been dead for years and the parlour was cleaned and panelled with matting on the floor and a rich Turkey carpet on the elegant oak gate-leg table with chairs set around a pretty fireplace. The steward led them in and offered them tea, wine or small ale.

Matthew, looking at Alinor's white face, ordered mulled wine and water for them all.

'Should you go to your bedroom, Mother Alinor?' he asked her. 'Should you lie down and rest?'

She shook her head. 'In a moment. I can't bear to go up yet. Everything is so different, it's like a homecoming and yet all strange ...'

'I can hardly believe it's mine,' Matthew said, looking out of the window over the new rose garden and the herb garden beyond. Beyond the herb garden was a high wall set with an inviting door. 'I'll go out and look around. I should see the coach into the stable, and the horses,' Matthew said. 'There might be our own carriage here. The lease said farm and stable equipment.'

'Then we could send the Avery carriage back to him at once,' Alys said. 'We wouldn't need it.'

'Nobody will know his name, if you're afraid of that,' Alinor reminded her. 'Nobody will see the crest and think of him. He went under another name then, and nobody will recognise us. It's like a dream, as if we are ghosts at our old life.'

'This is our life,' Alys said stubbornly. 'It is the old life that is forgotten, that is like a dream. It's him that's a ghost with no name.'

'What name?' Matthew asked. 'What ghost? Who went by another name then?'

'Sir James Avery,' Alys answered when her mother nodded that she might speak. 'He came here, years ago, under another name. He lied to us all. He was a spy.'

'Why?'

'It was the war,' Alinor told him. 'He had to hide who he was, and it ended badly.'

'He was a liar,' Alys said sharply.

Alinor smiled at her daughter. 'There were many lies,' she said gently. 'And most of them for love. And all of them either forgotten or forgiven. They are nothing to Matthew.' She turned to him. 'You go and explore your new country! There are no pasts or ghosts for you!'

He beamed at her and strode to the door. 'I can't believe it. I can't believe our luck.'

The two women exchanged a look as if they thought that luck had once been against them.

'You're a lucky boy,' Alinor told him, as if to defy chance itself. 'And now that we are here again, I begin to think that we are lucky too.'

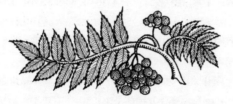

WINDSOR CASTLE, AUTUMN 1685

Livia was walking behind the queen and her ladies on the sloping paths of scythed grass that ran down to the river in the North Garden of Windsor Castle. The trees were changing colour, the dusty green leaves growing gold and yellow, the gardeners raking up heaps as bright as amber, the lads barrowing them away. The castle, beautiful as a fairy tale, rose behind them one terrace above another. The queen, who dreaded cold weather, was wearing a stole of the finest velvet thrown around her shoulders. Everyone was happy: the execution of Monmouth had confirmed the coronation, the country had backed the royals against a more beloved rival, the people had risen up – only to be crushed down.

Livia elbowed her way closer to the queen.

'The king is to give me some prisoners from the rebellion,' Mary Beatrice announced. 'And I shall give some to you.'

At once the ladies clustered around her. 'Oh please!' said one. 'I have to get money to pay my gambling debts, or my husband will send me home to the country!'

Livia laughed with the others and clapped her hands girlishly, but she knew the queen would reward her without asking.

'They're calling them the Maids of Taunton,' the queen said. 'The king has promised them to me – Maids for my ladies. A school of girls who went running after Monmouth, and embroidered him a banner!'

'Fools,' Livia said shortly. 'Won't they be executed?'

'Oh no! Girls still in school! Their teacher should have been burned for treason – but she died in prison: smallpox.'

'God moves in mysterious ways,' Livia said soulfully.

'By chance, the girls survived, and the king is to give them to me!'

'And will you give half a dozen of them to me?' the lady-in-waiting with gambling debts begged prettily.

'I will give you all one or two. My secretary Mr Nipho will see that they are transported and sold for us abroad – I think Barbados. He is managing it all.'

'And me! I want one!'

'And me!' the other ladies cried.

'How many young ladies are there to be transported?' Livia asked.

'About twenty, I think,' the queen said carelessly.

'And how much does each one make, when she is sold on the quayside?'

'There's a great demand for upper servants,' the queen said. 'Mr Nipho said we might get as much as twenty pounds each.'

'Oh! But how sad for them!' one of the ladies remarked. 'And how dreadful to be taken from your home.'

'And sold like slave on the dock!'

'They'll come home within ten years,' Mary Beatrice pointed out. 'It's not really slavery.'

One of the ladies managed an exaggerated shudder. 'I would rather die than be treacherous to my king.'

Livia gave her a hard look. 'I shouldn't think there will be many traitors ever again,' she said. 'Not now they have felt the king's mercy.'

Livia took the queen's arm and they walked on. 'He's giving me hundreds of prisoners,' the queen told her friend. 'Not just the Taunton maids, but ordinary men who served Monmouth. A small fortune in men. I will see you have some too.'

Livia pressed the queen's arm. 'My greatest reward is saving you when no-one else could.'

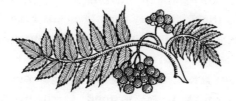

TAUNTON, SOMERSET, AUTUMN 1685

The judge, the clerks and servants and hangers-on, guarded on all sides by mounted cavalry as if advancing into a hostile country, swept into town, scattering claimants and mourners into the gutters, and took up their lodgings in the castle and every available room. Johnnie heard the uproar of their arrival as he was waiting for the broker in the common room of the inn. He could not reserve a parlour for his private use, every room in the house was serving as a bedroom, shared by two or even three or four strangers. Johnnie had managed to get a small bedroom cramped under the eaves, and he was already paying for two guests, saying that his servant would join him as soon as he could be found.

The two men found a corner of the parlour, and the broker outlined the business. 'You buy each man – or it might be a woman or child, I can't guarantee what you get, they're sold by the head and you only discover who you have when you've paid.'

'Can you at least guarantee they're not sick?'

'Who knows how smallpox spreads? And, of course, there's gaol fever now. Some are wounded . . .'

'Do you ship them anyway? Sick or well?'

The man spread his hands. 'I'm not the law,' he said pompously. 'It's the law that says they're guilty and whether they shall be hanged here or serve their sentence in Barbados.'

'Does the law ever say they're innocent?' Johnnie asked limpidly.

'Hardly ever,' he said cheerfully. 'Each prisoner is yours for ten pounds, and you carry the cost of shipping them. They're sold by my agent on arrival at Bridge Town in Barbados, for fifteen pounds, maybe twenty pounds each. That's a return that you can't despise, eh? The Royal Africa Company doesn't make more on their slaves than you will on yours.'

'If I took – say ten – I should want to pick them.'

The man frowned. 'Can't be done. There are hundreds to be disposed of, maybe even thousands by the time the judge has finished. People can't pick and choose their cargo. If I were to sell them to their own families, and they helped them escape, then it would be me dancing at the end of a rope, as well as them. This is business, Sir, not rescue. A young lady from London offered the judge a thousand pounds for her brother's life and was refused. That's a judge you can trust!'

'A thousand pounds?'

'She clung to the wheel of his coach and his servants whipped her off,' the man said with quiet satisfaction. 'But she got mercy.'

'Her brother was released, for a thousand pounds?'

'No! No! Hanged but excused drawing and quartering. That was the mercy. I suppose she thought it worth it to spare him pain. Young lad: William Hewling.'

'Can I see a list of names of those to be charged here?' Johnnie asked.

The broker grimaced. 'You can see those from Dorchester.' The man reached into his jacket and pulled out a crumpled packet of papers. The names were misspelled and crossed out, corrected and sometimes scratched out with a remark –'dead of wounds' or 'died'.

'And I'm still looking for the Indian servant,' Johnnie said, scanning the list for the name Ferryman.

'Would you pay a reward for him?'

'Not a bounty, he's not a runaway slave. He's a free – er – man.'

'A finder's fee then, like he was a horse?'

'Five pounds?' Johnnie suggested.

'You could hire a servant for a year for that!'

'I want this one,' Johnnie said, feeling his heart twist at the thought of her, in this dangerous town, where mercy cost a thousand pounds and bought a hanging rather than a disembowelling for a lad not yet twenty.

Johnnie, high up in the public gallery, pressed against the wall by the crowd, held one of his grandmother's pomander of herbs to his nose, and prayed that he did not catch a sickness from the people around him, or gaol fever from the pitiful prisoners crushed together on the floor of the court.

The Lord Chief Justice took his seat gingerly on a fat cushion; the gossip was that he was so tortured by a stone in his spleen that he could not sit or stand without pain, and the long days in the coach to get from town to town were agony to him. The country people said that he had sent so many good men to hell that they wished him the stone and the pox as well.

The clerk of the court announced the prisoners who were pleading not guilty; and to Johnnie's surprise, only four men came into court.

'Names?' the judge snapped to the clerk.

'Captain Abraham Annesley, William Cooper, joiner of Bridgwater, William Gatchill, yeoman of Angersleigh, and Simon Hamlyn, a tailor of Pitminster in this Hundred.' He paused, measuring the sour mood of the judge, high above him, behind an imposing raised desk. 'The Mayor of Taunton wishes to speak for Simon Hamlyn.'

Jeffreys heaved a sigh. 'Why?'

The mayor, wearing his chain of office over his gown, stepped up to the bench to address the judge and muttered earnestly.

'No, no,' the judge said loudly. 'Sit down, Sir. We have evidence against him.'

A lawyer stepped forward, hired by one of the families.

'Sit down, Sir, you have nothing to say,' Jeffreys raised his voice. 'Is there evidence for their guilt?' he asked the prosecutor.

In mute answer, Mr Pollexfen waved a thick sheaf of papers but did not trouble himself to show them.

'There's no time for me to hear them,' Jeffreys told the lawyer and the mayor. 'And certainly no time to read all this. I assume you don't want to be here for years? They are almost certainly guilty, and so I find.' He raised the gavel and smartly banged it down.

'My lord!' the mayor interrupted. 'This man is known to me as an honest tailor and is certainly innocent. He was nowhere near—'

'You brought him up before me, ahead of all the rest,' the judge turned on the mayor, suddenly enraged. 'It was you brought him before me! If he's innocent then it's on you – delaying the court. And telling lies! All lies! He can hang on Monday, and his blood is on your head.'

The prisoner buckled at the knees and the man beside him held him up.

'My lord!' the mayor expostulated. 'You can't hang a man for pleading Not Guilty!'

'No!' someone cried from the gallery, a young woman, her face stained with tears. At once, a guard barged through the crowd and thrust her out of the door. Everyone heard the clatter of her wooden clogs as he pushed her down the stone stairs.

The judge turned to the prosecutor. 'Isn't that evidence of guilt?' he demanded. 'Crying out? Contempt of court?' Hastily, he pulled on his black cap. 'Sentenced to be hanged and then drawn and quartered, the parts to be displayed at the gates or crossroads of their home towns,' he said briskly. 'All of 'em. Now bring up those who plead guilty.'

Johnnie thought there must be protest, but instead there was a sigh, a quiet indrawing of breath. Everyone in the gallery, everyone in the courtroom, even the condemned men had their eyes fixed on the judge, but no-one else cried out.

These were men whose hopes had gone down in the mud at Westonzoyland, whose future was ended in Judge Jeffreys' court, and whose last step would be taken on makeshift gallows. Some of them had marched with Monmouth from deep conviction, some had hoped to be on the winning side, some had gone thoughtlessly – as they might run after a fair. Some had not been there at all. No-one had imagined that the king would take murderous revenge on the humblest men of his kingdom. No-one could believe that the Lord Chief Justice of England, the greatest lawyer in the land, would come all the way from London to Taunton to hang a tailor.

FOULMIRE, SUSSEX, AUTUMN 1685

Matthew, up early, walked through the herb garden and out through the little door set in the flint-knapped wall. He found himself in a low-lying hay meadow, and beyond that a bank which rose steeply, to make a rough sea wall. Beyond it was a long sloping shingle beach and the mud, reeds and shingle islands of the harbour.

A scrawny haystack in the meadow showed the damp saltiness of the soil, but Matthew – a city-raised child – counted the stooks and thought himself rich: hay in the field, corn in the barns, sheep in the meadows, fish in the sea. And – more than all of these – rents every quarter day.

He strode towards the far drainage ditch where it was crossed by a single plank and saw his grandmother, poised on the little bridge, light on her feet as a ghost, looking out to the east where the sun was burning off the early morning mist.

'Ma Alinor? I didn't expect to see you up this early.'

She smiled at him, one hand resting on the rickety handrail, the other shading her eyes as she looked towards the mouth of the harbour, where the gilded crests of the waves showed that the tide was coming in. 'Oh, I always used to get up early – we started work at first light. I thought I'd remembered it so well but I had forgotten just how . . .' Her gesture took in the rising sun, etching shadows into the drainage ditches, sparkling on the ripples of the central channel. A thick flock of birds wheeled past them calling in bright high voices, the sunlight on their silvery wings flickering to white and then back to silver.

'What work did you get up for? I thought you were ferrymen.'

She smiled at him. 'Ferrymen and fishermen, and we gathered and poached and gardened and spun wool and did chores, whatever came to hand, anything to make a living. Alys and I worked at Mill Farm – which we passed yesterday evening – and I was a midwife to women all over the island.'

He had only ever known the two women in the warehouse, in their London life: his mother intent over the books, saving every penny, out on the quayside in all weathers, sending out carts to the shops and markets, watching the ships unload; his grandmother upstairs, too frail to work downstairs, grinding the herbs and distilling the potions that sold for a petty profit at the kitchen door.

'You were poor then?' he asked diffidently.

She nodded. 'Dirt poor. Your ma went to bed hungry more than once, Rob too. God forgive me.'

'I didn't know it was that bad.'

'We left here so that no-one would ever know. And no-one need know that it's us who've come back. We left as the poor Reekie family, two women accused and Ned unable to bear our shame; and – see – we come back as Peacheys – lords of the manor.'

'Accused?' he said nervously. 'What were you accused of?'

In the bright sunlight of the morning she laughed as if her old life had been a nightmare, forgotten at dawn. 'They said I danced with faeries, that your mother paid her dowry in faerie gold. They thought I was a mermaid or a witch. It was thirty-five years ago. It's forgotten.'

'I knew you were poor, but not accused. Ma never told me.'

Her smile was as bright as the morning light. 'Of course we never told you such a thing! You came to us years later as a baby and it was long ago and far away. We meant to never come back, though I missed it like an ache.'

He heard her Sussex accent, and recognised it for the first time in his life. 'You'll tell no-one that you've returned? You have no friends here?'

'I met the man that I loved here,' she confided. 'I brought him down this path, to this very field. When I came out this morning I half-expected to meet him. But I'm not the young woman I was then, and he is long ago and far away too. There's nobody else that I'd want to see again. It isn't the people I came back for ...' She gestured to the brightening horizon and the birds running at the water edge, in and out with the little waves. 'I've come back to the land, and the water and the sky.'

'People don't have ... anything against you?' he asked tentatively. 'Are there any old scores to be settled?'

'I think the millstones have been changed a few times in the last thirty-five years, don't you? It's all been ground down. We're all older – except you, my lamb, who is fresh and new – and all that is past can be forgotten. We sleep in the best linen where we were once the most despised squatters. And all this from the hands of a woman who seemed to bring nothing but trouble! Why wouldn't we be happy?'

It was like a call to live – 'why not be happy?' Matthew felt his heart lift like the wild ducks which suddenly arrowed overhead, whistling as they flew. 'Why not?' he exclaimed. He took her hand and kissed it. He felt her little bones beneath the thin skin; it was the hand of an old woman, but her grip was strong.

'This is your land now,' she told him. 'You take it, Matthew. And you be a good lord to the people, because once I was one of them, poorer than the poorest tenant on your land, and the most despised of women.'

TAUNTON, SOMERSET, AUTUMN 1685

Johnnie, in court for the trial of the five hundred men who had pleaded guilty on the promise of a pardon, saw the iron grille to the cells swing open and heard the soft low moan from the crowd as the fifty men stumbled and were pushed into the well of the court. Judge Jeffreys clambered onto his ornate chair with the thick cushion and grimaced with pain.

'Silence,' he said, though there was no word spoken.

'Pleading guilty, my lord,' the clerk said, a wary eye on his scowling face.

'Any of 'em seen marching?'

'Four, my lord.' The clerk passed a paper with four names.

'Any exaggerated treason?'

'Six, my lord, two carried a green flag for the traitor. One wore a green leaf in his cap.'

A little sigh breathed from the public gallery from those who remembered how the green flag of freedom had billowed in the wind, and how everyone had worn Leveller green.

'A green leaf, eh?'

'Just a leaf, your honour. No more than a leaf.'

'Anyone pleading right of clergy?'

'Three.'

'Denied anyway.'

'Yes, my lord.'

Jeffreys lowered his gaze to the accused men standing before him. One, a lad of about sixteen, was silently crying, his tears soaking his shirt collar.

'You've pleaded guilty and so I find you,' Jeffreys told them. 'The punishment for treason is death by hanging and then drawing and then quartering.'

There was complete silence in the courtroom.

'But His Majesty is merciful and may order you to be spared. He may. Or he may not. You're all sentenced to death, but His Majesty is a kindly king and may send a pardon for you.'

There was a murmur of meek protest. They had all pleaded guilty on the promise of a pardon. They had confessed and incriminated each other to earn a pardon. They knew from previous hearings that the judge always executed men who pleaded their innocence; but they had not expected his promise of pardon to mean nothing in this Bloody Assize.

Jeffreys banged the gavel for silence. 'I will hang you for interrupting me,' he told them. 'I shall send all your names to London, and the king will decide who dies. The rest of you will be transported. Your pardon will be that you are transported to Barbados rather than hanged here.'

He shouted 'Next!' to the clerk and the young lad let out a single sob of despair. A man put an arm around his thin shoulders as they were pushed out of the court.

'My lord, you forgot your hat,' the clerk reminded the judge.

'What? What?'

'Your black cap. For the sentence of death.'

'Ah! Yes. I've got it here. Might as well keep it on, eh?'

Johnnie craned forward to see the next group of prisoners being pushed into court. Among the bowed heads of the accused he caught a glimpse of dirty white linen: a bandage around a grizzled bowed head. It was his uncle Ned for sure, with his left ear bound up with a torn bloodstained piece of linen. He looked like all the prisoners, but a little lopsided, his head tipped a bit to one side as if he were injured. But he was at least standing, and apparently not wholly deaf, as his head came up when the judge asked the clerk if there were any prisoners guilty of exaggerated treason, or any that had been seen in arms.

'Four found in arms but wounded, and one of them taken up for dead on the battlefield,' the clerk said.

'Why didn't they hang him on the battlefield?' the judge complained. 'No need to bring him before me.'

'They thought he was dead, your honour.'

'Why bring him in then?'

The clerk had no reply.

'Better for him if he had been dead,' the judge glared at the prisoners. Ned kept his head down.

'Any exaggerated treason?' Jeffreys asked.

'Ten of them supplying food and mustering recruits,' the clerk said.

The judge waved away the papers with the names and straightened his black cap on his head. 'All guilty. All sentenced to hang. His Majesty will determine how many of you die, how many to be transported out of the kingdom and sold.'

FOULMIRE PRIORY, SUSSEX, AUTUMN 1685

In the steward's room that overlooked the drive at the front of the house, conveniently close to the garden door where the tenants came to pay their rents every quarter day, Alys was going over the books. At her side she had a dozen sheets of paper scribbled with the black ink of her notes and calculations. Before her on the well-worn round table was a pen and inkwell, all around her the books that showed purchases, sales, gifts of goods, tithes, loans, tenancy agreements, leases and rents. On the wall behind her was an old survey of the lordship of Foulmire, showing the border of the estate – cutting deep through the forest of Sealsea Island, stretching five miles across the harbour. Alys noted with a wry smile that the tenants of the tide mill and Mill Farm had bought themselves out of the lordship. She would not be able to walk into the tide mill yard with the lord of the manor, where she had been the most despised of the maids, her mother named as a coiner of faerie gold.

Alinor put her head around the door and came into the room. 'I knew you'd be here! D'you know it is the most beautiful day outside? Matthew and I walked to the shore and there were seals hauled up on the beach, sitting around together like old men in an ale house.'

'Aren't you tired?' Alys scrutinised her mother's flushed face.

'No. Not at all! I feel like I could walk forever. The air's so sweet, the wind from the sea blows right through me.' Alinor looked at the ledger. 'Rent books? How far back do they go? Have you found our name?' She pulled out one of the drawers of the table, each one labelled with a letter so that the steward could turn the table round and around and have the correct drawer in front of him. 'I remember standing in front of this very table and asking for time to pay.'

'You weren't the only one,' Alys said dourly. 'And they're still at it. Half of them are years behind.'

'It's a hard land to make pay,' Alinor replied. 'Dry in summer and wet in winter. But should you be looking at the books?'

'Matthew said I could,' Alys replied. 'And it's as well I did. It needs someone to get the place straight. The steward has been selling off timber from the forest and the crops in the fields. Matthew said I can dismiss him. And guess who bought Mill Farm?'

'Who?' Alinor spun the table one way and another, watching it turn.

'The Stoneys!'

At once, Alinor froze. 'Your husb—?'

Alys laughed. 'Aye! Who'd have thought it? The husband who left me between wedding and feast. He must have had me declared dead and married that girl – what was her name? – at the mill.'

'Jane Miller,' Alinor said. They both knew that Alys remembered the girl perfectly well. Jane who had been jealous of Alys' fair prettiness. Jane who had wanted Richard Stoney for herself, Jane who had finally netted him with the bribe of her dowry of Mill Farm, the tide mill, the granary and the quay, and promised him a steady ordinariness that his runaway first bride would have despised. 'However did they buy the lease?'

'They made money in that place, and they paid us a pittance. That's how.'

'They must think themselves halfway to gentry!'

'We've got a wharf,' Alys said, instantly competitive, making her mother laugh.

'Alys, our foster son is lord of the manor! We can't begrudge them their rise!'

'Nay, I don't. But, Lord! Richard Stoney's old cat of a mother must've been glad to see me go!'

'They never knew where we went, and they'll never know we've returned,' Alinor reminded her. 'They think we're dead and that's how we'll leave it.'

'There'll be stories about us,' Alys predicted. 'They'll say that we disappeared in a puff of smoke.'

'Or washed away,' Alinor smiled. 'Like most of my little house. Washed away and forgotten.'

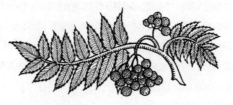

TAUNTON, SOMERSET, AUTUMN 1685

It seemed as if everyone in Taunton was gathered in the market square where one iron cage held the slumped body of the innocent tailor and the other Monmouth's unrepentant captain. The gibbet was still standing: today would be another day of execution for the prisoners sentenced to death. Smoke from the furze fires under the kettles of pitch for preserving body parts for display drifted a sulphurous smell across the market place. Judge Jeffreys had already left the town for Windsor, to report to the king that good work had been done in the heartlands of the Monmouth rebellion, and that the Bloody Assize would go on – like a murderous travelling show – to the other towns of the west country.

The Taunton town crier stood on the step of the gibbet so that he could be seen over the heads of the crowd, and heard at the farthest corner of the market place. The mayor, scowling with distress, stood beside him.

'Hear ye, hear ye,' the town crier called out. 'All the following are to die by beheading as befits gentlemen.' He read out a short list of names. Johnnie skirted the market place to get closer to the gibbet so that he could hear.

'All the following are to die by hanging, drawing and quartering, either here or at their towns or their villages as soon as may be conveniently performed.'

He read out eighteen names of local men into the stony silence.

'And the following have received the generous and gracious forgiveness of the king and are to be transported to the colonies as indentured servants for ten years.'

The town crier hammered the list into the post of the gibbet, bowed ceremoniously to the mayor and strode away. Johnnie shouldered his way through the crowd to get close enough to read the death list. His uncle's name was not there. He scanned hundreds of names on the transportation list, jostled by families of the condemned men, and then finally, he found it, smudged and hard to see, but there it was: 'Ned Ferryman'.

His first thought was that now he could go home, the bearer of terrible news. Ned would – once more – be exiled, far away, and he would certainly die in exile. Ten years' service in Barbados would kill him as surely as the hangman in Taunton market place. Ned's adventure and Johnnie's search were both over.

He turned to go back to his inn, pushing his way through the crowd, ignoring the occasional plea of 'Help me, Sir! Save a prisoner!' when he felt a light touch on his fingers, almost as if a hand had been slipped into his and, turning around, he saw a gown of reddish brown, a shawl of grey. The woman's face was completely hidden by the deep brim and wings of her sun bonnet.

'I can't help you,' he said harshly, and then she raised her head so that he could see her face, deep inside the brim of the bonnet – it was Rowan.

He wanted to throw his jacket over her head to hide her from anyone who might recognise her – surely everyone could see the high cheekbones and the dark eyes? He wanted to drag her away from the market place so that she would not see the pecked face of the tailor and the skull coming through the face of the captain in their iron cages. But then he saw the steadiness of her gaze and realised that she could walk through horrors without flinching.

Another glance at her told him that she had worked some magic and made herself almost invisible, even to someone who knew her, even to someone who loved her and was looking for her. She could pass for any poor woman in this crowd with her hard-worn clothes and her skin as brown as a ploughgirl. She could have walked past him every day and he would not have recognised her. Even her gait had changed: she shuffled in ill-fitting boots, her shoulders drooped as if she were used to the weight of the milkmaid's yoke, and her head was bowed like all the women in this town, like a woman defeated by sorrow.

'Follow me.' He felt he was choking on the words, as he led the way to his inn, through the front door and up the stairs to his bedroom, unnoticed by the landlord who was tapping another barrel of ale in the cellar.

Johnnie closed the door and turned to her. 'I've been looking for you for weeks.'

As soon as the door shut she became herself again. Her head came up, her gaze was direct. 'Is he on the list to die?'

'Were you with the army, Rowan? Were you seen with the army?'

'Is he listed to die?'

He saw that she would not speak of anything else until he answered her.

'No. Transported. Were you with the army?'

'Can you get him a pardon? He can't go.'

'Were you seen with him?'

She made a little gesture with her hand. 'I was his boy servant,' she said. 'Nobody would recognise me in these clothes. As soon as we can get him out he must see a doctor. He was cracked in the head by a cannonball, he lay like a dead man for hours.'

'You were never at the battle?' he asked horrified. 'He didn't take you into battle?'

'He lay like a dead man,' she repeated. 'And when he came to, I couldn't get him away. Will they forgive him, if you tell them how badly he is injured? Can you speak for him? D'you have money for a bribe?'

'You can't bribe the judge.'

She laid hold of his jacket. 'No, he's gone already. You'd have to bribe the jailors. He can't be transported, it will be the death of him.'

'I can't bribe the jailors. I can't break the law!'

'Then what did you come for?'

'For you!'

She was shocked into silence. He realised he had raised his voice. Downstairs, the rumble of the tap room and the parlour continued.

He took her hands and tried to draw her close to him. Seeing her in women's clothes for the first time reminded him that she was a woman, like any woman. She needed protection, she needed a husband, she needed a home. She was not the strange being – from another world – that he had first met. Now she was a poor woman, in a dirty sun bonnet and skirts. And she was grieving, he could see the strain in her face, she was thinner. He was flooded with sudden joy that he would save her from this terrible place, rescue her from this tragedy and take her home.

But she did not melt into his arms; she grew a little tense, as if ready for a fight, or to run away. He saw the way her dark eyes narrowed, taking in the room, marking the path to the window, the unlocked door behind her, the stool she could snatch up for a weapon, the jug of water she could throw in his face.

'I came for you,' he said, releasing her, gesturing that she should sit on the stool, seating himself on the edge of his bed and trying to look at ease, though his heart was pounding. 'Honourably! My grandmother Alinor sent me, she dreamed that Ned was hurt; I came to save you both. Now that there's nothing more I can do for him, I will take you back to London. It's what he would have wanted.'

She perched on the edge of the stool, ready to leap up and run.

'How have you managed?' he asked. 'You're thinner than you were. Where did you live for all these weeks?'

She shrugged. 'Different places.'

'How did you get these clothes?'

'I stole them.'

He was horrified. 'Rowan! For God's sake. You can be transported for stealing a shirt, just as well as for being a rebel!'

'Would I be on the same ship as Ned?'

'Of course not.'

She lost interest in his warning.

'We'll go to the high street and see if we can find a dressmaker to make you a better gown,' he said. 'And a cobbler for some boots.'

'D'you have the money for that?'

He smiled at her. 'I have the money for that,' he assured her. 'I am a wealthy man; to you, it would seem a fortune. I will spend it all on you.' He rose from the bed and offered his arm. 'Take my arm,' he urged her. 'I have said that you are my sister. You would take my arm.'

He felt a rush of protective love as she slipped her hand in his arm, and he led her down the stairs and out into the brightness of the afternoon.

'I will make you happy,' he told her.

'I don't think you can make anyone be happy,' she said. 'Doesn't it just happen? Or not?'

FOULMIRE PRIORY, SUSSEX, AUTUMN 1685

'I should be getting back to Lincoln's Inn,' Matthew said to his foster mother and grandmother eating a simple dinner in the grand dining room of the Priory. 'I can't be too long absent, I have to attend a certain number of dinners each term, and I'll have to go and see the Nobildonna.'

'I've got to get back to the wharf,' Alys agreed. 'Captain Shore'll be home this month, bringing Gabrielle and Mia. I must be there when they arrive. What d'you think, Ma? Great-grand-daughters? Does it make you feel old?'

Alinor smiled but said nothing.

'Shall we leave the day after tomorrow?' Matthew asked. 'I'll tell the coachman that we're ready to go home to London, and we can return the Avery coach to Sir James.'

They both turned to Alinor. 'Aye, it's time you two went home,' she said agreeably. 'But I'm thinking of staying here.' She smiled at their instant refusal. 'I know! I know you want me to go with you, but I'd like to stay longer.'

'Who will look after you?' Alys demanded. 'What if you're ill?'

'I won't be ill,' Alinor said. 'You've seen yourself how much stronger I am. I can breathe here, and I can walk out. I've been walking every day and I feel well. Alys, I know you worry for me. But I'm happy here. I've come home.'

'Of course you can stay,' Matthew said. 'And I'll come down again soon, anyway. But . . .' He glanced at his foster mother.

'How long for?' Alys demanded.

'Not too long,' Alinor replied. 'Not when winter comes. I don't want to be flooded, nor snowed in! But perhaps till December?'

'Months! And who's going to look after you?'

'There are more than enough of them. The cook's a good woman, and the maid Lizzie,' Alinor said. 'I can eat what they're having in the kitchen.' She saw her daughter's disapproval. 'I'll be served in the dining room!' she amended. 'I'm not forget-ting Matthew's place!' She looked from one to another. 'I can tidy and clean the still room, and weed the herb garden before winter. I can look over the linen, and get the chimneys swept and the covers off the furniture for when you next come down. It won't hurt the place to have one of us living here.'

'Won't you be lonely?' Matthew asked her.

Her smile was very bright. 'My dear, everyone I ever loved has walked on these footpaths. They walk with me, all the time.'

'You're thinking about him,' Alys said resentfully.

'Not about him now,' her mother said calmly. 'About him then, and the young lovers we were. And about you and Rob, my little children, and my Ma when she was young. I think about the past and it's as if it's the here and now. As if I am the girl I was then. It makes me happy.'

'I can see it suits you,' Alys said begrudgingly.

'Aye, it suits me,' Alinor agreed with a mischievous smile. 'And I'm going to stay an' all. So there's no need for you wear such a mope-face.'

Matthew choked on a laugh at Alinor's impertinence, and turned to his foster mother. 'She has become a girl again,' he told her. 'Next thing, she'll pull your braids. We'll have to let her have her own way.'

TAUNTON, SOMERSET, AUTUMN 1685

Johnnie wanted to take Rowan to London at once, but she refused to leave the town while Ned was in the jail of Taunton Castle.

'I came here for you, not for my uncle Ned,' he told her in the morning after he had spent the night hot with desire, lying beside her in the bed, clenching his hands together to stop him from reaching out to her, listening to her quiet breathing in sleep.

She was tying the waistband of her skirt over the linen shift she had slept in. She nodded. 'I know, you said.' She stuffed her hair inside her cap. He saw that it had grown and was nearly down to her shoulders. For a moment he thought he might reach out and touch it, imagining it silky and heavy in his hand. But then she pulled the ugly cap down over her forehead and his chance was gone.

'I couldn't bear the thought of you in danger,' he told her.

She pulled on the new boots he had bought for her and started to lace them.

'Rowan – I want you to come to me. I will marry you.' He gulped at the thought of his mother's outrage if she knew he was proposing to a runaway servant. 'I want you to be my wife.'

She was silent; he could not imagine what she was thinking. 'I know it's not a good time to speak . . .'

'No . . . no . . . I know that you people like to talk . . .'

'I've never known anyone like you. I offer you the protection of my name. Look! I've bought you clothes and I am housing you – like a husband already. Say you'll marry me, and we can start for London this morning.'

'Go without freeing Ned Ferryman?'

'My uncle was good to you, I know. But any debt to him is fully paid. And Rowan – he was guilty! His sentence is just. We can't save him.'

He could not read the blank face she turned towards him. 'I'm not free till he is free. If I agree to marry you, will you help me save Ned Ferryman?'

'Would you be freed by his death?' he confirmed, knowing that was the most likely outcome.

She did not flinch at the mention of his death, and that made him certain that she felt nothing more for Ned than an exaggerated sense of obligation, like a superstition, a savage superstition.

'I would be freed by his death,' she said solemnly.

'Then you are free now,' he said gently. 'My dear, he is certain to die within a year of getting to Barbados. The weather is too hot for an old man like him to work in the fields. The work is crushing, he won't survive it. Most likely he'll die on the voyage. I'm very very sorry, but it's true. You can mourn him as a dead man.'

He took her hand – it was icy cold, and he felt that familiar tension in her.

'You can do nothing more for him,' he told her. 'I can do nothing more. We've done all that could be asked of us. We can write to his master in Barbados and intercede for him. We can ask for him to have easy work. We'll do that. It shall be our first action as husband and wife.' He paused, looking at her wide eyes. 'And you will learn to take my hand and not look as if you are about to run away!'

He meant it as a joke, but he felt her return the pressure of his fingers and try to smile at him. He could hardly believe that she rested her hand in his, and he understood that this was her consent. 'There,' he said, as if he were talking to a timid animal. 'That's better. There. There.'

She asked if they might walk up to the castle in the afternoon and when they saw the many families keeping a vigil in the outer keep, praying for a miracle, he thought that now she would understand that there was nothing to be done.

'They're in there?' she asked a woman who was standing, gazing towards the archway of the gatehouse.

'They hold them in the inner ward, the cells are under the courtroom,' the woman said miserably, never taking her eyes from the arched stone gateway. 'They bring them up to the gatehouse to load on the wagons to go to the ports. In chains like slaves. My husband is in there now, in the gatehouse, waiting for the wagon. I hope to catch a glimpse of him as he goes.'

'Don't they let you say goodbye?'

The woman shook her head. 'Nay! They load the wagons under the archway and they drive past us without stopping, guards all round 'em. But if he looks up, he'll see me. He'll know that I'll wait for him.'

'How many guards?' Rowan asked.

'Dozens. They all come running out of the castle when the

wagons are leaving and hold us back, so we can't give them food or money.'

'Come away, Rowan,' Johnnie said quietly. 'We can't do anything here.'

Rowan smiled at the woman. 'God bless you,' she said gently. 'And your husband.'

Johnnie drew her away. 'Let's go back to the inn,' he said. 'We can't do any more for him.'

He saw the sudden determination in her face, like that of a man mustering for a forlorn hope. In all the time he had watched her, he had never seen her set her jaw like that, not like a beautiful girl at all, but like a fighter squaring up for his last bout.

'Rowan, don't look like that—'

'Can you give me money to bribe a guard? I just want to see him.'

'No,' he overruled her. 'I won't risk my life for him, and I won't allow you to risk yours.'

She looked at him with her dark forthright gaze. 'Not even for love of me, Johnnie?'

He nearly melted at her using his name for the first time, looking into his face, turning to him for help. But he knew best. 'No,' he said firmly. 'I'd do anything for you, but I won't take you into danger.'

He expected her to argue, but she gave a little sigh, as if the fight had gone out of her, and nodded and tucked her hand in his arm as if they were already man and wife. He led her back to the inn, brushing people aside, and helping her up the steps, warm with pleasure that she had her hand in his, that she was leaning on him, that he could guide her, direct her and protect her, now and for the rest of their lives.

'I shall order dinner,' Johnnie told her at the doorway of the inn. 'And you shall rest in my room while I hire a horse, and tomorrow we'll start for London. You must be tired.'

He took her bowed head for assent, and he saw her up the stairs to his bedroom with a new pride that he had courted her and won her and that her adventure was over.

Johnnie found the biggest livery stables in Taunton and spoke to the liveryman. 'A strong horse to carry two,' he said, flushing at the thought of Rowan riding behind him with her arms around his waist. 'A pillion saddle. D'you have such a thing?'

'Almost all our horses are hired,' the man said discouragingly. 'There's that many with their hearts broken going home to mourn. But I've got a steady old horse that'll take two.'

'I'm going to London. Where should I change him?'

'At Bath,' the man said. 'Go to the Blue Boar. You'll get another horse easily enough, and they know me there. They'll return him to me.'

Johnnie reached into his pocket, unbuttoned the flap and felt for his purse. 'Here is … here …' He felt in his deep pocket. It was empty. 'Good God,' he said, 'I've been robbed!'

'You have?'

'I can't pay you. I had all my money in my purse, and my purse is gone!'

'Try your other pockets.'

Johnnie was already thrusting his hands deep into his flapped pockets, and checking his belt and his breeches. 'I always keep it in my right-hand pocket. But look! Nothing!'

'When did you last have it?'

Johnnie hesitated, recreating in his mind the moment that Rowan was walking beside him, her hand in his arm, climbing the stone stairs to the inn, leaning against him as they went through the door. Her hand was in his arm, in his right arm, beside his pocket. He had held her against him, he had taken a moment to revel in her closeness …

'It's not lost. I've been robbed,' he repeated flatly.

'Someone in the crowd?'

'Someone in the crowd,' Johnnie said swiftly.

'Lord! These are wicked times. You'd think with a scaffold on every corner and a rotting leg at every gateway that men would reform.'

'You would,' Johnnie said quietly, a cold misery spreading through him.

'Best go to the magistrate. As if he didn't have enough to do.'

'Yes,' Johnnie agreed numbly.

'How will you pay your shot at the inn?'

'I have goods, I'll have to ask them to take my linen . . . I have a watch, I'll have to pawn it.'

The misery of having no money opened before Johnnie and reminded him of his mother's fanatical care that the warehouse should always turn a profit, that there should always be coin in the box. He felt the weight of a childhood fear of poverty, that sick sense that nothing could be done without money – and there was no money to be had. But even worse than that, was his certainty that it was Rowan who had robbed him.

'You'll need someone to vouch for you. D'you have a friend in town who can speak for you? Someone who knows you. Is anyone staying with you?'

Johnnie shook his head. 'I have no friend in this town,' he said miserably, knowing she was gone. 'I am here alone. I am quite alone.'

FOULMIRE, SUSSEX, AUTUMN 1685

Alinor opened the door in the flint garden wall and closed it carefully behind her. The meadow before her was bare of stooks; all the hay was piled into a clumsy hayrick for autumn, the shorn stubble dry and rough under her walking boots. She took the path to the sea bank thinking that she was walking through time as well as meadow grass. Years ago, she had run through this door to find the man she loved and tell him he was safe; she had risked her life to find him a refuge. James had said that he did not expect to find a woman like her in a place like this, and she had never known what he had meant. She had treasured the words of love and turned them over in her mind, but never asked him what he meant.

She smiled. Here they had climbed the bank together, and this was the path he had run, when he had come to see her in the darkness. To her left, too far for her to walk now, the winding track led under the down-swinging branches of the oak tree to her little cottage – little more than a shed, the pier extending out into the Broad Rife, her rowing boat bobbing at the end. They had gone fishing. They had lit a fire. He had been dazzled by her and for the first time in her life she had known herself to be desirable. For the first time in her life she had felt desire.

It was a lifetime ago, a long lifetime; and yet it felt to Alinor as if no time at all had passed, and she was still the young woman who had run along the shingle beach to meet him. Even now, decades later, she could remember the smell of his skin when she pressed her face to his naked chest, the heat of his fever. Even now, she felt her heart jump at the thought of his touch.

Now he was no longer a hidden priest and royalist spy in a wartime country, now he was a landowner and a gentleman, a married man, and his past forgotten. She expected nothing of him. All he could honourably do for her now was to loan her his carriage and send the note that she had crushed in her pocket. It read:

Thank you for accepting my carriage. I am glad to be able to take you to your home. I will come and visit you – unless you forbid me. You have my heart in your hands. Let me see you once more . . . James Avery

TAUNTON CASTLE JAIL, SOMERSET, AUTUMN 1685

Rowan hobbled into the outer keep of Taunton Castle as an old laundry woman with sore feet, her head bowed, unnoticed among the other market women and traders.

The men at the gatehouse to the inner ward, left behind to guard the prisoners while the main force rattled triumphantly back up the road to London, were miserable under the hatred of the local people. None of them could stand the stink of Taunton market place where trade was slight under the rotting corpses in the iron cages, and the tradeswomen treated them like invaders, pretended not to understand their speech and sold them spoiled food.

The trooper on guard swung open the wicket gate for Rowan, her newly cropped hair white with dusted flour under a big sun bonnet, a basket of linen on her arm and a big white apron wrapped around her bulky gown. 'Laundry for the prisoners,' she said to him in a voice that quavered a little with old age. 'Do they leave today, Sir?'

'Some of 'em do, Grandma.' He was surprised by her smile. 'I'm prisoner escort. Off to Bristol with them.'

'Lord! I nearly missed them! And I've been paid by their wives to bring clean linen to take with them.'

'Any good shirts?' he asked.

She gave him a knowing wink. 'You come down to the wash-house and pick out your own when you get back from Bristol.

The poor dears won't miss one or two,' she promised him. 'Can I take these in now?'

'That's the wagon!' he said, as the wagon rumbled up from the castle stables and halted in the gateway. 'You've left it too late.'

'It wouldn't dry!' she exclaimed. 'Oh, do let me run in and give them their linen quick.'

'Quick then,' he told her. 'And remember you owe me a shirt for this!'

'Bless you, bless you,' she said over her shoulder, as he opened the thick wooden door to the inner room and bolted it behind her. There were more than a dozen men crowded into the tiny space of the guard room. Rowan scanned every face and then saw the tattered bandage and the lined face of Ned Ferryman at the back. He was slumped on the bench. She said not a word but untied her apron and silently tore off her bulky gown.

She was wearing her old ragged boy's clothes underneath, as tattered as those of the prisoners. She pulled off her laundress's cap and bundled it with the apron. Still no-one in the cramped little room spoke; the men watched her in silence, knowing that she had not come for them, knowing that nothing could save them. Even Ned, who had risen to his feet at her entrance, was silent, watching her intently, as she pushed the gown and the apron into the basket and thrust it under the bench.

A shout from outside made him shoot a questioning look at her. 'Line up inside!' the guardsman yelled. 'Hands out in front of you! No moving! No talking!'

The prisoners stumbled into two lines, Ned in the back row. Rowan slipped out of sight behind him.

'What's to do?' he asked her, his voice low.

'Put on the clothes and walk out,' she whispered to him.

He turned incredulously to her – 'What?' – as she struck him, a clenched fist directly on the bandage at his injured ear. She felled him like an ox under a hammer. Silently, he crashed down to the stone floor, and she rolled his limp body under the bench. She pulled off his bandage and wrapped it around her own head, half covering her face and her whitened hair. She took his place in the back row and held out her roughened hands as the others did, when the wooden door opened and a new guardsman came in with shackles and chains.

She kept her head down as he went along the line locking on shackles and slipping the chain from one prisoner to another.

'Register!' the first guard shouted from the wagon outside.

The prisoners told off their names as they shuffled past the guard and climbed into the wagon.

'Robert Batt.'

'Richard Dyke.'

'John Jolliffe.'

'Bernard Loman.'

'George Ebden.'

'John Hooper.'

Then the second row went through the narrow doorway and climbed on the wagon.

'John Johnson.'

'Ned Ferryman,' Rowan said gruffly.

'John Denham.'

'John Meade.'

'Peter Ticken.'

'Nathanial Beaten.'

'Thomas Chin.'

'John Gould.'

The local blacksmith had made an iron cage and nailed it around the wagon. Their wrist chains were hammered into a staple set in the wooden floor. Rowan, looking at it, thought if they all pulled at once they might get it free, but then they would have to lever off the cage, jump together off the wagon, and all run together, still chained, matching their strides and all going in the same direction without pulling or checking. She would have done it with her own people who learned how to move as one from their earliest days hunting, but she knew it could not be done with these broken men who had, each one, been raised to think of himself as a solitary man, alone. She settled herself on the seat, dropped her head, and set herself to dream of her home, knowing that she would never see it again.

Minutes later in the guard house, Ned came round under the bench, to hear the rattle of the departing wagon, and saw at once the door of the empty room had been left wide open to air it from the stink of the prisoners, and that Rowan was gone. Cautiously, he rolled out and drew out the washerwoman's basket. Hiding behind the shelter of the open door he pulled on the big gown and tied the white apron. The wound in his head was bleeding again, but he tied the cap over it to staunch the flow and crammed the big sun bonnet on top of that. Deliberately, he did not think of his cold horror that she had taken his place, since her sacrifice would be for nothing if he did not get free. He did not give himself time to think, nor to feel fear. He hefted the basket on his arm, leaned it against his hip and stepped out of the door into the gateway.

The new guards were coming on duty, across the inner keep of the castle, complaining that they were not getting a ride to Bristol and back, complaining that everywhere in the town, everywhere in the whole country, smelled of death.

Ned did not shrink away from them to the town gate; instead he headed towards them, limping towards the inner keep of the castle, the basket on his arm, the wings of the big bonnet shading his face, praying that the blood from his head wound was not staining through the white cap. He ducked a little curtsey as he went past them, but they ignored him completely.

Ned went slowly across the inner keep and then swerved between the kitchen and the bakery. There was a broken wooden door, an old sallyport, set into a wall. Ned slipped through it. A small one-plank drawbridge crossed a nettle-filled ditch that was all that was left of the old moat. Ned hobbled across the market place and down a cobbled alleyway to a stable yard at the back of one of the grand merchant's houses. Ned looked left and right and then ducked into the yard and slipped through the wide doors of a hay barn.

It was piled high with stooks of fresh hay. Ned scrambled over them towards the back wall and dropped down behind them. He listened. It was all quiet in the yard: the horses were out at work, the stable boys mucking out the stables and barrowing the dung to the midden. He could hear the sound of someone working a pump and a gush of water. Carefully, he peeled the washerwoman's cap from his head, ripped it into strips and re-tied it as a bandage, ignoring the throbbing pain. He looked into Rowan's basket.

On top was a clean linen shirt, and below that breeches, a waistcoat, a jacket, a hat, hose and even shoes. There was a stone flask of small ale and a new-made loaf of bread and a slice of cheese. Under the clothes was a purse. Ned lifted it up, weighed it in his hand, untied the strings and looked in. There were five gold sovereigns. Ned had to blink away the tears from his eyes – Rowan had not just freed him, she had provided for him for weeks. He rubbed his face, and then pulled on the clothes she had stolen for him, and slipped the purse in the jacket pocket. There was a slip of paper left by the previous owner in the pocket. Ned pulled it out and read it.

> *Son,*
>
> *Your grandmother has been troubled by a dream and won't be turned from seeing you. Please come as soon as you can without inconveniencing the Company. Whatever she tells you, Do Not undertake to find your uncle Ned – wherever he may be.*
>
> *Your loving Mother*

Ned folded both hands over his mouth so that he should not make a sound, and silently laughed until his head ached so badly that he had to stop.

Ned located Johnnie without difficulty – there was gossip about the fine gentleman from London who had taken up with a doxy who had run away with all his money and his clothes and who would have to go with the landlord to the magistrate to arrange to have his debt paid on credit, and himself shipped to London.

Ned walked into the breakfast parlour of the inn, saw Johnnie and said loudly: 'Ah, there you are, Nephew! Your Ma is that worried about you! Sent me all the way from London to find you.'

'And good day to you, Uncle,' Johnnie said, recognising his own jacket, breeches and even his own shoes which were tight on his uncle's broad feet.

'This is for you,' Ned said, pushing Johnnie's purse across the table.

'Uncle! It's good to see you. Please sit down,' Johnnie said, indicating the high-backed bench. He called to the landlord for breakfast and said that he would be able to settle his slate – his uncle had providentially arrived from London.

'Londoner, eh?' the landlord said morosely, bringing the pot to the table and pouring them both a cup. 'I'll take the money for your lodging now, if you don't mind, your honour.'

Johnnie paid and the landlord served them with a side of ham, bread, eggs and cheese. Johnnie, looking pale and sick, had nothing but coffee.

'So, she got you out?' he asked very quietly, as Ned laid down his knife.

'Knocked me out and took my place,' Ned confirmed.

'She said she would be my wife. But that she had to pay her debt to you. She picked my pocket and stole my clothes from my room and she ran away. She only agreed to be my wife so that she could slip her hand in my pocket while I held her close.'

Ned shook his head, his eyes on the younger man's face. 'Bitter.'

'She's a savage.'

Ned's eyes were warm at the thought of her. 'For sure, she's not an English lady.'

'She's heartless!'

'Love isn't uppermost,' Ned tried to explain. 'She could love you and still have stolen from you. Doesn't mean she doesn't love you. Just means she had to do this first. Thing is – how do we get her free?'

'She'll survive,' Johnnie said cruelly. 'She said you were too frail.'

Ned absorbed the insult. 'She'll survive the voyage,' he judged. 'But not slavery; not if they put her in the fields.'

The landlord took the plates away and brought them mugs of small ale. Johnnie waited until he was out of earshot. 'I have no obligation to either of you.'

Ned smiled. 'None. You've done more than enough, coming here after me.'

'I didn't come after you.'

Silently, Ned drew the letter from Alys, telling Johnnie that he was not to look for Ned, and laid it on the table.

'I came here as my grandmother Alinor wanted, but hoping to find her,' Johnnie admitted. 'I only wanted to rescue Rowan.'

'You do know that's not even her name?'

'I don't care anymore,' Johnnie said. 'I don't care what her name is or what she wants. She's condemned herself to an early death, and she's damned herself to me and to God by her lies and deceit and theft.'

'Her soul's her own business,' Ned said gently. 'But I've got to save her life.'

'I won't be party to anything illegal,' Johnnie said.

'No,' Ned conceded. 'But would you help me get a pardon, or get her released?'

'Can't be done!' Johnnie said irritably. 'What d'you think I've been doing here for all this time in this stinking town? I couldn't buy a pardon for you. They're not for working men.' He glanced round. 'Guilty men,' he said accusingly.

'No, not for me, but she's wrongly arrested. Even under a Stuart we can demand her release?'

Johnnie hesitated. 'If someone would speak for her ... but why should I do anything for her? Why should you? She robbed me and she hit you!'

'Aye, she's bested us both, but I suppose that a blow doesn't end love.'

'Of course, I don't stop loving her because she stole from me. But it's against my better judgement. And you'll think I'm a fool.'

'I don't,' Ned assured him. 'Will you at least go to the castle, and see what port they've taken her to?'

'I'll do that,' Johnnie agreed reluctantly. 'You wait here and keep out of sight. Wait in my room. And for the Lord's sake, get a wash, change that bandage and wear your hat.'

FOULMIRE, SUSSEX, AUTUMN 1685

James Avery's carriage retraced the rutted track beside the harbour, the coachman driving with ill-concealed contempt for the poor road, the low hedges and the overarching sky. The tide was coming in and the seagulls were swirling in white flocks, fishing in the incoming water. The Broad Rife was spilling over its muddy banks, like a mirror to the blueness above. The coachman halted the horses at the wadeway and the driver beside him climbed down to ring the bell for the ferryman.

James was in such a dream of the past he was half-expecting to see Ned coming out of his door, wiping his hands on a cloth, and stepping down onto the flat-bottomed ferry, hauling it hand over hand on the overhead rope to the north side. But then he remembered those days were gone, Ned was gone, and there was a new ferryman in his place, and James would never again sit on his horse and look down the road to where Alinor, a young woman, her face bright with happiness at the sight of him, was waiting.

'It's not too high, you can drive across,' the ferryman yelled at the coachman.

James let down the window and felt the soft salty air against his cheek. 'What d'you think?'

The coachman tightened the reins. 'There oughter be a proper ford. There oughter be a bridge.'

James closed the window and sat back. 'It's the tidelands,' he repeated. He closed his eyes and he could hear her voice: 'The harbour moves in every storm. The sea breaks into the fields and takes back the land. The ditches make new lakes. These are the tidelands: half tide, half land, good for nothing, all the way west to the New Forest, all the way east to the white cliffs.'

He could hear her voice as if they were on the bank of the harbour, on the brink of love, then the coach turned left off the road, and right towards the Priory, and before he could compose himself into the important man he now was, he had arrived like a love-sick boy.

He did not know who to ask for, he did not even know how to announce himself. He stood hopelessly in the lamplit doorway while some servant – a footman? A steward? Surely, they did not have a chamberlain? – raised the lamp and said: 'We were expecting you, Sir James,' and stepped back to admit him.

He recoiled from the hall. Where there had been a flight of stairs leading down to plain stone slabs, with a suit of armour at the bottom and an open fireplace billowing hot smoke, the hall was now floored with polished wood and the fireplace had been reduced in size and fitted with a neat grate. The old tapestries had been stripped from the walls, and there was painted wooden panelling in its place, with some blotchy landscapes of French gardens. The double doors to the chapel where he had served Mass as a secret priest were shrunk to a modern door frame, a single door, and the room was now a dining room with a good table and half a dozen chairs. The manservant led the way to what had been Sir William's gun room overlooking the garden, and opened the door and James found himself suddenly in a pretty parlour, and at the fireside, there was the woman he had loved for so long.

Alinor rose as he entered and stood still, one hand on the mantelpiece, one on her heart.

Neither said a word.

'May I get you some refreshments, Sir James?' the man said into the silence.

James nodded, but found he could not speak at the sight of her, at her steady grey eyes on his face, at his sense that the years were falling away from them both and they were spinning back to their youth, both of them beautiful, both of them innocent, both of them so much in love. 'Wine,' he said, without taking his eyes from her lined face. 'A glass of wine.'

The servant crossed the polished floorboards and poured two glasses, set a bowl of dry biscuits on the table, put another log on the fire and reluctantly retired. Neither of them spoke, until the door was closed behind him.

'To see you here!' James said.

Her mischievous smile was quite unchanged, her merriment shone through her old face. 'I know! Who'd have dreamed it?'

'You are comfortable?'

She laughed at him. 'You mean: do I feel out of place?'

'Do you?'

'No. Not at all! I feel at home.'

She seated herself and made a gesture that he should sit. He took the chair and thought it so odd that she, who had been little more than a beggar, born in the ferryhouse a few miles from here, should reign in the parlour like a queen, while he, a gentleman from generations of gentry, should be as awkward as a schoolboy.

'You were kind to give us a lend of your carriage,' she said politely.

'You're welcome ... at any time ... please let me send it for when you go home ...' he started.

'Nay, I won't go back to London until winter comes.'

'Really? You like it so much here?'

'It's my home.'

'And nobody ...' He did not know how to ask if she was notorious.

Her face, as open as he remembered, turned to him and her smile was as sweet. 'Nobody remembers,' she said. 'It's probably a legend now, like the hushing well in the harbour. Long gone and forgotten.'

'The hushing well has stopped?'

'The harbour's changed many times since you and I were last here. There's no memory of the hushing well, it's fallen silent.'

'The people at the mill ...' He could not remember their names, only their avid faces as they clamoured for her guilt.

'The daughter Jane – you won't remember her – has bought out the lease.' Her smile invited him to wonder at the changes since they were last here. 'She and her husband would be the last people in the world to speak of us. Their marriage would be overset if Alys reappeared. There's a new family at the ferry and no-one thinks of the old Ferrymans. No-one would link that family, that lowly family, to the Peacheys.'

'You pass off as Peachey?' he asked her, shocked that she should take a gentry name.

She shrugged. 'Not I! It was your own wife, the Nobildonna, who chose the name for herself and so gave it to Matthew. Called herself da Picci as luck would have it – and now everyone assumes we're distant cousins of the old Peachey family.'

'And this place was Matteo's choice?' he asked incredulously.

'We call him Matthew,' she corrected him gently. 'Aye, he chose it, God bless him, as a gift for me: him that owes me nothing. But it'll prove good. His Ma can advise him about the land, Alys knows every yard of every hedge.'

214

'I didn't think you would receive me,' he said, hoping they could speak of themselves.

'Your wife got Matthew the house,' she pointed out. 'Does she know you've come?'

He flushed at her directness. 'I am not obliged to tell her anything. But I did tell her I was coming.'

'She didn't mind?'

'She made no complaint.'

Again, the light of laughter came into her eyes. 'Not quite the same thing!'

'No. But this is important to me.'

She folded her hands in her lap and turned her grey gaze on him. 'What is it, James? That you have come to me, after all this time?'

Now that he had her attention, he found that he did not dare to speak. 'It is . . .' he began. 'It is about myself. Forgive me. My physician tells me that I have a problem in my heart,' he said. 'The beat is irregular. It does not go as it should.'

She said nothing.

'He tells me that, one day, it may just stop.'

'Stop?'

'Yes. Just stop beating.'

She frowned, looking at the fire as if she might see his future in the embers. 'And that is fatal?'

'Yes,' he said. 'Fatal.'

She nodded, saying nothing.

'In a way I'm glad,' he said hastily. 'For so many years I thought of your suffering, the water in your lungs, your struggle to breathe. Now I feel that I am a little like you. I too am under a sentence of death. I'm not surprised. My heart broke that day, when you were half-drowned. I truly believe that it has never beat in time since that day. My doctor cannot tell me how long I might live.'

She waited.

'Months rather than years, he thinks.'

The log shifted in the grate and sent a shower of sparks up the chimney. He thought that if he had not been a fool and a coward, this might have been their parlour, and the wood in the grate might have been logged from his forest and dried in his wood store, and they might be facing his death after a long life together. They would have had their own children to inherit his fortune, and she would have held his hand as the light went to darkness.

'I am sorry,' she said levelly.

He wanted to kneel at her feet and put his face in her lap. He wanted to feel her cool hand on the nape of his neck. 'If I were to kneel at your feet, I wouldn't be able to get up again,' he said, trying to make a joke of the pain in his heart.

'Did you come here to kneel at my feet?'

He flushed, feeling the heat rise in his face as if he were still a young man with a strong heart. 'Yes. I suppose I did. I came to beg your forgiveness—'

'You did that, and I forgave you.'

'And to ask if I might spend the rest of my life with you? Here with you? In the house as a friend? If I might live my last months with you?'

He saw her eyes warm at the thought of it. 'Ah, James – I don't know—'

'You're thinking of Alys,' he said suddenly. 'But she can have no objection. She's not your keeper. And Livia won't care. We don't live as husband and wife, she thinks of nothing but her place at court. I am free, Alinor. I have been freed by this promise of my death. Let me come to you.'

Still she said nothing, her grey eyes on his pleading face.

'I love you,' he admitted, very low. 'I have never stopped loving you.'

She was as quiet as a deer in the woods, watching silently falling snow.

'Do you love me?' he demanded. 'Have you loved me for all these years?'

She blinked as if he had pulled her from an inner vision. 'Oh yes,' she said, as if it were unimportant. 'I never stopped loving you. But as for your living here, I should have to think about it.'

'Of course!' he said hastily. 'Of course.' He had expected her to turn to him, that he would reach for her, that he would hold her in his arms once again, that, he would feel her body against him and smell the perfume of her hair. He had thought she might cry at this happy ending of their story. But she was far away, seated in her chair, dreamily watching the fire.

After a while she gave a little sigh and rang a small bell that stood on the table beside her. 'I have to go to bed,' she said, as if they were not in the middle of a conversation – the most important conversation of his life. 'Ask them for anything that you want. They will serve you a supper. Please excuse me.'

'But I thought—' He jumped to his feet and took a hasty step towards her. She put out her hand and he stopped at once, as the door opened and a maid came in.

'Lizzie, I need to go to bed,' Alinor smiled at the girl. 'And when you come down again please serve Sir James his supper and show him to his room.' She turned to him with quiet confidence, as if she had been giving orders as the lady of the manor for all her life. 'Shall we take breakfast together at ten?'

With the maid in the room he could do nothing but bow. 'Goodnight,' he said formally, though he had hoped she would be in his arms and he would spend the night in her bed.

'Goodnight,' she said; she had no such thought.

REEKIE WHARF, LONDON, AUTUMN 1685

Captain Shore's ship, *Sweet Hope*, nosed towards her home wharf, the Captain on the bridge in his best coat and hat, bellowing orders to his crew to get the lines on the quay capstans, and loose them from the barge which had towed them in.

Alys stood on the quay, proudly watching her husband's ship come in. She waved to his stocky figure on the bridge, and then gave a little gasp as she saw two girls beside him.

'Captain Shore, are those my grand-daughters?' she shouted at him.

He waved his hat like a boy and yelled: 'Ahoy there! Two precious cargos from Venice, Miss Gabrielle and Miss Mia! Safely delivered and undamaged by salt water.'

She had to wait until they had the gangplank run ashore and as soon as it was extended from the ship she ran up it, and onto the deck, to draw the two girls into her arms. 'Welcome! Welcome to your home! Welcome to London! Welcome to England!' she cried, then she turned to her husband and beamed at him. 'And welcome home to you, Captain Shore.'

He brushed the two girls aside and kissed her on the mouth. 'Glad to be home,' he said shortly and then he went for'ard to check the lines and that the rope fenders were out to protect the ship from the wall of the quay.

Alys looked at the two girls, the grand-daughters she had never met. Gabrielle was the older, a girl of thirteen, with the dark brown hair, strong mouth and straight gaze of her mother. Her sister Mia, only a year younger, took after the Italian side of the family with a caramel skin, black hair and eyes and a sidelong smile.

'What a pair of beauties you are!' Alys exclaimed. 'I can't believe this is the first time we've met! I've thought of you so often, and prayed this day would come . . .' She drew them to the head of the gangplank and then hesitated. 'Your Ma will have told you what to expect? We don't have a great London house, this is a working wharf and we live beside the warehouse.'

'Ah, we know, we know!' Gabrielle assured her. She spoke with a slight Italian accent that made Alys shiver for a moment thinking of the calculated charm of the Nobildonna, also from Venice, who had come to the warehouse saying that it was her sanctuary, and then nearly destroyed it in her determination to rise higher.

'Ma told us all about her childhood here,' Mia chimed in. 'And at home, though it's a great house, we have the stone masons working in the rooms below, and the studio is next door. We both work there, we're not idle. In Venice, everyone works. Ma says it's only in London that people like to pretend their money fell down with rain.'

'It's true,' Alys agreed, leading them down the gangplank. 'But your Ma says you want to study here?'

'She said English girls are allowed?' Gabrielle asked her.

'You can start at your uncle Rob's house with his daughter's governess, and then go to school, and nobody knows more about herbs than your great-grandmother. She's not at home right now, she's in the country ... And so here is your new home.'

She opened the front door. 'Mind the ledge – that keeps the floodwater out.'

The girls stepped over the threshold into the hall.

'Here's the parlour.' Alys gestured to the room on the left of the front door. 'That's where we eat. To the right here, that's the warehouse. At the back is the kitchen, and beyond that the yard and the stables. Upstairs: your bedrooms.' She led the way up the tightly turned wooden stairs.

The girls exchanged a glance; this was very unlike their home in Venice where the floors were marble and the ceilings high and the walls panelled or painted with frescoes.

'You're both in the spare bedroom next to me,' Alys said, showing them their room. 'It's your mother's old room when she was a girl, and while my Ma is in the country you can have her room as your sitting room.' She opened the door to the room with the glazed balcony that looked out over the two aspects: the Neckinger drain and the River Thames.

'Pretty,' Mia said, admiring the lightness of the room and the view of the river. 'When will our great-grandmother come home?'

'She'll want to see you at once, so perhaps we'll go down to Sussex in a few days' time and bring her home with us. Gracious!

I've been waiting for you for so long that now you're here I can't believe it. You'll be hungry, I'll get Cook to serve an early dinner. Captain Shore always has roast beef on his first night home.'

Alys left them in their room and went downstairs where the lumpers were unloading the girls' luggage into the hall and the cargo into the warehouse. 'There's a jug and bowl for you to wash your face and hands,' she called back up to them.

The two girls drifted into Alinor's room which overlooked the quay and watched the men throwing the sacks of silk from hand to hand, rolling the casks of fine wines, and heaving crates of statues and paintings on barrows to take them into the warehouse.

Captain Shore stood at the entrance to the warehouse double doors checking everything off his cargo list with a custom officer agreeing the tally. As the girls watched from the upper window, they saw Alys come to the warehouse doors and direct where things should be stored.

'She's nothing like Mama,' Mia said. 'But just as Mama described her. Busy, hurried, nice.'

'Thank God we're out of Venice,' Gabrielle said. 'Every day we were further away I felt more and more free. Look at her down there, giving orders, raising her voice! She runs the wharf, Mama said, not Captain Shore.'

'Mama said London is full of women with their own businesses. What if we were to be wharfingers ourselves!'

Gabrielle shook her head. 'Physicians,' she said. 'I want to study herbs with our great-grandmother and doctoring with Uncle Rob.'

'And there's the exhibitions and the studios and the libraries, churches and concerts,' Mia pointed out. 'And women can go to them. We can even walk out alone.'

'It's like a new world,' Gabrielle said. 'Streets everywhere, roads everywhere, horses everywhere. And everyone speaking English and sounding like Mama!'

'A different world and yet a homecoming,' Mia said.

ON THE ROAD TO LONDON, AUTUMN 1685

Johnnie hired a coach to take him and Ned to London. 'We can't do any more here,' he told Ned. 'She'll be held at Bristol till her ship, the *Rebecca*, sails. All the Taunton prisoners are the property of the queen and she's giving them to her favourites. And that's where we get our chance. The courtiers are selling pardons!'

'They are?' Suddenly interested, Ned turned from watching the granite walls of Taunton high street jolt past the window.

'Far beyond the price of common people, but for gentry or lords who can raise the funds, who'd rather pay than see a cousin or a younger brother in such a state, they're selling a royal pardon for a couple of hundred pounds.'

'I've not got that sort of money,' Ned said. 'Nowhere near.'

Johnnie scowled. 'We might be able to bargain it down. Livia Avery is a favourite of the queen, if we could get her to intercede for us.'

'What sort of king enslaves his own people?' Ned demanded. 'Why should we pay for our freedom?'

The coach went faster, swaying on the straps as they joined the highway, but neither man noticed.

'Your crime made you the property of the king,' Johnnie the merchant-trader asserted. 'This is not tyranny but justice.'

Ned rested a hand on his shoulder. 'Lad, I was fighting injustice before you were born, I will be against it until the day I die. If we have to pay a tyrant to free Rowan, I will. But I would free all slaves, if I could.'

'Slaves are property, it's not about justice but about wealth. And you'll never change that. Someone owns everything.'

Ned shook his head. 'It's the nature of the world that we've chosen to make,' he said stubbornly. 'Because men like you want it that way. But I don't want it that way, and there are men like me, and women, who would rather not own another, not profit off someone's misery.'

'Then you'll live and die a poor rebel in someone else's coat,' Johnnie predicted. 'Like you are now. Riding in my coach with a mouth full of treason but nothing in your pocket. The very food in your belly, I bought you.'

'It's going to be a long, long journey for you if you're counting the pennies at every stop,' Ned observed unruffled. 'And I thank you for my coat, though it wasn't your gift. The shoes I stand up in were stolen from you by a girl with a greater heart than yours. Her land was taken and her people enslaved by men who think – like you – that they have a right to everything. And sorry I am, to see a man of my own family – and we were a poor family ourselves – become one of them.'

'Being poor is the very reason we're driven to make money and keep it!' Johnnie exclaimed. 'I was raised by a mother who used to look in the cash box every Sunday night to see if she could send me to school with a penny for my schooling the next day! She swore, and I swore, that the cash box would never be empty. Her life's work, and mine, is to make the fortune that you so despise.

'You're playing an old song, Uncle! It's not freedom from a king that matters now, it is the freedom to make money. You went to war to change the king but the king matters less than profit. The true king of England is not Charles or James or whoever comes next. The true king of England is wealth. And we can all see the good of that. We're all loyal to that.'

'Not me,' Ned said imperturbably. 'Still not me.'

FOULMIRE PRIORY, SUSSEX, AUTUMN 1685

James, in the grand guest bedroom at Foulmire Priory, slept badly, listening, as he always did, to the thud of his heart, wondering if it was speeding or slowing or even missing a beat, and if this was the night when he would hear it stop. He woke late, got dressed and slipped out of the front door to walk around the garden. The kitchen garden had been replanted with herbs and there was a new rose garden, but the door set into the wall leading to the hay meadow was the same. He remembered waiting in the meadow and letting her go in alone, because he served a cause that was greater than them both; and his moment of revelation when the door opened and she came out, her carefree smile, her confident stride telling him that she was safe – and his realisation that there was no cause in the world greater to him than the turn of her head and the light in her grey eyes.

He heard the bell in St Wilfrid's church tower strike ten as he went back through the little door, across the garden and into the front door. Alinor came down the stairs wearing a gown of slate grey with a white cap on her silver hair. She had a hand on the bannister and with her other hand she steadied herself with a black ebony cane. Seeing her in the morning light, her little grimace of discomfort at every step on the stair, reminded him that they were old. He told himself he should have put passion aside long ago, and that he only burned for her now like a young man because they had parted so abruptly, as such young lovers. They had longed only for the next day and the next night. There had been no familiarity to wear off passion, no daily life to erode desire. He could not see her as a woman of sixty-four, he could not imagine his death without her at his side.

He reached his hand to her. 'You look like you did when I first saw you in the churchyard,' he said.

She smiled. 'Doesn't it sometimes feel like yesterday? Or even that it'll all happen for the first time, tomorrow? I forget it was the past, I've lost the sense of time.'

She took his hand, and at her touch he was certain that she would come to him, that they would be lovers again. He knew he only had to draw her to him and she would yield, as she had always done before. He led her into the dining room which was laid for breakfast. She offered him small ale or milk, and he took the small ale for the remembered taste.

'Is this your brewing?' he asked.

'Lizzie does the hard work. But I cut the herbs and taste the brew.'

He carved slices of ham and the maid brought boiled eggs in their brown shells. Alinor ate a little meat and a sliced apple. She drank a glass of milk as he revelled in the normality of sitting at a table with her and eating breakfast and seeing her smile. She said: 'Shall we walk out? I think it's going to rain later on, there's a dark cloud out to sea, and the wind's getting up.'

Together they went through the front door and without saying a word turned to the path through the herb garden.

'Do you remember . . . ?' he began. He was thinking of the days when he had been sick with fever, isolated in the loft above the stables, and she had washed him with cool water and wrapped him in clean linen. He had longed for her with a mounting desire like a second fever, and she had laid her cool body against his and they had lost all sense of themselves as a poor woman and a wealthy young man but become, somehow, one complete being.

She smiled. 'Of course I do.'

They walked through the garden brushing against the overgrown herbs. She ran her hand through the spikes of rosemary and gave him a twig for the sharp perfume. Without speaking again they went through the little door in the wall of knapped flints and out into the sea meadow.

She hesitated on the threshold. 'I can almost see us here.'

'A woman like you, in a place like this,' he quoted himself and she nodded.

He tucked her hand into his arm and she walked with him towards the plank which crossed the drainage ditch to the bank beyond. He helped her up the steps in the bank and at the top they looked over the harbour at low tide. Ahead of them, the Broad Rife was running deep with brown river water and in the distance she could hear the roar of the tide mill like receding thunder.

'I've thought about what you want,' she said, her eyes on the far horizon where she could see a darker line that meant rain.

He knew, with complete certainty, he would live with her for the rest of his life. He savoured his joy and hoped that he would live long. The thought of lying with her again filled him with a sense of life renewed; he wanted to hold her gently in his arms and kiss her closed eyelids and whisper that he loved her, that he had always loved her, and that the years apart would be forgotten.

'James, I'm sorry, but you can't come and live here with me,' she said coolly. 'It's not possible. And you can't visit again.'

He was astounded. 'Alinor!'

She looked at him steadily with her grey gaze. 'I am, I'm truly sorry.'

'But why not . . . ?'

'What happened between us was like a death,' she told him slowly. 'What happened at the tide mill that day . . . it can't be undone.'

'I know!' he said eagerly. 'I know that! But we don't have to spend the rest of our lives apart just because we made a mistake . . .'

'I'm that sorry to refuse you,' she said gently. 'Especially here and now, where I could refuse you nothing.'

'We could bring back that time!'

'Nay, you know you can't bring back time by wishing.' She turned and started to walk inshore, along the top of the bank, the meadow on her left, the harbour stretching to the horizon on her right. He followed behind her, remembering other times when he had followed her worn boots and trusted that she would take him safely through the quicksands and the mudflats and the deep pools. They came to the lane which led from the harbour to the little church and walked side by side, in silence, past the mound of the old ruined castle, to the low flint wall of the churchyard. She paused at the lich-gate.

'D'you attend every Sunday?' he asked her.

She nodded. 'Imagine! We're in the first pew at the front. I think Matthew has the right to appoint the vicar.'

He was not to be distracted. 'When I die, I should like to be buried here.'

He was glad to see he had startled her. 'Here? Not in your family vault at Northallerton?'

'My body has to go there, the funeral will have to be there, and the reading of my will. But I should like my heart to be buried here. In the same grave as you.'

She laughed out loud, and then clapped her hand over her mouth. 'Oh no!' she said. 'I'm sorry, I shouldn't laugh. I know it's not funny. Not funny at all!'

At his grave face she could not stop herself; her laugh pealed out again. 'No, James, really! Think how horrible for the Nobildonna! To have her husband divided! And how could she explain it to your family and friends? And how should I bury a part of you? And if I'm already dead and it's poor Alys, she would be so furious and ... anyway ... why?'

'I want to lay in the same ground as you,' he said stiffly. 'I thought my heart could be buried beside you.'

'But won't that ruin the resurrection of the body?'

He was suddenly furious that she was such an ill-educated woman, wise only in superstitions and fables. That she laughed when something struck her as funny, without considering how she appeared, without understanding that it was not funny; not funny at all. That she was a common woman from common stock and, although he loved her, she would always disappoint him.

'That's heresy,' he instructed her.

'Is it?' she asked. 'I wouldn't know.'

'No. But I know, and I am telling you.'

She shot an amused smile at him and turned from the lich-gate and started to walk back to the Priory. 'I've got to rest now,' she told him pleasantly as they walked up the drive shaded with overhanging trees. 'I have to cosset myself like an old plough horse. I can't go too far.'

They walked to the great front door, which was not opened at their approach as it should have been. James had to step forward and open it for Alinor and they went into the hall. 'No servants?' he asked.

'I don't like them waiting around for me,' she said simply. 'I can open my own doors and light my own fire.'

He thought she was ill-served, and if she had been his wife, she would have had a maid to walk behind her, carrying her gloves; but he said nothing.

'Will you eat before you leave?' she asked simply.

'Before I leave?' Obviously, he could not stay. But he had thought he would choose the time of his leaving. 'Will I see you again before I go? At noon?' he asked, holding onto his dignity.

She had no idea that she had offended him. She was trying only to see that he had dinner before he left.

'At noon,' she agreed, and wearily started to climb the stairs.

BERRY STREET, LONDON, AUTUMN 1685

The hired coach drew up outside Johnnie's little townhouse on Berry Street.

'Are you sure you don't want to go on to the wharf?' he asked Ned. 'You can have the carriage.'

'Nay, I'll come in with you. Happen Sarah's girls will be in my old room already, and if I'm here, we can start raising the money for Rowan's pardon at once.'

Johnnie paid off the coach, picked up his portmanteau and opened his own door.

'I don't like servants in the house,' he explained to his uncle. 'I'll send for my housekeeper now.' He whistled for a link boy, gave him a small coin and an instruction and then showed Ned into the narrow hall.

'When Mrs Wales comes, she'll make up a bed for you. She just lives down the street, she'll be here in a moment. And tomorrow we'll go to court. She'll know where they are, St James' or Windsor.' He smiled. 'She's a great enthusiast for the royals.'

'Papistical?'

'Fashionable. She likes the clothes.'

'We can't go tonight?'

'Easier to get admittance in the morning, and we'll have to smarten up. We won't get in if we don't look like gentlemen.'

The front door behind Ned opened, and Johnnie's housekeeper bustled in and dropped the two of them a curtsey. 'I came at once,' she told Johnnie. 'I've been in every day to dust. I didn't expect you to be away so long.'

'I was detained,' Johnnie said shortly. 'This is my uncle Mr Ferryman. Can you make up a bed for him in my dressing room, and send out to the bakehouse for dinner for us both? And I'll have a bath.'

'Yes, Sir,' she said. 'I'll get the hot water on at once. Shall I bring some wine and biscuits to the parlour?'

'Yes please,' Johnnie said, and the two men went into the little room at the front of the house, overlooking the street.

'I'll light the fire,' Ned said, looking at the kindling ready laid in the grate. He smiled at the housekeeper when she demurred. 'Nay, it's no trouble.'

'I've got your letters, Sir,' she said to Johnnie, bringing them in on a leather tray.

'I'd better send a note to my grandmother to tell her you're safe,' Johnnie said to Ned. He turned over his letters. 'Oh, this one is from Ma,' he said, surprised, and broke the seal. 'She's not at the wharf, – whoa—' He broke off. 'We've been away too long, Uncle! All sorts of changes. Matthew's been given Foulmire for services to the queen, and they've gone down there in the Avery carriage!'

'What?' Ned demanded incredulously.

'See for yourself.' Johnnie flicked the letter into Ned's hands.

'Sir James Avery?' Ned demanded. 'He's the very one we should see about getting a pardon for Rowan.'

'D'you know him?' Johnnie asked curiously.

He saw one of Ned's rare smiles. 'We were on opposite sides of the king's war,' he admitted. 'But he owes my sister his life.'

'I thought they were enemies? Ma and Grandmother and the Nobildonna and Sir James?'

'Your grandma hid him when he was a royalist spy,' Ned said shortly to Johnnie's shocked face.

'She did?'

'And he betrayed her. It was years later that the Nobildonna turned up, dumped Matthew on them, nearly ruined the business and scooped him up. They never spoke after that. But if your Ma and grandmother will use his carriage now, then I can ask him for a favour. Besides, he's the only man we know at court.'

'We could ask the Nobildonna?'

'Her, I wouldn't trust at all.'

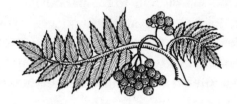

FOULMIRE PRIORY, SUSSEX, AUTUMN 1685

James Avery ordered his carriage to the door of Foulmire Priory when the stable clock struck twelve; rebuffed and offended. She could not have been more clear that he could not live with her at Foulmire. He would not invite her to his home in Northallerton, or even to his great house in London. She had laughed at the thought of his heart being buried with her. She refused to speak of love; she had grown old and heartless, she had never had an education – and now she had no wisdom either.

The servants laid out small ale and the interminable ham and bread at the parlour table. When he heard her light step on the stair, he rose from the table for courtesy to greet her and lead her to a seat at the fire. But when he saw the pallor of her face he was filled with tenderness.

'Was I wrong to come to you? Was it too much for you?'

She smiled up at him, as if she were glad of his touch on her hand, and the way he put a cushion behind her back. 'Nay, I slept like a baby,' she said. 'It's such a treat to take a nap in the day, and not be up at dawn to work! Of all the things that have come to me in this life, to have a comfortable bed and good linen is the greatest!'

Every other woman he had ever known had risen late and rested before dressing for dinner. 'Your life hasn't been easy,' he said. 'I will never forgive myself that it was not easier.'

'Not so, I've been lucky,' she said.

'I'm glad that our parting didn't ruin your life,' he said, thinking that it had.

'It didn't ruin my life. It took a turn, that was all.'

'Then we can part as friends?'

She nodded. 'We are friends.'

'It may be that I don't see you again before I die,' he warned her.

'I understand,' she said steadily, as if death were not a terror.

'Can we part as lovers? I will think of you on my deathbed as the only woman I ever loved, the great love of my life.'

She sighed, as if she were sorry to refuse him even this. 'Not really, James. For it's not true.'

'I loved you then, and I love you now! With all my heart!'

'It wasn't all your heart,' she said very quietly. 'In that moment, when you should have stepped forward and claimed me as your lover, and the child that I carried as your own, you did not love me then, James. In those long moments, you loved someone more than me.'

'No-one!' he exclaimed, startled. 'No-one but you! Ever!'

'Yourself,' she pointed out. 'Your honour? Your self-regard? I went to trial by water rather than shame you. But you let them drown me, rather than own me.'

He was appalled that she had thought this of him, for all these years. 'I was so wrong! I was so mistaken, Beloved. I was so young, and such a fool! But you said you forgave me? I thought I was forgiven?'

'I do forgive you; I gladly forgive you. Who am I to judge?' she asked him. 'It's not my forgiveness you need.'

'Then whose?' he cried out. 'Who did I injure more than you?'

'Yourself.'

'Forgive myself?' He had always thought of her as an ignorant woman. Now he was as baffled as if she were a philosopher.

'I loved a young man who was ready to give up the world for

me; but then – when it mattered – he wasn't there,' she told him. 'The young man, that day at the tide mill, wasn't the man I loved. Perhaps he was never real at all, and I dreamed him, and put it on you.' She showed him a rueful half-smile. 'I'm sorry for that. It's not fair to forge a dream of someone, and then press it – like a seal into hot wax – into another's face.'

He shook his head; he was completely bewildered.

'Maybe that dream was one we both had?' she went on. 'Perhaps you dreamed of a young man like that, dreamed of being him, dreamed that you were him? Perhaps the tragedy – the real tragedy – is that you weren't able to be him– when your trial came. When a man like him would've faced down shame, he wasn't there. It was only you. And you couldn't rise to it.'

She looked inquiringly into his face, to see if he understood her, to see if he heard the truth of what she was saying. 'Perhaps you need to forgive yourself, James, for not being him. And forgive me, for asking too much of you. And when you've forgiven, then you can let him – the dream-him, and the dream-me, and the dream life that we didn't have – slide away into sleep.'

'The sleep of death,' he said bitterly.

'Perhaps we shall dream of each other in the sleep of death,' she agreed pleasantly. 'Perhaps in death, we shall meet and be our dream selves, our best selves.'

He was choked with remorse. He bent and took her thin hand and put it to his lips. 'I hope so,' was all he could say, not knowing what he was saying, and he turned and went from the room. She stayed where he had left her, listening to the wheels of his carriage crunch on the gravel, and the sound of the horses' hooves, until he was gone.

WINDSOR CASTLE, AUTUMN 1685

Johnnie was hesitantly walking up the long approach to Windsor Castle. On Ned's insistence, they had taken the stagecoach to Windsor from London, and got down at the inn. Now he wished they had hired a coach. There was a queue of coaches down the long drive, waiting at the door for admission, servants shouting names, coachmen holding horses as they pawed the ground, double guards on duty and footmen opening the doors of carriages and ushering guests drowned in silks and furs and sparkling with diamonds through the great double doors of the castle.

Ned cast one aggrieved look at Johnnie. 'Is it always like this?' he asked. 'The country mad for wealth and show?'

'No, no, there must be some kind of ball. What a night for us to choose! We'll never get in.'

'Better now, than at any other time,' Ned reassured him. 'Look, isn't that gentry folk getting in over there? Maybe they've come to watch, and we can join with them?'

Johnnie glanced over to the side entrance where gentlemen and ladies dressed in their best but far short of the extravagant excess of the courtiers were being allowed to enter on foot. Clearly, there were merchants and Windsor gentlemen and their families and even visitors from London come to the palace to watch the dining and dancing.

'Some sort of ball?' Ned asked the man who came up behind them.

233

'I'd say so!' he laughed. 'The queen's birthday and they say the king can't do enough for her: she's banned him from her bed for straying, and he's got to win her favour if he wants a son to come after him.'

'No, that's not it,' said a woman, turning round. 'He spends all his time with that ugly Lady Sedley.'

'I heard that the queen was sick to death,' another gossip observed. 'And she can't bear a child anyway.'

'Then how come she's dancing at her own ball?' someone asked.

'Anyway, the queen's birthday,' Ned said, grasping the one piece of reliable information from this flood of hearsay and gossip. 'Lucky that we're dressed for it.'

Johnnie had bought his great-uncle a good coat with a fine waistcoat to go underneath, breeches, stockings, shoes and fine linen; he himself wore his best velvet jacket with his embroidered silk waistcoat and his lace cravat.

'This is nothing,' Johnnie said. 'Barely respectable.'

'Good enough to get us in,' his uncle reminded him as they stepped towards the footman at the door.

'Who can vouch for you?' the man demanded.

'We're guests of Sir James Avery,' Ned said confidently. 'Where'll we find him?'

'He's at dinner,' the man replied. 'You can watch from the back of the hall.'

He waved them in the general direction of St George's Hall and the swell of noise guided them as they followed other smartly dressed men and their wives who had come to see the king and queen take their dinner. They were shown into a vaulted hall filled with tables for courtiers. At the far end was a high dais and on it a grand table loaded with silver and gold ewers and salt cellars and decanters.

The trumpets blared and the court turned to the entrance and sank into bows and curtseys as the king and queen walked in, their favourites behind them. The queen was draped in the finest of silks, a long train billowing behind her, jewels at her neck, twisted around her dark ringlets, in her ears, on her fingers and around her waist. Her hand barely touched the king's as he led her through the great hall. She turned her head away from him and ignored his court and his advisors, acknowledging only those on her own side, her ladies and the gentlemen of her household, and her particular favourites. She did not throw one look at him, not even when he whispered something in her ear and helped her up the shallow stairs to the dais. He handed her into her seat and she never once met his eyes. A manservant drew out her chair and presented her with a silver ewer of hot water and a towel. She dipped her fingers, she wiped them on the finest linen, she sat in her great carved chair. Still she did not look at her husband.

The king, red-faced in a glorious silk jacket of peach embroidered satin, awkward and pretending to be easy, addressed a remark across the high table to some men in the hall, smiled at their jests and drank heartily. The queen beside him was like a woman made of ice.

The king's confessor rose to his feet. There was a small rumble of dissent from people watching at the back of the hall, deeply suspicious of a roman catholic reading a Latin grace at the king of England's dinner.

'They'll push it too far,' Ned said with quiet satisfaction in Johnnie's ear. 'They always do: the Stuarts. They never understand what's staring them in the face. They always think they know better. They always think they can dance over hard ground.'

'For Christ's own sake!' Johnnie hissed back. 'Can you stop your mouth for once? We've come to court as supplicants, we want a royal pardon. Don't you dare say another word!'

Ned was silent. Johnnie glanced sideways at him to see if his uncle was offended.

Ned winked at him. 'Cavalier,' he said, quite unrepentant. 'Poodle.'

The two men watched the courtiers in silence as the dinner concluded.

'Look!' Johnnie said. 'It's the Nobildonna.'

Ned saw a woman of extraordinary beauty, her gown tailored so tightly that it gripped her slim waist but slid off her shoulders, showing her neck and the top of her breasts, loaded with diamonds. She had diamonds in her black hair and in her ears that caught the light and sparkled when she turned her head. When she rose and mounted the dais to lean over the queen's bare shoulder and whisper in her ear, all eyes followed her.

'Lord, I've never seen such a thing before,' Ned said like a man observing an exotic animal. 'Is that really her?'

Johnnie was awe-struck. 'Yes, that's her. She always was—'

'Better speak to her husband before she spots you,' Ned said, completely indifferent to the woman's compelling presence. 'She doesn't look like a woman for honourable business.'

'Again!' Johnnie made a muffled complaint. 'Keep your opinions to yourself!'

'Oh aye,' Ned said, nearly laughing. 'I'm mum.'

'Please leave me to do the talking,' Johnnie said nervously as they went down the stairs from the gallery and looked through the open double doors to the great hall. He hesitated at one of the footmen beside the open double doors. 'Can you direct me to Sir James Avery?' he asked.

'That one,' the man said, nodding him inwards.

Sir James, in a dark silk jacket with a gloriously embroidered waistcoat, silk breeches and diamond buckles on his shining shoes, was in conversation with two men, but he turned as Ned and Johnnie approached. 'Good evening, gentlemen,' he said courteously. He glanced over the two of them. 'Do I know you? May I serve you?' His dark gaze narrowed and returned to Ned. 'Have we met?'

'Sir, I have the honour—' Johnnie began as agreed, when his uncle interrupted him.

'Ned Ferryman,' he said bluntly. 'We've met. You'll remember.'

A deep flush rose in James Avery's face. 'This way,' he said shortly and drew them both into an antechamber. 'Is it Alinor?' he demanded as the red velvet curtain fell closed behind them. 'I just left her! Does she want me back?'

Johnnie looked from one man to another, marvelling at the stubborn calm of his uncle and the trembling hands of the greater man. 'We haven't come about her, Sir.'

'Ah, you lent her your carriage and felt she was obliged?' Ned asked cuttingly.

Johnnie made a little exclamation of protest. 'No offence ...'

Sir James nodded, paler than ever. 'I asked her if I might call. But what do you want from me, Mr Ferryman?'

'We want a pardon,' Ned told him bluntly.

'Perhaps I should explain ...' Johnnie began but neither man even looked at him.

'The rebellion?' James guessed. 'You were mixed up in that? Will you never learn?'

Ned smiled at him, quite unrepentant. 'Happen I won't. We can't all turn our collar to the winning side.'

'Excuse him!' Johnnie blurted. 'Forgive us!'

Neither man heard him.

'Anyway, you're far off. The pardon's not for me.'

'If it's for a man witnessed in arms at Westonzoyland, I can't help you,' James told him. 'The king is ... the king is ...'

'Vindictive,' Ned finished the sentence as Johnnie made a little gasp of disagreement and grabbed his uncle's arm to silence him.

Sir James scowled. 'He's not granting pardons for exaggerated guilt,' he said shortly.

'But he *is* granting pardons? And some of the lords and ladies here have been given prisoners, and they're selling them back to the prisoner's families and friends who can raise money?'

Sir James nodded. 'Very few.'

'The prisoner that we're asking a pardon for is owned by Her Majesty.'

Sir James turned to a writing table in the corner of the room and made a note of what Ned was saying. 'Was he seen in arms?'

'No. He never took up arms.'

'Is he awaiting transportation or execution?'

'Transport. He's at Bristol port.'

'And what's his trade? And what is your interest in him?'

'He's a Christian Indian servant. What we'd call a Praying Indian. Innocent of rebellion in New England too. He was my servant. I brought him into England when I came home—'

'And took him straight into a bloody rebellion,' James finished his sentence.

Ned shook his head. 'No, Sir. Not us, Sir. We landed in the west country and he was arrested in error.'

'An error?'

'You may not be aware,' Ned explained with biting contempt, 'but they arrested everyone, and hanged most of them without trial—'

'He *is* completely innocent,' Johnnie interrupted. 'I can vouch for him, Sir James.'

'And his name?'

'Ned Ferryman.'

Sir James put down his pen and looked at his old adversary. 'He has your name? What is he? Your son?'

'He was my servant, he knew no other English name. He couldn't say his own name, could he? Of course, he gave mine when they asked him.'

'Did you send him in your place?' Sir James asked scathingly.

'No, Sir,' Ned said flatly. 'I wasn't in the rebellion and neither was he.'

'And you injured your head ... how?'

'I fell off a horse,' Ned said. 'Will you represent us or not?'

'We would be most grateful, Sir,' Johnnie added. 'I am Mrs Reekie's grandson, Johnnie Stoney at your service. You won't remember me; but we met at the wharf ... and at your wedd— ... I was there when ... At any rate, your wife, Lady Avery, was kind enough to help me start at the East India Company. I am sorry to have to come to you again but—'

'Of course, I remember you,' James said shortly. He stared into Johnnie's face as if trying to trace a likeness. 'You're a grown man,' he said almost to himself. 'And I've never known you, and now it is too late for this too.'

'Yes, Sir,' Johnnie said uncertainly. 'I was most grateful for my place in The Company. You spoke for me.'

'I'm glad I could be of service to you,' James said slowly. 'I would have done more if I had been asked. But she . . .' He turned to Ned: 'Your sister knows I'd do anything for her. Did she tell you to come to me? Does she want this servant freed?'

'I ask you in her name,' Ned said, knowing the potency of the appeal.

'You'll tell her that I did it for her?'

'I'll tell her we owe you a life.'

'Will you tell her that I am trying to be the man she thought I was? Even though it's so late, I am trying.'

Ned looked at the other man as if he pitied him. 'I'll tell her that.'

'I will discover the price of a pardon and send a note to the wharf.'

'We're very grateful, Sir,' Johnnie said politely. 'We appreciate your patronage. We acknowledge—'

'Don't take too long about it,' Ned interrupted. 'They're throwing them on board like cargo. We've got to get the pardon and get it to Bristol, before the *Rebecca* sails.'

Sir James nodded. 'I'll write as soon as I have spoken with the queen.' He hesitated. 'Don't be hopeful,' he said. 'They are only selling pardons for gentlemen, and they are expensive.'

Johnnie bowed low and led the way out of the room.

Sir James watched them go, the ink drying on the nib of his pen.

FOULMIRE PRIORY, SUSSEX, AUTUMN 1685

Alinor had been waiting all day, going from door to window in the Priory, not leaving the cold stalks of the autumn garden for fear of her guests arriving to find her away from home. The maid Lizzie, taking away an uneaten meal, pressed her to at least take a bowl of soup. 'You'll tire yourself out, Ma'am.'

Alinor took it in her hand absent-mindedly, and ate a few spoonfuls looking out of the window.

'I can watch for them while you eat,' Lizzie offered. 'Coming by hired coach, are they? And Mrs Shore bringing her grand-daughters?'

Alinor nodded.

'They'll not find husbands in Sealsea,' the girl warned. 'Nobody here but fishermen and farmers. And most of them half-wits.'

Alinor knew it was pointless to say that the girls were looking for something more from English life than husbands. 'Was that a carriage?'

'Yes! Yes! It's them, turning in the gate.'

Alinor rushed to the door, limping without her stick. Lizzie followed behind her. Alinor threw the door open as the carriage drew up. The hired coachman pulled up the horses, the footmen jumped down from behind to let down the steps and the two girls, Gabrielle followed by her sister Mia, came tumbling out of the carriage, Alys behind them. Alinor had a confused sense of an old memory breaking into the present: she felt again her joy in her own children, her daughter and her son Rob, the delicious smell of young hair and young skin, the tousled gleam of young curls and the brightness of a young smile. She felt as if she held the future of the family, the future of England, when her arms were around both girls and they were bobbing like apples on a springing bough to kiss her cheek and lay their heads on her shoulders.

'Gently! Careful! You'll bowl her over!' Alys protested as if calling off puppies. She steadied her mother as Alinor laughed. 'You'll never be English ladies if you fling yourselves on your friends like that.'

'Let them!' Alinor held the fresh rounded bodies to her. 'We've got so much time to make up.' She led them into the parlour, but the girls could not sit still; they roamed the room admiring the paintings on the panels and the little grate.

'Fancy that we never met you before, but I feel I know you, Mama talks about you all the time. About you and Grandmama . . . and now we are here? And was this your home when you were a young woman?'

Alinor laughed at the babble of the two girls. 'No, this wasn't my home. We weren't wealthy like this, we had a little house near here.'

'Oh! A cottage!' Mia said. 'The little country houses are so pretty!'

'Not quite like that.' Alinor met Alys' amused gaze over the heads of the two girls.

'And what shall we call you?' Gabrielle asked. 'We could call you Great-Grandmother? In Italian it is Bisnonna.'

'I'd like to be Bisnonna,' Alinor smiled.

Mia clapped her hands. 'Bisnonna dearest! Can we look around?'

'Of course. You can go anywhere you like. Would you like to see your bedrooms? Would you like a rest?'

'They never rest,' Alys said grimly as the girls dashed out into the hall and ran up the stairs to see their bedrooms. 'I swear, Ma, I feel about eighty. And they never stop talking.'

'Do they think we're the Peachey family? The lords?' Alinor asked.

Alys smiled. 'I don't know what they think! They can't imagine a past further back than yesterday, and I am so old in their eyes that they must think you came out of Eden.'

'So I did,' Alinor said with a gleam of a smile. 'In a way, I did.'

'I've seen Ned,' Alys told her mother, pulling a note out of the pocket of her cape.

'I thank God,' Alinor said fervently. 'And his girl?'

'Trouble, as I thought. It's all about her in the note.'

'Ah.' Alinor put a hand to her heart. 'Thank God Ned is safe at least. And bless Johnnie. And forgive me, Alys, for sending your son after my brother.'

'This is even worse,' Alys told her grimly. 'Rowan has got herself arrested in Ned's place and is to be transported as a rebel and the two of them – Ned and Johnnie – are running all around London trying to raise money to buy her out. I said to Ned, you can look at the books yourself, you can look in the chest. We've got nothing to spare until we've sold the Venice cargo, and then we have to lay out on the next voyage. I can lend you a pound or two, but how're you going to pay it back?'

'I've got some money,' Alinor offered.

'Not enough. He's going to need much more than the twenty pounds she'd get on the quayside at Barbados. We don't even know how much yet: it could be a hundred. He'll have to let her go, and comfort himself that she was going to be transported when Ned found her, anyway.'

'She can't be transported, a girl like her. And if she's in prison in Ned's place, then we have to free her, if we can.'

'Well, we can't,' Alys snapped. 'And my guess is that she'll fall on her feet like a cat.'

Alinor smiled at her daughter. 'You're angry because Johnnie disobeyed you and chased after her, and he's not going to marry an heiress, or some rich City widow,' she said accurately.

'He'd be mad to marry her, and mad to buy her out, and mad to do anything but forget her,' Alys said roundly. 'And he's not mad usually, he's the only level-headed one of the whole family.

So I expect him to come to his senses. And you can tell your brother to come to his senses too.'

BERRY STREET, LONDON, AUTUMN 1685

Ned was waiting in Johnnie's house for him to come home from his work at the East India Company, when he heard the front door open. He went into the hall.

'Any luck?' he asked.

'And good evening to you,' Johnnie said irritably.

'So: no?' Ned said, not in the least apologetic, as Johnnie put his hat on the hall table and took off his thick coat.

'I am a bachelor,' Johnnie said dampeningly. 'I live alone for good reason. I like to come in, light the fire, light the candles, take a glass of madeira and then go out for dinner later. Without anyone chattering in my ear.'

'Quicker we raise the money, quicker I'm gone,' Ned said. 'Don't be precious, Nephew.'

'Oh, for God's sake!' Johnnie snapped. He pushed open the door to the little parlour and saw that the fire was already lit in the grate, and a glass of madeira stood on the side table beside his chair. 'Oh,' he said. 'That's different.'

'Changed your mind about being a bachelor?' Ned asked, pouring himself a glass of wine and sitting in the opposite chair. 'See what a comfortable pair we are together! Now, did you raise any money today?'

'I've got the promise of ten pounds,' Johnnie said. 'That's an advance on my salary and a loan on some trades that I'm doing.

But that's all I've got so far. This place is rented, so I can't get a loan against it. If I took all my cutlery and tableware to pawn, I would probably get another four pounds or so – but how would I ever get it back?'

'We'll have to borrow from the warehouse,' Ned ruled.

'It's all very well to say, but how are you going to pay it back?' Johnnie argued. 'You know my Ma can't stand debt.'

'She's my niece . . .'

'You're a bad uncle to her, if you take her money. It's hard earned, and there's never any guarantee of more . . .'

Ned exclaimed and strode to the window, twitched back the curtain and looked out. 'You live well,' he said. 'These curtains alone . . .'

'Rented,' said Johnnie.

'Can you not forward sell some of your goods from the Company? You bring in your own silk and jewels, don't you?'

'I do,' Johnnie said. 'But what if that ship sinks or is hit by pirates, or just meets contrary winds and comes in late?'

'Then what?'

'Then I'm ruined,' Johnnie told him.

'But what are we going to do?' Ned demanded simply. 'We have to have a small fortune by next week. Sir James says it could be as much as two hundred pounds!'

'Inconvenient, isn't it?' Johnnie asked nastily. 'You despise the whole idea of making a fortune, and you loathe the rich. Now, you rather need a fortune, and you have no rich friends.'

'She is innocent, that should save her. If your world is as well ordered as you say, then an innocent woman would be freed.'

'It is well ordered,' Johnnie said stubbornly. 'It puts a market price on freedom. Our trouble is we can't afford it. That's our fault, not the market place.'

'You'll have to get a reduction,' Ned decided. 'We'll separate, and go about our work in our two worlds. I'll go to Bristol, and find a magistrate who will listen, tell him that we've got an innocent lad imprisoned. You go back to Sir James and get a reduction on the pardon. Bring it to Bristol, as soon as you can.'

'I'll try and get a reduction,' Johnnie agreed. 'It's the only way.'

'Wait – how much of this wine have you got in your cellar?' Ned demanded, holding up his glass. 'And what else do you have down there?'

'A couple of casks.'

'What are they worth?'

'Now, Uncle!'

'What are they worth?'

'About four pounds,' Johnnie said sulkily.

'Well, you can sell them tomorrow, for a start.'

Johnnie was about to argue and then, suddenly, he laughed. 'Lord, what a Cromwell you are!' he said. 'I'll sell them back to my wine merchant on the way to St James' and we'll see what price the queen has put on Rowan's freedom.'

Ned took a gulp from his glass.

'For Christ's sake, make it last,' Johnnie said. 'This is our last bottle.'

BRISTOL JAIL, AUTUMN 1685

Rowan, locked in a stone-walled room with twenty other prisoners, had no idea that Ned was ceaselessly trying to find a way out for her, did not think of the outer world at all.

When they had been led into the cold church she had flinched from the high walls and the vaulted ceiling, but she thought that it would be a hard place to guard and there would be a chance for her to slip away. They were still chained one to another like slaves, but her eyes darted around the shadowy corners, taking in the great nave, the wooden pews, the stained glass windows and the many doors leading to vestry and chapel and cloisters.

Then she saw they were being driven and dragged to a great metal enclosure at the side of the church and inside that was a narrow stone stair, winding down into darkness. She hesitated, peering into the cold shadows below her, but the man ahead of her in the line jerked on the cuffs on her wrists and the man behind her pushed her on. There was nothing that she could do but go down, her chains clanking on the stone, her way lit by the flickering of a torch held high by one of the guards.

The flaring light showed a huge square room, hollowed from the reddish rock beneath the church, the walls perforated by dark doorways, and inside them, stone slabs holding rows of coffins. It was the crypt of the church, where the nobility of Bristol had their family tombs.

'God save us,' one of the men said to the guard. 'You'll never leave us down here with the dead!'

'You'll be fed,' the young guard said.

'For pity's sake!'

Rowan looked around: there was only a single source of light, a grating high up in the wall, the early morning light shining through in a narrow beam. She kept her eye on it as she seated herself, her back against the cold stone, and let it dazzle her, so that she could forget where she was.

The stone of the walls, the stone on the floor, the roughly carved ceiling above them was a dull red colour, the only sound was a booming echo of the shouted orders in the hall. They were not chained, as black slaves would have been chained, waiting for a voyage. And they were not beaten, as black slaves would have been beaten. And there were no children, dying of hunger, crying for pain, or calling for their mothers. Rowan told herself that it could have been worse.

She let her eyes get accustomed to the shadowy light as if she would never see daylight again. She taught herself not to listen for anything, but to let her ears fill with the sound of defeated men in a hollowed-out stone cave. She could not rid her mouth of the bland taste of oats and water, and she never thought of spicy hot meat, or the piercing sweetness of fresh-picked berries. Her sense of touch – when her fingers only found cold stone walls – her strength that had let her run all day, her joy that made her laugh at nothing, her optimism that turned her to the sun every morning, slowly drained away and Rowan let herself quieten, like an animal in captivity goes as weak as death, when it cannot bear its life. Rowan surrendered one sense and then another; and the men around her knew her only as the lad who never spoke, never listened and never looked up.

FOULMIRE, SUSSEX, AUTUMN 1685

Mia and Gabrielle, determined to explore all of Sealsea Island, persuaded their grandmother to hire two steady horses with pillion saddles and went behind two grooms down the road to Sealsea village, across to the fishermen's hovels at East Beach, deep into Sealsea Forest, and north across the wadeway to visit Tide Mill Farm.

Everywhere they went, they were greeted with smiles and courtesies, as the foreign cousins of the landlord's family. Nobody had known before that the Peacheys had Italian cousins, but with a foreign queen on the throne and a papist school opening in Chichester it was impossible to be sure of anything, anymore. And the girls were smiling and pretty and spoke English as well as any Londoner – which was to say fancy, and without the Sussex drawl – but they could be understood and they said 'hello' and 'please', waved at the tenants' children and paid for crossing the wadeway or for cups of ale, which by rights they need not have done.

The girls rode behind the grooms along one of the logging tracks through Sealsea Forest, looking at the boughs overhead interlaced, and the yellowing leaves sifting silently down through the quiet afternoon air. It was still, as only an autumn afternoon in England can be still, the air cool but unmoving, the leaves the only movement in the vaulted wood, the flicker of their fall the only sound. The regular scrunch of the horses' hooves on the track, and the occasional cry of a seagull from the nearby shore sounded strangely loud: as if the whole world, trees, birds and little animals, were settling themselves down for the sleep of winter.

They pulled up the horses in a clearing and stood for a moment, taking in the tall trunks, the silence, the glimpses of the unending sky through the gold and yellow leaves which still clung to the tops of the trees.

Mia lifted her head. 'What's that smell?' she asked the stable boy.

'Woodsmoke,' he said. 'Charcoal burning.'

'Oh! Can we see?' Mia asked.

The two grooms shrugged and turned the horses down a little track, following the grey smoke which lay between the trees like mist. The horses snorted as they came into a clearing and the sound alerted the charcoal burners who turned to see two big horses, and the two girls on pillion saddles behind their grooms.

'Good day,' an old woman said as she straightened up from a mound of dry turves and earth and came to the horses' heads. Her lined face was deeply blackened with soot, her clothes and her hair dusted with dark powder. 'Good day to you. Are you lost?'

'No,' Gabrielle said. 'We're riding home, to the Priory, when we smelled the smoke. Are you burning wood for charcoal?'

'Aye, that's what we're doing, and we have a licence from the manor, and all. Are you the new landlords? Sisters to the new lord. Mr Peachey, isn't it?'

'We're his cousins,' Mia said. 'Can we see?'

The old woman laughed. 'Not much to see here.'

Mia tapped the groom on the shoulder and he got down from the saddle and turned and lifted her down, and then helped Gabrielle to the ground. The grooms stood, holding the horses as the girls went closer to the pyre.

'Hot work,' Gabrielle remarked, looking at the woman and her family who carried on working as if the visitors were of little interest to them. They all had blackened hands and faces from the soot, and their clothes would never be clean.

'Hot and dirty,' the woman said. 'And ill paid. But it keeps us fed. That, and brush gathering, and nutting, and mushroom picking, and berry picking. We have a licence for the rights.'

'I thought it was free,' Mia said. 'Aren't berries free?'

'Nothing is free.'

'And you live here?' Gabrielle asked, looking doubtfully at the little hovels built from branches and the leather sheets.

'In summer it's easier to keep the fires in. But in winter we live in a house at the edge of the woods and come out to the fires. Would you like a glass of small ale?'

Gabrielle was sure that they should not stay, but Mia said: 'Yes please,' and in a moment they were served with earthenware cups of small ale.

'I can tell fortunes,' the woman offered quietly. 'Or I can tell stories for a penny?'

'I think we should . . .' Gabrielle began.

Mia reached into the pocket of her jacket and produced a penny. 'Tell me a story. D'you know one of long ago? About the monks in the Priory?'

'Ah, a long-ago story,' the woman said. She took her seat on a fireside log, and the girls sat beside her and looked at the smoke escaping in wisps.

'There was a mermaid here once,' the woman said. 'Came out of the sea.'

The girls nodded; daughters of Venice, they had heard many stories of mermaids and strange creatures from the deep sea; there was no reason to disbelieve mermaids on an island named for seals.

'Came out of the sea on Midsummer Eve, years ago, looking for a lover. Came out of the sea where it laps up against the churchyard wall. St Wilfrid's church, you know it?'

'Yes,' Mia said. 'Just across the field from the Priory.'

'The mermaid was longing for love, she was lonely in the sea, she wanted a man to love her, one that could hold her and take her, not some cold fish-man. She wanted to be loved so much that she grew feet where her tail should be, and she came out of her world and she walked – oh! Her feet were that sore! She hobbled through the lich-gate to the churchyard and she took a seat on the stone bench in the porch. Still there now. You've seen it?'

The two girls nodded.

'She knew that if she waited there and faced the moon and turned her head to look over her shoulder at midnight, she would see her lover coming to her, with no shadow behind him.'

Both girls were completely silent, listening.

'The bell in the tower struck twelve notes, she counted them, it was midnight. She came out of the porch and faced the moon. She turned her head to look over her shoulder, away from the moon, and there she saw him.'

'Who was he?' Mia whispered.

'To her, he was the man she had dreamed of all her life under the water longing for a man. But – he was not a dream but a man in real life, a priest from the Priory, and he'd never seen a woman before, so he didn't know from her grey eyes and the streaming golden hair all wet on her shoulders, and the shimmer of her gown like scales, that she was no real woman but a mermaid, one of the faerie folk, that no man should touch. He didn't know that he shouldn't even look at her. Not even for a moment. He fell in love with her like that!'

The woman snapped her fingers. 'The moment that he saw her, though he didn't know what he was seeing. He fell in love with someone who wasn't even there! He fell in love with a beautiful woman when before him was a mermaid who could not be satisfied with the sea, standing on her bleeding feet. And she fell in love with him like that—' again she snapped her fingers, 'thinking that here was a handsome man, a man who would give her a baby and a family and would stay with her forever, and love her forever, and never fail her. She thought he would take her away from the sea and cure the coldness in her heart. She didn't know he was a priest, and his love and his faith and his heart were already promised to God and couldn't be claimed by any woman – and never ever by a mermaid.'

The girls could not drag their eyes from her old lined face.

'They lay together and he gave her a child, and then they parted – she to the sea and he to the Priory – but they knew that they would be together again, that they had a love, an unbreakable love.

'One night, before her time, it was the night of a full moon, a harvest moon, and a flood tide, she came to find him. She came into the harbour on the crest of the high water but the current swept her right past the Priory, right past St Wilfrid's church. The tide went so fast that she couldn't swim against it and it washed her right through the sluice gates into the millpond, and then, as the tide turned and the water ebbed, the great water gates swung shut and captured her, in the pond, swimming round and round with her hair streaming behind her in the weedy water and her pale face shining in the moonlight, crying for her lover to come and save her.'

'Did he?' Gabrielle asked, her voice a whisper. 'Did he save her?'

'The miller came and saw a mermaid in his pond and crossed himself and blessed himself and sent at once for his landlord. His landlord came – that would be one of the Peachey family – and he brought his priest, not knowing what he would find. And the Peachey lord ordered that the mermaid be netted and drawn out of the water and as she came out, all naked and shimmering with scales, her feet started to grow, and she stood up before them, like a beautiful woman. They dropped the net in their fright, and she saw her lover the priest, and he saw her, and he knew that he must speak for her, and say she was a mortal woman and his wife. And she knew that she must speak for him and claim him from the church and the world of men.'

The girls were rapt, even the charcoal burner family sat on their haunches and listened to the old story, their eyes on the little wisps of smoke escaping from the turves banked around the fire. The grooms stood by the horses, half-listening as the woman paused.

'But she didn't speak for him,' she said with a sigh. 'She didn't want to shame him by claiming him before all the people who knew of him as a priest. She didn't want to betray him and she was ashamed of herself, a mermaid with sore feet. She stood before them, naked with her hair streaming down her white back, with her poor feet bleeding onto the stones of the tide mill yard, and she looked at him with her great grey eyes . . .'

'And did he . . . ?'

'He said nothing. He didn't claim her. He couldn't be the man that she needed; that he thought he was. He stood silent, though he knew her, and knew she was with his child, and he loved her. Truly, he loved her . . . But not enough.'

Gabrielle blinked tears from her eyes: 'Oh . . . not enough.'

'What happened next?' Mia whispered.

'They said that she must be proven to be mermaid or woman. The tide was on the ebb and some said just throw her back in the harbour and let her swim away. But others said they must save her if she was a woman, and return her to the sea if she was a mermaid, and others just wanted a show – like people do sometimes.'

'They did a trial by water?'

'They did. They took her arms and her poor little feet and they tied her flat on one of the blades of the waterwheel so that it would turn and take her underwater and bring her up again. They thought that if she drowned, then she was a woman who had sinned, and God was taking her to Himself; but if she came out alive, then she was a mermaid, and nothing to do with God nor Man. So they laid her on the mill wheel blade and all the while the man who loved her, watched them do it, and said not one word.

'They opened the sluice gate so the water poured into the

millrace, they took the brake off, the mill wheel turned and she went over the top and down into the pouring water of the mill-race, underneath the water as the wheel turned, and then she came up again, out of the other side. Three times they put her deep under the water and three times the mill wheel turned and brought her up again, and when they brought her out the last time she was white and blue and her little bleeding feet were still.'

'She was drowned?'

'Of course she was drowned, and the priest her lover lifted her off the blade of the mill wheel and walked with her in his arms down the road to the wadeway and walked deep into the ebbing waters of Broad Rife till everyone thought he would be swept away with her. Then he let her go. And her body with the streaming golden hair turned over and over and sank into the dark waters. And she was never seen again.'

BRISTOL JAIL, AUTUMN 1685

Ned, arriving in Bristol, the greatest provincial slave-trading city in England, found that not one magistrate in the city was prepared to review a transportation. No magistrate wanted to overturn a sentence handed down by the newly appointed Lord Chancellor, and none of the magistrates – all wealthy on slavery – were worried about a wrongful transportation.

'What about the Habeus Corpus?' Ned demanded of one clerk. 'I demand that this Ned Ferryman be brought into court.'

'He's already been in court and sentenced,' the clerk reasoned. 'He's a prisoner, he's got no rights.'

'You've got the wrong man!'

'Who is he then?' the clerk was momentarily interested.

'A servant, an Indian from the Americas. Arrested in error.'

'Should have said so at the trial.'

'You know they were hanged if they pleaded not guilty.'

The clerk shrugged. 'You say, he's an Indian?'

'Yes – a praying Indian. A Christian. From New England.'

'Then he's not an Englishman – habeas corpus don't apply. An Indian's got no rights: no more than a woman or a child or an idiot. Only his owner could demand sight of him, and his owner would be punished for his crime. Are you his owner?'

'No,' said Ned, seeing the trap opening before him.

'Thought not.'

Next morning Ned went to Bristol jail and found that the city-appointed head jailor of Newgate prison had not yet finished his breakfast in his house, and was not to be disturbed.

'Brother,' he said to the scruffy guard standing before the castle jail, 'I've come ahead of a pardon for one of the Monmouth rebels. He's innocent and the pardon will set him free. Can I see him and tell him it's coming?'

'They're not kept here. There's too many of 'em for the jail.'

'Not here?' Ned exclaimed, his heart sinking. 'But he was sent from Taunton to Bristol. Don't tell me they're shipped already?'

'Some of 'em,' the man said indifferently. 'Some of 'em gone, some of 'em waiting for ships. Some of 'em dead from gaol fever. There's too many of 'em, that's all I know.'

'I know there are many,' Ned said steadily. 'Help me, Brother, I beg you, in the name of the Lord. Where are they? Those that are not yet shipped out?'

'St Mary Redcliffe.' The man jerked his thumb in the direction of the towering spire. 'In the crypt, poor bastards. Pushed down into the crypt, sleeping alongside the dead.'

'Thank you,' Ned said heartfelt. 'At the church? How can I get to see him?'

'You can't,' the guard said. 'If we let one man see his family, we'd have the city filled with crying widows and children. They're down among the dead for a reason. They're as good as dead.'

'But I have a pardon for him!' Ned exclaimed.

'Better show it to the master of the ship. He'll release him to you, if your pardon's good.' The man paused. 'Is it good?'

'It will be, it's coming from London.'

'Then it's no good,' he said gloomily.

'It is, I tell you!' Ned snapped.

'A pardon coming from London is no good for anyone. One in your hand is what you need. And you haven't got that.'

REEKIE WHARF, LONDON, AUTUMN 1685

The hired carriage was drawn up before the narrow door of the wharf and Alys helped her mother down the steps. Gabrielle and Mia stepped down after her and went either side of their great-grandmother to help her over the cobbles and into the little parlour.

'I don't need to be hauled in like cargo,' Alinor protested. 'I'm just cramped with sitting for so long.'

'I'll get you a glass of hot ale,' Alys said, looking anxiously into her mother's pale face. 'That carriage was cold.'

'Should've sent for the Avery carriage,' Alinor said mischievously, taking her seat by the parlour fire as the girls took their seats at the table.

Alys came in with a glass of ale for her mother. 'Ma, have this, I'll be back in a moment. There's a muddle in the warehouse that I must see to straight away.'

Alinor took the cup with a word of thanks.

'Has our Nonna always run the wharf?' Gabrielle asked.

'Ever since we came here,' Alinor replied.

'And have you always dealt in physic?'

Alinor nodded. 'When I was younger, I worked as a midwife too. That was a great joy. To help a woman to give birth and keep her safe, to help a child come into the world.'

'Not like business,' Mia suggested.

Alinor smiled. 'No. Business is very orderly; your grandmother is good at it because she likes things in the right place, and sold at the right price. But I like a world that is a little . . . unruly.'

'How unruly is your world?' Gabrielle asked cautiously.

Alinor hesitated before she replied. 'Well, remember I was brought up by a woman who could barely read or write. She was a wise woman. I was raised by her to observe the laws of this world, but to know that beyond this world is a place that is quite different, with laws that we don't know. That we don't begin to know.'

'Like mermaids?' Mia asked. 'And faeries?'

Alinor's smile was warm. 'Like mermaids,' she agreed with the girl. 'And faeries.'

A tap at the front door interrupted them and the girls jumped up as Johnnie came into the room.

'Ah, Johnnie!' Alinor said gladly. 'Here at last! And these are your nieces, Mia and Gabrielle!'

The girls swept him a curtsey and Johnnie bowed to them. 'I'm glad to see you here,' he said kindly. 'My own sister's girls.' He smiled at Gabrielle. 'You take after her,' he said.

'Would you go to the counting house and tell your Grandmother Alys that Johnnie is here? And ask Tabs for another glass of small ale. You'll take a small ale, Johnnie?'

He nodded. 'I'm here to see Ma,' he said shortly. 'I'm trying to raise money to free Uncle Ned's lad.'

His grandmother looked grave. 'Have you not got enough?'

He shook his head. 'I've less than half of it. I've asked for a reduction but the queen's secretary is asking an impossible price. I'm hoping that Ma will change her mind about lending me some.'

'I have ten shillings I can give you,' she said.

He knew he should not take it from her. 'I don't like to take your savings ... but I will take it for her.'

'Oh Johnnie, do you love her?'

'I do. God knows why. She tricked me and she stole from me, but I can't bear the thought of her in prison, transported. God knows what she's suffering now, she's a creature of the wild, she should be—' He broke off and Alinor laid her hand, thin and brown-spotted, over his.

'Nay, don't think like that,' she said gently. 'She's a young woman of a different nation, with a different life. That's all. If you think of her as a wild creature, it's no better than thinking of her as a savage. She's your equal, she may even be a better person than you. Rescue her, if you can; but don't think of her as a creature in a trap, and don't do it for her gratitude.'

'She'll owe me a debt! The debt of her life. That's how she thinks,' he protested.

'She might – but you shouldn't. Free her for love without a price. It never works if a man thinks he's doing a woman a favour. He's not her better, he shouldn't set himself up as that. Don't you think that, Johnnie. Not you, who had a sister who was your equal neck and neck all through your childhood.'

'It hardly matters if I can't get her pardon,' he said miserably.

'Can Rob lend you any money? Can he borrow from his father-in-law?'

'He's given me a couple of pounds. That wife of his, the goldsmith's daughter, she's as tight-fisted as her father. My Ma is my last chance.'

The store was crammed with crates and barrels and sacks of goods; a shopman's wagon was waiting at the open door to the yard, arguing about a load.

'Ma,' Johnnie said, coming into the cold warehouse and shrugging his coat closer around his shoulders. 'I know you're busy, but I have to ask you for a great favour.'

'Wait a moment,' Alys said. She spread the loading manifest on the tailgate of the wagon and went through each item with the man. He agreed with the total, tipped his hat to her. 'You're allus straight, M's Shore, I should 'a known 'twas my mistake!'

She gave him her strong handshake and then turned to Johnnie. 'What is it?' she asked, instantly concerned. 'And why aren't you at work yourself?'

'I'm still on leave – they've agreed I can take as long as I need. I've been running round the City trying to raise money to free Rowan. I need about eighty pounds.'

Now he had her attention. 'For her pardon?'

'The queen is selling only a few pardons, at a great price. It won't be less than a hundred and twenty pounds and I have raised only forty.'

She spread her arms to gesture to the goods. 'I haven't got it, Johnnie. All this belongs to the investors who took shares in the voyage, it's not ours.'

He nodded. 'I wondered if you would borrow it for me? From the next?'

'Send Captain Shore out in a mortgaged ship?' she asked him, genuinely shocked. 'Johnnie, we never trade in debt. We only did it the once, and the Nobildonna nearly ruined us. I don't dare, Johnnie. I'm sorry to refuse you, Son. But I can't.'

'It's not debt,' he said. 'It's credit. Everyone trades on credit.'

'They're one and the same to me,' she said staunchly.

'Then what am I to do?' he said simply. 'I can't let her be sold like a slave on the quayside!'

She was flushed with distress. 'It's not your doing!' she exclaimed. 'It's Uncle Ned's doing. And hers. She took his place in prison. It's him who should free her.'

'You know he hasn't a penny in the world.'

'That's his choice too,' she said firmly. 'He believes in a world without masters or lords. He believes in a world without rich and poor. But we live in a world where money is the greatest master.'

This was so much in agreement with Johnnie's view that he could not argue against her. 'He's waiting for me to come to Bristol with a pardon. He expects me to raise the money.'

'I doubt that,' she said dourly. 'He knows we're not a family that has ever had money.'

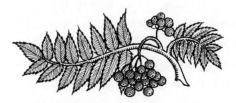

ST JAMES' PALACE, LONDON, AUTUMN 1685

Livia, the queen and a woman wearing a cloak with her hood pulled over to hide her face were alone in the queen's bedchamber, the door firmly locked on the other ladies-in-waiting.

'This is Mrs Cellier,' Livia introduced the hooded woman. 'You can take your hood down,' she told her. She turned back to the queen. 'She's a highly regarded midwife, and of the true faith.'

The queen extended her hand and Elizabeth Cellier kissed it. 'A great honour,' she said.

'Her Majesty has conceived before, but miscarried,' Livia said when the queen was silent.

'How many miscarriages?'

'Five,' the queen said quietly.

'And she has also lost four babies at birth, and a little girl at four years old.'

'God's will,' Elizabeth Cellier said piously and crossed herself.

'It is God's will that I have a live son for England,' the queen stated.

'It is indeed,' the midwife said. 'Has He blessed you with good health?'

It was obvious to anyone that God had not blessed the queen with good health. Her face had lost the rounded prettiness of the girl who had come to England to give England a roman catholic Prince of Wales. She was pale and thin, and she gathered her velvet stole around her as if she felt cold in the overheated rooms.

'I have faintness,' she said. 'And I am tired. I am only happy when I am riding, and I have not ridden since I fell at Windsor.'

'Not tired when riding?' the midwife asked.

'No, for then I am free, and thinking of nothing. I am just riding, galloping, and no-one can keep up with me, and no-one can talk to me and no-one can blame me—' She broke off.

'Her Majesty is not a happy wife?'

The queen bit her lip and shook her head in silence.

'His Majesty is not attentive?' the midwife asked tactfully.

The queen turned her head away, but Livia said shortly: 'He is not.'

'Her Majesty's courses are regular?'

'Not timely,' Livia said. 'And that gives us false hope too – and then disappointment.'

'The king must be welcomed one week after the course has ended,' the midwife said. 'Other times are less propitious. So it is not too onerous for him.' She did not so much as flicker a smile, and both women were equally grave. 'The field has to be ready for the sowing,' she said. 'Once a month at the right time is all that it needs. If there is vigour on the one side and willingness and agreement on the other.'

'Is there anything you can do to increase agreement?' Livia asked. 'And vigour?'

'I can give you some herbs to brew into a drink to encourage both of their Majesties,' Mrs Cellier said. 'A hot drink like a wedding ale. To encourage good cheer, and to make the husband eager and the wife fertile.'

'Lady Avery will take the herbs,' the young queen said, her head turned away and her cheeks burning red with shame. The midwife bowed and Livia guided her to the doorway where she handed over a purse of herbs.

'There'd better be nothing in this that is dangerous,' Livia warned her bluntly. 'If she gets ill then I will be in terrible trouble, but you're a dead woman.'

'Nothing but thyme to boil in sweet wine. She should take honey and pepper every day, and she should eat hare and venison, male meat, the pizzle and the parts. Can you order that for her?'

'Of course I can,' Livia said. 'She's the Queen of England. I can get almost anything in the world but a son in the cradle!'

BRISTOL, AUTUMN 1685

They loaded the prisoners at dusk, to take advantage of the empty quayside. Everyone who could shelter from the grey driving sleet had left the wet cobbles of the quay and the heaving murky water where the *Rebecca* pulled at the mooring ropes. She was Bristol-built, square of beam to sit on the mud of the port when the tide went out. 'More room below,' Ned said miserably. 'At least she'll have more room than slaves.'

The prisoners were the last of the cargo and the captain ticked them off the loading manifest as they came down to the quayside in chains. Johnnie and Ned in the shadow of a doorway could hear him count them off in numbers, as they went past him, no longer prisoners with names, now they were freight. If Rowan died at sea, they would never be able to discover it. No-one would report it. It would not matter except as a loss of profit that had already been calculated – a number of prisoners always died at sea.

There was a high unearthly scream from somewhere inside the hold of the ship.

'Good God!' Johnnie said. 'What was that?'

'Horses,' Ned said grimly. 'They're loading her with horses, for a two-month voyage, in high seas.'

The chained line of prisoners passed under a flickering torch and up the gangplank. Ned and Johnnie could not see which was Rowan. The flame of the torch leapt and was quenched in a gust of wind.

'Is that her?' Johnnie demanded as the line went up the gang-plank. 'Is she even there?'

Ned sighed: 'There she is.'

She was a little shorter than the men chained either side of her, and slighter. She walked with a short stride, as they all did, hobbled with iron chains on her ankles; but her shoulders were set and her head was up, and she was looking around, all the time, for a way out.

Ned could not bear it. Johnnie's restraining hand could not stop him lunging forward. She saw the movement in the shadows and turned to look. She saw him. Their eyes met across the wet quay but she made no sign of recognition, she did nothing to draw attention to him. A very tiny nod of her head was the only movement that she made, as if she were thanking him for showing himself, telling her that her sacrifice was not for nothing. He was not dead of his wounds, he was not recaptured. She was going into servitude, but she had freed him.

Then the man before her jerked on the chains that joined them wrist to wrist and she made a little grimace and followed him up to the wooden gangplank, and then stepped down to the deck, and then she hesitated, just for a moment, as the dark hatch yawned before her, and the smell from the hold hit her.

She took one look at the sky, ravelled with dark clouds, and the moon coming up as if to print the grey and blue-black colours in her memory, and then she stepped in, and went steadily down, until all they could see was the top of her dark head, and then she was gone.

Johnnie put a hand on Ned's shoulder to pull him back into the sheltering doorway and felt at once that something was wrong. Ned turned to him, his face drained of colour and his eyes black, and his knees bowed and he slid down to the wet cobbles.

HATTON GARDEN, LONDON, AUTUMN 1685

Thirteen-year-old Hester, Rob's daughter, was waiting anxiously for her cousins, at the window of the parlour that overlooked the street. Her governess, Miss Prynne, was laying out books suitable for young ladies, on the parlour table. Her mother, Julia Reekie, was unwell, resting on the day bed in her bedroom with the blue silk curtains drawn against the bright light, and a cold cloth on her forehead.

'Is that them?' Hester peeped out of the window. The iron clamp on her leg knocked against the edge of the seat and Miss Prynne frowned at her.

'Take care!' she said sharply. 'No-one wants to hear you clanking!'

The girl blushed scarlet as she settled herself in her seat, facing the room, trying to bring her feet neatly together. One foot was encased in a heavy leather boot braced with a metal clamp, and a raised heel to correct her club foot. Facing the room like a demure young lady she still craned over her shoulder to see the stone steps to the street, and the plainly dressed woman and the two girls who rang the bell.

'It's them!' Hester went to jump down from her seat, but a long look from the governess kept her still as the footman slowly walked the length of the hall and opened the front door.

'Mrs Shore and Miss Gabrielle Russo and Miss Mia Russo,' she heard Alys say to the footman who bowed and showed them into the parlour.

Miss Prynne rose from her seat at the table and curtseyed to the visitors. 'How do you do?'

Alys nodded in reply and then turned to Hester. 'Hello, my dear,' she said kindly. 'And here are your cousins, Gabrielle and Mia, who've been longing to meet you ever since they came to London.'

Hester slipped down from the seat, curtseyed to her aunt and then went to her for a kiss. She turned to the girls. 'I am so glad you are come! So glad!' she said.

The governess raised her pencil-thin eyebrows. 'And what do we say?' she questioned.

'Oh! Please, won't you sit down, Mrs Shore?' Hester said quickly. 'And will you take some refreshment? A glass of lemon water? A small ale? Or chocolate?'

'You can call me Aunt Shore, I should think,' Alys remarked, one eye on Miss Prynne to see if she would object. 'And I'll take a small ale. What would you like, girls?'

'Lemon water,' Mia answered for them both. 'How old are you, Cousin Hester? Do you speak Italian?'

'I'm thirteen,' the girl said. 'But everyone says I am small for my age. But I am fourteen in three months.'

'Same as me,' Mia said, pleased.

'And I can read Italian quite well, but I don't speak it. Do you speak both?'

'And French,' Gabrielle said. 'But we weren't ever really taught, so it doesn't count. Papa speaks Italian to us and Mama English.'

'My father said that you are going to school?' the smaller girl asked.

Mia nodded. 'We hope so. But he said we can study with you first. I think he's not sure that we're clever enough.'

'Oh really!' Alys exclaimed. 'I'm sure Rob didn't say such a thing!'

'Gentlemen have a low opinion of the abilities of women,' Mia said with a cheeky smile at her grandmother.

'Of ladies, you mean,' Miss Prynne corrected.

Mia turned her dark head and looked at the governess. 'Are women different from ladies?' she asked limpidly.

The governess flushed. 'Of course!'

'Less or more clever?'

'Now, Mia,' Alys interrupted.

The governess rose to the challenge: 'No female can challenge the intelligence of a male,' she ruled. 'We are called the weaker sex for a reason! But we can be educated – I may say that I am an example of that!'

'And anyway, I'm sure Rob just meant that you should have a chance to learn from Miss Prynne before you go to school,' Alys said.

'I can't prepare a young lady to compete with a young gentleman,' Miss Prynne said icily. 'I would not know where to begin.'

'Are you not well read?' Mia asked bluntly.

Miss Prynne flushed scarlet and Gabrielle leaned gently against her sister's shoulder.

'*Smettila*, stop it,' she said so quietly that only Mia could hear.

'You misunderstand me,' Miss Prynne said, her voice growing a little shrill. 'I know what is expected of students at the great colleges – Oxford or Cambridge or the colleges of law – my own brothers attended Oxford. But I would have no idea what is learned by young ladies at a school run by a master's wife. Does she teach classics? Rhetoric? Literature? Philosophy? However does a wife find the time?'

'Can you teach all them?' Mia inquired. 'Because I would like to learn them.'

Miss Prynne showed her a completely false smile. 'Why would a young lady want to learn Philosophy?'

'Why not?'

'Mia and Gabrielle are unusual girls,' Alys intervened. 'You will make allowances for them, I hope. They are scholarly. And their mother could not satisfy their desire to learn in Venice. That's the very reason they have come to us. That's why my brother Rob said that they might study with you. I do hope that they can share Hester's lessons with you.'

'I can teach them,' Miss Prynne confirmed. 'But I don't know if dear Mrs Reekie would want them preparing for serious academic study in our house. She asked me only if they might share Hester's morning lessons, and perhaps read some of the improving fables suitable for young ladies, from the doctor's library.'

'I could start on Philosophy . . .' Hester whispered, her admiring gaze on Mia and Gabrielle.

The footman returned and served the guests. The matter might have been left there, but Hester shot a longing glance at her aunt Alys.

'I am sorry that my sister-in-law is not well enough to see us today, but my brother – Doctor Reekie – assured me that you were capable of teaching all these subjects to the girls.' Alys sipped her small ale and found it bland. 'So I will leave them here this morning, and you can see how you all get on. I'll come back at half-past two and you can tell me if they can be taught and if you can teach them.' She rose and stood as squarely as she would stand on her own quay, agreeing a deal, her feet slightly astride, her chin jutting. 'Is that agreeable, Miss Prynne?' she asked.

A half-hidden gleam from Hester and an outright wink from Mia confirmed that they knew Alys was on their side. Miss Prynne rose to her feet. 'Of course, I shall do my best,' she said. 'But I don't know if it is what Mrs Reekie intended.'

'Not here, is she?' Alys pointed out. 'So let's give it a go and see what everyone says when I come this afternoon. Perhaps she'll be up by then. Girls – you do your best, and Miss Prynne will do hers, and we'll see what you all make of each other.' She put out her hand to Miss Prynne with a smile. 'I know they're in good hands,' she said.

Miss Prynne's limp hand disappeared into Alys' firm grip.

'Good day!' Alys said cheerfully, opened the door herself, before Miss Prynne could ring for the footman, and left them.

'Well . . .' Miss Prynne said, casting around for some excuse.

Hester slipped into her seat at the parlour table, and silently Mia and Gabrielle took off their bonnets and capes, and took their places. The three girls looked expectantly at the governess, waiting for her to begin. Miss Prynne cast around for the most discouraging topic she could think of.

'If you want Philosophy,' she said, 'I shall read you the first chapter of Thomas More's *Utopia* and you shall write for me a full page on your understanding of what you have heard.'

She disappeared from the room to go to Rob's library next door and reappeared with the book in her hand.

'Is that Saint Thomas?' Mia asked.

She hesitated. 'I believe in the papist religion he would be regarded as a saint. We have nothing to do with the papist religion in England.'

'What about the king? Isn't he roman catholic?'

'Do the English not have saints?' Gabrielle asked.

'Oh, don't we?' Hester could not contain her interest.

Miss Prynne scowled over her pince nez at the three of them. 'That is History,' she said damningly. 'And rarely suitable. This is Philosophy, and perhaps too difficult for the young female mind. I shall continue without interruption if you please: "I was colleague and companion to that incomparable man Cuthbert Tonstal, whom the King, with such universal applause, lately made Master of the Rolls . . ."'

Rob, coming home at six o'clock, found his wife getting up for the first time in the day, the governess in a state of exhaustion, and Hester, half-hidden by the turn of the stairs, lying in wait for him.

'May my cousins come again, Papa?' she asked him, catching him as he was going into his dressing room.

'Good God! I thought you were a footpad! Jumping out at me like that!'

She giggled. 'Don't be silly, Papa,' she said severely. 'I wanted to see you, before you talk to Mama.'

'Why?' he asked, scanning the flush in her face and the brightness of her eyes. He put his hand on her forehead. 'You're not feverish?'

'No, no!' she exclaimed. 'I'm well! My cousins came today: Gabrielle and Mia. And they made Prynne teach us Philosophy, and she hated it. But it was truly interesting, and they know so much already, I'm so behind, Papa! And we read a book from your library – a proper book – not a chapbook for children with a moral at the end. And Aunt Shore came to fetch them, and she was so funny, Papa. She said she can't be running in and out of London every day, that she has work to do, but if they are to come regularly, she will send them in the wherry on their own. Prynne nearly died of shock, but Aunt Shore just smiled and said, "Why not?" She left her love for you and sent up her good wishes to Mama.'

'Did your Mama not see her?'

'No, she didn't come down at all, and Prynne said just as well – because Aunt Shore is in trade—' She broke off, looking at him anxiously. 'But I thought it just as well that Mama didn't come down because she doesn't like me going into your library. Prynne chose this book to put us off Philosophy, but really, it didn't, Papa. And Mia understands everything anyway.'

'She does, does she?' Rob smiled at the sudden vivacity of his daughter. 'Well, it certainly looks as if you've enjoyed their visit.'

'And they're so funny,' Hester told him earnestly. 'Mia can wink! I nearly laughed out loud.'

'They're not to distract from your lessons,' Rob warned. 'They're not rowdy?'

'Oh! No! No!' she promised him. 'Mia winked when Aunt Shore said that we might learn difficult things. They want to study. Can I study with them?'

He put a gentle arm around her slim shoulders. 'I can't say "no" to you,' he told her. 'But you must do your exercises and walk out every day as well. I want you strong, as well as clever. And we can't upset your mother. Don't you start winking!'

She flushed with pleasure as a thought came to her. 'I could walk them to the New Canal after our lesson every day? That would be more walking than I do now.'

'You'll have to have Prynne or a footman to go with you. And stop if you get overtired.'

'Oh yes! Papa! Yes!'

He smiled. 'When do they want to come again?'

She gave a little gasp. 'The day after tomorrow, if you say so?'

'I'll send a message to the wharf,' he said easily. 'And you and Miss Prynne can meet their wherry at the Holborn water stairs.'

'They can come on their own in a wherry?' she confirmed.

'Why not?' he chucked her under the chin. 'Since they are philosophers who know so much already?'

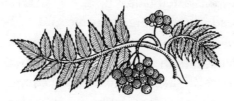

REEKIE WHARF, LONDON, AUTUMN 1685

The hired carriage from Bristol drove through the Reekie gates and halted in the yard. The lad jumped down onto the cobbles, opened the door and let down the steps.

'Wait,' Johnnie told him and went to the back door. 'Here, Tabs, come and give me a hand. Susie, fetch my mother and someone to help carry. I've got my uncle in the coach and he's in a bad way.'

'Lord save us,' the cook said and came out into the yard and peered into the coach.

Ned was propped on the seat, his body slumped. His face was frozen in a scowl, his forehead was puckered, his eyelids closed, his colour as pale as a drowned man.

'God bless us, is he dead?' she whispered.

Alys came out into the yard with one of the lumpers from the quayside.

'Lord save him,' she said quietly. 'Poor Uncle Ned.'

'He's had some sort of seizure,' Johnnie told her. 'The Bristol surgeon said to treat him like a drunk man. Handle him carefully, get him into his bed, and hope that he comes round. We should put him in a chair to carry him. Where's he to go?'

'He'd better go in your grandmother's room for now. I'll send the warehouse lad for Rob.'

The lumper from the quay and Tabs brought a sturdy high-backed chair from the kitchen and Johnnie went inside the coach and took hold of Ned's shoulders. The lumper lifted his legs and the two of them hauled him out of the carriage and seated him in the chair.

'Does he have a wound?' Alys asked, looking doubtfully at the grey colour of his twisted face.

'Only his head, from before,' Johnnie said. 'The surgeon said it was a seizure inside his brain and it might right itself in time.'

He straightened up and nodded at the lumper. 'You take the back of the chair, I'll take the front. We'll carry him in and up the stairs. Keep it tipped back so he doesn't fall forward.'

'Aye, aye,' the man said.

The two of them lifted the chair and carried it into the house, the women bringing in the bags from the carriage while Alys paid off the hire. Carefully they made their way up the tight turn of the narrow stairs. Alinor opened the door to her room and had them lay him on her sofa.

She spoke not one word of shock, but took his wrist and felt his pulse, steady and strong, put a hand on his pale face and felt he was cool but not clammy. She touched, with deep tenderness, the twisted grimace on his face.

'I've sent for Rob,' Alys told her. 'Are you all right Ma?'

Alinor nodded. 'D'you know what caused it?'

'He saw Rowan loaded onto the ship as it set sail,' he said. 'He fell down as if his heart was broken.'

BRIDGETOWN, BARBADOS, WINTER 1686

Rowan, half-starved and shaking from the fever that she had caught in the jail at Bristol, shaded her eyes from the blinding light of the Caribbean sun, and fell back when someone – she could see nothing more than a looming shadow before her – slapped her hand away. 'Show your face, lad,' he growled. 'Open your mouth.'

She opened her mouth and then gagged when a dirty fist was pushed into her face and strong soiled fingers jiggled her teeth.

'Not bad,' the voice said approvingly. 'What age are you, lad?'

'He's about twenty,' someone volunteered. 'One of the Monmouth scum.'

'As if we didn't have scum enough!' the man complained.

'Look, d'you want that lad or not?'

'Is he an English boy?' the man asked, taking a pinch of Rowan's cheek and squeezing it to see the colour. 'Looks brown. I'd take him for an Indian.'

'He's from Bristol,' the captain replied. 'Who knows?'

'I'll take him.' The man was like a thick tree, blocking the sun. In his shadow, Rowan stole a quick upward look. Blinded by the sunlight, she could see nothing more than a flushed red face, a shock of grizzled grey hair and a broad-brimmed hat.

'Property of the queen, price is twenty pounds,' the captain said.

'I'll give you fifteen,' the man said, unmoved. 'God bless Her Majesty. We both know he'll be dead in a year.'

'He's indentured for ten,' the captain pointed out. 'And from the west country – he'll likely know how to fish and farm. Worth all of twenty pounds. And he's not been beaten or broken.'

'Yet,' one of the men said with a short laugh.

'What good is fishing and farming to me? He won't know how to boil sugar.'

'If he can feed himself, it saves you the trouble,' someone said judiciously.

'I'll give you seventeen pounds in sugar,' the big man said.

'Done,' the captain said and spat into his palm, as the man did. They slapped palms together and the captain crossed off Rowan's number in his ledger and unchained her from the manacles.

'How d'you want him?' he said. 'Roped?'

'Just the hands,' the man said. He leaned towards Rowan and glared into her face breathing a gust of sour rum. 'I'm Mr Peabody,' he told her. 'You call me Sir. You follow me back to my farm and you'll have a little cabin of your own, for a fair day's work. You run away and I'll set the dogs on you and beat you when I get you back. You work hard and you get your cabin at the end of your service and ten pounds to start you off. Work hard, and you might make a fortune here. Cheat me or steal from me, and you're dancing at the end of a rope and no-one will even ask after you. Agreed?'

'Yes, Sir,' Rowan said.

The man checked. 'That's not a west country voice,' he accused her. 'You've got learning?'

'I can read and write,' Rowan said shortly.

'What was your trade?'

Hunting, Rowan thought. Fishing. Running, hoeing weeds beside my mother, playing with my sisters, swimming in the river, trading with the village, weaving, making wampum, singing, making pots, playing in the snow, praying to the Gods, dancing. Out loud she said: 'I was in service at a London wharf.'

'I might make you a house servant,' he promised her. 'Or a clerk. Or an overseer. If you can read – which I doubt.'

She did not argue, though he glared at her. 'Don't you get above yourself,' he warned her. 'You're the lowest thing there is – a rebel.'

Still she said nothing.

'Lower than a slave. And there's nothing lower than a slave but a dead dog,' he amended, twitched the rope that the captain had tied around her wrists and gestured that she should follow him down the ladder to the waiting rowing boat.

She found her legs were too weak to manage the ladder, not even her hands could grip. She slithered down and would have fallen in the boat but her new owner pushed her roughly on the bench. 'You a cripple?' he demanded.

She shook her head.

'Lad's still got sea legs,' the boatman said.

'Did I ask you? Tell them to row us to shore.'

The white boatman nodded at the black rowers and they took up their oars. Cautiously, Rowan raised her head and, squinting against the dazzle of the water, looked ahead. She had never seen a sea this colour. The depths were nearly indigo, but close to shore, breaking on white rocks, washing on white sand, the water was a deep turquoise. They were headed towards a stone quay built of bright white rock, beyond were wharves and warehouses like a miniature Boston or London, fine buildings with wooden shutters barred against the brightness and the heat. The men, boys and women arduously rolling barrels of rum and sugar along the stone quay were all black, slaves from Africa, and the terrible stink of a slave hulk blew into the port from the looming ship anchored outside.

Rowan hunched her shoulders against fear and slumped in her seat. Beyond the warehouses were shops where the shutters were propped open, and goods for sale displayed inside the darkened rooms. Every other house was an inn, or a tippling house. Men sprawled in the gutter, unnoticed by passers-by who stepped over them. In one alley Rowan saw three or four men swaying from side to side locked in a drunken fight.

Some gentlemen had dressed with absurd grandeur, high beaver hats, embroidered silk waistcoats, thick gold-buttoned jackets, clocked stockings, thick breeches and ornate shoes, red-faced from the heat. A few poor white men had scraps of clothing, a ripped shirt and torn trousers, or clung to a tattered jacket which showed the ghost of frayed embroidery. The black slaves were mostly half-naked except for a few ornately dressed house slaves who waited outside the tavern for their masters, sweating in full suits of livery. One black coachman wore a white curled wig, a tricorn hat and a gold braided suit, as he held the reins of a pair of matching grey horses before a grand carriage.

There were black women on every corner, selling little goods off trays tied around their necks, or standing tall with towering baskets of fruit and pitchers of rum balanced on their turbaned heads. Others, in tattered finery with gowns pulled down low to show their breasts, were strolling up and down the streets outside the tippling houses, waiting to be called into the darkness within.

The noise was appalling. Barrels were rolled along the stone quay by gangs of slaves, there was a constant screech of the sledges on the slabs of white pavers and the rattle of the wheels of carts drawn by iron-shod oxen harnessed in pairs, mules pulling wagons and horses before carriages. Pairs of running slaves were harnessed to drag carts of sugar from distant farms into town, and behind them rode an overseer on a horse, yelling them to go faster and cracking his whip. The smell of spice and decay, sugar and sour rum hit Rowan and made her retch. She clamped her fist over her mouth and fought to be silent. The black rowers looked at her without seeing her, their eyes as blank as the dead.

The rowing boat nudged against a step of coarse-stoned white stairs. Rowan's owner twitched at the rope that bound her hands and she staggered to her feet. To save herself she clutched at the shoulder of one of the black men and he flinched from her touch, as if from a blow. She straightened up and climbed out of the rocking boat and up the stairs to the top of the quay. Her legs were in spasms of pain by the time she reached the top where a silent black man was holding the reins of a fine-looking horse. Another man laden with sacks of goods stood beside him.

'You take this lad and start for home,' Mr Peabody ordered. 'I'll catch you up.' He turned to Rowan. 'No tricks, mind, or they'll tell me at once. I'll be right behind you, and if I have to chase after you or send the dogs – you'll be sorry.'

He nodded to the men. 'Take him home,' he told them. 'I'll take a drink and then follow you.'

The silent man swallowed down his thirst and handed over the reins. Mr Peabody led the horse to the doorway of the tippling house, yelled for a slave to hold the horse while he went inside and paid no more attention to them. Rowan, hardly seeming to look, scanned the quay, the alleyway, the river below her for a way to escape. She glanced up to find the silent black man looking at her.

'There's no way,' he told her in a deep voice, speaking English. 'There's no way to your home but death.'

ST JAMES' PALACE, LONDON, WINTER 1686

Triumphant against the rebels, unchallenged by parliament, the west country studded with gallows, the north thanking God to be spared an invasion of Scots, King James knew his reign to be blessed by God. Confidently he appointed his favourite roman catholics to any state post they wanted, priests to protestant colleges of Oxford and Cambridge, papist army officers over the heads of those who had served him loyally against the Duke of Monmouth. The emergency army, wholly under his command, was never to be disbanded: he was free to persecute protestants at home like the French king attacking the Huguenots, or send his men and arms abroad to support roman catholic tyrants against their people. When the parliament reached sticking point and finally refused him, he closed it down, just as his brother and grandfather had done – and sent the MPs home.

He ordered the opening of monasteries and convents, oratories and chapels in every city in the land, and each new foundation opened a school – the children of England would be taught the king's faith, not the country's. He requested a Papal Nuncio from Rome and the Pope sent him the aristocratic Ferdinand d'Adda, naming him as an English archbishop.

At this, the very pinnacle of his triumph, the king had the woman he loved at his side. Catherine Sedley was at every court function, at every ball, at every gaming table, at every dinner. She might curtsey to the queen – who seemed to grow paler and thinner every day the bawdy laughing woman strolled into court – but everyone was waiting, on edge, for the day that Catherine would overstep the line and openly insult the younger woman. Why would she not? She was notorious for her quick wit, her coarse humour, her jokes about religion, her sexual innuendo, her free and easy laughter. As the great rooms of the palace echoed to her crack of laughter, and roar of appreciation, the queen grew more and more silent. As Catherine was every-where, showing her bony shoulders in revealing dresses, laughing in the king's face, refusing to attend his oratory and still escaping criticism, the queen was less and less seen at her own court.

'You cannot let her take over!' Livia exclaimed in the queen's privy chamber, all but hiding from the party in the presence chamber where they could hear Catherine Sedley yelling for candles to light the table as she was – 'for once, for the love of God! Any God!' – winning. 'You must go out there and call for music, make them move the gambling table, turn them into our rooms again. These are our rooms – not hers!'

'Is the king playing at her table?'

Livia crossed the room, opened the door a crack and peered through. Catherine Sedley was dancing on a chair in triumph, the king sneaking a glimpse of her calves, and laughing in delight at her irrepressible joy. 'For the love of God, deal my cards!' they heard her scream. 'I have the luck of the devil tonight!'

'Yes.'

'Then I can't make them move the table, can I? And if I call for music, he will dance with her.'

Livia closed her eyes, thinking of the romp that Catherine made of any dance. 'You have to fight her. I'll help you. We'll fight her together. We'll get her disgraced. There must be something we can do to pull her down. She says herself she's not beautiful. It's not possible for him to prefer her to you.'

'She claims to be funny, and he likes that. I was raised to be a queen, not a jester. And anyway, I have nothing to laugh at.'

'He does his duty by you?' Livia asked. 'For all that he's with her every evening? He does his duty when he comes to your bed?'

Mary Beatrice turned her head away from her friend's anxious scrutiny. 'He does it.'

'Does it properly?' Livia pressed.

'I suppose so. It hurts enough.'

'He hurts you?' Livia was shocked.

Mary Beatrice shrugged. 'My whole life is pain.'

Livia saw the deathly pallor of the younger woman and the shadows under her eyes like violet bruises. 'I know,' she said tenderly. 'I know you are living in pain. But it will get better, my dear. The kingdom is at peace, our enemies routed, you will conceive a child—'

A raucous scream of joy and a scatter of applause interrupted her.

'I suppose she has won,' Mary Beatrice remarked. 'I think he loses to her on purpose to give her money.'

The door from the public rooms opened and one of the ladies-in-waiting came in. 'Father Galli asks to be admitted,' she said, curtseying to the queen.

'Of course,' Livia answered for the queen, gesturing that the new priest should come in. 'Now here is a friend,' she said to Mary Beatrice. 'Here is a comforter.'

The dark-robed man came into the room, bowed to the queen and then, as the two women knelt before him, made the sign of the cross over their bowed heads.

'Amen,' they said devoutly.

The queen took a seat, as the priest stood before her.

'I have bad news,' Father Galli said, his eyes on the queen's pale face. 'His Majesty has decided to honour Catherine Sedley. She is to be the Countess of Dorchester.'

Livia gave a shocked gasp, and whirled around, to see the queen paler still.

'Why?' she asked simply.

Father Galli shrugged. 'I believe she asked for the honour, and he said "yes".'

'This is how we create an order of nobility?' the queen cried out. 'Some commoner – a woman without a husband even! – just demands a title?'

Father Galli folded his hands inside his sleeves and clasped them as if in prayer.

'How did you advise him?' Livia asked quietly.

He turned to her as an ally. 'I made no comment. I thought it best to speak first with Her Majesty.'

The queen turned away from them, her head bowed as if it were she who should be ashamed. She walked to the window and drew back the curtain, leaned her hot forehead against the cool glass. 'This is a terrible insult to me,' she observed, her voice drained of emotion. 'She was my maid of honour, and now she is made a countess?'

Father Galli bowed his head too. 'An insult to us all,' he said. 'It's well known that Lady Sedley makes a mock of us and our faith.'

'I will not bear it.' The queen dropped the curtain and turned back into the room. 'I cannot bear it. I cannot bear any more.'

The queen's musicians in her own presence chamber burst into a dance and at once the thud of heavy feet dancing drowned out the queen's voice. 'I cannot stand the noise she makes. How loud will she crow when she has ermine on her shoulders and a coronet on her head?'

'If we asked the king to give a lesser honour . . .' Livia started.

'The papers are already drawn up,' Father Galli said. 'He told me to tell you now, before it is announced to the court this evening. It will be in the news-sheets by tomorrow. They have set the type.'

'I am going to retire,' the queen said quietly as the thud of dancing feet grew louder as the movement of the dance took the court close to the privy chamber door and then away again.

'To bed?' Livia came towards her. 'I'll come with you. I'll send for your ladies.'

The queen shook her head with sudden determination. 'No, retire from my duty. I am going to leave court, and leave the king, and go to a convent. I always wanted to take holy orders, I always knew I had a vocation. God called me to England, the Holy Father told me to be queen, the King of England chose me as the bride for his brother. But if I cannot be queen in my own kingdom – the chosen companion of my husband and mother of his children – then I shall go to where I want to be. I shall go to a nunnery.'

'You can't,' Livia said flatly.

Mary Beatrice rounded on her. 'I can.' She looked at Father Galli. 'No-one can stop me taking my vows, can they?' she asked.

'It will jeopardise the King of England,' he told her earnestly. 'Without you as queen how will he get an heir? He cannot hold England to the true faith without a son to inherit. If you abandon him to that harpy, we have lost His Majesty to sin and England forever.'

For once she was defiant. 'It's his choice. You tell him! Tell his new confessor, Father Petre, that he must hold the king to his vows if I am to stay! If he chooses her over me, then I choose God over him. And no-one – no-one – will blame me.'

BARBADOS, WINTER 1686

Mr Peabody's plantation was in St Thomas Parish, Barbados, half a day's gruelling walk for the slaves, a pleasant ride for Mr Peabody, who would only leave the tavern as the sun began to set and the day began to cool. It was a trial of endurance for Rowan, who set off, the rope from her hands tied to the waist of one of the black slaves, in the burning sun of two o'clock in the afternoon.

She could not walk for more than twenty minutes without stumbling; the slaves who walked with her, carrying goods for the plantation strapped on their backs or balanced on their heads, waited patiently until she struggled to her feet again. Her feet, softened by the months of sitting in prison, blistered within the hour, and her wasted muscles screamed with fatigue. One of the slaves clapped his own ragged hat on her head to keep the sun from beating down on her bowed neck, but none of them could shade her from the burning sun on her arms, on her legs below her tattered breeches. When there was water in the ditch at the side of the cane fields they stopped to let her soak her bleeding feet, or scooped water on her neck, but her shirt and breeches dried out in moments as soon as they were in the full sun on the white road.

When she said 'thank you', grateful for their patience, they did not reply. They looked away from her, even when they rested beside her. They were so silent that she thought they did not speak English, but then she heard one say quietly to another, 'He'll not live long,' and she realised that they saw her as a ghost – half-dead already.

Every time she rose to her feet after a rest, she thought of the turtle who struggles so hard on land, who will get trapped by a stone and baffled by shifting sand, but in deep water is as smooth and easy as a swimming bird. She called on the spirit of the turtle to walk with her, to loan her his indomitable courage and his blindness to defeat. When they doused her, she thought of the cool water of the morning prayer, and that this land – where the sun was so bright in the afternoon would be cool and beautiful in the dawn – and that perhaps she would be able to rise early, to pray to her Grandfather Sun, perhaps she would be on the east of an easterly island, and a child of the Dawnlands again.

Then the man gently twitched the rope at her sore wrists, and she walked behind him, her eyes on the white road and the pale colour of the soles of his bare feet, the scars left by the manacles of his enslavement, and she walked on.

As the road climbed higher, they came to plantations where harvest was starting – weeks of frantic work to cut a year and a half of growth. One cutting gang was working beside the road and as Rowan and the slaves trudged by, they could see the ripe canes tumbling down, an overseer seated high on a horse, a whip coiled at his side, and men and the strongest women hacking frantically at the cane with broad flat blades, the second gang coming behind them, gathering up the canes and dragging and carrying them to the cart at a half-run. The carter stood on top of the load and caught and stacked canes with desperate haste. They had been working since dawn. Rowan could tell from the dark stains of sweat on turban and gown that they were beyond exhaustion, on the edge of collapse, but the overseer watched them and shouted if anyone seemed to be slowing, cursing them, swearing that this field would be cut and milled in a day, before it dried, or he would see them whipped.

A cart rumbled past them, pulled by oxen, each chewing a leaf-top of cane, with the driver shouting to them to get out of the road, he could not be delayed for a moment! On every hill, rising above the cane, Rowan could see the sails of endless wind-mills turning and turning, as if even the wind was enslaved.

Hanging over every plantation was the haze from the fires in the boiling house, stinging smoke tainted with the sickly sweetness of boiling sugar. To Rowan, stumbling behind a slave, hearing the bitter working chant from the harvesting gang in the deep crop behind her, they were the sounds and smell of hell.

WHITEHALL PALACE, LONDON, WINTER 1686

There was a tremendous scene between the king and queen, when the king's confessor knelt to him begging him to give up his adulterous affair, and the queen stood by her oath to leave him if Catherine Sedley was not dismissed from court. Furious at being cornered, torn between love for his mistress and the demands of his marriage vows, the king collapsed into penitent tears and the new Countess of Dorchester, Catherine Sedley, started an interminable process of her long farewell.

The queen and her ladies found that the Sedley woman could not be persuaded to go until a suitable destination was found for her. Firstly, she refused to go to France for fear, she said, of being kidnapped into a convent.

'As if they would want her,' Livia said disdainfully.

Similarly, she could not go to Portugal or Spain. She pointed to the arrival of the Huguenot protestants from France, terrified refugees, fleeing into exile for their faith. 'I can't go to a papist country!' she told everyone. 'It's to send me to my death.'

'Perfect!' Livia whispered.

Someone suggested Holland, and at once she wanted letters

of introduction so that she would be received at the court of William of Orange and his wife, Princess Mary of England.

'As though I would put her in my stepdaughter's court!' the queen said.

Then the newly-minted countess took to her bed and announced that her distress had caused a miscarriage, she had lost the king's child. It had been a boy, she was certain. God had blessed her with a half-royal prince, and if she had not been cruelly persecuted and separated from the baby's father, she would have presented him with a son.

Livia came into the queen's chapel to find Mary Beatrice on her knees. Her pale face was twisted in pain. 'Did God give her the king's child?' she demanded. 'Would He do such a cruel thing? Has He turned His countenance from me?'

Ahead of them was the glorious altar, carved in wood and painted in gold. Above them were radiant windows streaming with colours that dappled the priceless marble floor with colour. Only the queen was pale in the joyous brightness of her chapel. Livia knelt beside her.

'Probably lying,' Livia said cheerfully. 'Just refusing to leave, one excuse after another.'

'He'll never make her leave if she's ill,' the queen predicted. 'And if she goes on saying she has lost a protestant heir, the whole country will be on her side.'

'A protestant bastard. And dead, anyway.'

'They'd prefer a protestant bastard!' the queen exclaimed. 'They wanted Monmouth instead of us.'

'Well, he's dead too,' Livia said ruthlessly.

Catherine Sedley finally left court, in a procession as grand as any royal princess. Four full-sized coaches harnessed with teams of horses drew up outside the palace. Streams of servants with endless bags and baggage loaded the carriages and climbed in themselves. Her entire household, from her chamberlain to her lowliest maid, all had to accompany the royal mistress, all of them had to travel in the grandest of style. Finally, Catherine herself, heavily veiled and wrapped in priceless furs, got into the first carriage. They put up the steps, shut the door, the footmen swung up behind, the coachman cracked his whip, the six bay horses strained at the harness, and at last, with a rumble of wheels as loud as the crack of doom, the woman was gone.

Mary Beatrice did not watch from a window with Livia. She lay in her beautiful bed, the thick embroidered curtains drawn around her, the room in an early dusk because she could not stand the light. The rumble of wheels penetrated the deep silence of her room, and she could hear the shouts of well-wishers calling the countess to come back soon.

'Has she gone?'

Livia came from the window where she had been spying on the ostentatious farewell. 'She's gone. You've won. There's every reason for you to be happy.'

Mary Beatrice raised herself up on one arm and looked at her only friend at court. Her dark eyes were huge in her pale face, violet shadows from sleeplessness smudged on her cheeks. 'Do I look happy?' she asked.

PEABODY PLANTATION, BARBADOS, WINTER 1686

Rowan's first days at Peabody Plantation were taken up with learning her way around the house and grounds, and identifying who people were, and what threat they posed to her. Most were black enslaved men and women; there were very few children. They watched her out of the corners of their dark eyes, as a new and unknown threat to them. They avoided her as if she were cursed, and never spoke to her, flinching if she spoke to them. Rowan realised that her caramel skin and her dark straight hair identified her as one of the owners, the kidnappers, the killers – to be avoided at all times.

She was housed with other white indentured servants, many of them Irish, captured or shipped from the prisons of Dublin. Their house was nothing more than a one-roomed cottage, built of rough blocks of coral, quarried from the steep cliffs of the creek, thatched with the leaves of plantains. The floor was tamped-down earth; the men slept on beds of sugar cane leaves and ate from a common pot of loblolly stew made from boiled maize and root vegetables, occasionally enriched with a slice or two of meat from the big house, or fish they had caught. They relieved themselves against the outside wall of the hut, and every now and then ordered a slave to dig a pit for their dirt. They washed rarely, slept almost naked for the heat, and wore broad hats and tattered shirts and breeches to work. They insisted on wearing shoes, however ill-fitting, telling Rowan that there were worms that would eat into your feet and leave you lame for life.

After the first night in the fetid cottage with the snoring, exhausted men, Rowan, terrified of them discovering she was a woman, was determined to get away from the stink, the certainty of a fight and the threat of rape.

The slave huts were worse-built than the servants' cottages, plank walls and a leaf roof but better managed. Black couples lived together as husband and wife, in their self-built hut. The single women lived in one larger hut and the single men lived in another in a compound some distance from the main house. They all grew vegetables and fruit to eat and to sell, and they kept their huts scrupulously clean. They built and managed a hospital hut to nurse a constant stream of sick slaves: dying from overwork or infected with wounds from a beating or a branding.

Once a week the slave quarters were searched from roof to floor for weapons or stolen goods; every so often an enslaved girl would disappear from her sleeping hut and come back bloodstained and tearstained and mute, raped by the white men servants, by the overseer or by Mr Peabody himself. Occasionally there would be a public whipping for some offence, or the blacksmith might be ordered to brand someone, or wound them. Rowan realised that the white masters ruled by the constant threat of terrible violence.

If Rowan could have moved in with the women slaves she would have done so, but by passing as a white male servant at arrival she was now forced to live with the white men. There was privilege attached to this – as a white servant she could beat a black woman without fear of punishment – but she could not speak to them or eat with them, and she would never be allowed to live with them.

The first day that Mr Peabody recovered from his drunken bout in Bridge, he sent for Rowan.

'You gotta come to the big house,' the black maid told Rowan, finding her sharpening the blades of the sugar cane billhooks. 'Come quick. He don' like waiting.'

Rowan went as fast as she could, hobbling on sore feet up the stone path from the servants' cottages to the walled garden. Mr Peabody was in the shade of a great tree, its enormous trunk swelling behind him, its canopy casting a welcome shadow over him, a long cool drink of rum punch in his hand.

Rowan stood before him and pulled off her hat.

'You said you can read?' He tossed a news-sheet to her. It was an old *London Gazette*.

She took it up, and squinted at the travel-stained paper:

'"Right truly and right well beloved cousin and counsellor, right trusty and right well beloved counsellor, right trusty and entirely beloved—"'

'Skip that bit! Skip it!' Mr Peabody grunted irritably. 'Go down. Read on.'

'"We greet you well. Whereas by our letter of the 21st day of August last past, we were graciously pleased to inform you of our designs in order to the ease of our roman catholic ..."'

'Same as usual then, more comfort for papists. I see you can read. Who taught you?'

'My mistress, Alinor Reekie. I was a clerk at the Reekie warehouse, I noted the goods in and out,' Rowan lied, wondering what service would earn her a bed inside the house, away from the men. 'I worked as a house servant too,' she said. 'In the kitchen and serving. I helped the cook.'

He laughed abruptly. 'You want your feet under my table!' he accused her.

'I'm going to die out here,' she told him frankly. 'And you'll lose the money you paid for me.'

'If you want soft living, you should've thought of that before you turned traitor.'

She bowed her head. 'I'm not a thief.' She knew they feared theft, second only to rebellion. 'And I can fire a musket. I can serve in the militia against the slaves.'

''Cause you fired one for that damned traitor, Monmouth!'

'No. Never. I was captured by accident on an errand.'

He thought for a moment. 'You'll work as hard as a slave in the house as you would in the field, don't think you'll get off lightly. You'll clean and wash and wait on me, you'll run with messages, you'll write my letters. You'll be up at dawn to serve my breakfast and you'll clear up after I've gone to bed.'

Rowan nodded. 'Yes, Sir.'

'And you'll guard the house and grounds. Every other night.'

'Yes, Sir.'

'Harvest is starting, and I'll need white men to oversee the gangs. Can you do that?'

Rowan thought that she was about to sink lower than she had ever been: a white man, sharing in white violence. 'Yes, Sir.'

'Go into the house and tell Cook to find you some half-decent clothes. And get a wash, you stink. You can serve dinner, and if you're any good, I'll have you as a servant: a footman.'

Rowan bowed and headed for the house. It was built with the same coral stone as all the other buildings but edged and trimmed with a handsome deep red brick. It was a grand two-storey house with a gable over the two upstairs windows, surrounded by formal gardens, standing high above the low-roofed slave huts and outbuildings. It was pretty: neat as a doll's house, looking over a long green vista of fields. Rowan knew not to enter through the front door but went around the side to find a back yard, and outbuildings: bath-houses, a necessary house, a bakery and a kitchen, shaded by the canopy of a huge broad-trunked tree which slumped, fat and comforting, in the centre of the yard.

Behind the house was a working yard: a smithy, the sprawling sugar factory shady and quiet now before the start of harvest, and over them all a squat windmill, with the sails idle. It was like a little English estate transported under burning sun, nightmarishly changed into a place of torture. Through it all, through every sunlit vista, there was the stench of slavery, of fearful sweat, of bruised and bleeding flesh, of grief.

The smell of roasting meat drifted into the yard making her stomach grip with hunger and her dry mouth water. She followed the haunting scent to the open door of the stone-built building opposite the main house, across the yard. The black woman cook was basting a hog on a spit turned by a tiny black child, his eyes squinted against the unbearable heat of the fire, his hands and arms scarred from earlier burnings from the spitting fat.

'I'm to have half-decent clothes, and wash. I'm to serve dinner,' Rowan said, looking away from the little boy.

The cook looked up. 'Yes, Sir,' she said.

'Where can I wash?'

She pointed to the bath-house on one side of the yard. 'In there.'

'And clothes?'

'I get them for you.' She poured a ladle of fat over the crispy skin and spoke quickly and fiercely to the exhausted child who nodded and turned the spit. She went in the back door of the house and came out with a pair of baggy sailor's trousers and a clean linen shirt. 'Here.'

'Whose are these?' Rowan asked, taking them.

'The last one. He dead.'

Rowan nodded and crossed the yard, relieved to find the little bath-house had a door that latched shut, and a tap and even some lye soap and a rough towel. She felt safe to undress, wash her body and her hair, forcing herself not to scratch the itch of lice on the nape of her neck. She checked her feet for chigger worms, towelled herself dry and pulled on the clean clothes. She had never thought that she would enjoy dressing as a white man, but the smell of sun-dried linen made her think longingly of laundering for Ned, and sleeping in clean sheets. She wrapped her baggy linen shirt closely around her skinny body and buttoned it up to the neck. She rolled up the trousers at the waistband and tied the cord tight so that it sat on her hips. She stepped into ill-fitting shoes.

Back at the kitchen Cook was hurrying to prepare an extraordinary array of dishes for just two people: the Master and Mrs Peabody. There was stewed saltfish arranged on a trencher with fruit, there were thick slices of the roast pork and crackling with roasted potatoes and boiled carrots, there was a chicken pie, and as Rowan watched, she drew a dish of creamed eggs from the oven. 'Go! Go!' she said, waving Rowan towards the door. 'Take it while it's hot!'

Rowan seized the roast pork tray and stepped into the blinding sunlight and went quickly across the yard and into the big house. The dining room was down a short corridor to her left – at the front of the house – and as she put the dish on the table the front door opened and Mr Peabody came in the house and took his seat at the head of the table, mopping his sweating face.

'More punch,' he ordered, putting his glass down at his place.

A black woman slave who had been laying the table ladled the drink from the cooler on the sideboard, and turned back to the sideboard to open a bottle of ratafia and one of madeira.

'Pour it! Pour it!' Mr Peabody snapped.

Rowan went quickly out of the room to fetch more dishes as Mr Peabody flicked out a napkin of the finest damask and tucked it in his neckcloth, under his chin. In the kitchen Rowan picked up the pie and the vegetables on solid silver salvers and hurried back to the dining room.

A lady was coming slowly down the stairs, in a white gown of heavy silk with a silk stole thrown over her bare shoulders, diamond earrings in her ears and thick diamond bracelets on her arms. She completely ignored Rowan, who fell back from the doorway, and drew back her chair. She sat without a word of thanks, but she widened her eyes at her husband.

'He's new,' she said and gestured, without speaking, for a glass of ratafia.

'Trying him out.'

She nodded and they sat in silence while the black woman slave passed dishes one to another.

'It's hot,' she remarked to her husband.

His face was buried in his wine glass and he did not reply.

Rowan fetched more dishes, found space for them on the overladen table, and then handed them to Mrs Peabody and her red-faced husband. They served themselves from the dishes that Rowan held out. The slave poured the wine and water in a constant supply, and when one of the serving platters was empty she nodded at Rowan to take it out to the kitchen.

'They ready for the next course?' Cook asked.

'They've not finished everything.'

'You take these and put them on the sideboard. Corree knows when to put them out.'

Rowan took another array of plates, baked cheese, sugared apple, a dish of pears, meat pie and a syllabub. She loaded them on the sideboard and received empty platters from Corree. There was no sound in the room but the loud screeching of the birds in the tree outside, the insistent cooing of the doves, the loud clink and scrape of knives on plates and the noise of Mr Peabody chewing, and greedily gulping wine.

'Excellent dinner, my dear,' he said as Corree and Rowan replaced the dishes with the second course.

'Cook does it,' Mrs Peabody said disdainfully, reaching for the meat pie. 'Did you see Mr Hendon in Bridgetown?'

Samuel Peabody nodded. 'Can't help me,' he said. 'He's got the same problem as everyone. When the cane's ready for harvesting he's got no spare time in the boiling house. He's harvesting next week, same as us.'

'So what'll you do?' She hardly seemed interested.

'I'll have to send to England for the rollers and everything and extend our mill as soon as harvest is over. God knows how much it will cost, and how I will get anyone who knows what he's doing.'

'My Papa said a man was mad to live on the sugarlands without a big enough mill.'

'He said that after we were married,' he told her with quiet resentment. 'Before then, he told me that I could always use the family mill. I didn't know then that your dowry of sugarlands with only a small mill was like a gold mine without a shaft. If I'd known . . .'

Rowan, replacing the empty syllabub bowl with a glass dish filled with preserved cherries, shipped from Boston, wondered what Mr Peabody would have done if he had known.

Dora Peabody laughed at her husband. 'Nobody could know that my brother would sell up.'

'Your brother knew, Madam. Your father knew. Which is why they are sitting in a huge pile of a house in Kent, with a seat in parliament, and I am left trying to make sugar without a big enough boiling house, an old mill and no way to hire the equipment they sold!'

There was a silence. 'So, will you plant coffee instead?' she said indifferently.

'Sugar,' he said dourly. 'Nothing pays as well. And I'll draw up my own plans to enlarge the mill.'

She laughed as if she knew he could not. 'And how are you going to do that?'

He flushed sweaty red and nodded at Rowan. 'He can draw them.'

Dora Peabody turned her pale blue gaze. 'The new one?'

'Can read. Says he can write. Can you draw? What's your name?'

'Ned Ferryman,' Rowan said. 'I can draw.'

'There you are then,' Mr Peabody said to his wife. 'I'll draw up my own plans, I'll buy new rollers, triple rollers. I'll enlarge my own boiling house. I'll make my own sugar. And I'll live long enough to tell your father to his face that he sold me a pup when I married you for two hundred acres and an old mill.'

Dora smiled down the laden table at the man she had married for his name. 'I'm sure you will,' she said pleasantly. 'Now, I'm taking a nap. It's so hot.'

'Can we eat?' Rowan asked. The half-empty serving dishes were like a torture for her to carry back to the kitchen.

'We can eat some,' Cook ruled. 'The meat has to be served cold this evening. But you can get a slice of the end. The fish goes to the servants. The scraps go for the slaves' loblolly.'

Rowan took a slice of the pork from the trencher. The juices rushed into her mouth; it was still warm, tasting of herbs and a little hot seasoning. The fat from the meat was like an elixir of life and she chewed slowly, savouring every moment of it. She closed her eyes. The taste reminded her of her home, of pork traded from the English, roasted over the fire.

'You sure are hungry,' Cook remarked. 'Here. Take some carrot too, and some fish. Don't gorge on meat.'

The carrots were boiled to blandness, but the fish was fried in salted butter. The skin was blackened and crispy, the flesh thick and white. It tasted like the fish they used to barbecue on sticks of pinewood. 'Good,' Rowan said, her mouth full.

The cook laughed at her and turned to give the child a little plate of food.

'Don't you tell I give you meat,' she warned Rowan.

Rowan shook her head. 'Can I drink?'

'Water won't hurt you,' Cook replied. 'Comes from the well.' She gestured to the green glass jug that they had brought from the table. Rowan took a long cool draught.

'Now you help clear up,' Corree spoke for the first time. 'And you got to be waiting when he wakes up. You're his man-servant.' She paused. 'He says you're his valet.' She drew out the word with evident amusement. 'Vallaaay. You know what a valet does?'

Rowan shook her head.

'That don' matter. Neither does he.'

Rowan was given a bed of old cane straw with a square of sail-cloth for a sheet in the house servants' hut at the back of the yard. She would share the hut with Cook, the spit boy, Corree and another maid called Bonny. She was so relieved to be out of the men's cottage that she did not complain that she was given the smallest bed at the doorway.

'What do I do now?' Rowan asked.

'Master'll sleep till sunset,' the girl said. 'You better rest. You look a funny colour.'

Rowan looked at the back of her hand.

'Your face. Like a ghost.'

'I feel like a ghost.'

REEKIE WHARF, LONDON, SPRING 1686

Johnnie, hurrying from his work with the East India Company in Leadenhall Street, a letter crackling in his pocket, strode to the river, summoned a wherry with a shrill whistle and directed it to the Horsleydown Stairs.

At the warehouse he put his head around the door of the counting house. 'Ma – I've come to see Grandmother. I've got news of Rowan, and she'll want my uncle Ned to know.'

His mother came out into the hall, wiping her hands on her apron. 'What news?' she asked shortly.

'She's been sold to a Mr Peabody, he's got a sugar plantation in the north of the island. So at least we know she survived the voyage. She's alive! I came as soon as I got the message.'

'God bless her,' his mother said unenthusiastically. 'Thanks be. So – we are satisfied now?'

He shook his head. 'I'm going out there,' he said. He put his hand out to stop her instant disagreement. 'Let me tell Grandmother first, and then you can break a peal over my head. But I think I should, Ma. I can't settle till I know.'

'Since when was she your burden?' his mother began, but he had slipped upstairs to where Alinor was sitting in the table at her window, and his uncle Ned was propped up on the sofa, his eyes closed, his limbs limp.

Johnnie beckoned Alinor from the room with a jerk of his head and whispered the news to her.

'You shall tell him yourself,' she said.

'Can he hear?'

'Surely.' She took Johnnie by the hand and led him up to the sofa. Ned, shaved and neatly dressed, looked as if he were sleeping, but Johnnie knew that he never opened his eyes.

'Ned, here's our Johnnie with news of Rowan,' Alinor said. Johnnie noticed that she did not speak with special distinction, nor did she raise her voice.

'He can understand?' he confirmed.

She smiled at him. 'He's in there,' she said gently. 'He's just the same as ever. He'll speak when he can.'

Johnnie looked doubtfully at the waxen pallor of the older man.

'Ned,' she said again, even more quietly. 'Here's Johnnie. He has news of Rowan. Of Rowan.'

Only Alinor could have seen the tiny signs of awareness in his face at Rowan's name.

'Go on, Johnnie, tell him!'

Alys appeared in the doorway, a hot drink in her hand. 'Should he have this?'

'In a minute.' Alinor took it from her.

Johnnie pulled the letter from his pocket. 'She's alive,' he said. 'At any rate, she survived the journey.'

Ned's eyes were still closed.

'She's been sold to a planter on Barbados, Mr Peabody.' Johnnie proffered the letter to Ned's sightless face, and then showed it to Alinor instead. 'The captain writes his name clear. Peabody's Plantation, in St Thomas' Parish.'

With enormous effort Ned nodded his head. They could see the muscles in his face strain as his eyelashes fluttered. Slowly, his lips moved, he took an effortful breath, then he spoke. 'Rowan!' he said.

Johnnie shot a glance at his grandmother. Alinor and Alys were holding each other, arms around each other's waists, watching Ned.

'Is that his first word?' he asked, quite awed.

'Praise God,' Alys whispered.

'I knew it,' Alinor said quietly.

'She got there in January, and she was sold on the quayside,' Johnnie went on. 'I had this from the captain of her ship. He doesn't tell me more than that.'

With enormous effort, Ned raised his hand.

'Take his hand,' Alinor prompted Johnnie.

Johnnie stepped forward and took the work-hardened hand in his own soft palm. He had expected his great-uncle to be as cold as death, but his hand was warm. This was a living man who would recover.

Ned's faint grip slowly tightened.

'He'll want to know if you're going to her?' Alinor guessed.

'Aye, we all want to know that,' Alys said under her voice. 'And some of us have an opinion.'

'I am going to her,' Johnnie told Ned. 'I love her – you know that. I'm going to take some stock and set up a little shop, high-quality goods, things that the planters love: silks from our warehouse, and some chinaware, silverware, maybe even some antiquities from Venice. And Mother Alinor will give me some herbs and seeds. I'll set up a little business and I'll buy Rowan out of service on the plantation. I'll buy her servitude. She can keep shop for me, till her time is up.'

The animation left Ned's lined face. He tried to shake his head.

'Leaving your job in the Company?' his mother demanded.

'They'll have me back, Ma. I'm getting leave, not retiring,' Johnnie said firmly. 'So don't try to persuade me.' He spoke more gently to Ned. 'I won't do anything illegal. They're very hard on anyone helping servants escape. I'll get her safe, but I can't set her free. I won't break the law. She'll have to serve her sentence. Ten years.'

Ned was fighting to speak, his eyes still closed but his eyelids fluttering.

'Be calm, Brother. It's the best we can do for her,' Alinor said, coming forward to give Ned the drink. She glanced at Alys. 'Is there laudanum in this?'

'Two drops, as Rob said.'

Ned stirred, tried to speak and Alinor turned to him. 'Hush now. Don't try to do too much. Here's you spoken your first word – praise God for that – and here's Johnnie with the best news we could have hoped for. She's alive and he's going to find her. Rest now.'

PEABODY PLANTATION, BARBADOS, SPRING 1686

Rowan lived her days to serve the sugar harvest, in step with the windmill that turned night and day, the thwack-thwack sound of the sails going through her brief dreams like a beating. The roar of the milling was constant, and the noise of the wagons coming from fields to mill yard and back again, feeding the mill with an endless supply of sugar canes and bringing wood to stoke the fires hotter and hotter under the boiling kettles.

Under a huge yellow moon the slaves cut cane in the fields, slashed the top leaves, trimmed the sticks, bound them into stacks and loaded them onto groaning donkeys and on carts drawn by paired oxen who went by moonlight down the white road back to the mill. As the harvest wore on, and the cutting gang went deeper and deeper into the fields, the journey grew longer and longer down the white stone road; even the animals were exhausted, a mule died in traces. There was no time to eat, gangs were allowed only a few hours' sleep. Slaves staggered like dead men and women from field to their huts and out again. Whenever they stumbled the overseer, high on his horse, would shout a warning and then his horsewhip would crack and someone would cry out in pain. The field gang cut cane all day, every day, and into most of the night. The first gang went out earliest and cut and trimmed the cane, the second gang of older and weaker slaves bundled it and loaded it on the wagons. As soon as the cane was cut it had to be crushed into pulp, or it would dry out and the sugar at its core would be lost. Nobody could slow, nobody dared to weaken. They had to keep up with the rollers in the mill, they had to be as machines themselves – never resting and never stopping, they were ground down like cane.

The wagons unloaded at the back door of the mill, the yard men throwing stack after stack up to the platform where the men slashed open the stack and thrust the cane into the relentless rollers that split the thick stems open and crushed them. They milled the canes through the night, each man terrified of being dragged into the rollers and losing a hand, even an arm. Draining away, below the rollers, was a brown stream of juice, running into the boiling house where it was ladled into the copper kettles.

Smoke from the fires beneath the kettles filled the boiling house, drifted across the yard. In the tropical heat, the endless task of stoking the fire was unendurable. The youngest men and women were tasked with keeping the fires red hot, their faces wet with sweat, their hands pock-marked with burns. Above them, the sugar boilers stood over the open kettles of syrup, skimming the foam, watching the roll of the boil, ordering the pour from one kettle into another as the syrup was purified until finally it was tested by the sugar maker, rolled between his scarred fingers, and poured into a stone cone lined with plantain leaves, to drain until it was crystallised and dry, the drained liquor collected for distilling into rum.

In the rush of harvest, even Mr Peabody rose early and came out into the fields to watch the crop being hacked down, trimmed and loaded, strolled into the boiling house to see the big kettles simmering, swore that it was too hot for a white man to bear, and went back to the big house. He ordered Rowan to walk with him, to learn the process so that she could draw a new design of a bigger and better rolling mill, so that she could write the letters to order new parts from England. 'I'm going to make this go faster,' he promised himself. Rowan looked around at the men and women running to match the speed of the rollers, sweating to feed the fires of the boiling kettles, skimming the simmering syrup. 'I am going to speed this up,' Mr Peabody said.

AVERY HOUSE, LONDON, SPRING 1686

Avery House was going back under wraps. The holland covers were over the beautiful damask chairs in the drawing room, the chandelier in the gallery was bagged in muslin, the kitchen cupboards swept clean of anything but bottled fruit and vegetables to avoid attracting mice, and a housekeeper and her husband were retained for the light tasks of keeping the house clean, locking up safely and guarding against fire and burglars.

James Avery, on the doorstep, watching his goods being loaded in his coach, was surprised to see his wife Livia stroll around the corner, richly gowned in a blue velvet outfit trimmed with fur, her maid a few steps behind her, a royal footman bringing up the rear.

'I thought I might catch you before you left,' she said carelessly to her husband. She threw a quick curious glance at the carriage. 'You're going now?'

He nodded. 'As you see.'

'And the poor house all shut up again.'

'You have no use for it.'

She could not resist brushing past him to peer into the interior of the coach and saw only James' cash box, his writing box and his box of medicines on the silk upholstered seats.

'So she's really not here? She's not going with you?'

Grimly, he shook his head.

'I would have sworn you would have taken her with you, though you told me she would not.'

'I don't lie,' he said conversationally. 'And she does not change her mind.'

'I don't see why not,' she said reasonably. 'If you're both so near to death as you think? If you loved each other so much?'

His crooked smile showed the pain that her words caused him. 'I love her still,' he said quietly.

'But not enough?' she taunted.

'Not enough,' he confirmed.

She laughed. 'Ah well, if you won't quarrel with me then I shall have to send you away with my good wishes. I shan't come to Yorkshire in the summer, you know, we are going to Bath for the queen to take the waters. God knows what will happen.' She lowered her voice. 'They're barely talking and she is worse than ever. It's only the priests that are keeping them together.'

He looked grave. 'I hope her health improves. I have said my farewells to her and to the king, but you might tell her that I wish her very well.'

She gave him her impudent smile. 'The best thing you can do for her is leave me with her,' she said. 'No-one else makes her happy.'

'I am glad she can find any happiness,' he said, still not rising to the bait of her teasing. 'And you may stay with her. I don't want you at my home, not even at my end.'

He took her gloved hand and raised it. He barely touched the perfumed leather with his lips. 'Goodbye,' he said formally. 'I doubt we will meet again.'

'Not in this world,' she said, as if his death meant nothing to her.

'I will be with her in the next,' he said with certainty.

She laughed in his face. '*Allora!* You are very sure. But anyway . . . your will is unchanged? I have my dower as agreed? If you do . . . if you happen to . . .'

He laughed as he turned and climbed the steps into the carriage. 'My dear, you never disappoint me!' he told her. 'It is as we agreed. If I should die this summer, you will have my name, the Dower House for life, and your dower.'

She flushed. 'The entail?'

'The estate goes to my cousin. Matteo gets nothing.'

'This house?' She gestured to the grand London house.

'Goes to my cousin. I assume – as I have always assumed – that Matteo's father will provide for him, or you will.'

'Oh! His father?' she said smiling, as if it were a private joke. 'Would you like to know his name? To take to your grave?'

'Whoever he is does not matter to me anymore.'

The footman folded the steps into the carriage and closed the door. She stepped forward and James lowered the glass of the window so that she could whisper.

'You have no jealousy?' she asked. 'Is that why you won't leave your own stepson a bequest – what about the house? Avery House? You could leave it to him and prove to me that you are not jealous?'

He shook his head, leaning back against the silk squabs of the carriage. 'I have only loved one woman, and that was never you. I feel nothing – no jealousy, nothing. And I won't leave Avery House to Matteo, for – whoever he is – he is not an Avery, and I respect my name.'

Pale with irritation, she stepped back, and James raised the window at once. The footman swung up behind and the coach moved away.

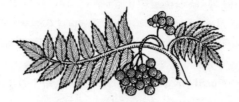

HATTON GARDEN, LONDON, SPRING 1686

The two girls, Mia and Gabrielle, escorted by their cousin Matthew, arrived at Rob's front door, as the waiting footman threw it open.

Mia turned on the step to Matthew. 'Why don't you come in?' she asked.

Hester appeared in the hall behind her. 'Oh yes, do come in, Cousin Matthew.'

Matthew hovered, torn between wanting to stay with his cousins and fear of intruding.

'I don't—'

'She never comes down in the mornings,' Gabrielle told him. 'It's only Hester and her governess in the mornings. And he's always out.'

Matthew grinned at her quickness in understanding him, pulled off his hat and stepped into the hall.

'Come into the library,' Hester invited them.

The three visitors followed Hester down the hall to the large panelled room at the back of the house where tall windows overlooked the gardens. Matthew looked around, seeing the walls of books, the bright fire in the grate, the jug of lemon water, the biscuits and the glasses. 'This is nice,' he said.

'Better than your little crow's nest?' Mia teased him. Turning to Hester she said: 'Matthew has a bedroom where he is supposed to study at the top of a winding stair at Lincoln's Inn. He's something between a clerk and a kestrel.'

'I wasn't allowed in here at all till you two came,' Hester said.

'Why not?' Gabrielle asked.

Hester opened her mouth but could not embark on the lengthy explanation of why her Mama did not want her educated beyond the limits of genteel ignorance. 'There's no point,' was all she said.

Matthew understood, but the Venice-born girls did not. 'You need to be able to calculate at least,' said Gabrielle, the Venice trader's daughter.

'And to read a map, and speak languages,' said Mia. 'At least Italian and French.'

Hester flushed. 'Mama says that elegant manners are more important than books,' she said. 'And Miss Prynne teaches them in the parlour.'

'Oh stuff!' Mia said.

Matthew frowned at her. 'That's not elegant speech for a young lady.'

She gave him a cheeky smile. 'I don't want to be elegant; I want to be well read.'

He gestured to the heavy grandeur of the room. 'But here, Mia . . . and with . . .' His gesture took in Hester, 'you have to . . .'

'Are you going to finish any of those sentences?' she challenged him.

'He means to say that you may not corrupt me with your careless speech when in my father's library,' Hester said solemnly, causing them all to collapse into giggles, Mia clapping her hand over her mouth and Matthew waving his hands at them: 'Hush! Hush!'

'Not corrupt!' Gabrielle hissed, catching her breath. 'Not corrupt, Hester. That's much worse. We're just . . .' she looked for the words, 'making you more commonplace,' she finished.

'Less ladylike and more sensible,' Mia added.

Matthew nodded. 'And you shouldn't,' he told the two older girls. 'Hester here has been raised very carefully, as her father wants. You shouldn't come in here and laugh at that.'

Hester flushed, looking up at him. 'I'm not dull.'

She caught his attention. 'I didn't mean that! You're not dull, Cousin Hester. Actually, you're rather exquisite.'

She flushed a rosy red and Gabrielle and Mia looked at her with new attention.

'Anyway, we don't come in and laugh at ridiculous things, truly we don't,' Mia assured Matthew. 'We just do our lessons, and she likes that – don't you, Hester? She was lonely in this big house with nobody but her governess to talk to – anybody would be – only seeing her Ma in the afternoons, and her Pa out with his patients all day. We're company. And anyway, we're family.'

Hester swallowed a rush of emotion. 'I like them very much,' she assured Matthew. 'And of course, we're all family. I'm going to ask my Papa if I can visit the wharf. Would you take me to visit, sometimes?'

'I shouldn't even be here,' Matthew said, more and more uncomfortable at these challenges to the silent authority of the house. 'I'm only supposed to bring them to the door.'

'Are you going on to Lincoln's Inn?' Gabrielle asked him. 'Staying there tonight?'

'Yes, but I'll meet you at the Holborn Stairs to walk you here on Thursday,' he told her, and saw a little colour rise in her cheek. 'Tuesdays and Thursdays.'

'All right,' she said.

'Please come in, on Thursday morning too,' Hester told him.

'Thank you,' Matthew said awkwardly. 'But perhaps I . . .'

'Why ever not?' Mia challenged him. 'We're all cousins, aren't we?'

He looked from one young face to another. 'Not really,' he said. 'You three are cousins but I'm only your foster cousin. So I shouldn't visit Hester unless her father invites me. And not without a chaperone.'

Hester's face cleared at once. 'Oh, I'll ask Papa to invite you,' she said simply.

'What's wrong with that?' Mia demanded, seeing he was not reassured.

'I don't know what he'll say,' he confessed. 'It's not as if I was really a member of the family.'

Gabrielle gently touched his shoulder, as if she could not stop herself. 'Doesn't matter to us,' she told him. 'You can still walk us here. If we have to say goodbye on the doorstep then at least we've seen you.'

'But if he only walks you, then when will I see him?' Hester asked plaintively.

Mia looked from one to the other. 'You're in demand,' she said to Matthew with a knowing smile. 'A seller's market.'

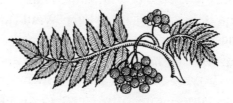

REEKIE WHARF, LONDON, SPRING 1686

Johnnie's trade goods for Barbados were packed and ready for shipping at Reekie Wharf. Sarah had sent a new consignment of silk and china from Venice, and a collection of small furniture pieces, writing boxes, pot-pourri boxes, trinket boxes and sandalwood chests for hats and gloves.

'They're hard to pack safely,' Alys said, going through the cargo manifest. 'She's put them inside one another wherever she could and sewed them into oilcloth. But you'll have to keep them dry, or they'll warp on the way.'

Johnnie nodded.

'And your grandmother has made up a stock of tisane bags, and put up some seeds of herbs for you to sell. She's sent cases of bottles from the still room at Foulmire.'

'Do we have any of my uncle Ned's herbs left? The sassafras?'

'Yes. I've given you a barrel. But I don't know what they grow themselves.'

'They've turned over the whole island to sugar,' Johnnie told her. 'That's what one of the sugar merchants told me. They grow nothing but sugar on every field. It pays so well that they neither make nor grow anything for themselves. That's why it's so profitable for us to trade there.'

'Until the crop fails on them,' she said sourly. 'Like the coffee did. Like the tobacco did.'

'Sugar won't fail,' Johnnie promised. 'Everyone wants it, and only the Sugar Islands can grow it. Only slaves can brew it. The wealth of the planters has to be seen to be believed, he was telling me.'

'The great men are wealthy, but what about the others?'

Johnnie checked. 'You're not becoming a Leveller like your uncle, are you, Ma? If there weren't rich and poor, how would any of us make a profit?'

'There's such a thing as usury profit,' she said. 'Grievous profit.'

'I'm going to put my profit to good use,' he protested. 'I'll buy Rowan out of her service and she can manage my warehouse for me, the profit will set her free and make us a living.'

'You won't stay there till her time is up,' she said flatly. 'Not for ten years. Say you won't. I didn't raise you to see you go overseas to a fever coast for half your life.'

'No, no,' he assured her. 'I'll come home as soon as I've found her. Then I'll go out again when it's time to fetch her. We're traders!' Johnnie told her. 'We're bound to go where the market goes. And there's nowhere in the world richer than Barbados.'

ST JAMES' PALACE, LONDON, SPRING 1686

The court was in a solemn mood, attending the opening of yet another new chapel near the palace, this one commissioned and sanctified by the Papal Nuncio, Ferdinand d'Adda. A long procession of clerics and priests preceded the king and queen down the aisle. The choristers took their places in the beautifully carved wooden choir stalls, the priests behind the gilt rood screen, the king and queen in thrones on the chancel steps, the court in strict order of precedence in the pews: ladies before the lady chapel where a statue of Mary smiled down at them, gentlemen behind the king on the west side.

Only a few members of court were brave enough to refuse. Lord Middleton prided himself on his ignorance; Lord Peterborough, ostentatiously crossing himself, would keep his pew in his parish protestant church, St Margaret's Westminster, so that he could return to the fold at any time. Anyone who wanted royal favour or even a place at court rushed to be baptised into the faith. Even Nell Gwynne who had called herself the 'protestant whore' now attended the royal chapel, knowing very well that a woman has to work to keep the favour of a king; on her back or on her knees alike.

Livia – doubly blessed in being born roman catholic and being the queen's most intimate friend – knelt behind her royal mistress the picture of devotion, her gaze raking the congregation but her attention always returning, anxiously, to the queen at her prie dieu. She was proudly upright, her eyes on the monstrance;

but Livia knew that it was only determination that held Mary Beatrice up through long ceremonial occasions like this one.

Livia thought that the royal observers who predicted that the queen would die and that James would marry the daughter of the Grand Duke of Tuscany were probably right. And then, thought Livia grimly, if my own husband dies and leaves me as the Dowager Lady Avery, with nothing but a miserable dower house in Yorkshire – what future is there for me? My walk behind her coffin will be the last time I am close to the Queen of England. A new one from Tuscany is not going to need me to hold her in bed at night while she cries for loneliness. I will have nothing for myself, and nothing to give Matteo. Can it be that I have done all that I have done, to win nothing more than Foulmire Priory for him? For the woman my husband loved instead of me? Have I been through all this, to end up as a respectable widow, scraping a living on my dower, in a damp manor house on the edge of a bottomless mire?

REEKIE WHARF, LONDON, SUMMER 1686

The whole family turned out to see Johnnie off on his great adventure. The young man, who had said that he would never stray from his desk at the East India Company, was leaving his country for the first time. His ship, the *Bonaventure*, stopped at Reekie quay to load his goods. Alinor with Ned, seated in a chair from the parlour, were already on the quayside to say their farewells; Alys, Matthew, Gabrielle and Mia were lined up beside them. Even Rob took a wherry downriver from his patients to shake Johnnie's hand and give him a bottle of laudanum for pain and fever.

Matthew glanced at Mia. 'I should like to travel,' he said. 'Maybe go to Italy, maybe see your home?'

She shrugged. 'It takes forever and you have only a cramped cabin and when there's a storm, you are thrown around like a pea in a rattle.'

'But to see the world!'

'I swear all you see are waves.'

Matthew stepped up to Johnnie. 'Good luck, Uncle Johnnie,' he said, slapping him on the back. 'Good luck.'

Johnnie laughed, hugged Matthew, kissed his nieces, and paused before his mother, Alys.

'Now here's the manifest,' she said business-like, handing over the list of his cargo. 'All safely stowed.'

'Ma,' he hesitated.

'God speed,' she said tightly. 'Send us a message as soon as you're safe into Bridge.'

'I will, I will.'

Her face was set firm against emotion, her jaw clamped so that she did not cry out to him not to go.

'I love you, Ma,' he said simply. 'I'll come home again.'

'God bless,' she said shortly, hugged him, and stepped back.

Ned could stretch out a hand but could not frame words. His dark eyes stared up at Johnnie as if there was much that he would say.

'I'll find her,' Johnnie promised. 'I'll find her, and I'll make sure that she's safe. When she's served her time, if she wants it, I'll marry her and bring her home. If she wants something else, she can say. She'll be free.'

Ned nodded, his hand tried to grip.

'You can trust me.'

Johnnie kissed his grandmother. 'Grandmother . . .'

'I've packed you a case of herbs for the journey,' she said. 'Don't drink the water anywhere that the air smells rank. And boil all the water that you use.'

'I know.'

She looked at him, as if she would see past the quayside and the waiting ship to his future. 'Goodbye, my dearest boy,' she said solemnly. 'We won't meet again.'

He checked. 'Grandmother!'

She smiled at him, quite unafraid. 'I think not, Johnnie. But you remember this – great wealth or position is not a right, and you don't deserve it however hard you work. It is chance, and the labour of others that brings a man wealth. Don't forget that others have earned your fortune for you. Never imagine you deserve it.'

'I will! I promise! I'll remember this. And I'll make a fortune and bring it home to you!' He bent down so that Ned could hear his promise. 'I'm going as a trader, not a planter. I'm going to free her, not to enslave anyone. Don't fear for me.'

Alinor nodded and held Ned's hand as Johnnie ran up the gangplank and they loaded it behind him; the girls and Matthew waved. Johnnie stood at the rail and waved to them until the barges drew the ship into mid-river and then he threw a triumphant salute to the shore and went down to his cabin.

FOULMIRE PRIORY, SUSSEX, SUMMER 1686

As soon as she had seen Johnnie set sail Alinor was anxious to take Ned to Foulmire – their childhood home.

'On your own?' Matthew asked.

Alinor smiled at him. 'There's a house full of servants.'

'Of course,' he hesitated. 'Does Ma say it's all right for you and Uncle Ned to go?'

'You know full well she doesn't!' Alinor told him with a

twinkle in her eye. 'But I'm going if you say I may – it's your house, Matthew, I'm not going to take squatters' rights.'

'No! No! Of course you can go. I'll hire a carriage to take you. But what if Uncle Ned gets worse while you're down there?'

'He won't get worse,' Alinor said confidently. 'He's going to get better.'

The carriage journey was hard for Ned, jolting on the poor roads. Alinor had told him where they were going; but he made no sign of understanding, and lay across the seat, his eyes closed against the bright light and the pain.

Only when the carriage stopped at the causeway did he open his eyes when the briny air flooded into the carriage and the wide sky arched over them. He heard the crying of the gulls and the twitter of the little terns over the bright water of the harbour. Incredulously, he turned his head to Alinor and met her radiant smile.

'I've brought you home,' she told him.

Every night as she put him to bed, she prayed for Rowan's safety, naming her clearly in the prayers and Ned said 'Amen', the word more distinct and his voice stronger every night. Every day, she walked beside his wheeled chair, showing him the lush growth of summer in the tidelands, the scramble of dog roses through the hedges, the thickness of the grass in the meadow and the lambs prancing in the fields like little dancers. Huge flocks of seabirds came and went with the tides and the little terns hovered over the blue waters of the harbour and nested, laying eggs like speckled pebbles on the shingle banks, so that Alinor stopped walking there until the tiny birds were fledged and flying, skimming the water like silver-winged swallows. She talked to Ned all the time of the little changes in the garden and on the land and at sea, until slowly, over the summer, he learned, like a child, to walk and speak again.

On Midsummer Eve Alinor went to the churchyard at

midnight and stood in the graveyard while the bell in the tower tolled twelve times. She looked towards the graveyard, her hand shading her eyes, dreading that someone she loved would come slowly through the gravestones. She was afraid she would see her brother Ned, as a warning that he would not outlast the year. But deeper than any other fear was that she would see her lover James Avery come slowly through the moonlit churchyard where he had once walked before.

But she saw no-one: not Johnnie at sea nor Rowan, enslaved, so far away. Content that her family and those she loved would live another year, Alinor went home under a huge round strawberry moon so bright that she blew out the lantern and walked along the hedgerow, a silent white-winged barn owl going before her, a moon-shadow behind her.

REEKIE WHARF, LONDON, SUMMER 1686

Twice a week, on Tuesdays and Thursdays, Alys put Mia and Gabrielle into Mr Jonas Rode's wherry and waved them off from the Horsleydown Stairs, watching him row upriver, sometimes going easily with the tide, sometimes working against it. Where the water was rough under London Bridge, he set them on shore and picked them up again on the far side at Beaufort Waterman's Stairs, even when they begged him to let them shoot the bridge in the boat, like daredevils.

'And have your grandmother gut me like a pilchard?' was all he would say, rowing them upriver past the old dock of Queenhithe, and Puddle Dock.

'And here we are, Venice itself!' he announced proudly, every time that he turned the wherry into the New Canal.

Dutifully, the two girls laughed at his joke; but it was true that the broad quays on either side of the wide water had been designed to resemble the pavements of Venice, the water and the bridges to resemble the canals. The New Canal in London was not nearly as busy as the Grand Canal in Venice; there were no gondolas arrowing through the water, no queues of *sandoli*: flat-bottomed boats carrying goods to market; there were no singers warbling in closed cabins, or beautiful masked women parading on the quaysides. To the girls it was eerily quiet, a beautiful broad waterway through the city, passing under one elegant new bridge after another, between wide wharves of stone, fronted by warehouses still standing empty, as tenants swore the rents were overpriced. At Holborn Stairs, Mr Rode the wherryman held the iron ring to keep the craft against the steps, glaring upwards to make sure that Matthew was waiting to meet them.

'Aye, there he is,' he would say. 'Always punctual, I'll say that for him. Young ladies, you can disembark. All ashore!'

'Thank you,' Gabrielle said politely as Mia stepped from the wherry and went up the steps to Matthew.

'And I'll be here to take you home an' all,' the wherryman assured her. 'Don't you step into another boat. I am to come for you. Your grandma, Mrs Shore, paid me for the return journey.'

Grandly, Matthew offered his arm to each girl and escorted them along Holborn, past vendors of little goods, milk maids and beggars, across the busy thoroughfare to the quieter and more elegant area of Hatton Garden. They walked three abreast, Matthew in the middle with the girls on either side of him, and more than once, some street wag shouted: 'Don't be greedy!' Or 'Share 'em out!' Both girls, strictly raised by their mother, neither glanced nor responded to cat-calls, and though Matthew bristled slightly at the impertinence, he felt a hidden glow of pride that he was escorting two pretty girls. They were good companions, striding easily at his pace, always chattering, whether it was news from the warehouse, what they were studying, or gossip from the scandal sheets about the royal court.

'How d'you even know such things?' Matthew demanded when they gave him the details of the queen's dress at a dinner where she had eaten nothing.

'Prynne gets the news-sheet, and hides it from Hester, in a Latin book in the doctor's library,' Mia said demurely. 'We read it when we're supposed to be drinking chocolate and resting from the enormous effort of reading a book.'

Matthew could not contain his laughter. 'You are a pair of romps.'

They paused to cross Hatton Garden to Rob Reekie's door which proudly showed the doctor's special brass door knocker.

'I'll come home again on Thursday to walk you over,' Matthew promised. 'But after that, Trinity term ends for the summer.' He hesitated, suddenly awkward, intensely aware of the two girls. 'Shall we all go down to Foulmire and stay with Mother Alinor and Uncle Ned? They're down there for the summer.' He felt himself flushing and looked from one bright face to another. 'I mean … I am going … I have to go anyway … would you like …'

'Oh yes!' Gabrielle said. 'I do love it there. Do let's go.'

'You do?' Matthew asked, trying to recover.

'I do too,' Mia said quickly, and her sister glanced at her.

'We both do,' Gabrielle assured him.

'I'm sure Mother Alinor would be glad to see us,' Matthew said.

'Why would she not want us?' Mia demanded. 'We're very charming.'

'You are!' he smiled.

The footman opened the door and the girls turned to go in. Matthew looked up and saw Hester, waiting at the window. He waved to her.

'I wish Hester could come too,' Gabrielle remarked.

'She'd never be allowed,' Mia said quickly.

'It's a pity,' he remarked. As he walked away he glanced back. Hester was at the window watching him go. She raised her hand.

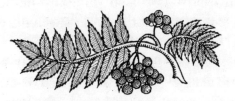

PEABODY PLANTATION, BARBADOS, SUMMER 1686

Rowan, now better fed and better housed than the other white servants who worked in the garden and stables, and far better treated than the slaves, was still exhausted at the end of every day, and aching with weariness at dawn. She slept in snatches through the night, cross-legged on the floor of the hall, as Mrs Peabody would not allow her on the chairs, as if she were a dog with fleas. She dozed with a musket laid across her lap, getting up every so often to walk the outside perimeter of the gardens, looking into the outbuildings, into the eerily silent mill standing over the cold boiling house, and then walking down the white stone track to the slave quarters looking for any light, or any disturbance, any thieves or rebels. She could feel the grief in the hot still air of the night; sometimes she heard sobbing.

At dawn, her watch was over, and before she rang the bell to turn the slaves out of their quarters, Rowan went through the cane fields to the creek that cut through the fields on the east side. This was the only place in the plantation that she ever felt that she could breathe. The steep craggy sides of the cliff that fell down to the river were too sheer for any crop; not even the English could drive slaves down the rock face and make them hoe. Here, the old thick jungle of the island could not be cleared; the water trickled out of the side of the rock and dripped down in little waterfalls to the river below. Rowan scrambled down to where clear water trickled into a little pool, stripped naked and paddled into the water, faced east and looked at the lightening sky through the canopy of trees.

'Great Spirit, Mother Earth, Grandmother Moon, Grandfather Sun, I thank you. I pray to the four directions.' Carefully, she bowed to the rising sun and then in all directions. 'I thank you for all my relations: the winged nation, the creeping and crawling nation, the four-legged nation, the green and growing nation, and all things living in the water. Honouring the clans: the deer – *ahtuk*, the bear – *mosq*, the wolf – *mukquoshim*, the turtle – *tunnuppasog*, the snipe – *sasasō. Keihtanit taubot neanawayean.*'

She knew there were no bear here, no wolf, that the turtles were overturned and scooped out of their shells while alive, the snipe shot for amusement, but she whispered their names and honoured them and saw the sun filter through the ceiling of leaves. She heard the monkeys chatter high in the treetops and the insistent calling of the doves. For a moment, her bare feet in the stream, the patter of cold water on her head, running down her face and neck, Rowan was one of the People, and when the sun rose over the side of the creek she knew she was once again in Dawnlands.

'You go all that way to wash in a stream?' Cook asked, as Rowan came into the house servants' hut, in a damp shirt with wet hair, smelling of clean water.

Rowan nodded.

'Why you don' wash in the wash-house?'

'I like the spring water.'

'At dawn? You say prayers?'

Rowan nodded. 'I'm baptised,' she said hastily. 'I'm Christian.' Passing for Christian, like passing as white, was a slim guarantee of safety against abuse. Being Christian and white was to claim the master status – one of the owners of everything: a servant, not a slave.

Cook hunched an irritable shoulder. 'You think I care? I don' care. I jus' going to tell you that there's a slave woman who comes out of her hut at dawn and faces the sun and washes and prays too.'

'Is there?' Rowan was suddenly attentive. 'Prays and washes in the morning?'

'So – you want to know now?'

'Does she wash in the creek?'

'How she going to get to the creek? She's a slave. Can't go nowhere but from hut to cane field and back again. She wash' outside her hut sayin' things. I seen her.'

'Where is she?'

Cook pulled on her skirt, thrust her feet into painful clogs. 'She'll be goin' to the fields now,' she said. 'Workin' all day. Comin' back at dusk. Growin' her own food. Feedin' her child. Sleepin' if she can. Cryin'. Like all of us.'

Rowan was already out of the door, striding towards the slave huts. She knew her way around them, as she searched them with Mr Peabody once a week and patrolled them every night. She had never seen anyone who looked like one of the People; but she had been too ashamed to raise her eyes from her own ill-fitting boots except to rake over some poor stores, or poke the end of a whip into a bed of corn cobs.

She hesitated outside the women's quarters. There were well-tended gardens growing cassava for bread, plantain, papaya and pigeon peas, in straight rows, scratched into the earth, to make weeding and watering easier. But one garden was a tumble of plants grown together, corn tall and straight, the bean plants scrambling up the stems of the corn, fat pumpkins throwing their vines across the soil and blocking weeds. Thousands of ants that were everywhere on Barbados swarmed across the leaves of the pumpkin but did not climb the stalk of the corn to spoil the cobs nor the beans that twisted around the stalk. Rowan stared disbelievingly. It was her mother's garden, her grandmother's garden, the garden they made in the woods in a clearing every spring: the garden of the three sisters. A garden of three plants based on the three stars that came out to tell the People when the ground was ready for planting. The three sisters were the stars in the sky, the three sisters were the plants in the garden: corn, beans and pumpkins, that gave a complete meal from one garden, that supported each other and even fed the soil. Only one of the People would make a garden like this, the three sisters' constellation only shone on the Dawnlands, only the People had been taught to see the stars and plant the gardens.

'Whose is this?' she called out to a passing black man.

He stopped at once and replied, his eyes on the ground, obedient to the slightest word from a white man.

'It' her',' he said simply, pointing through the doorway of the women's quarters. 'Kitonckquêi.'

'Kitonckquêi?' Rowan yelped at the Pokanoket word for 'ghost'. 'You sure?'

'Sure,' he said. 'Sure.'

He waited until Rowan made a gesture to release him and then he set off at a run to catch up with the gang of slaves headed for the cane fields. The women were coming out of the hut to follow the field gangs, tying their heads with strips of old linen, some of them pulling on hats. All of them were bowed with pain, some of them hobbling from old wounds from land crabs, some of them with brands on a cheek or forehead. They flinched when they saw a white boy standing in their gardens; someone muffled a little cry that he would kick the plants over.

'Which is Kitonckquêi?' Rowan demanded. She shuddered as she said the word. 'Which one calls herself Kitonckquêi?'

A ripple of fear and concern moved down the line. Someone pointed, someone said something very quietly. One woman, a hat shading her head, a young boy beside her, put the child behind her as if to shield him from the malevolent white gaze.

'I, Kitonckquêi,' she said.

Rowan waved the others to go to work, to leave them alone. Kitonckquêi pushed her boy after them, as if the gruelling cane fields were safer for him than standing before a young white man. She raised her head to look at Rowan and they saw each other, for the first time. Each of them took in the straight black hair, the brown skin, the direct gaze, the unmistakable poise of a hunter: each saw another one of the People.

'*Nenomous*,' Rowan said falteringly in her own language, looking into the half-starved face for recognition. 'I am of the People. *Tow wow* – I am your sister. I am *Squi minneash sookenon*, daughter of *Séquan wuskuhwhan*.'

The woman looked at her incredulously, stared as if she would see through the signs of privilege – the boots, the clothes, the hat. She stared at Rowan's deer-black eyes, saw that she stood, even in a man's old boots, as a girl who has been raised barefoot, saw the slope of her shoulders and the starved thinness of her face, heard the beloved words of her own people. The words that the victors declared should never be spoken.

'I am Caskwadadas,' she said quietly.

'Why call yourself Kitonckquêi? Why name yourself for a ghost?' Rowan demanded. 'Why name yourself as a dead woman?'

The woman shrugged, her spread hands indicated the tiny garden, the poor crowded hut, the desert of green cane all around them. 'We are all dying here,' she said simply. 'The only question is the hour of my death.'

Rowan took a breath. 'I am Red Berries in the Rain,' she repeated. 'Grand-daughter of Quiet Squirrel. We lived at Norwottuck and in summer, at the sea. Are there others of the Dawnland here?'

'Not here,' Caskwadadas said. 'There was one and he died. I have to go,' she said, looking up the white dusty road after the field gang. 'I will be beaten if you make me late.'

'I'll come and say I delayed you . . .' Rowan offered.

The woman shook her head. 'Better that I am not seen with you,' she said. 'Alone, you pass as white, just as I pass as living.'

'But I must see you again!' Rowan said urgently. 'We are the same people. Perhaps I can help? They think I am an Englishman, that my name is Ned Ferryman. I work in the house, I can bring you food.'

'Can you bring food for my son?' For the first time she looked into Rowan's eyes.

'Yes, I can. I will.'

'Can you come tonight?'

'Tonight, before moonrise, at the darkest time.'

The woman nodded and started after the slave gang.

'I will come,' Rowan promised. 'I will bring food. You are not a dead woman. You are not alone.'

She said nothing and Rowan watched her hurry after the field gang. Her head bowed but her stride was long and smooth, the lope of a hunter.

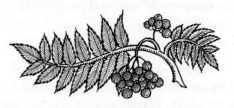

ST JAMES' PALACE, LONDON, SUMMER 1686

The queen's drawing room reception was a formal event held every month, for the court to spend the evening in conversation, flirtation and conspiracy, with card tables for those who had nothing to say. Visitors from the country could be presented to the queen and meet their town friends. Young men and women entering society could be presented by parents or sponsors, make their bow to the queen and sometimes glimpse the king who often dropped in to see men of influence or visiting ambassadors.

Mary Beatrice had loved the drawing rooms when she was a young duchess, not much older than the girls who now came to make their curtsey to her. In those days she had been the prettiest girl in the room and the centre of attention. King Charles had petted her, her husband, his brother, had kissed her hand before everyone, and even her sister-in-law Queen Catherine had smiled on her.

Mary Beatrice had held few drawing rooms of her own, since her coronation a year ago. With a rebellion in the north and west of the country, and bitter opposition in the heart of the city, the councillors had advised it was not safe. The king's attention was completely claimed by his religious advisors, his new army, and – until the start of this year – his mistress Catherine Sedley, so she had not wanted to open her doors to the elite world or to hear the gossip.

'But you are queen, and should be seen,' Livia told her.

'You're bored of these four walls,' Mary Beatrice said, looking around at her beautiful bedroom. She was seated before her mirror as the lady-in-waiting inserted false ringlets of hair into the queen's rich tresses and secured them with diamond pins.

'I want to see you at the heart of your court enjoying yourself.'

She managed a smile. 'I can't enjoy myself.'

'You might,' Livia encouraged her. 'And the king might visit.'

Mary Beatrice picked up a hand mirror and looked closely at her powdered face and then turned to see the back of her hair. 'Very pretty,' she said indifferently, to the lady-in-waiting who held a comb for any last-minute changes. 'I'll go like this.'

She stood; a maid of honour threw a fur-trimmed stole around the queen's bare shoulders and adjusted it so that it framed her shoulders, her neck and her beautiful face. Livia felt a pang of envy for the silk embroidered stole, the flawless beauty of the skin. She stepped forward and put a kiss on the rouged lips. 'You're irresistible,' she told her. 'I want to keep you all to myself.'

Mary Beatrice laughed and led the way through her privy chamber to the drawing room. They could hear the musicians playing as the double doors opened and everyone turned. All the women dropped into deep curtseys and the men bowed. Livia, following the Queen of England, the most favoured of all the ladies-in-waiting, smiled this way and that, sometimes nodding to total strangers, to demonstrate her wide acquaintance. 'How do you do?' she said to a slightly familiar face. 'Good day,' she said to another. She drew the gaze from the pale queen who settled herself on her throne without a word to anyone, as Livia, beautifully at ease, took her place standing beside the queen and looked around with all the confidence of a woman who knows that she is the favourite.

Livia nodded to the footmen at the doors to admit anyone who was dressed elegantly enough to indicate wealth. English nobility, ambassadors and their ladies, visiting lords and royalty were admitted without question and came up to the queen, seated on her blue silk chair, to be greeted with her sweet smile. City gentlemen who had made a fortune might be admitted if their jackets were richly embroidered and their shoes studded with stones that passed for diamonds. Only ladies of known good family could waft in past the equerries who knew one carriage from another and would turn away anyone of inferior status.

'May I present Lady Winterton and her daughters, Miss Sarah Winterton and Miss Winterton?' One of the courtiers stood forward and three ladies, the girls walking with studied care, curtseyed without mishap and stood, mute, before the queen. Livia smiled graciously, the queen asked them a question each about the weather, and if the streets were crowded, and the three curtseyed again and drifted off to one side to whisper to each other and look around.

The next to come forward to curtsey was a young lady from the Sugar Islands, her gown the finest that would be seen that day, her face thickly powdered to whiten her skin, darkened from the constant sunshine. The queen inquired of her mother if their journey had been long and arduous and was assured that it had been easy, they would do it again, they intended to visit England regularly, it was their home after all ... Livia feigned interest, gently gestured when they should step aside and, glancing up to see who was coming next, was stunned to see the doors opening on Catherine Sedley.

There was a gasp of amazement. Catherine did not bother to hide her amusement.

'You didn't expect to see me so soon?' she demanded of the room and sashayed forward to curtsey to the queen. She dipped down as low, as courtesy demanded, but came up beaming.

'Lady Sedley? We thought you were in Dublin,' Livia said sharply as the queen froze.

'I couldn't stay there forever,' Catherine said frankly. 'I couldn't abide it. I missed you all too much.' She laughed loudly at her own joke. 'Why should I not come home? I've got a beautiful house in London standing empty and all my friends are here. And people missed me. I can name one who did!'

'Was your journey an easy one?' the queen whispered, overwhelmed by the cheerful defiance.

'Just as easy as it was going,' Catherine declared. 'The king sent his own carriages for me. I travelled like royalty, with outriders all the way.'

Mary Beatrice went white and leaned back into the throne as if she were fainting. Livia stepped before her to shield her from the court. 'I'm sure we're very blessed in your return,' she said acidly. 'We are all very happy to see you again even for a short stay.'

'Oh no—' Catherine began.

'I am sure it will be a short stay,' Livia repeated, making the woman laugh out loud.

'I'll come and go as I please,' she said. 'I'm a free-born Englishwoman and I shall do as I please. I have Magna Carta to defend my rights, I am not an Italian with no law to defend me.' Her bright gaze raked the room, spotted a few priests. 'Or a poor papist who has to do as the priests say.'

Livia stepped down from the dais and took Catherine firmly by the elbow. 'How completely fascinating,' she breathed. 'You must tell me more. Over here. In the window embrasure. Out of the way. So we're not centre of the stage. *Allora!* What a surprise you are!'

The thunderclap that broke over the king's head at the triumphant return of his mistress was delivered by his confessor, his chaplain and the Papal Nuncio himself. It was enough to send Catherine Sedley to a discreet country house outside London – Ham House on the river bank at Weybridge – but not enough to drive her from court. Instead, the king's hunting trips often took that direction and he did not come back for the rest of the day. It was an open secret that she returned his visits, coming to court in the afternoons, entering the palace by the back stairs, spending half the day with him in the rooms belonging to Mr William Chiffinch, the page of the back stairs whose entire life was devoted to hiding secret visitors: priests, spies and the king's mistresses.

Livia held the deserted young queen while she cried, rocked her as if she were a child. '*Silenziosa*,' she said. 'Hush. Your heart will mend, you're young. You are the queen. She is nothing to you.'

'She is everything to him! He wouldn't have had her back if he could have been happy without her. He has been wanting her and missing her for all this time. I wish I was dead, and then he could marry her!'

'If you were dead, he wouldn't marry her,' Livia said, knowing full well that princesses were being lined up all around Europe for the king's next wife; the daughter of the Grand Duke of Tuscany was buying furs for the cold English winters. If this frail young woman died of a broken heart then her place would be taken within a year. 'She's a mistress, she'll never be queen.'

'Why does he want her so much, and not me?' Mary Beatrice's face was tragic, her dark eyes brimming with tears, her mouth trembling. 'What is wrong with me, that he cannot love me?'

Livia, overwhelmed with pity and tenderness, drew the young woman into her arms again, kissed the tears on her wet eyelashes, her soft mouth, kissed her hot cheeks, her perfumed neck, pulled down the ribboned neck of the gown to kiss the tops of her rounded breasts. 'He's mad,' she said, caressing with her lips. 'He must be mad not to prefer you to every woman in the world.'

'Do you really love me?' the queen asked pitiably.

'I do,' Livia swore. 'I will be more faithful than any husband. I am yours till death.'

PEABODY PLANTATION,
BARBADOS, AUTUMN 1686

It was planting season in the cane fields, and the first gang was digging out holes for the new canes. The field looked like a chess board, divided into deep squares, the sides heaped high with a bank of earth. They laid the cane pieces along each square and filled them up with muck from the night soil pit and the stables. The stink was unbearable: the night soil seeped into their hair from the baskets on their heads and could not be cleaned from their fingernails. Little cuts became raw and poisoned, people got ulcers at their mouths and eyes and a vomiting sickness.

Rowan was afraid that Caskwadadas would get sick, as she raked and watered the dung pits. Every night Rowan paused in the dark shadow behind the women slaves' shed.

'*Tow wow*,' she whispered, 'Sister,' and Caskwadadas would appear in the doorway like a shadow, and then blend with the shadows behind the hut.

Rowan would pull a stolen bundle of food from the pockets of her baggy breeches and Caskwadadas would take it with a word of thanks.

'You are well?' Rowan asked in their language. 'It is easier now?'

The woman nodded. 'It's better with the food. But my son – Wómpatuck – he's getting too old for the women's hut and working beside me. They'll take him away when he is twelve and make him work with the men.'

Rowan hissed through her teeth. 'I didn't know they did that.'

'He'll have to go into the men's huts and work in the men's work gang. He can't do it. He can't carry the weights they have to carry, he can't load the cart. He can't bring in cane, not even in the second gang. He's too light, and he's too short.'

'Can you lie about his age? Keep him with you another year?'

'They know his age well enough. It was only that he was too young to wear black warpaint and fight to the death that they did not kill him at Montaup. They sent him here instead, to die from overwork.'

'What can we do?' Rowan asked.

'You would help me?' the woman asked.

Rowan nodded.

'But why?'

'*Nenomous*,' Rowan said softly. 'I am your People. *Tow wow*, I am your sister. Wómpatuck is my brother. You are all the family I have left.'

'It's too great a risk for you,' Caskwadadas said. 'You're safe where you are. You're fed, you are clothed. You're not beaten, you don't work in the mill or in the fields. They think you're a man, they don't take you into their hut when they want. Mr Sir doesn't rape you.'

'But I'm not free,' Rowan said, thinking of Ned and the green flag of liberty. 'And we are the people of the Dawnland. Of all the peoples in the world we – the first to see the sun – should be free.'

The woman looked doubtful. 'I thought only that we might get Wómpatuck into hiding. Do you mean escape?'

Rowan caught her breath at the thought of escape, of doing something more than enduring, of being, once again, an actor in her own destiny, not subject to someone else's whim. 'Is it even possible?' Rowan whispered. 'Mr Peabody makes me guard the huts but no-one has ever run away?'

'It is possible.'

'You've known someone escape?' Rowan demanded.

The woman nodded.

'They got away? And stayed free?'

'For months,' she said. 'Then one of them was brought back.'

'Punished?'

'Flogged to death.'

The two women stood in silence, Rowan looking into Caskwadadas' eyes. 'Even so,' she said quietly. 'How would we escape? If we dared to do it? If we dare?'

She was calling, knowingly, to the courage of the People. Caskwadadas might have named herself Kitonckquêi, a dead woman, a ghost, but beneath her despair was a longing to live, and a hunger that her son should live.

'How might we get Wómpatuck away? A ship from Bridge?'

Decisively, Caskwadadas shook her head. 'Not three of us. Not without money.'

'Then how?'

Slowly, as if she hardly dared to dream of escape, she whispered: 'There are caves.'

Rowan felt excitement, deep in her belly. 'Caves?'

'There are caves, not far from here, many caves interlinked, very deep and the white men don't go in them. Some of them are high up in the cliffs of the deep creek – not the one nearby, the big one further down. Our little river flows into it.'

'In the forest?' Rowan asked. The floor of the creeks was impenetrable, with great trees that thrust upwards, tangled with creepers blocking out the sun. The tropical birds screamed from the trees at sunrise, the animals and insects, the life of the forest buzzed and rustled and hummed as if the plantations had not made a desert of green to the very brink of every clifftop, as if the white man had never come to destroy Barbados. Rowan had gone no further than the little creek that cut through the Peabody fields but she had seen others: on the way from Bridge they had arduously crossed two river valleys, down one side, across the river, and slowly climbing up the other. They were too steep for horses or even mules – the road to Bridge ran around the deep creeks and central hills.

'The forest,' Caskwadadas added. 'Have you been there?'

'Only to the edge of our creek by the fields. Does it join with the others?'

'I think they all flow into another and then to the sea.'

'They're all clean water? And we could hunt? And forage?'

'It won't be like home,' Caskwadadas warned. 'I don't think there are any deer. And the white men have eaten all the wild hogs.'

'There's fish in the ocean and turtles and crabs and shellfish,' Rowan said. 'We won't starve.'

The two women fell silent, watching each other.

'He'll die here,' Caskwadadas said flatly. 'The black men die of overwork, and they are stronger and taller than my son will ever be. He will not survive one harvest, not two.'

'Have you seen the caves?' Rowan demanded. 'We have to be sure we won't be found.'

'I've never seen them. We walked here in chains and we went up and down through a little creek. I saw how thick it was then, how wild, and that was just a little creek, not deep. The white men don't go into the big creeks at all, they can't get through the jungle, there are no paths for them. But I've heard people talk of them. They say you can hide there. They say people have run away and hidden there.'

'We could go,' Rowan said.

'If we even try to go we can never come back,' Caskwadadas warned. 'If they recapture us, they'll beat us till the skin is flayed from our backs and maybe brand us. Or maybe take off our toes so we can't run away again. They might rape me so I'm with child and can't go. And if they discover that you're not a white man, they'll rape you and then kill you. We go once, and we never come back. We die before they bring us back.'

Rowan nodded at the brutal truth. There was no law against a white man killing a slave. Any one of the legal punishments would be fatal for a slight twelve-year-old boy. His mother would kill him herself, rather than return him to slavery. Rowan gritted her teeth in a grimace. 'I don't know what we should do,' she confessed.

Caskwadadas watched the younger woman, wondering if her spirit was broken, as so many had been broken. 'Be brave,' she whispered. 'Be brave *Squi minneash sookenon*. And I will be brave too. I shall not be Kitonckquêi: a dead woman. I shall come back to life. And I shall save my son.'

'I'm one of the People,' Rowan agreed. 'I was brave from birth. The white men have taught me nothing but defiance.' She nodded. 'I hate this life. I would rather die trying to escape than live here forever.'

'Of course.' Caskwadadas smiled for the first time – a smile like a sunrise. 'That's why we cannot be enslaved. That's why slavery will end, some day, for all of us. No-one, whatever their colour, deserves a master. We all long to be free.'

'I'll find the caves,' Rowan promised. 'I'll get out somehow to find them and see if they're safe.'

'Quickly,' Caskwadadas told her. 'Go as soon as you can.'

FOULMIRE PRIORY, SUSSEX, AUTUMN 1686

Daily, Ned was stronger, walked further and talked more clearly. The arrival of Matthew, Gabrielle and Mia was a huge spur to his recovery as they chattered constantly and asked him a dozen questions a day about what life had been like on the tidelands in the old days.

'I reckon they think we were here with the Saxons,' Ned remarked to Alinor. 'Mia asked me what king was on the throne when I was born, and was it Elizabeth?'

Alinor gurgled with laughter. 'They're very tactful with me. They think I live in a world of faeries and mermaids and they don't want to spoil it for me.'

Ned chuckled. 'They asked me if you had once had a love, a great love, like from a fairy story.'

'What did you tell them?'

'I told them "yes, in a way". Was I wrong?'

She shook her head, her eyes warm. 'No, you were right. It was a great love. It makes me happy now, to think that I had it. Even if it was for so short a time.'

'You don't regret it? It cost you so much?'

She smiled and shook her head. 'I'm glad to have loved like that. Even if it was not forever. It is still something – to have loved a man like that. Someone so strange as to be almost from another world.'

She saw the tenderness in his face. 'You're worth ten of him.'

'I was lucky,' she corrected him. 'I was luckier than him to know that it was the love of my life, while he thought it was something that could be made ordinary. He always wanted to fit me into his life. But our love could never have been in his world. It really was part of mermaids and faeries.'

They were silent for a moment. 'You'd best drop a word in young Matthew's ear that there's to be no mermaids and faeries for him this summer.'

Alinor knew at once he was referring to the two girls. 'I don't think he could choose between them. They're such friends.'

'You'd better tell him they're not for the likes of him. And the Lord knows, we don't want his mother the Nobildonna calling on our Sarah as his mother-in-law.'

'She'll have a duchess lined up for him,' she predicted. 'But I'll remind him that he's too young to be thinking of love or marriage; and they certainly are.'

Alinor waited until they were all four walking in the herb garden. Mia and Gabrielle were ahead of them, with a pair of scissors and a basket, cutting leaves for drying and for flavouring oils. The girls were in plain country dresses, their faces shaded with the enormous sun hats that their mother had sent from Venice and insisted that they wear to keep their skin as fair as possible. Alinor and Matthew could hear their voices but not make out their words. Alinor saw how his gaze followed them, and his smile.

'They're lovely girls,' she said. 'They've brightened your uncle Ned's visit here. He suggested a game of cards this evening, and that's the first time he's felt well enough to play.'

'That's good,' he said courteously. 'Do you want us to lose to him?'

She smiled. 'No. He'd not want an injustice, even at the card table.' She nodded towards the girls. 'They'll start school in the Michaelmas term,' she said. 'You won't have to take them to Rob's house anymore. You'll be spared the walk.'

'I like taking them,' he said. 'And I've promised to take them to visit Hester even after school starts.'

'I'm glad,' Alinor agreed. 'I'm sure she's enjoyed their company. But don't get too fond of them, Matthew. They're too young to be thinking of marriage, their father wouldn't like it, and for sure, your mother the Nobildonna would never forgive us if she thought we had entrapped you.'

'Entrapped me!' he exclaimed.

'You're quite a catch now,' she told him with a smile. 'The heir to all this.' Her gesture took in the beautiful walled garden, the old house, and the broad sky above them. 'The name that you carry, and your education, especially if that leads you to higher things. You don't come from a trading family like us; no doubt your mother has plans for you.'

'They'd never think of me anyway.' He turned to her and caught her hand. 'Mother Alinor, d'you not see a great love for me?'

She closed her eyes and put her fingers to both her temples, and then opened her eyes to laugh at him. 'I do! I do!'

'Who am I going to marry?'

'A princess,' she told him. 'Nothing less would satisfy your mother.'

His dark gaze rested on the girls, who were coming towards them down the path, their baskets heaped with the violet heads of lavender flowers. 'I know it's not possible,' he said quietly. 'I know that.'

DEEP CAVE, BARBADOS, AUTUMN 1686

Dora Peabody's dog, a bad-tempered pug named Troilus, ran off following a scent one afternoon and she declared that she would not sleep all night unless he was returned. Someone must be sent to find him and bring him home. Samuel Peabody started to say that nobody could be trusted to go running through the plantations at dusk and that no doubt the little brute was off chasing rats and would return, but Dora showed him a sulky stubborn face.

'My Papa gave him to me,' she said. 'He's very valuable. He won't be chasing rats, he'll be lost.' She pointed a silver fork at Rowan. 'He can go after him,' she said.

'He does the night watch on the house and patrols the slave quarters,' Samuel Peabody protested. 'He can't go off the plantation at night.'

'Why not?' She turned to Rowan. 'You'd find little Troy for me, won't you? Find him for me?'

'Yes, Ma'am,' Rowan answered promptly, and when Samuel Peabody glowered at her, she said: 'If you wish, Sir.'

'Oh go,' Mr Peabody said irritably. 'Go now, if you're going. Take a musket with you and keep a sharp eye. I'll have to sit up myself tonight,' he complained to his wife. 'I'll have to sit up to make sure that you sleep safely, while the man who should be on watch is chasing off after a little dog.'

She smiled, quite untroubled by his bad temper. 'Yes, you will,' she said. 'Papa always said that a good planter checks the slave quarters twice a night. You should be doing it yourself every night anyway.'

Mr Peabody turned to Rowan. 'Here—' He handed her the key to the gun cupboard. 'And if you see any black man off his plantation, you arrest him and bring him in here.'

'Cook will give you some meat to tempt little doggie,' Dora said. 'And he comes to call. Make sure you call "Troy-Troy-Troy" like that. He always comes when he's called.'

'Not this afternoon, he didn't,' Mr Peabody said disagreeably. 'Actually, I've never seen him come when he's called . . .'

Rowan went out of the dining room to the back hall, opened the gun cupboard and took out the musket, filled her pockets with balls and a powder horn, locked it up again and took the key back to Mr Peabody.

'Back by dawn,' Mr Peabody said. 'And take a torch and light it if you're on the road after dark, so no-one shoots you. Don't go wandering onto anyone else's plantation, or talking to anyone's slaves or they'll slit your tongue for a trouble-maker, white or not.'

Rowan nodded, hiding her contempt, and went out of the room, leaving Bonny to finish serving dinner.

The sun was low in the sky, sinking golden in rosy clouds; the burning heat of the day had gone off a little but it was still hot. Rowan went at a steady pace, away from the main road between cane fields where the slashed crop was already springing up, past the cane holes where the new canes were growing, proof that there would be another harvest, the cane would grow and be cut and replanted every year, the slaves would die and new ones would be bought. The cycle of sugar and death would go on as long as it showed a profit, and sooner or later Caskwadadas and her son would go down to death, unnoticed, among the millions of others.

Rowan loped on until she could see the top of the nearby forest, half a mile from the house. It seemed incredible that their little creek might lead to a greater river and caves buried among other plantations, unknown to the planters; but Mr Peabody had no curiosity about anything other than growing sugar and selling it in Bridge, and Dora Peabody had been taught from childhood that the sun would turn her skin an ugly brown, and that the fields were no place for a lady. She never went beyond the garden unless it was in a carriage to Bridge for shopping, church services or parties. She never went out but under a parasol and a hat. She visited neighbouring planters on special occasions, but their plantations were all beside the main road, far from the creeks that wound through the island. The valleys in the centre of the island and the many steep tributaries were an untouched ribbon of wildness in an island where all the flat land had been carved up between white owners, and arduously cleared by their slaves.

Rowan called 'Troy-Troy-Troy' as she trotted down the road, the musket slung over one shoulder and a candlewood torch on the other, until she was so far from the house that Dora Peabody would not hear. Then she stopped calling and increased her pace until she reached the end of the cane fields and the track ended abruptly in a rough turning circle for the cane carts, and before her was a tumble of rocks, dumped after filling potholes in the track, and beyond them the ground fell away so steeply that the tops of the trees growing far below showed their heads beside the cane. Rowan went cautiously to the edge and peered down. Branches and creepers hid the valley floor, but from the distant sound of water she thought this creek must be hundreds of feet below. There was no way down, the cliffs were sheer, and though there were creepers and weeping figs trailing across the rock face and rooting in every crevice, there was no way of telling if they would hold her weight. Rowan went along the edge of the field, sometimes pushing her way through sugar canes which were planted up to the very brink of the cliff, until she found a tiny trace of a path, almost lost to sight, which the wild hogs once followed to get down to the water in the bottom of the creek, and which the monkeys might scamper up, single file, to raid the sugar cane.

It was no more than one footstep wide, hardly visible. Setting one foot before another Rowan traced her way, tracking the path as it wound its way down, past the rock face, around thick roots, so close to the edge of the cliff that a pebble slipping under her foot rattled hundreds of feet down into the valley below, making her hug the stone of the cliff wall even tighter. She trailed her hand along the wall for the sense of safety, and then suddenly, she stumbled, as her hand felt nothing. There was a deep gap behind the creepers; she had nearly fallen into it. Her heart pounded with fear that she was balanced on a concealed stone bridge, a void on her right, a deadly drop masked by creepers on her left. Cautiously, she balanced herself, and parted the leaves of the rope-like vines. A shallow gap was hidden behind the vegetation, a hollow in the rock. Rowan slipped between the strong cords of the roots but found the back wall only a yard or two from the entrance. She turned in disappointment to go back to the path when she heard – only she could have heard it – the tiniest noise of a drip of water falling into standing water, and an echo. It came from behind the rock wall.

The setting sun shone on the opposite side of the creek, Rowan and the cave were in shadow. She realised that the cave faced east; anyone facing out would be the first to see the dawn. She stepped into the hollow, crouching low, and felt her way all around the back wall. At the furthest point, low on the wall, no bigger than the burrow of a rabbit, was a hole in the soil, and as Rowan bent to look, she could smell the cold scent of water on a cool breath of air coming from inside. Tentatively, she brushed her hands against the hole. The sandy soil collapsed upon itself, making the mouth wider. Rowan pushed some more and heard the earth falling away inside, falling into another cave, hidden beyond this one. Now she was digging with her hands, dragging soil outwards, widening the hole until she could get her head and shoulders into the opening and look inside.

She had to blink until her eyes could make out anything. She was on the brink of a huge opening, below her a lake of dark water, so black that she could see nothing but a dim halo – the light from behind her head reflecting off still waters. The little drips of water all around the cavern only accentuated the deep silence. It was cold, blissfully cold after the sweaty heat of the sunset. Rowan felt as if she had plunged into the river at her home, into darkness, into memory, into a new life.

She wriggled her way back out of the hole feeling the rock scrape against her back and picked up her musket and the torch of candlewood. She rammed the rod down to make sure it was unloaded, and then blew on the flashpan to clear it of any black powder. She put a scrap of charcloth in the pan and, holding the gun at arm's length, pulled the trigger. The flint dropped and scraped and planted a tiny glowing spark on the charcloth. Patiently, Rowan breathed on it and then put the tip of the candlewood in it. The wood glowed and caught light. Holding it before her, Rowan once again pushed herself into the hole and looked around. The flame flickered and then burned, telling Rowan that there was good air in the cave. She watched it for a moment, seeing that it was favouring one side: there was an air current in the cave, blowing towards her. So, there was another entrance somewhere to her right, somewhere in the darkness.

Immediately below her was a little ledge, just wide enough for her to crawl, and beneath the ledge a cascade of silver white rocks, which caught the yellow flicker of torchlight and threw it back, as mirror-bright as ice, luminous in the darkness. Someone, years ago, centuries ago, had cut steps into the white rock and the constant seep of water had trickled over them for hundreds of years until now they were almost-invisible footholds for tiny feet. Rowan reached down to touch, almost expecting the cascade of stone to be cold as snow, as if this were a winter world of darkness and ice inside the island of heat. Her fingertips felt a wet slippery surface, smooth as marble, wet, but not icy. She cupped her hand into the first indentation; it could serve as a step for anyone with small bare feet, anyone brave enough to climb down to the darkness of the lagoon.

She pulled the musket through the hole and slung it over her back; she took the shaft of the flickering torch in her teeth, pulled off her ill-fitting shoes and left them on the ledge as she lowered herself gingerly over the side. The light of the torch on the rocks was dazzling, so near to her face, but below the blaze, her feet scrabbled for foothold in total darkness. She found the first step and rested, the toes of her right foot gripping as hard as she could, while she lowered herself down and ran her bare left foot over the smoothness of the rock until she found another half-smooth step below, and then another and another. Rowan crept down, poised like a lizard, on the sheer white cliff, peering into the darkness below.

The wet white wall thickened like an old tree trunk as she reached the floor of the cave, and Rowan stepped off the last step into a shallow lagoon of cold water over silky white sand. The water came to her knees and Rowan bent down, holding the torch aloft, and took a handful and tasted it. It was cold and clean, with the sharp refreshing taste of water filtered through miles of stone. Now the torch reflected off walls of white stone that surrounded the cave. There were two arched tunnels that led off into the darkness, one to her right, where she could see the clear water gently flowing out of the white sand lagoon, and one where the water was flowing in, from the back of the cave. She went to take a step, to paddle towards the exit, following the water, when her foot sunk deep in the silky sand and she gave a sudden gasp of fear.

She was in quicksand: both feet had been sinking impercep-tibly as she had stood still, but as soon as she lifted one foot to take a step, her weight had driven the other deep into the soft silt and she was knee-deep, and then thigh-deep, falling forward. Instinctively, she plunged the torch down to support herself and the flame went out at once, the complete darkness like a thunderclap. She levered herself back towards the cliff and the hidden steps, one hand outstretched in the darkness to where the cliff had been. Her fingers scrabbled over the invisible rock to find the tiniest indentation where she could get a grip and haul herself out of the steady suction which was holding her legs and dragging her down.

She fastened on a tiny crevice with the fingertips of her out-stretched hand and, pushing off the sinking torch with her other hand, managed to get one foot out of the water and onto the rock and then drag the other from the suction of the sand. It was like fighting with an invisible being; she forced herself not to thrash and kick. Steadily, Rowan strained against the quicksand, and with a sickening noise of yielding, her foot was free. In total darkness, clinging to the rock, Rowan trembled with exhaustion and shock.

She drew a breath, she tightened her fingers and toes in their holds, she took a sobbing breath, and then – despite her fear – she laughed out loud. Her laughter echoed eerily off the walls, off the vaulting ceiling of the cave. She laughed at herself, at her predicament, she laughed at herself, a child of the wild places, stepping into deadly quicksand like a fool, extinguishing her only torch and leaving herself in total darkness, stuck at the bottom of a cliff which she would have to climb blind; but more than anything, she laughed for joy at being, at last, in deadly danger caused by herself – her own actions, not a victim of a man's malice, but in danger on her own account, by her own doing. She thought that if she died here, in the darkness, unable to find her way up the cliff, unable to climb it with her bleeding fingers and feet softened and blistered by shoes, that she would die a free woman, and the water would drip over her and make her a woman of stone; a woman of unyielding stone.

HATTON GARDEN, LONDON, AUTUMN 1686

Reluctantly, Mrs Julia Reekie agreed to take Hester for a visit to her cousins at Foulmire Priory, driven by curiosity to see what sort of inheritance the Reekies' poor foster boy Matthew had managed to secure. Her husband Rob had been infuriatingly vague about his former home, saying only that when he was a boy his mother Alinor had sent him to study at the big house with the squire's son. Rob claimed he could remember nothing about the house and grounds.

'Oh, you know,' he said to his wife as they sat together in the parlour one evening, waiting for the tea tray to be brought in, 'just a rambling sort of place. It was once a priory, rebuilt, I suppose, a hundred years ago. Walter and I spent most of our time in the library with our tutor – not that there were many books, the squire was a sporting man.'

'Why didn't you go with the son to university?' Julia asked.

'I was a study companion for the country, only for that summer,' Rob explained. 'They paid me well, and then they paid for my apprenticeship to the Chichester apothecary. I was never of his world, I was a hired companion.'

She was always offended by the poverty of his early life; her gesture with her fan told him to avoid the Chichester shop, or any mention of a wage.

'But how is it that Matthew, your sister's foster son, inherited it? That's what I don't understand.'

He laughed shortly. 'Nobody understands that! It was his mother, the Nobildonna. She got him to do some great favour for the queen – you know how these things work.'

She did not know, she longed to know. But she kept her face quite impassive.

'I think Matthew took the queen's goods into safekeeping at the warehouse, during the Argyll riots, something like that.'

A wave of her fan told him that she did not want to hear about the warehouse.

'Anyway,' he said, keeping a wary eye on the languid movement, 'the queen offered a reward, so the Nobildonna asked for a manor house. Matthew thought of the Priory so he could take his foster mothers to their old home – a generous thought.' He glanced at her blank face. 'At any rate, the Nobildonna got the

Priory for Matthew and he has invited the girls to stay for the summer. And now they have invited Hester.'

'I don't know that it won't be too much for her,' she said.

'She doesn't need to wear her brace in the day anymore, and her maid can put it on at night, just as well as here.'

'She can't possibly keep up with those two lumping girls.'

'I'll ask Alys to make sure she does not get overtired. But I'd recommend exercise. It will strengthen her, and the country air is undoubtedly better for her than town.'

'Certainly, I'd like to see your childhood home.'

'My actual home wasn't the Priory. It was a very poor cottage by the ferryhouse.'

'I don't want to see that,' she corrected him, trying to smile. 'I'd like to see the Priory.'

'Why don't we all go, and if you are satisfied that Hester will be happy, we can leave her there, till they come back to London?'

'What about Prynne?' she queried.

'She can come, if you wish? But she's not a very merry companion.'

'To chaperone Hester with the foster boy, and anyone else they meet. She cannot be allowed to make the acquaintance of anyone ... unsuitable.'

'Alys will keep an eye on her,' he said, trying not to bristle at her snobbery, remembering that it had been his own choice to marry an Alderman's daughter. He had not realised that rising socially with Julia would be so effortful and involve so much separation from his past and from his family. When he had married her, a pretty heiress, he had never dreamed that her careful gentility would come to grate on him quite so much. 'Alys knows that Hester is carefully brought up,' he said patiently. 'Gabrielle and Mia are clever girls and quite suitable companions.'

'Clever girls!' she repeated with an artificial shudder of horror. 'Heaven save us from a clever girl!'

'I hope not!' he exclaimed at last. 'Hester has a good brain and should learn how to use it. Her cousins have come to England for the sole purpose of studying. There's nothing unladylike about it.'

The door opened and Miss Prynne came into the room followed by the footman with the tea tray before Julia could lower herself to argue with her husband.

'Here you are, so comfortable!' she said inaccurately. 'Shall I pour tea for you, dear Mrs Reekie?'

Julia nodded, as if she were too exhausted to raise the silver teapot herself.

'We were just agreeing that we will take Hester for a stay with her cousins at the Priory,' Rob said, accepting a cup. 'So you can take a holiday, Miss Prynne. Hester will not need you in the country.'

'That will be a great pleasure for me, and more importantly an enjoyable holiday for Hester,' Miss Prynne said. 'Unless you want me to go with her? To keep her in mind of the little elegancies of life?'

Rob Reekie made a small cough indicating contempt for the small elegancies of life.

'That's not necessary,' Mrs Reekie said, frowning at her husband. 'You can have a month off, Miss Prynne, and come back to us at the end of September.'

Miss Prynne, looking at Julia's icy expression, thought if she might ask to be paid for her holiday time; and then thought that she would not.

DEEP CAVE, BARBADOS, AUTUMN 1686

Rowan climbed with meticulous care up the wet ledges of the cliff, her eyes wide against the darkness. As she neared the top it was only slightly lighter and when she broke through the earth burrow to the outside, she was in darkness, the moon and the stars blotted out by the thick jungle canopy. Grimy and exhausted, her fingers bruised and her feet bleeding from scrabbling on the wet cliff, Rowan collapsed on the floor of the little entrance cave and slept like an exhausted dog.

When she opened her eyes again the rising sun was shining on her, like a message of hope. She sat up and looked around at the little sheltered spot, bathed now in a warm golden light. 'Why, this is Dawnlands,' she said wonderingly. 'This is a Dawnlands. Just like my home.'

She turned back and reached into the cave to wet her hands in the water sliding down the cliff edge, and rubbed her face, the back of her neck and her throat, as a token gesture of the ritual bathing that she would have done at home. She turned north and south, west to the back of the cave and then east to face the sun, and she smiled into the growing light, as it pierced through the canopy of trees to shine on her. 'Great Spirit, Mother Earth, Grandmother Moon, Grandfather Sun, I thank you. I pray to the four directions.' Reverently, she bowed. 'I thank you for all my relations: the winged nation, the creeping and crawling nation, the four-legged nation, the green and growing nation, and all things living in the water. Honouring the clans: the deer – *ahtuk*, the bear – *mosq*, the wolf – *mukquoshim*, the turtle – *tunnuppasog*, the snipe – *sasasō. Keihtanit taubot neanawayean.*'

She did not know how to make the prayer fit this strange land, where there were neither bear nor wolf, nor even many deer. 'I honour the monkey and the hummingbird, the insects that bite and the leaves that heal. The great fish of the ocean, and the many turtles of the sea.'

She finished the prayer and sat under the arch of the cave. Consciously, she rested her strained muscles and her painful feet until she was ready to move again and step into her ill-fitting shoes and pick up her musket. She climbed down to the first level of the cliff where the ground levelled out before it tumbled in a precipice of rubble and trees down to the river below. She plucked a twig from a tree and broke it so that it formed a Y and then taking two short arms and letting the other long one twist to point upwards or down she imagined the cave beneath her feet and started to make her way through the forest, visualising the flow of the sapphire blue river underground. It was hard walking, climbing over fallen trees, ducking under vines, the forest floor sometimes soft with fallen leaves or a mass of crumbling stones. The sticks twisted in her hand and the pointer stick turned down showing her the path of the underground river, many feet below her. She went through the tangle, never breaking anything, never tempted to thrust her way through, threading like a needle through fustian, over rocks and under branches, wriggling through gaps in the foliage and stumbling over rough ground, choosing a path that followed wherever the stick strained in her hands and pointed down.

She walked for hours, until the sun was fully up and she was thirsty, looking around her all the time for another cave entrance to admit her to the caverns below where the cold river ran in the darkness. Then, ahead of her, she saw what looked like a spring, bubbling up in a pool and overflowing in a waterfall to the river below. She went to it, smelled the water, noticed the bird droppings at the edge where they had drunk and bathed and then took a cautious sip. She recognised at once the icy sweetness of the cave water: this was water that had filtered through the thick rock, that had dripped from white stone to stone. It was not a spring, welling up from the earth, it was one of the overflows of the underground river that she had been following.

Rowan knelt down to the pond, drank deeply, feeling the coldness of the water in an ache behind her eyes, and the chill of it in her belly, and then sat back on her heels, peering through the leaves to see the height of the sun in the sky, guessing that it was nearly midday.

She turned and looked more carefully at the pool. It bubbled up in a bowl of the white rock; behind it was a rubble of tumbled overgrown rocks, and behind them, hidden, was a wide dry cave. Rowan clambered cautiously over the rocks and found herself in a cleft, tall enough for her to stand. A fissure in the rock admitted her to a cave deeper in the cliff. Behind that, was a low tunnel leading to another cave, and a tunnel leading from that. The further she went from the entrance, the darker it became until she did not dare to go any further in case the ground fell away beneath her feet in a cliff inside the cliff. She had a sense of a series of galleries and caves and the river running through some of them and falling away to leave them dry.

She turned and found her way back to the cave, and then the crack to the cleft in the rock and then the entrance cave behind the spring. She squatted behind the spring watching the water bubble up, scenting the air, very sure that no white man with his tobacco smoke, his sweat and his stinking woollen clothes had ever been here.

She squatted on her heels. She had not been so happy since before the war and before her capture. She knew that she had found another entrance to the cave system and she was confident, given the scanty flow of water in the spring, that there were other streams, perhaps many others, draining into and flowing from the great underground river. This would be her refuge and her new home. She felt entirely free. She curled up at the back of the cave, and she was asleep in seconds.

She woke as the sun was going down and stretched out her aching muscles before getting to her feet. She was ravenously hungry, but she ignored the ache in her belly, pushed her sore feet into her shoes and started the arduous climb up to the top of the creek, noting the way by every outcrop of rock, and occasionally twisting a twig or breaking a leaf to mark her path. No white man would have even seen the little pointers that Rowan laid down as she walked, but she was confident that no white man would try to get down here to the creek.

It was nearly two hours before she emerged into the Peabody cane field, and again she looked around her carefully so that she would know the way when she returned. Then she set off with her steady lope towards the plantation, ignoring the growling hunger in her empty belly and the pain of her bleeding feet.

Caskwadadas was awake at the first sound of a barred owl, the owl of her homeland that she had never heard in Barbados. Quietly, she slipped away from her sleeping son and ducked below the low doorway of the women's hut. The night sky was speckled with thousands of stars, so many and their light so bright that she could make out Rowan against the wall of the hut, half-hidden by the shadow from the overhanging reed roof.

'*Tow wow?* Sister?' she asked.

Rowan answered, low voiced, in their own language. 'I have found a cave, it has two entrances at least, it has fresh water and good air. It's well hidden. I'm not coming back here again, except for you and Wómpatuck. I will come back for you when you want – or we can leave now.'

Caskwadadas did not hesitate. 'Now,' she said. 'I'll wake Wómpatuck.'

She turned and went back inside. Rowan waited motionless in the shadow of the hut.

In a moment, Caskwadadas and her son were beside her, dressed in their work clothes – a ragged shirt and breeches for the boy, a tattered dress and a cloth turban for his mother. She wore broken-down boots on her feet, the child was barefoot.

Rowan nodded and led the way; they fell in behind her in single file, the boy then his mother, pacing themselves so that nobody walked in step. Even the child, Wómpatuck, walked in Rowan's footprints but at a different pace. It made their passing almost silent, a single track of blurred footprints. Rowan felt her heart lift that she should be walking once more, as her people walked, that she was going into the forest where she belonged – even though it was a strange forest in her enemies' land; still she felt that she was going home.

FOULMIRE, SUSSEX, AUTUMN 1686

Julia Reekie was not impressed by the bumpy road from Chichester to Sealsea Island, and she was horrified by the Sealsea ferry. The tide was in, and the Broad Rife filled with swirling brown water as the water draining from the harbours was pushed back inland by the incoming tides from both sides of the island.

'This was my uncle Ned's house and ferry,' Rob said, amused by her dismay. 'And his father's before him.'

'Surely it isn't safe?'

'Safe enough. They'll take the horses out of their traces and take them over first, then they'll take the carriage. It's no worse than the Lambeth ferry. You can sit in the carriage, you'll hardly know it's on the water. It's all over in minutes.'

'Can't we go round?'

'It's an island. You have to cross the water to get on it.'

'There should be a bridge.'

'So everyone has said since the Saxons. I did warn you, my dear.'

'But how was I to know!' She looked despairingly at him. 'It's not safe for Hester.'

'It's perfectly safe for us all,' he ruled. To Hester he said: 'Come and watch them loading the horses on the ferry, and I will show you the harbour.'

Hester glanced at her mother for permission and climbed down the steps. Rob tucked her hand under his arm and led her around the carriage and showed her the track to the tide mill, the bell to call the ferryman, the ferryman coming to load them, hauling the ferry hand over hand on the overhead rope across the Rife, and his little house on the far side. 'That was where my uncle Ned lived,' he told her.

'And where was your Mama's house? My grandmother's home?'

He gestured further down the bank of the Broad Rife. 'Down there, tumbled down, I think.'

'Poor Papa,' she said sympathetically.

He laughed. 'Yes, I was poor, but very carefree.'

'I'm so glad to see it,' she said earnestly.

'You can say if you want to come home early, or if you want to stay.'

'I can tell you that already, I will want to stay,' she said, blushing a little. 'Matthew told his mother we are all staying till the end of the month.'

'Of course . . .' He was irritated that Livia would know he was visiting Matthew's house.

The ferry had taken the two pairs of horses over, and now Tom Drydale the ferryman was hauling it back for the carriage. The coachman, the footmen and the ferryman rolled the wheels so that the carriage was settled amidships on the flat barge, and Hester and her father climbed inside to sit with Julia, who clutched Rob's hand in pretend terror for the entire length of the crossing. As he had promised, it was not long before they were on the other side, bowling through the stone pedestals of the Priory gate, and drawing up before the open front door.

'And here we are!' Rob said heartily.

The footmen jumped down, opened the door, let down the steps. Rob dismounted and held out his hand to help Julia down, as the front door behind him opened. He turned with a smile, expecting Matthew, but, to his horror, it was Matthew's mother, the Nobildonna herself, dazzlingly beautiful in a dress of peach silk with cream lace, who stood in the doorway, her eyes bright with amusement.

'Dear Mrs Reekie, dear Doctor Reekie, and you must be Miss Reekie! Welcome to Fairmere Priory, welcome to my home.'

Julia Reekie's curtsey was perfectly judged, the correct height of obeisance from a considerable heiress of the City of London to a lady of the court, a close friend of the queen, and her hostess. Hester beside her curtseyed lower. Livia turned her confident smile on Rob who was lost for words. Speechlessly, he took the hand of the false wife who had betrayed him and left him for dead, and bowed.

'And here is my son, your friend, Matteo Peachey,' Livia said smoothly; a gesture of her fan brought Matthew forward to make his bow to Julia and Rob and to greet Hester. Rob and Matthew exchanged a glance of mutual horror. Matthew shook his head very slightly, as if to say that this was none of his doing, and he had not known his mother was coming.

'Come in! Come in!' Livia urged them. 'You must be so tired from your journey. Did you have to take the ferry? Such a ridiculous performance, is it not?' She turned to Julia. 'Will you take a dish of tea, Mrs Reekie?'

'Oh, tea!' Julia said faintly.

'I have brought some from London! The footman will take your luggage. Matthew – take Miss Reekie to find her cousins, and show Doctor Reekie the gardens, I am sure he is longing for a walk after spending so long in the carriage.' Livia swept Julia away to the parlour leaving Matthew, Rob and Hester in the hall.

'Uncle Rob!' Mia broke the stunned silence, coming into the hall from the garden door, followed by Gabrielle.

'And Hester!' Gabrielle said, kissing her cousin. 'We've been waiting for you this whole afternoon.'

Both girls curtseyed to Rob and he kissed their cheeks. 'How long has Lady Avery been here?' he asked urgently. 'How long is she staying?'

Mia's dark eyes widened. 'Isn't she a goddess?' she whispered. 'You should have seen her hat.'

'Her ladyship came today, just to welcome you and Mrs Reekie,' Gabrielle said, silencing her sister with a glare. 'I believe she is to stay only till tomorrow.'

'I didn't know,' Matthew said shortly, blushing to the roots of his hair. 'She didn't say she was coming.'

'No matter,' Rob said kindly to the young man. 'You couldn't stop her. Nobody could. Lord! Is my sister here? Have they met?'

'No! Ma Alys is at the wharf.'

'Thank God for that at least – but – has she met my mother?'

Matthew looked completely at a loss. 'We all had lunch together,' he volunteered. 'Mother Alinor, the Nobildonna, Uncle Ned – and us three.' He was completely nonplussed. 'Mother Alinor was just herself, very calm, very pleasant. She put the Nobildonna at the head of the table as if she came every day, and after lunch, Mother Alinor said that she always takes a rest in the afternoon, and then she just went off! Uncle Ned too. He hardly said a word. But we're all to have dinner together.'

'Dinner?' Rob repeated. The two men exchanged an aghast look.

'Except Uncle Ned,' Mia added. 'He said he would rather be hanged.'

Rob choked down a laugh.

'But what is the matter?' Gabrielle asked, looking from Matthew to Rob. 'What's wrong? Why should the Nobildonna not come to her son's house? Why is it such a surprise? What would be so awful if she had met our grandmother Alys?'

Matthew tried to smile at her. 'Nothing's wrong,' he told her, glancing at Rob. 'It's just that I've never seen them together, except the once, when she came to the warehouse on royal business. It's like two worlds colliding.'

'The stars are shaken in the firmament.' Rob recovered, and chucked Hester under the chin. 'Nothing to concern you. We all quarrelled very badly once; but it was a long time ago and clearly it's all forgotten and forgiven. I'll go and see the horses stabled. Hester, you can go with your cousins.'

'I'll come with you, Sir,' Matthew said quickly. 'And then perhaps you'd like to come to the library for a glass of wine?'

'I would,' Rob said earnestly. 'I truly would.'

Dinner at the Priory was an informal family meal; but with a guest from court and Julia Reekie present, Alinor summoned her son Rob to the parlour to consult him on etiquette.

'We can't lay on a show,' she said simply. 'We can't pretend we're anything we're not – but I don't want to be rude. Should you take Lady Avery in? And Matthew take Julia? Cook'll do her best, but there won't be enough dishes for a fine dinner like she's used to, and there's no bakehouse or pastry-maker for miles. The wines are good, I know that, as they're in the cellar already. But we don't have sweetmeats or anything but fruit.'

'I'm not taking her in to dinner,' he refused flatly. 'We'll just go in, and sit as we like. Don't put her at the head of the table ... it can be Matthew at one end and you at the other – if Ned's not joining us?'

She laughed. 'He's sworn off.'

'Well, don't put her beside me. Or opposite me. Spread the children out between us—' He broke off. 'Ma – what's she even doing here? What does she want?'

Alinor had a twinkle of laughter in her eyes. 'Ah, Rob, she's a rarity! I should hate her; but I can't. She just arrived all smiles, and brought a great dressed turkey from London that's too big to cook for tonight, and a caddy of the queen's own tea. She chattered away to the girls in Italian, and was sweet as sugar to me and Ned.'

'I can't stand to see her!' he burst out.

His mother looked at him. 'It's her son's house. She got it for him.'

'You should never have let her come to the wharf. This is what comes of having anything to do with her!'

'Nay, this is what comes of raising Matthew as our own. We always knew she might come back for him. We knew she was a woman who would stoop to anything. That's the risk we took for love of Matthew.' She stole a quick measuring look at his angry face. 'Have you told Julia anything at all about her?'

'Only that she caused trouble for me in Venice, years ago. I told her father the Alderman all about it when we drew up the marriage contract – told him that I had been tricked by Livia into an invalid marriage. He told me to say nothing about it. Not to anyone, not even Julia. He said Julia would only be upset by it, and it was old history, and I should forget it.'

'Should you tell her now?' she asked.

'Ma, I can't now,' he said as frank as a boy. 'She looks down on me as it is. I'm not going to tell her that Livia tricked me, and then Alys. I'm not going to tell her that Livia cuckolded me, and had me locked up, that I could have died but for Sarah coming for me—' He broke off, his face dark with anger.

She put her hand on his. 'Son, if you're not going to speak of it to Julia, then don't think of it. Livia's not going to bring it up! Not now that she's Lady Avery gracing the court and so close to the queen. We'll all do what your father-in-law Alderman Johnson advised: forget the past.'

He turned to the window to stare out at the rose garden and the flutter of falling petals from late roses. 'Sarah will never forgive us for letting her girls near Livia.'

'Sarah'd understand that we can't stop Livia coming to see her son in the house that she got him,' Alinor said steadily. 'And anyway – she's not staying. We just have to get through dinner, and through breakfast tomorrow, and then she'll go. I think she just came for curiosity, to see the girls with Matthew.'

'Hester is to have nothing to do with her.'

Alinor smiled and put her hands over his. 'She'll see her at dinner and that's all. Probably never see her again in her life. You do what your father-in-law said: forget the past.'

DEEP CAVE, BARBADOS, AUTUMN 1686

The two women and the little boy reached the spring water cave as the sun was rising. For the first time in years, Rowan faced the rising sun and said her prayers in a soft chorus with other voices. She splashed the water on her face and breast and heard the others beside her washing too. For a moment, she was back in the Quinnehtukqut river with her mother and her grandmother, her sisters and her brothers, the people from her village with a sense of herself as one of a community, not a single individual like a lonely white man. Then she came back to herself and these two who had survived, and showed Caskwadadas the cleft in the rock, the dry cave behind it, and the gallery behind that.

'I think there are many caves, and many ways through the rock,' she said quietly, her voice echoing in the dry still air.

Wómpatuck's eyes were bright with excitement, shining in the darkness of the cave. 'Can I go and explore?' he asked.

'Not till we tie a twine around you, so that you can find your way back,' Caskwadadas said. 'And no further than this cave, till we know our way round.'

'There are steep cliffs,' Rowan warned. 'And a quicksand.'

'A quicksand in the cave!' He was thrilled.

'All the safer for us,' Caskwadadas said. 'If we can find a hiding place behind the quicksand, we could never be taken.'

'I know. But first we have to find some food. I've eaten nothing for two nights.'

Caskwadadas fished into a pocket and pulled out some pone

bread wrapped in plantain leaves. 'I saved this from my dinner. You share it with the boy. And then we'll go deep into the caves and sleep till dusk. They'll be looking for us today, but the next day or the day after they'll give up. They'll go first to the nearby farms. Most runaways hide in the slave houses and then go to Bridge and try to get on a ship.'

Rowan took a tiny piece of dry bread and ate it slowly, sipping the spring water from the palm of her hand as she ate. 'People get on board a ship and get home?'

Caskwadadas nodded. 'Very few. Usually they are found. But somehow, we have to get back to our lands. We can't stay here hiding forever.'

'We go home?' Rowan whispered as if it were a promise.

'We go home,' the older woman answered. 'Now: you sleep, I'll watch. Then the boy can take his turn to watch.'

'He won't fall asleep?'

'He was born one of the People,' Caskwadadas said. 'He won't fall asleep.'

Caskwadadas was right. The Peabodys decided that the new servant must have had an accident looking for the dog. They squabbled briefly about whether he should have been sent out at all and Mr Peabody ordered a search party to shout and listen for Rowan at the upper part of the creek where it brushed against the cane fields and Dora Peabody said they should look in the cane fields for the pug as he was far more valuable than an indentured servant.

Mr Peabody rode to the neighbouring plantation to tell them of the runaways – a slave and her boy – and stayed for a grand dinner; but no-one searched the little creek near the house, and would not have dreamed of hacking their way through to the deeper forest. The overseers could not ride their horses on the tiny wandering tracks, and they would not dismount and walk in the blistering heat. They could not send slaves without an overseer, for fear of them running off or plunging to their death over the cliffs, and the woman they called 'Kitonckquêi' and her son were not worth more than a day's absence from the fields, which were growing high and needed constant weeding.

The overseer swore that the mother and son had just run off, as Indians were always running off to die in the forest. 'They'll get lost and starve to death,' he assured Mr Peabody as he rested in his chair in the shade after dinner.

'Forest has got fruit trees, hasn't it?' Mr Peabody demanded irritably. 'They can eat them?'

'Half of them are poisonous, and you can't live off berries and nuts,' the man from Bristol told the man from London.

'True.' Mr Peabody was pleased at the thought. 'She'll starve to death out there and her brat with her. Serve them right.'

FOULMIRE PRIORY, SUSSEX, AUTUMN 1686

Julia, in a dream of snobbish delight, ate dinner with the best friend of the Queen of England, and found, as they drank tea together after dinner, that they shared an extraordinary number of opinions, likes and dislikes. Encouraged by Livia's smiling interest, Julia told her about her childhood home in Cheapside in the City, her father's membership of the Goldsmiths' Company, and the development of his business which was now lending money so far afield that they were issuing their own receipts for deposits in London which could be cashed in the West Indies, and taking in monies there, that could be drawn on in London by returning planters.

Livia was fascinated; but said that she, herself, knew nothing about business. She said that although trade in the City was a very good beginning for a family, she could not bear to live on a wharf.

'The noise!' Julia shuddered. 'I try to visit only on a Sunday when it is quiet.'

'Yes, but then you have to attend St Olave's church,' Livia whispered with a smile.

Julia widened her eyes to show her disdain for the wharfingers' parish church. 'Oh, I know! The sermons! The vicar is halfway to being a dissenter.'

'I go to the queen's chapel,' Livia told her.

'I've heard it is very beautiful?' Julia asked longingly.

Livia threw up her hands in a pretty gesture. 'The paintings! The music! But you must hear the choir. You could bring Hester.'

'I don't think Doctor Reekie would ...' Julia knew that Rob would not like his daughter to attend a roman catholic church. But the temptation of the court was too much for her. 'We should be delighted. Delighted!'

'I'll write you a note,' Livia promised. 'Are you attending a drawing room this season?'

Julia's family had never had an invitation. 'Hester is too young as yet,' she said quickly. 'I want her a little older before she goes out in society.' She hesitated. 'So wealthy an inheritance can be a burden ...' she hinted.

'You are your father's only heir?' Livia asked acutely. Her dark eyes strayed across the parlour where Rob and Matthew were playing Game of Goose, bending over the board with the three girls. Mia's laugh rang out and she slapped Matthew's hand away from her winnings.

'Exactly,' Julia confided. 'As Hester is ours. I shall have a puzzle when I plan her marriage. I know no young man whose fortune is her equal.'

'I can advise you,' Livia offered. 'I know everyone. And with no daughter of my own, I shall take an interest.'

Julia was briefly silent, awed by the prospect opening before her.

'And she is a little lame?' Livia mentioned quietly.

'It's nothing!' Julia was quick to assure her. 'She wears a brace at night only till she is fully grown. Her foot will come straight, we are assured of it. And it's not . . .' She could not find a polite euphemism. 'It's not in the blood,' she flushed. She wanted to say that it would not be passed on to any future noble children; but she saw a reassuring nod from Livia and realised that the older woman completely understood.

'And anyway, a generous dowry would compensate . . .' Livia smoothed over the moment.

'And your son, Matthew?' Julia asked brightly. 'Such a promising young man! Has he nearly finished his studies? Will he be attending court?'

'Of course, I expect him to receive some sort of post, at court or abroad. He has this house, Fairmere, but a young man needs his own house in town. He's in chambers in Lincoln's Inn at the moment.'

'Avery House?' Julia ventured.

Livia smiled. 'Of course: Avery House in time.'

Prospects of social rise shimmered like a mirage before Julia. 'They're very young yet,' she said irrelevantly.

'Both of them, far too young to think of marriage!' Livia smiled, equally insincere. 'But it's natural for a good mother to look ahead.'

'Yes,' Julia agreed. 'Indeed, yes.'

It did not occur to Julia that night to ask why such a devoted mother as Livia had left her son at Reekie Wharf. It was not until after a night filled with dreams of the queen's drawing room, and Hester with her club foot magically straightened, walking without a limp down the aisle of the queen's chapel, marrying into the aristocracy, that she asked her husband to give her a moment before he went down for breakfast. Julia had a tray with her breakfast cup of chocolate and some pastries on her bedside table; she gestured that Rob should sit in a little chair opposite her bed.

'I have to go down,' he said unwillingly.

'I just want to know how Lady Avery came to know your family,' she said.

He had expected the question sooner or later. 'You know that she trusted Matthew with them when he was just a baby? She didn't want to take him to Yorkshire.'

'They were not his wet nurses?' Julia was horrified at the thought. 'They did not actually . . . ?'

'No, no. She came to the wharf when she first came to London. She had their direction from me. You know that we knew each other in Venice. Her husband the Signor Fiori was my patient.'

'Oh, Venice,' Julia said vaguely. 'But was there not some trouble between you?'

'A disagreement,' he said. 'Very bad. But she went to them anyway. She didn't tell them what she had . . . how she had offended me.'

Julia was not interested in Rob's past. 'So she stayed at the wharf before her marriage to Sir James Avery?'

'Yes,' he said shortly. 'Ma and Alys took such a liking to Matthew, he was a tiny baby then, that when she wanted to leave him with them for the first months of her marriage, they kept him; and then he just stayed on. She visited once, I think; she paid for his keep and his education. Sir James was his manucaptor at Lincoln's Inn.'

'His what?'

'His patron, his guarantor. He is his stepfather.'

'Sir James acknowledges him as his stepson?'

'Yes, as you see. And she got a royal favour – Matthew chose the house that he wanted.'

'And who is his father?'

Rob checked in his smooth explanation. 'She took the name of Picci, and now Matthew spells it the English way: Peachey,' he said awkwardly.

'His father was a Venetian prince?'

'Her first husband was Signor Fiori.' He evaded the question but she did not notice.

'And anyway, as the queen's companion . . .' she said vaguely.

'We will not befriend her,' he said shortly.

'My dear, we could not!' she explained. 'Any invitation would have to come from her, from the palace.'

'My dear friend, I am so pleased to have met you.' Livia advanced on Julia with her silk-gloved hands held out. 'It's been such a delight! But I promised Her Majesty my prompt return.'

'Of course,' Julia said. 'We should not detain you.'

'But you must stay as long as you like, and you can safely leave Hester here with her grandmother.' Livia waved vaguely at the garden and the woods beyond the drive. 'She will like it, I am sure.'

'We will,' Julia said. 'Hester is very fond of nature.'

'And I will visit you in London,' Livia promised her.

'Please do – you have our address?'

'Matthew can bring me.'

'Oh yes! Do come with Matthew,' Julia urged her. 'The dear children . . .'

The carriage door was open. 'Hired,' Livia said darkly. 'Sir James has our own carriage in Yorkshire. I so rarely need one, living in the palace.'

'We are going to set up our own carriage. I keep asking . . .'

Alinor came down the stairs, in a dark navy dress, leaning on Gabrielle's arm, as Matthew came through the garden door with Hester and Mia to say goodbye to his mother.

'Be a good host to your foster family!' Livia told him. 'We must repay them for all the kindness they have shown you in the past. Now kiss me goodbye.'

Warily, Matthew approached his mother and bent his head

so she could kiss him on the forehead. She kept hold of his arm, so he led her to the carriage. 'Goodbye,' she said, climbing the steps. Her dark assessing gaze swept over Alinor and Julia, and the three dazzled girls. She kissed Matthew again, on both his cheeks. 'Such a pleasure!' she said gaily. 'I am so sorry to leave.'

The footman put up the steps and Matthew closed the door of the coach. The Nobildonna dropped the glass of the window to wave to them. As if under a spell they all smiled and waved back, until the carriage had gone down the drive, around the slow curve to the gates and was out of sight.

DEEP CAVE, BARBADOS, AUTUMN 1686

With meticulous care, never leaving so much as a footprint or a bent twig to show their passing, Caskwadadas, Rowan and Wómpatuck hunted, gathered, fished and trapped, going to and from the spring water cave at dawn and dusk every day, sleeping through the day with one of them on watch, coming out in the darkness of night when they puzzled over the mixture of stars: those they knew, and those that sat on the horizon and were strange to them. Occasionally, they heard a gang of slaves carrying casks of sugar up and down the arduous paths, further down the creek, at one of the flatter parts where the assingoes could trace a winding path down the slope, and the slaves could creep over the rocks on sore feet. No-one ever came to their part of the creek where the steep cliffs made passing impossible, and the thick jungle hid them from the fields above.

Both the spring water cave and the quicksand cave emerged

in the cliff face on stone, and so it was easy to leave no marks at the entrance. If the planters had hunted with dogs, they might have tracked them; but there were no foxhounds or staghounds or even bloodhounds on Barbados, and the gang which went out after runaway slaves with their half-wild dogs worked out of Bridge and never came near the creeks. The English were afraid of the wild, and so convinced that the heart of the island was an impenetrable jungle, crowded with strange trees with poisonous fruit, that they left it alone.

There was much that was familiar to the little family. They gathered pitch pine to make torches for light inside the cave, just as they would at home. They ate fruit that grew wild in the forest: cherry, soursop, papaya, prickly pear and golden apple. They dug the roots of the cassava, crushed and drained and dried it to make pone. They caught land crabs, and fish in the river, and netted doves, they ate nuts and roots, and big cockroaches and broke into the big colonies of ants for food. Within weeks Wómpatuck had filled out and was stronger, his skin glowing, his hair glossy, and his mother and Rowan were thriving.

In the daytime they stayed in the shelter of the cave. They used the time to slowly penetrate the cave system, to discover the galleries leading from one cave to another, roped up with vines from the weeping fig trees, their way illuminated by the flickering light of candlewood. They found their way through the rock to the quicksand cave, and beyond it to more caves. They laid a bridge of canes and palms across the quicksand to get across, and then they sank rocks as stepping stones, in a random pattern that lay invisible under the water, to make a hidden path that only the three of them knew.

'If we are ever raided,' Rowan said, 'we go across the quicksand to the caves beyond and nobody could follow us.'

They went past the quicksand, deeper into the caves, paddling down a river which dropped out in a waterfall from a seashore cliff into the sea and they climbed down the cliffs to gather seagull eggs, down to the sands to catch a turtle.

They did not fear the cold in this forest. 'There's no winter here,' Caskwadadas told Rowan. 'Sometimes it rains a lot, and sometimes there is a terrible wind. But there is never snow. We'll never wear fur here.'

'Wómpatuck is named for a snow goose, but will never see snow?' Rowan asked. 'That can't be.'

'We can't stay here forever. Wómpatuck has to be a *Pinese*, he has to become a man. He has to take his first deer, he has to run with the wolves and taste the snow.'

'I know,' Rowan said, looking at the boy. 'I don't forget.'

BRIDGETOWN, BARBADOS, AUTUMN 1686

Johnnie had expected his arrival in Barbados to be busy; but the town of Bridge was a roar of confusion. The arrival of a ship from England was an occasion for anyone hoping for letters or a payment from home to crowd down to the stone harbour and drink in the many tippling houses and gentlemen's clubs while waiting for the ship. By the time the ship had anchored and the passengers and goods had been ferried by smaller boats to the quay, there were riotous arguments and fights, and a drunken welcome on the quayside.

Johnnie felt very alone amid the bustle and noise. He saw his trade goods safely into a locked warehouse, paid the duty to the harbour officials and accepted the captain's advice on the best hotel. A slave boy from the boarding house carried his bag and led the way, and Johnnie followed him along the cobbled quay, his hat pulled down to shade his eyes from the glare that bounced off the painted walls of the warehouses. He was overwhelmed by the stink of the salt water swamp that lapped around the bridge crossing the river, and he had to hide his horror at the sight of mutilated slaves, who limped after him offering to carry his goods, or begging for charity.

To his surprise the inn was a replica of a London boarding house, complete with a host swathed in a green apron in the tap room, and his wife who showed Johnnie to a small clean room. 'One of our best rooms,' she said. 'And you can take it for yourself alone. You don't have to share.'

'Thank you,' Johnnie said.

'Paying in silver or sugar or note?' she asked.

'Silver – I have no sugar.'

She laughed at the newcomer's answer, the frill on her white cap bobbing around her flushed red face. 'You will!' she told him. 'Or you'll take a note of hand for it. It's the easiest way to make money in the world. You buy sugar at harvest time, you keep it cool in your store, and you sell it six months later, when the price has gone up again.'

'I have an interest in sugar,' Johnnie admitted. 'Do you know of a sugar planter by the name of Mr Peabody?'

''Course I do!' she said instantly. 'Doesn't he choose to stay here whenever he comes into town? Wasn't he here just last month?'

'Was he?'

'Oh aye. Are you a friend of his?'

'No, no,' Johnnie said, realising that he did not want to tell the hotel keeper of his hopes to free Rowan. 'I just know his name. From the captain.'

'I can introduce you when he next comes to town,' she promised. 'Are you making a long stay with us, Sir?'

'I'm setting up a small warehouse for goods,' Johnnie told her. 'My family trade in silks and antiquities and elegant furnishings and I am opening a shop here, like the Royal Exchange that we have in London.'

'Pretty things?' she said eagerly. 'New things? London fashion?'

'Just what the ladies were wearing in London as I left.'

'May I have a sight of them?'

'When I open my store. They're all in bond right now.'

'Well, you've come to the right place,' she assured him. 'Half the island has pockets bursting with money and nothing to buy.'

'And the other half?' Johnnie asked, smiling.

She laughed in his face. 'The other half are goods, themselves. We have our trade too, Sir! But they're all lost souls.'

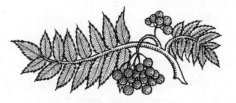

WHITEHALL PALACE, LONDON, WINTER 1686

The magnificent chapel that had cost thousands of pounds in marble and gilding, in the heart of the royal palace of Whitehall, was finally completed and Father Petre, rising unstoppably in the king's favour, was to be Grand Almoner.

A great procession to midnight Mass was led by the Duke of Norfolk bearing the sword of state, to lay on the altar to show the kingdom of England's obeisance to the Church of Rome. But at the doorway to the roman catholic chapel, the duke hesitated, checked like a horse that refuses a jump.

'Go on!' the king said impatiently, just behind him, weighed down with robes of gold thread.

'I can't,' the duke said unhappily. 'Forgive me, Sire. But I can't do it. I cannot go in.'

'Go in! Go in!'

He was visibly distressed; the sword of state, held before him, shook in his hands. He had planned to do this ceremony, he had thought he could bring himself to it. Now, he was trapped between his loyalty to the king and to his faith. 'I cannot, on my soul, enter a roman catholic church.'

The king was speechless for a moment then he burst out furiously: 'Your father was a better man, and would have gone further!'

The duke bowed. 'And your father would not have gone so far.'

There was a little gasp from the courtiers who were close enough to hear. The queen stepped forward. 'If you will not come in, you can stay outside,' she said sharply to the duke. 'You will not be missed.' She gestured to the many courtiers waiting to enter.

He bowed low to her, and he turned to the king. 'I surrender the sword of state, and my commission in the army.' His voice was trembling with emotion as he resigned from his duty and abandoned his family's tradition. James had none of the charm of his brother or his father. Either of them would have rescued the man from the conflict of his loyalty to his religion and to his king, neither of them would have put him in such a place, but James pushed past him without a word, and went into the chapel, the queen and court following.

It was a blaze of gold, illuminated by thousands of candles, the choir were singing an anthem – it was a glorious moment that James was determined should not be spoiled by someone's conscience. He, himself, was utterly convinced that this was the will of God.

The service was – as Livia had foreseen – long and filled with ritual, the priests almost invisible behind the richly gilded rood screen, the sermon a lengthy attack on the heresies of protestant-ism. Even the queen, the most devout of women, was tired by the time the Mass was over and she could return to her bedroom.

The ladies responsible for undressing her opened the cedar-wood chest and took out her fine nightgown, as she sat before the looking glass while another lady unpinned the jewels from her hair and gently removed the false ringlets.

'What is it?' Mary Beatrice asked Livia. 'I can tell that you are waiting to say something.'

'I'll wait a little longer,' Livia said. 'If I may.'

The queen shrugged off her gown and stepped into the night-robe. They put a warm wrapper around her shoulders and she took a seat beside the fire. 'Now go,' she told them and turned to Livia, who took a seat without waiting for permission.

'You may not like the news I have, but I swear it does you no harm.'

The younger woman's face was grave with worry. 'It's not Catherine Sedley? He's not bringing her back to court?'

'No, no, not as bad as that.'

'What then?' The queen flushed, and Livia slid onto her knees beside her chair and took her thin hands in a gentle grip.

'His sons by Arabella Churchill are coming to court this week,' she said. 'The old mistress isn't coming, don't fear her – she's married off and grown plain. But her bastard royal sons: James and Henry are invited. By the king.'

Mary Beatrice went so white that Livia tightened her grip. 'Why now?' she demanded. 'He said he would never bring them to court. He said he would never grieve me with the presence of his bastard sons, before I had one of my own!'

'They're not going to stay,' Livia told her. 'He's granting titles. He's going to give James Fitzjames a dukedom. He's going to make him Duke of Berwick.'

'This is to declare him as his son?'

Livia could not deny it.

'So he has given up all hope of having a son from me. And now he tells the world.'

Livia rose up and poured her a glass of red wine. 'The king is coming to you this evening, you might make a baby this very night. Giving the Churchill bastard a dukedom is no more than finding him a place in the world. His brother Henry is to go to sea. We can't stop the king acknowledging his bastards, but any

365

child you have will take the throne, even if there are a dozen bastard dukes.'

'It's what he thinks of me that matters,' the queen said miserably. 'And when he makes his bastard a duke he tells everyone that he has given up on me.'

BRIDGETOWN, BARBADOS, WINTER 1687

Johnnie planned to open an Exchange like the new markets that were springing up in London: big buildings where small tradesmen could rent space for their own shops. He rented a warehouse on Exchange Street, near the merchant meeting house, where all the great planters, exporters of sugar and captains of ships gathered to do business. It was an elegant street, broad and wide with stone buildings, rebuilt with slave labour after the town's disastrous fire. The paved street was wide enough to take two carriages passing by, so Johnnie was certain that ladies would drive by the open doors and be unable to resist the temptation to step inside. At the rear of the building were great doors that opened wide enough for a wagon to enter from the quay which was only yards away.

Here, with almost no competition, with customers desperate for English goods, Johnnie unpacked a selection of housewares, small pieces of furniture, textiles, luxury goods and fashionable accessories. He had dried herbs, salves and remedies from the Priory still room set out in a display on a small gate-leg table that was for sale, as were the hangings behind it. Silks from Venice, forwarded by Sarah and packed by Alys, were hung on all the walls; Johnnie hoped to introduce to Barbados the fashion of curtains at the windows where – surely – they did not need shutters against cold winds? He had rolls and rolls of light fabrics, muslin and silks for bed hangings, as everyone had told him that the gnats and mosquitoes were an agony at night. Johnnie thought that billowing bed curtains might keep the insects out, and even if they did not, they would add London elegance to a faraway room.

Rob had guaranteed a loan from his father-in-law, the Alderman goldsmith, both of them eager to invest in the Sugar Islands. Johnnie had bought everything from trimmings for hats and headpieces, leather and silk gloves, lace for collars, embroidery threads, expensive linen for luxury petticoats, and ells of fabric for dressmakers and tailors. He had several muffs and matching capes. After fifteen years in the East India Company trying to persuade the inhabitants of India to wear English wool, Johnnie was delighted to find that the English in Barbados did not dress lightly for the hot climate but wanted to wear what the English wore in England; and he could sell heavy tweeds as well as he could sell light silk.

Nothing was made on the island but sugar and rum: everything had to be imported. Johnnie could have sold butcher's knives and blacksmith's rasps. He could have sold bridles and harness for ox and horses, of course he could have sold the tools of slavery – branding irons, whips, chains and manacles, instruments to pierce the tongue or knives to cut off ears or pierce cheeks. But his main stock in trade was fabric and fashion for the ladies of the island who had almost nothing to do but dress and sit in shaded rooms, and hope that they were in the fashion of the English court, though inevitably trailing some months behind.

From the very first morning, when Johnnie spoke severely to the two slaves loaned to him from his hotel, and threw open the doors of his store, he knew that he would make his fortune. The carriages were drawn up outside, the ladies poured in, followed by slaves to carry their purchases, avid for anything new from England, desperate for new materials, colours and patterns, greedy for as little as inches of lace to trim a collar or a ribbon for a hat. There was nothing to do on Barbados but visit other plantations and drink. They had enslaved thousands of men and women and made themselves into bored and lonely prisoners of their own wealth.

The first months went by in a whirl. Johnnie sent a stream of letters to Alys with lists of goods that he needed to replace his sold stock. He paid his takings into the Bridge goldsmith and sent the receipt to Alys for her to draw on the Alderman's bank. The evening that the innkeeper's wife mentioned that Mr Peabody was expected the following day, Johnnie had already earned enough to buy Rowan into his own service and place her as his indentured servant, to run the shop until her ten years were up. Then he would free her, marry her, and make a huge profit in one single brilliant venture.

Mr Peabody came in his carriage with Bonny seated on the box beside the black coachman, and a black enslaved footman clinging on the back. Johnnie encountered him in the parlour of the hotel.

'Forgive me,' he said with a warm smile. 'The landlady said that a gentleman was staying, and I was avid for company.'

'Eh? Mr Peabody said, looking around from squeezing limes into a bowl of punch.

'Johnnie Stoney, London merchant,' Johnnie introduced himself, coming into the room.

'Samuel Peabody, planter,' the man replied. 'Good to see a new face. Will you take a glass? I'm just making a glass or two. My own rum, from my own plantation.'

'I'm grateful,' Johnnie said, secretly adding fruit juice and boiled water to the stiff mix, so that he had a chance of remaining clear-headed while Samuel Peabody became gradually more red-faced, sweaty and drunk.

'Coming to plant sugar?' Mr Peabody asked. 'Manage a plantation?'

'No. I have a little shop, fancy goods.'

'Have another,' Peabody served them with another two glasses. 'Just as well. Sugar's a game for an experienced man. Experienced, you know?'

Johnnie nodded.

'Have another, eh?'

Johnnie accepted a glass and diluted it again.

'The trouble with this place,' Samuel told him. 'You won't know, coming as you do from London, not yet seasoned, knowing nothing but the old country ... The trouble with this place is ...' He had lost his thread. He blinked owlishly at the punch glass in his hand. 'Bowl's dry,' he announced, and raised his voice and bellowed for Bonny to bring more rum and lemons and sugar.

'Do you have a very large plantation?' Johnnie asked politely, and Mr Peabody explained that it was his wife's dowry and not nearly big enough for a man of his ambition, but that he would buy more land whenever there was any to be had. He would buy a new mill with triple rollers as soon as he completed the design. The rich old families, like his father-in-law, might sell up and retire to England, but the new men, the brilliant young men like himself, had to compete for land on a small island and speed up the harvest to make a profit.

'They've got to go faster,' he insisted. 'Faster.'

'How I should like to see it,' Johnnie hinted.

Samuel Peabody declared that nothing was easier. Nobody in England had manners anymore, but Johnnie would find that in Barbados the traditions of old England – he waved his hand to indicate some fabled time – possibly Good Queen Bess – were maintained and any man was given a great dinner at any man's door.

'White men,' Johnnie confirmed.

'Rich men,' Samuel agreed. 'Not scoundrels . . .' Again he lost his complaint in the bottom of the punch bowl. 'Good health.'

'I may visit you?' Johnnie pressed.

'You go to any house, any house in Barbados and you'll find a welcome,' Mr Peabody told Johnnie fondly. 'Glad to see a new face. We don't stint . . .'

He poured another cup of punch. 'There's so few of us,' he said thoughtfully. 'We have to stick together.'

'Few of you?' Johnnie thought of the crowded street, the babel at the quayside, the sweat of all the bodies crushed together and the churn of men running after profit.

'Few of us planters,' Samuel Peabody explained. 'Few of us masters.'

Johnnie realised he meant white men, and that living with hundreds of people he was lonely; drowning in wealth, he thought himself hard done by.

'There's so very many of them . . .' Samuel complained.

'But it's you who bring them in? You buy them in? More and more every year? They would not be here if you did not order them to be kidnapped from their homes?'

'I don't think anyone realised how terrible it would be,' Mr Peabody confided damply, his eyes watering.

'For the slaves?'

'For us. For us! My God – trying to live like this? Live like it, and make it last forever? Setting the laws so they're never freed, can never escape. Setting the punishments so we can kill them rather than they endanger us? Always looking behind, never anyone you can trust . . .'

'It's bad?' Johnnie queried, seeing his host dissolve into tears of self-pity.

'It's the finest life in the world,' Samuel Peabody contradicted himself with drunken insistence. 'It's England as it was! As it ought to be. The most beautiful houses, and the most beautiful women, there's nowhere that people live better, there's nowhere richer – nowhere. It's the richest country in the world! And it's tradition. It's natural that one race should rule another.' He drank deeply. 'But it's like eating children,' he said, mumbling without meaning. 'It might be the sweetest flesh in the world but sickening. Sickening!'

'You eat children?' Johnnie asked, horrified.

'We eat sugar. And sugar eats them. We eat up the children of Africa.'

Johnnie waited in case he said more, but Samuel Peabody was fast asleep. Johnnie went to the parlour door and opened it. Mr Peabody's black slave woman was sleeping, propped up against the door jamb. She leapt to her feet, rubbing her eyes, when she felt the door move. She saw Johnnie standing in the doorway.

'He's asleep.'

She nodded and turned to go towards the kitchen to fetch slaves to lift the big white drunk man into bed.

'He invited me to the plantation. Will he remember that? And then he was unhappy,' Johnnie told her.

'He'll remember he asked you,' Bonny told him. 'He'll forget he cried.'

'He cries often?'

She shrugged. 'Why not?' she asked him. 'Shouldn't he?'

Mr Peabody returned to his home the next day but left an invitation for Johnny to visit in a scrawled note.

What a night of it! Look forward to seeing you at Peabody Plantation. In St Thomas' Parish, anybody will tell you where. Come anytime.
  Samuel Peabody (Gent.)

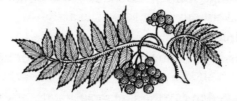

PEABODY PLANTATION, WINTER 1687

Dora Peabody was delighted to have a house guest to break up the monotony of her days, and even more pleased by the gift that Johnnie brought: some little cakes of scented soap from Venice. She sat with the men as they drank the last of the wine after the long extravagant dinner, and only went to bed when Samuel said that they would have a bowl of punch as a nightcap.

'Goodnight,' she said, giving her hand to Johnnie. 'It's such a pleasure . . . Such a . . .' She was nearly as drunk as her husband. Bonny came in silently, and helped her to bed. Johnnie and Samuel took their seats in his library, two comfortable chairs before the empty cedarwood shelves.

'M' father-in-law's library,' Samuel said, seeing Johnnie looking at the echoing space. 'Took all the books when he went back to England, and I'm not much of a man for reading.'

Johnnie accepted a glass of punch. 'Me neither. I never went to college.'

'I read law for a term,' Samuel reminisced. 'But I'd no real use for it. I always knew that I'd come out here, or the Americas. Second son, you see – nothing left to me but a good name. I knew that I'd always find someone who wanted a good old name to attach to new dirty money. A true match,' he said. 'A true love match: old name, new money.'

'How many slaves d'you have here?' Johnnie asked, trying to turn the conversation towards Rowan. The thought that she might be somewhere on the plantation, nearby, made his head spin as much as the drink.

'About two hundred,' Mr Peabody said thoughtfully. 'Overseer counts them every day so he knows exactly.'

'Two hundred?'

'Give or take. Mind!' He raised a fat finger at Johnnie. 'I didn't buy them all,' he said owlishly. 'Most of them came with the land, part of her dowry.' The stubby finger jabbed upwards in the direction of Dora Peabody's bedroom. 'But so many of 'em died off. I had to buy a few, about a score, and about half a dozen white servants. I like a few white servants to keep the place safe. Even the scrapings of the poorhouse, whatever. Even rebels. Even Irish. You've got to have enough white men to hold the blacks down. You always have to keep that in mind.' He blinked at Johnnie as if he might have argued. 'We've put angry natives into an empty country,' he said. 'Madness. There was nobody here when we first came here. Think of that? Virgin land. But now we're as surrounded as badly as any New Englander, overwhelmed by savages. We've imported our enemies.'

'It's not a risk, buying English rebels?' Johnnie prompted.

'They don't last,' he complained. 'They can't stand the field work, and half of them have no trade. And they die of the heat. Or they wander off and get lost. Just last year I had one out looking for Dora's little dog. Did he come back as he'd promised?'

'Did he?' Johnnie prompted when it seemed that Samuel Peabody had fallen asleep.

'No!' he said with a start. 'Didn't find his way to my neighbours, didn't stroll off to Bridge. Vanished off the face of the earth.'

'Drowned?' Johnnie suggested.

'Only if he went all the way to the headland and fell off into the sea.' Samuel pointed out. 'Didn't drown in the pond for sure. Not deep enough. Only the black women drown in there when they tie themselves to the anvil and haul it from the farrier's.'

'What was his name?' Johnnie asked.

Samuel Peabody scowled with the effort of remembering. 'I bought him off the *Rebecca*,' he said.

Johnnie felt himself grow cold in the heat of the library.

'Young lad, lean as a lop.'

'Off the *Rebecca*?'

'Aye. Would've been one of the rebels. Said he was just a servant following his master. But they all say that.'

'What was his name?' Johnnie repeated.

'Ferryman.' Samuel found the name with quiet triumph and did not notice that Johnnie had clutched the arms of his chair and was staring at him, as he searched for the Christian name.

'Ned Ferryman.'

'You're quite sure?'

Mr Peabody had drifted off; he came to with a jolt. 'Sure? That he's dead? Oh yes. If he didn't break his neck in a fall or die of heatstroke, he couldn't live here. Nothing but cane! Nothing to eat!'

'You've made a desert,' Johnnie said. 'And filled it with enemies.'

'Ha! Ha! Y'know that's very true. Yes, we have.'

FOULMIRE PRIORY, SUSSEX, SPRING 1687

Ned and Alinor, returning to the tidelands for the second summer, saw the little terns settling on their nests of pebbles, hovering over the waters, and welcomed the first swallows swooping in and out of the Priory stables where they had nested for generations. They walked through the herb garden and Ned laughed as Alinor threatened him with comfrey soup.

'No, I'm well,' he told her. 'I swear I don't need it. You've made me well again.'

She smiled. 'It was your own stubbornness. I prayed for you and fed you, but it was you that grabbed the side of the bed and heaved yourself up, and took another step every day.'

He had a lopsided smile now. 'I'm well enough to take ship,' he told her.

'Back to New England?'

He shook his head. 'Barbados.'

He saw her hesitate. 'What is it?' he said flatly. 'Tell me! Has he found her?'

She hesitated. 'Sit down.'

'If it's bad news, tell me now!'

She pressed him into the seat at the end of the path.

'Tell me quickly, Alinor, is she dead?'

'I am afraid so. I am sorry, my dear.' The shock on his face was too much for her. She stood behind the seat so she should not see his face twisted with pain. She rested her hand on his rigid shoulder. 'I am so sorry, Ned. I only had the letter from Alys this morning.'

'I can bear it,' he said tightly. 'Sit beside me. What did he say? Exactly?'

'That he went to the plantation where she was working and they said she'd gone out looking for a stray dog and met with an accident. Her owner offered a reward for the musket she was carrying but nobody came forward, and they haven't found it, though they searched the slaves' huts.'

'D'you have the letter?'

She produced it from the pocket of her cape, and he looked through it. Johnnie was ordering more goods for his Bridgetown warehouse, especially light goods that were easy to ship. Fabrics and ribbons and lace. Pins and needles, embroidery scissors and silks. At the end of the order, he wrote of the loss of Rowan.

'So they didn't look for her. Sounds like her owner just asked at his neighbours, and Johnnie just asked him.'

'I'm sorry, Ned, I think that she's gone.'

'Do you?' he demanded, returning the letter to her as if it were valueless to him. 'D'you really think so? D'you feel her death, Sister? In your heart?'

She was still for a moment, her grey eyes hazy and unseeing, as if she were listening for a silent call.

'Last midsummer, we were here,' he pressed. 'On Midsummer Eve. You'll have gone to the churchyard? You'll have waited and watched at midnight, to see those that would die this year. Did you see her then?'

She shook her head. 'No-one came, thank God, though I was looking for your spirit as you were so sick, and for—' She broke off; she would not tell her brother that James Avery thought his heart was broken. 'And for another. But no-one came. Not you, not him, and not Rowan.'

'I won't believe it till her body's found,' he decided. 'Alinor, this isn't a girl who tumbles off a cliff looking for a dog, she wouldn't drown in a lake trying to rescue it. It's my belief she's run away, and she's living wild somewhere.'

'Johnnie says there's nowhere for slaves to run, the whole island is given over to sugar cane.'

'I've seen her hide on the shadow of a rope,' he said, his eyes warm. 'In Amsterdam, I once saw her disappear in the corner of a room. I don't believe she's dead. She'll be in hiding somewhere. I'm going to her.'

'D'you think you can find her?'

'Nay! Not I! I won't see so much as her shadow unless she allows it. Nobody will ever find her. But I'll go there, and make a bit of a noise, and she'll come to me if she wants.'

'But she might already be with Johnnie. She might have been hiding on the plantation and be with him now. She might be safe, and his letter on the way.'

'I don't know what there is between her and Johnnie,' Ned said steadily. 'I've never even seen them together, and she's never spoken of him to me. None of my business. If she comes out of hiding and goes to him ... it doesn't matter to me, Sister. I want her to please herself. In all fairness, I know that he loves her.'

'Like you?' Alinor asked.

'No! Never. He loves her as a man loves a woman, as a young man loves a young woman, and that's good and right for him. But I love her as if she were a star in the sky. I love her as if she were the wind blowing over the water. I don't need to own her, I just want her to be in the sky, moving over the deep, I just want her to shine.'

REEKIE WHARF, LONDON, SUMMER 1687

The carriage hired to take Matthew, Mia and Gabrielle to the Priory brought Ned back to the warehouse on the return journey. Despite Alinor's concern, he travelled alone and arrived on an unseasonably cold rainy day and climbed down the steps without help.

'Now here's a grand sight,' Alys greeted him in the yard. 'Look at you! Not a mark on you.'

He lifted the floppy greying fringe of hair to show her the white scar where the cannonball had struck his head. 'Your Ma has been basting me with arnica beeswax,' he said. 'And lavender, and comfrey. I swear to you, I went to bed some nights as sweet as a pomander.'

Alys laughed. 'Did she feed you nettle soup? She always fed me nettle soup if I had a fall.'

Ned smiled. 'I've come here to escape the nettle soup. Don't remind me of it. The stench! And that green colour! And fish – I had fish for dinner every day. I am like to grow fins.'

Alys laughed and led him into the house. 'Come and have some small ale after your journey – are you allowed small ale?'

They walked past the open kitchen door and Ned called a greeting to the cook Tabs and the maid Susie. 'I am allowed small ale, but no strong liquors,' he said. 'I am allowed a glass of wine and water with my dinner. I pity those children, with her for the summer, she's a tyrant.'

Cook came in with two glasses of small ale and Alys sat at the parlour table and Ned at the empty hearth. 'Jests aside, you are well, Uncle? You look better?'

'I am. I'm well enough to sail. I'll take a passage to Barbados.'

Alys grimaced. 'All that way on the off-chance that she's alive?'

'Gladly. I owe it to her.'

'Johnnie was very sure that she was dead.'

'That's not a girl who gets lost in a forest.'

'Uncle Ned, I don't want Johnnie stirred up about her all over again,' Alys told him bluntly. 'He's making a fortune there, he sent home two barrels of sugar.'

'Slavery money.'

'Profit. It's all slavery. There's no free labour in Barbados.'

'Alys, I wouldn't distress you for the world, and I won't trouble him. But it's my duty to see she's safe. I'll go as soon as I can raise funds for a passage.'

'Half of London's going out with the new governor for Jamaica – you could probably get on the frigate.'

'Who is it?'

'Christopher Monck the treasure hunter.'

He gave a comical yelp of dismay. 'Drunk Monck!' he exclaimed. 'I last saw him drunk as a lord in a little town in the west. Wouldn't come over to our side, couldn't lead his men. Good for nowt.'

'Did he see you?' Alys asked, immediately anxious. 'Did he get your name?'

'Nay, he won't remember me, he won't remember anything. It wasn't his finest hour. But I might get a place in his train.'

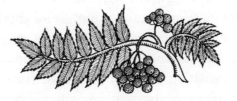

FOULMIRE PRIORY, SUSSEX, SUMMER 1687

'When I was a girl,' Alinor told Mia, Gabrielle and Hester, 'we believed that if you picked a rose on Midsummer Eve it would stay fresh and blooming till Christmas Eve.'

The girls were in the still room, a tray of beeswax before them, putting honeysuckle flowers face down into the wax to drain the perfume; the heady smell filled the room. Matthew was at the stone sink, carefully washing the flowers and putting them to dry on muslin.

'And did it?' Gabrielle asked.

Mia made a face at her. 'Of course not.'

Alinor smiled. 'I never picked a rose on Midsummer Eve,' she admitted, 'so I don't know.'

'Why not?' Hester asked.

'I didn't have a rose garden then,' she said. 'And I was too busy to pick roses from the hedgerows. But we could do it this year and see.'

'What other things can you do for midsummer?' Gabrielle asked.

'It's a lot about love,' Alinor cautioned them. 'So of no interest to serious girls like you.'

'Should I leave?' Matthew asked, looking up from the sink full of flowers.

'No, stay,' said Hester.

'I have no time for love,' Gabrielle told them.

'Nor I,' said Mia immediately.

'Mama says that she will decide all about it,' Hester said.

'And it is indelicate for a young lady to ask. But do tell us, Grandmother!'

Alinor laughed. 'My, you make me feel old!' She moved the full tray to the rack and put out another for them to put clean flowerheads into wax. 'If you pick St John's wort and put it under your pillow without telling anyone, picking it in the morning of Midsummer Eve with the dew on it, picking it in secret, then that night you will dream of the man you will marry.'

'St John's wort? Do you grow it?' Hester asked.

'Little yellow flower, in the herb garden,' Gabrielle told her shortly. 'Is it all love potions for girls?'

'Young men can conjure their sweethearts too,' Alinor offered.

The girls turned to Matthew. 'Say you'll try!' Mia urged him.

'What does he have to do?' Gabrielle asked.

'He has to go to the herb garden before the clock strikes twelve on Midsummer Eve,' Alinor said.

'Oh no, I would be too afraid,' Matthew told them, drying his hands. 'I wouldn't dare.'

'Then he has to pick a leaf of sage for each tolling of the bell.'

Matthew rolled his eyes in a parody of terror.

Alinor laughed at him. 'And then when he picks the last leaf at the last bell he turns around and his future lover is standing behind him.'

'A ghost?' Matthew quavered.

'A vision, or even the real woman.'

'Terrifying!'

'No, but really, I don't think you should do that,' Hester cautioned him. 'Because it would be too easy for someone to creep up on you—'

'I'm not going into the herb garden at midnight if someone is creeping up on me—'

'Not to attack you. But to cheat you into thinking that you were destined to marry them.'

'I'm not going to marry anyone who creeps up on me,' Matthew protested. 'Mother Alinor, this isn't going to work! It can never have worked! People would always have had to marry madwomen!'

'You could try rosemary,' Alinor said, turning to Gabrielle. 'You take a plate of flour and put it under a rosemary bush on Midsummer Eve. In the morning you will find your future husband's initials written in the flour.'

'That's a pretty one,' Hester said.

'Could we do that?' Mia asked, her eyes shining. 'Just to see, of course. Not that I believe in it!'

'But I don't want to marry a man who goes around at midnight writing his name in plates of flour,' Gabrielle objected.

'Besides, he'll bump into Matthew's mad wife, creeping up on him!' Mia laughed. 'Is it all pretend?'

'It's all about looking into your own heart, and then reading whatever you want in leaves and flour and dust,' Alinor ruled.

'Grandmother, have you ever told fortunes?' Hester asked her.

Alinor's face was grave. 'No sensible woman would ever do so. Even now, it's not safe. When it's wrong you're taken for a fool; and if it comes right, then you're taken for a witch.' In the brightness of the sweet-smelling still room, with the untroubled young faces before her, she spoke without a quaver in her voice. 'I was wrongly accused once.'

'What did they say?' Mia asked.

'That I had a purse of faerie gold,' Alinor smiled, refusing to remember the fear. 'That I was a mermaid from the sea.'

'Was there a priest?' Gabrielle asked acutely.

Alinor gave her a little smile. 'Once there was.'

'Was there a true love?'

'As true as it could be.'

'But have you ever known Midsummer Eve foretelling come true?' Mia asked.

'Well, of course people make wishes come true. There's no magic in that – just desire.'

'These young ladies are too young for wishes,' Matthew said firmly, and Alinor shot a smile at him.

'Just so.'

Alinor guessed that curiosity would get the better of the girls, and she watched from her bedroom window as they let themselves out of the garden door and crept into the herb garden with a basket of goods. She picked up her cape, drew it around her shoulders and put up the hood. The garden was light with the eerie luminous gleam of midsummer night, a pale sun almost white, hidden by the flat silver sea, the moon high and golden, rising over the trees of Sealsea Forest.

Alinor went down the stairs, holding to the bannister, picked up her cane by the front door, opened the door without a sound and felt the warm air on her cheek. A barn owl called plaintively from somewhere in the garden and an answering cry came from the wood. Alinor smiled, imagining the girls clutching each other in fright.

The drive of white shingle gleamed in the half-light and Alinor walked away from the house, past the tall gateposts and took the path to church. She paused at the lich-gate, remembering the time she had waited in the churchyard on Midsummer Eve. It was so long ago that it seemed as if another woman had walked in the moonlight and waited in the porch to see a handsome young man coming towards her. Alinor put her hand to her heart, remembering how it had speeded the moment she had seen him, all those years ago, and then she stepped out of the shadow of the lich-gate into the eerie dusk of the silent graveyard.

She was alone; the upright headstones were solitary, casting dark shadows on the bleached grass, the carved crosses hid no-one. The only large memorial was dedicated to the Peachey family, at the far end of the graveyard in solitary grandeur, and there was no-one standing in its shadow.

Alinor's feet made no sound as she walked to the church porch. In the distance she could hear the softest whisper from the harbour as the tide crept in, silvery under the light sky, and the babble of a few sleepless birds. She seated herself on the bench of the porch where she had waited nearly forty years ago, and looked out through the archway down the path, towards the sea, for the ghosts of those she loved, that would come to say farewell as they would die this year.

From the bell tower in the graveyard she heard the slow clank of the mechanism winding up to ring the bell. Twelve times the hammer hit the bell, the sound ringing out into the grey night as if it were calling someone from far away. Alinor rose to her feet, like a girl will stand to see her lover, until at last he came, walking between the graves, his feet on the ground making no mark, and there was no sound when he reached the stone step of the porch.

All her heart was in her smile. 'James,' she said. 'I am so glad you are come to me, at last.'

He was a young man, as handsome as the priest from the charcoal burner's story with long dark hair tied back at the nape of his neck and dark eyes set in a pale face, and when she put her hand out to him she saw the scratched hand of the fisherman's wife that she had been forty years ago. 'I knew we would meet again,' she said simply.

He nodded. 'I knew it too.'

'Did you forgive yourself?'

'At the end. At the end I became the man I hoped to be.'

'I love you, James,' she said simply. 'I loved you truly.'

He smiled at her, that young smile: filled with joy and confidence, his eyes warm upon her face. 'I loved you,' he told her. 'Not enough then. But I learned. And now I can love you again.'

She knew better than to try to touch him; she sunk down to her seat and smiled up at him until he grew ghostly and she could see him no more, then she gave a deep sigh and rested her head on the stone wall and fell fast asleep.

That was where they found her in the morning.

WHITEHALL PALACE, LONDON,
SUMMER 1687

A letter from Matthew saying that his foster grandmother Alinor had died, and would be buried next to her parents in the St Wilfrid's churchyard, arrived at Whitehall Palace at the same time as bad news from Rome. Duchess Laura, the difficult bad-tempered mother of the queen, had died and Mary Beatrice, shocked with grief, losing her refuge from her unhappy marriage, ordered the whole court into the deepest black mourning. Livia thought it painfully ironic that she had to go into deepest black as if she were mourning Alinor: the one woman in her life that she had never been able to seduce, defraud or even confuse.

Servants were to wear black gloves, black armbands and black sashes. Ladies of the court were to wear no colour for a month, and no beauty spots or rouge; the gentlemen and lords were to wear black or grey for Duchess Laura. The embroiderers and haberdashers ran out of black thread and black velvet and Julia's father loaned the guild of haberdashers a thousand pounds to buy French silk.

It was a sign of how unpopular Duchess Laura had made herself that some of the ladies and lords at court refused to go into full mourning, and the Dowager Queen complained that when her mother died, there had been only partial mourning for a short time. and she would wear dark colours, but neither she nor her ladies would go into black.

Livia did not hesitate: the shape of her face, an exquisite oval, was enhanced by a high black neckline, the lines around her eyes and forehead were obscured by a little veil. Her dark eyes under her hat with dark feathers and black crystals, sparkled ambivalently, as if filled with tears or perhaps promise. She drew the best of the black gowns from the royal wardrobe the moment she heard the news, and she wondered how she could keep them in her cupboard after the official time of mourning was over.

So she was already dressed as a widow when she received the news from Yorkshire that her husband Sir James had died in his sleep on Midsummer Eve. She read and re-read the letter with increasing incredulity, then she took Matthew's note telling her of Alinor's death and re-read that, looking at the date, seeing that they matched exactly. James and Alinor, lovers for all their lives, had both died on Midsummer Eve. She had no doubt that they had died together, at midnight. She told her maid she was not to be disturbed and she retired to her room and locked the door.

'She's grieving for her husband,' the other ladies told the queen who had taken to her enormous gilded bed in her luxurious new apartments to cry for her mother. The young queen forced herself up, threw a black robe around her black nightgown, and went through the shaded silent palace to her friend.

She listened at Livia's door for heartbroken sobs, but instead heard the rapid stride of footsteps up and down, up and down the length of the room, echoing on the wooden floorboards, dulled by the expensive rugs. She tapped on the door.

'I gave orders I was not to be disturbed!' Livia snapped from inside the room.

'It's me, the queen,' Mary Beatrice said, her voice choked with grief. 'Please let me in, Livia.'

She heard Livia's heels click across the floor and then the door was flung open and Livia, tragic in black, sunk into a curtsey. Mary Beatrice rushed into the room and lifted her up to hold her as tightly as a lover.

'I came as soon as I heard,' she said. 'I got up at once. I knew you would be miserable.'

'Yes,' Livia said, still white with anger.

Mary Beatrice peeped into her friend's scowling face. 'We can grieve together,' she promised. 'To think that I will never see her again . . . now, when I need her so much! When I have lost the love of my husband, to lose my mother as well!'

Livia wrenched her expression into mournful serenity. 'It's terribly sad,' she managed to say.

The two of them sank onto a sofa before the fireplace. Mary Beatrice sobbed into Livia's shoulder and the older woman smoothed her hair. 'We should pray for her,' she said after a little while. 'We should go to your chapel.'

'Yes, yes,' Mary Beatrice said. 'But the soul of your husband! He was not of our faith.'

'I'll have Masses sung for him anyway,' Livia said vindictively. 'He was so heretical . . . d'you know I believe he commanded the hour of his death, he timed it so that he —' She broke off in the face of Mary Beatrice's tearstained bewilderment. 'Nothing. Nothing. I am distracted with grief. He believed he would be reunited with his loved one in death,' she said.

'It must be true,' Mary Beatrice said. 'I know I will see my mother again. I know I will speak to my mother again.'

Livia silently gritted her teeth at the thought of what she would say to James if they met in the afterlife. 'And now I shall have to go to Yorkshire for his funeral. And the reading of the will.'

'Oh, don't go!' Mary Beatrice said, holding her tighter. 'I can't bear to be alone.'

Livia tightened her grip. 'And I can't bear to leave you,' she assured the younger woman. 'I won't go till after tomorrow. I won't leave you at once. But they can't conduct the funeral without me, and I have to be there for the reading of the will.' She let her voice tremble with a real sense of loss. 'The estate is entailed. It won't even come to me. I will have nothing but a life interest in a pokey little dower house. But surely, he will have left me something more? Otherwise, I won't be able to afford to attend court.'

'Oh no!' Mary Beatrice said at once. 'No! No! I shall give you a post, I shall give you a salary. I shall give you access to the royal wardrobe all the time, not just for mourning. You must come back. If you have to go to Yorkshire, all that way, then you must come back.'

'I shall have to hire a carriage—'

'Take mine! Take one of the royal coaches.'

'Thank you,' Livia said smoothly. 'I would serve you in rags, you know.'

'I shall pay you,' the queen assured her. 'I shall see that you have a generous salary. Trust me. Promise you will come back. Promise me that you will never leave me.'

They held hands. Livia had the sense of the solemnity of an oath.

'I promise I will never leave you,' Livia swore. 'Whatever becomes of us both. We will be together, one heart, one fortune.'

'I promise,' the queen whispered, and slid into Livia's arms.

Livia rocked her like a hurt child, soothing herself, comforted that even if Alinor and James had managed, somehow, to die at the same time on the same night, as if holding hands on a journey together, then at least nobody would ever know.

FOULMIRE, SUSSEX, SUMMER 1687

The bell in the tower of St Wilfrid's church tolled steadily for all the morning, as the plain coffin was carried from the Priory, down the lane to the church and set before the altar.

The priest, even though he was wearing a surplice and vestments, censing the church and dousing the coffin with holy water, still conducted a service as simple and reverent as Ned could specify and Alys agree. Mrs Julia Reekie, now the only Mrs Reekie, in the first pew beside her husband and daughter, expected a coffin with brass ornaments and great handles, a choir in the church, and all the tenants in black gloves; but Rob and Alys had refused everything but a plain funeral from the Book of Common Prayer.

Matthew as the lord of the manor stood by the coffin to say a few words about the woman who had raised him as her own son. Mia, Gabrielle and Hester held hands in the second pew, willing him to get through the speech they had composed with him.

'My foster grandmother was born a poor woman,' Matthew started. Julia, behind a veil, closed her eyes briefly in horror.

'She was a woman of great gifts,' Matthew went on. 'All of us have known her wisdom and some of us have been lucky to have her advice. She was a natural healer, with an understanding of plants and herbs, and her son and her great-grand-daughter have followed in that practice.'

Briefly he glanced towards Gabrielle and to Rob. He noticed that Julia Reekie had fixed him with an unwavering gaze, her eyes wide in warning, but took no notice.

'She had a great love of this land and this sea – the tidelands – and we are glad that she was able to spend her last years here. She leaves a large family – we are spread across the oceans – we loved her very much, and each one of us is a better man or woman for having had her raising.'

'God, keep him from saying anyone's surnames! Or that they came from here!' Julia prayed fervently that the history of a poor family would be buried forever with Alinor.

'She was kind enough to raise me with her daughter as their foster son. We are all the better for her wisdom and her compassion and her understanding of this world and the next. She had a strong belief in the life after this one . . .'

'Stop there!' Julia whispered into her clasped hands.

'She sensed the other world, just through a veil, all around her, and neither time nor miles nor even death could part her from those she loved. She knew she would be reunited with those who love her in heaven.'

Gabrielle had been following along the words Matthew was saying, and now he was finished, she looked up, her eyes brimming with tears, and he saw the love and sympathy in her face. He bowed his head to the coffin, he put one gentle hand on it as if to say farewell, and he laid a sprig of rosemary, cut from the Priory garden that morning, to promise remembrance.

Julia flinched at the unconventional herb; but thought it might be safely overlooked when Rob stepped forward to place a bouquet of lilies, brought from London at enormous expense, at the foot of the coffin.

'God bless you, Ma,' he said quietly. 'Thank you, for all you did for me. I know how much ...' He could not say more. He stepped back to his pew.

Slowly, the mourning bell started to toll and to everyone's surprise, Ned stepped forward, holding Alinor's herb basket, her pruning knife and her hoeing stick. Gently he placed them on the coffin, to be buried with her. Julia Reekie pressed her gloved hands to her lips to stifle a quiet moan at the eccentricity. The vicar looked inquiringly towards the young lord; Matthew nodded permission. He guessed this was a ritual from Rowan's people and that his grandmother would understand it, as she had understood Rowan.

The door at the back of the church opened, and a man in green livery came forward. Matthew recognised with dread the Avery uniform, and was afraid that his mother the Nobildonna had sent an ostentatious wreath tied with black silk ribbons and a card with flowery writing. But it was not. It was a spray of wilted white roses.

Only Alys recognised the white roses of Yorkshire and knew that James had cut flowers in his garden in the night before he died, to send them to the woman he loved; and that the bond which had held them throughout their lives, had not been severed by death.

FOULMIRE PRIORY, SUSSEX, AUTUMN 1687

The summer was ending, the Michaelmas term starting, and Matthew was not sorry to be going back to London with Alys and Gabrielle and Mia. The Priory was strangely empty when Rob, Julia and Ned left after the funeral. All of them had a place or a time of day where they looked for Alinor, all of them had to remember that she would not be seen there again.

'You will come and visit again, even though she's not here,' Matthew said urgently to the two girls as they walked at sunset along the little path that led from the seashore, across the hay meadow where the aftermath grass was showing green through the stubble, through the door set in the flint-knapped wall. Matthew held the door for them to pass through into the garden. 'You will come again, even though she's gone?'

'Of course,' Gabrielle said with her ready sympathy. 'We wouldn't leave you here, all by yourself.'

'Won't you marry?' Mia demanded and then blushed at herself. 'I mean . . . well! won't you?'

Matthew laughed, equally embarrassed. 'I suppose I will,' he said awkwardly. 'I suppose I can. I have a house, and I'm qualified as a lawyer. If I get a pupillage I will start to earn money . . . I can. You're right. I could marry.'

Gabrielle looked from Mia to Matthew and back again, as if she had never really seen them before. 'Your mother perhaps has plans for you.'

'She's never said anything.' Matthew still had his eyes on Mia's face.

'She'll perhaps invite you to court to meet ladies,' Gabrielle persisted.

Matthew glanced at her. 'I hardly saw her through all my childhood,' he said. 'I doubt I would have met her even now, but she needed someone to serve the queen, and she knew I could get her a ship. I'm grateful for the Priory, of course. But it was the queen's gift, not hers. She didn't come to my grandmother's funeral, she didn't show that respect for the woman who had fostered me from babyhood. I don't see that she should choose my wife. I can choose my own wife.'

Mia was looking down, her colour rising.

'Shall we go in?' Gabrielle asked.

'Oh yes,' Matthew said as if he had forgotten that they were walking home. He gave his arm to them both and they walked through the herb garden to the rose garden and to the garden door.

Gabrielle turned to Mia the moment that their bedroom door was shut. 'You like him,' she said bluntly.

Mia's eyes flew to her sister's face and then she turned and sat before the mirror and twisted the ringlets in her hair.

'You do?' Gabrielle pressed.

The young woman nodded at her reflection. 'I do,' she said seriously. 'Truly I do. Very much. I didn't think of it until now, just that I am always so pleased to see him and so happy when I'm with him. But when he spoke of a wife, I suddenly realised that I would hate her! I couldn't bear anyone else to marry him, I couldn't bear for anyone else to live here. I feel like this is my home, and he is mine, and nobody can take him away from me.'

'I understand,' Gabrielle said slowly.

'Of course, he's handsome,' Mia conceded as if explaining

to herself and not to her sister, who stood silently watching her. 'And so good natured! He has the sweetest temper. I don't think I've ever seen him even moody.'

'Me neither.'

'I like it when he smiles at me,' Mia confessed. 'There's something about the way he smiles at me. I thought he was smiling at us both? But perhaps he is just looking at me?'

'I always thought it was at us both,' Gabrielle agreed.

'But he was talking of me, wasn't he? Just now? In the meadow, as his wife? He was thinking of me, wasn't he? It was unmistakable?'

'I thought so,' Gabrielle said quietly. 'I certainly thought so.'

Mia turned on her seat and caught her sister's hands. 'Don't think I'm leaving you!' she said. 'If he marries me, we'll all live here together, and you can work in the herb garden and still room and treat the tenants, and I can read and study in the library and he can go up to London when he has a case, and the rest of the time we can be happy! Wouldn't we be so happy? Just like we are now?'

'I think you would be very happy,' Gabrielle said with a little smile, her eyes on her sister's bright face.

'He'll love us both!' Mia declared with a little laugh. 'And we will both of us love him!'

'Yes,' Gabrielle said, keeping her thoughts to herself. 'Perhaps.'

BATH, SOMERSET, AUTUMN 1687

The queen was so grieved by the loss of her mother Duchess Laura that the court physicians and advisors all agreed that she should go to Bath to see if the waters improved her health and if she regained her spirits in the pretty spa town. The queen wrote urgently to Livia in Yorkshire, begging her to come to Bath, and when Livia walked into the queen's rooms in the beautiful sandstone building, Mary Beatrice ran to her and fell into her arms.

'My dear, you look so sad!'

'I grieve for us both,' Livia said elegantly.

'I'm happier now that the first shock is over. But you? And the funeral?'

'He left me nothing.' Livia neglected any description of the funeral, and went straight to the will.

'Nothing?'

'Nothing but what he was bound to give me by the terms of our marriage contract. A horrid little dower house, and some rents.'

'And the new lord?'

Livia had allowed herself to dream of the new lord, in case he was rich with another estate, in case he was unmarried, in case he was attracted to her. 'A very uninteresting man,' she said since none of those things had proved to be true, and he was happily married.

'But you are back with me for good?'

'Alas, my darling, I cannot afford to live at court. I am so sorry, I don't know which way to turn.'

'I shall give you a post and a pension,' the queen ruled. 'Don't even think about it. I will see to it at once. And you must enjoy yourself here, it's such a happy town and my good doctor has forbidden me to do anything but take the waters and amuse myself. Don't even think about money, I shall give you everything: clothes from the royal wardrobe, jewels from the treasury, and a pension for life.'

'Oh, very well,' Livia said reluctantly. 'I'll try to be happy.'

In the morning, Livia and the queen went to the Cross Bath and prepared to enter the famous waters. In the heated stone-walled dressing room Livia stripped the younger woman naked, and draped her with a yellow cape that fastened up to her neck, for complete modesty.

'You come too!' Mary Beatrice said. 'I'm not going in without you.'

Livia laughed, and as Mary Beatrice waited, she slipped off her gown, her petticoat and, standing shamelessly naked, pinned up her long dark hair. Only then, with a little glance down her curvaceous honey-coloured body, did she put on the voluminous yellow cape. With an attendant on either side, they went out of the queen's dressing room and down the stone steps into the hot sulphurous water. The capes filled with water and billowed around them, the hot water rose up their legs, over their bellies, up to their necks.

An orchestra played in the gallery, the notes echoing around the stone bath, and ladies and gentlemen looked out of the arched openings to the bath below, where the queen and her ladies, all draped in the capes, stained yellow by the mineral waters, were walking around in the water or sitting on the pedestal of the central cross.

'*Allora!* It is like the moat of hell,' Livia remarked. 'Why does it smell so terrible?'

Mary Beatrice giggled. 'It's the smell that shows it is good for you.'

Livia thought that a cattle stall smelled much the same, but she admired the glow in Mary Beatrice's face. 'Certainly, it suits you.'

Mary Beatrice waded around, an attendant on either side so that she should not slip as she took great strides, held up by the water. She laughed with pleasure, she lay on her back and let herself float as they supported her head in warm linen pillows. Livia bounded towards her, supported by her attendants. She could feel the hot water all over her naked body. It was deliciously sensual, especially for the two young women who never swam, and only ever bathed in a restricted tub. They held hands, they gambolled around like children, they danced to the music, their capes billowing around them, weightless in the hot water.

'Don't splash me! Don't splash me!' Livia begged. 'I don't want to taste it.'

'You'll have to drink a glass of it!' Mary Beatrice explained. 'It's part of the cure.'

'No! No! I am well! I assure you I am in the best of health.'

Mary Beatrice took her by the shoulders and put a warm damp kiss on her mouth. 'As anyone can see,' she said. 'You are a most beautiful widow. Swear to me that you won't remarry, I don't want to share you with anyone.'

In the afternoon they went riding in carriages at the slow pace of a marching band preceding them playing tunes as they took in the views from the high hills of the town. In the evening the queen dined in public and received guests, playing cards and making conversation while the musicians sang harmonies, and sometimes the orchestra played for dancing.

Anyone could see that the queen was returning to health, at last. She gained a little weight, the colour came back to her face. Under Livia's steady adoration and tenderness, the applause of the citizens of Bath, and the absence of rivals, especially the hated Catherine Sedley, she transformed from an infertile neglected wife to a young woman with hopes for the future. The news that Princess Anne had lost another baby prompted a letter of condolence written by Livia, and secret renewed hope that Anne would never give England a protestant prince.

Nor did Mary Beatrice miss her husband. James was to join her at the end of the month after a progress to the heart of the country: visiting Oxford to threaten the Fellows of Magdalen College with his displeasure if they did not appoint a roman catholic president, to Chester demanding an address of loyalty and that they convert a church into a roman catholic chapel. The king on progress made enemies everywhere he went.

'So he is happy,' Livia said acidly.

Mary Beatrice smiled. 'Perhaps we will both be happy,' she said like an optimistic child.

CHRISTOPHER MONCK'S TOWNHOUSE, LONDON, AUTUMN 1687

The Royal Society were taking an interest in Barbados and the Sugar Islands as a miraculous source of what seemed like unending wealth. Was it possible that one tiny island was the only place in the whole world that could grow it? Was it possible that only the Barbados planters could farm it? Could it be true that only African slaves could make it? Was it truly an elixir of life which had to have an alchemical combination – the rich soil of Barbados, the blood of black slaves and the expertise of white greed? The Royal Society agreed that Christopher Monck, whose only interest was making easy money and drinking himself into a state of complete unconsciousness, was the ideal man to survey the Sugar Islands and answer these pressing questions. No sooner appointed, Christopher Monck slid the task over to his personal physician, who suggested that he should have an assistant. Alerted by Alys, Ned applied for the post as an experienced collector of rarities.

'Can you draw specimens and describe them and so on, and so on?'

Ned stood before Christopher Monck in the handsome library, a chart of the Sugar Islands spread on a table before them.

'Yes, Sir.'

'And you can identify new leaves and flowers and herbs and so on, and so on?'

'It's what I did in New England, Sir,' Ned confirmed. 'I would go out all spring and summer into the forests, and send home what I found. Sometimes I dried it, sometimes I sent seeds or roots. I packed them in sand in barrels to keep them dry. I could do the same at Barbados.'

'Yes, yes. Ever find any treasure? Ever any word of any treasure?'

'No, Sir, I've never found treasure.' Ned gritted his teeth on his distaste. 'We don't all have your skill, Sir.'

Christopher Monck beamed and took a glass of brandy by way of celebration of his skill at treasure hunting. 'Here,' he said, suddenly troubled, blinking at Ned. 'Haven't I seen you somewhere? What's your name?'

'Edward Stoney, Sir.' Ned gambled on a drunkard's unreliable memory. 'I was in your troop when you marched out against Monmouth.'

'Ha! He was sorry he came against me!' Monck had forgotten that he played no part in the royalist victory. 'But what were you doing in Somerset, and so on?'

'I landed in Plymouth from New England and volunteered at once,' Ned said.

'Good man.'

'And so on,' Ned prompted.

'Yes. Yes. Well, we sail from Portsmouth on the tenth?'

'The twelfth I think, my lord.'

'Exactly so. Make sure you have the right day. I brook no delay! On a frigate and so on.'

'Yes, Sir,' Ned said politely.

WHITE HART INN, LONDON, AUTUMN 1687

Ned, loading bags on the roof of the passenger coach drawn up in the courtyard of the White Hart Inn, looked down to see Alys with her two grand-daughters Gabrielle and Mia beside her. She was holding a covered basket. He climbed down. 'It's good of you to come to see me off,' he said.

'Ma would never've let you go without this.' Alys pressed the basket into his hands. He peeped under the linen cover and saw a box of fever tea, comfrey salve for his old wound, tisanes against quatrain fever and sachets of herbs. There were seeds for planting in labelled purses. Some of the labels were written in Alinor's careful hand.

'Those were collected by Bisnonna herself,' Gabrielle told him. 'And I made the fever tea according to her receipt, just as she would have made it.'

'You have her receipt book?' Ned asked.

'She gave it to me,' Gabrielle said. 'Is that all right, Uncle Ned?'

He nodded. 'I'm glad we have another healer in the family. You use it, Gabrielle.' He turned to Alys. 'I'm sorry to be leaving you so soon after the loss of her, Niece.'

'Aye, I miss her, but I don't grieve. Once she was back on the tidelands she was happy. And she said goodbye to the love of her life.'

'I've got the love of my life to find again,' he said, smiling at the two girls. 'I owe someone my life. I'll settle my debt to her before I come home again.'

'God bless and keep you,' Alys said. Ned eased himself down from the coach step and took her in his arms, widening his embrace to include the girls.

'And give my love to Johnnie,' Alys reminded him. 'There's goods loaded for him on the next ship to Barbados and a letter for him in the basket. Tell him that we miss him and we're looking for him.'

'I will.' Ned climbed the steps to the coach. He had an inside seat by the window.

'Look after yourself!' Alys said. 'Come home safe!'

He smiled and waved as the other passengers got in. Alys and her two grand-daughters stood, arms around each other, as the last passenger climbed inside. The door was slammed shut, the coachman took up the reins, shouted at the horses to be ready, and then the coach rocked and moved off.

BATH, SOMERSET, AUTUMN 1687

The post from London brought a letter for Livia as she sipped tea and ate cakes in the queen's drawing room at Bath.

Dear Signora Madre,

I am pleased to tell you I have got a pupillage at Raynold and Barr, a senior law firm, and I will now practise as a lawyer and be paid a fee. Your late husband Sir James was so good as to remember me in his will and I am now in a condition that I can support a wife.

I am going to propose to Miss Mia Russo, whom you met

when you were last at the Priory. I cannot properly tell you
how much I love and respect her. I should have been glad to
come to speak of her, but I believe you are with the queen at
Bath until later this month.

I shall write to her father Sn Felipe Russo for permission to
address his daughter with a proposal of marriage as soon as I
have your blessing.
Your obedient Son,
Matthew Peachey

'Lord, no!' Livia exclaimed, reading the letter and then re-reading it. 'Fool that I am not to have foreseen it!'

She scanned the letter again. 'Typical of James to give him enough to make him think he can marry and yet not enough to keep a wife. Ridiculous.'

She flicked the page with her finger as if she would dust the words from the paper. 'I'd like to see Felipe's face!' she remarked. 'Ha! Or the pert girl he married, Sarah. Lord! The daughter of Sarah the milliner and Felipe Russo the mountebank as a wife for my son? I think not!'

She set the page on her lap and gazed at it.

'Bad news?' asked one of the ladies-in-waiting, passing by her chair.

Livia looked up with her most charming smile. 'My son, writing to me,' she said. 'He is such a joy!'

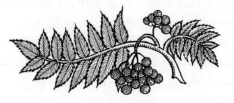

THE COFFEE HOUSE, SERLE COURT, LONDON, AUTUMN 1687

Livia sat in her preferred seat in the coffee house, away from the central table where the clerks and the lawyers exchanged notes and read newspapers, close to the stove for the warmth, in the discreet high-backed settle.

Matthew came into the room and was greeted with new respect by the owner Mr Hart. 'Mr Peachey, Sir,' he said in greeting. 'Lady Avery has just arrived.'

It had not taken Mr Hart long to learn that the newly qualified Matthew was the only son and heir to the queen's favourite, Lady Avery, owned the family seat of Fairmere Priory in Sussex and would doubtless inherit Avery House in London.

'Shall I bring coffee over, Sir? And pastries?'

'Yes, yes,' Matthew said, hurrying to greet his mother.

She did not rise to greet him but merely looked up at him. He was struck once more by the classic loveliness of her face, set off now by a black collar and a tall black hat with inky plumes that curled around the brim and rested against her perfect cheek, reminding him that she was still in mourning for Sir James.

'*Signora Madre!*' he said. He bent to her and she kissed his forehead. 'I am sorry for your loss.'

'Your gain. He left you five hundred pounds. Have you had it yet?'

'Yes, a draft to my bank. It was very good of him! I did not expect it.'

'He did not surprise me with a legacy, I am sorry to say.'

Matthew was silent for a moment while Mr Hart himself set the cups and poured coffee and left a large bowl of sugar on the table. Matthew thought that his mother did not look like a woman disappointed in her inheritance. The hat and the cloak were new, and she wore black opals in her ears and at her throat. '*Signora Madre*? I should be glad to give it to . . .'

She shook her head. 'I don't complain,' she said. 'Your gain is my good. We are as one.'

He blinked a little at learning they were, once again, a couple with a shared endeavour.

'But five hundred pounds is not enough for you to marry a girl without a fortune.'

'Mia Russo . . .'

'I thought that she had come to England to study and to write? I was specifically told that she was not looking for a husband?'

'Yes, that's true.'

'There is no money to be made from writing. Especially for a woman.'

'The playwrights—'

'Need not concern us. Are you suggesting that you should marry a shameless woman who writes for the stage? A scribbling bawd?'

'She need not write for the stage! As my wife she will—'

'She cannot be your wife, my Son.'

'I can support a wife.'

'Not in the style that anyone would wish for you. But in any case, she is not my choice. She is completely unsuitable.' She lifted her veil and drank her coffee. He had to curb the rise of his temper.

'Forgive me, Nobildonna, but she is the daughter of a good family in Venice, and the grand-daughter of my foster mother. She cannot be completely unsuitable.'

She touched her mouth with a black-bordered handkerchief. 'I shall speak to you frankly,' she said simply. 'Her father Felipe Russo was the steward of my late husband Signor Fiori.

A well-known thief. He stole from the prince's antiquities collection.'

Matthew gaped in horror. 'No!'

'He had access to all the house—' She raised the handkerchief to her eyes. 'I was a young widow. The very night that my first husband the prince died . . . Felipe Russo ravished me.'

She had knocked the breath out of him like a blow. He glanced around, terrified that someone would hear of her shame. 'He forced you?'

'I could do nothing. I struggled in vain . . . He overpowered me.'

'Lady Mother! Mother!'

She nodded, her face half-hidden by the handkerchief. 'I never wanted you to know. But now I see that I must sacrifice my pride for your safety. You cannot marry Felipe Russo's daughter, either one of his daughters, because he is a rapist, and she may be your half-sister.'

Matthew felt sick; he reached for the cup of coffee and downed it in one gulp. At once it surged back up into his mouth and he coughed and fought the need to spit. 'Forgive me,' he said, making himself swallow, choking on rage and horror at what he was hearing. 'It cannot be so!'

'You think Sarah his wife might have played him false?' his mother considered. 'She was a very forward young woman, and Alys her mother gave her no guidance. But there's no way of knowing. Safer by far to assume the girls are your half-sisters.'

'No!' he yelped. 'I don't suggest for a moment . . . I only meant . . . this is unbelievable!'

She put her silk-gloved hand over his. 'I know. We will never speak of this again. Only a mother's love would force me to admit my shame.'

'Why did you not denounce him?'

She shook her head. 'Who would believe me? A young widow and her husband's handsome young steward? The Fiori family would have accused me of stealing the antiquities myself, and seducing the thief.'

'But how could you bear to meet Gabrielle or Mia? Why didn't you tell Ma Alys as soon as you came to London? She'd never have let her daughter Sarah marry a man like . . .'

She shrugged and tucked her handkerchief in her black sable muff. 'How could I speak without destroying you? How could I name you – an innocent baby – as the bastard of my royal husband's steward? And again – who would have believed my word against Felipe Russo? Sarah Stoney was besotted with him, together they had released Rob Reekie from imprisonment. They came to England in triumph, as heroes! How could I stand against that noisy joy and say – no! no! – he is the wickedest of criminals?'

'You met him afterwards?' he asked in horror. 'You saw him, when they came home? Uncle Rob was in prison?'

'On my wedding day to Sir James,' her voice trembled. 'Can you imagine? He came to interrupt my wedding and to ruin my happiness. But he did not dare to confess what he had done. And what could I say before Sir James and them all? What could I possibly say that would not have led to dreadful violence, terrible grief? It was a tragedy in the making.'

Matthew felt it was a tragedy fully made. 'I am dishonoured,' he said. 'A child of a rape.'

She nodded, her dark eyes filled with tears, fixed on his young face.

'Nobody can ever know,' he said slowly, realising that he would never be able to share this burden, not even with the young woman he loved. 'I can't tell anyone, least of all Mia or Gabrielle.'

'No-one,' she said. 'You cannot tell the girls that their father is a vile rapist. It would destroy them. You should never tell the world that you do not know your own father. And you can never tell a soul of the stain on my honour. The shocking stain of violence on my pure honour.'

'I should punish him?' He searched for a sense of outrage as preferable to his sick sense of shock. 'I should go to Venice and challenge him?'

She pressed his hand. 'That would only expose and shame us all. You and me – the innocent victims, and the other innocents:

his poor sons, his poor daughters, dear Mia and Gabrielle, his innocent wife Sarah, even his mother-in-law – your foster mother, poor Alys! I have held this secret to my heart for years, to protect all of them and you. Now I share the burden. And you will keep it with me.'

He dropped his head into his hands. She watched him, judging his reaction, and was pleased to see that he did not sink into self-pity; but raised his head and said: 'I am sorry that I forced you to tell me this, Lady Mother. May I ask one more thing: are you certain that this man, this criminal, is my father?'

Her large black eyes met his without flinching. 'Son, I am so very sorry. I cannot know. I was attacked the night of my husband's death. I cannot know for sure which man was your father. My husband was a great man, bearing a long honourable name. He may well have left me with you – his parting gift. His family would not believe it, they did not accept me, but nobody can know for sure.

'I gave you the name of your foster family to hide my fears. I called us da Picci – in the Italian way of speaking – and I would have changed your name to Avery when I married Sir James if only he had agreed to it. I have only named this crime to you now to save you and the girl from the terrible sin of incest. For all I know, Mia Russo is your half-sister.'

'She's not to blame!' he said.

'Only one man is to blame,' she said steadily. 'The rapist: Felipe Russo. And God will punish him. Not us. So you will have to meet Mia as a friend, and never tell her, nor Gabrielle, nor even Alys, what I have told you today.'

His face was anguished. 'I had thought I would marry her!' he said. 'I was going to write to him as my father-in-law!'

She was tender. 'My Son. It has cost me greatly; but I have saved you.'

WHITEHALL PALACE, LONDON, AUTUMN 1687

Livia was diverted from her plans for Matthew by undertaking the work of moving the queen's household into her newly renovated apartments at Whitehall Palace. The rebuilding of the palace had been so elaborate and so rich – gilded and painted ceilings, glorious antique hangings, five different marbles on the floors and the walls – that it was not even finished now, years late and way over the planned cost. 'But worth it!' Livia exclaimed. 'This is a bedroom fit for a queen indeed!'

'And it has a deep-water bath!' Mary Beatrice came running through the adjoining rooms. 'Come and see, it's wonderful. I can almost swim in it! And water piped to it, hot water! Nobody has to carry it in! I can lock the door and bathe in complete solitude.'

Livia followed her into the lavish room; gold-framed mirrors surrounded them, throwing their images back and back until they looked like a dozen women in a golden maze. The queen closed the door so that no-one could hear her whisper.

'I think I have news,' she said, holding Livia's hands and drawing her close to whisper. 'I'm not sure.'

'News?' Livia breathed, instantly alert.

'You know my courses are changeable, but I think I have missed two. And I feel strange in myself. Like I did before, when I was with child. I can't bear the smell of hot chocolate in the morning and my breasts are tender. Livia, I think I may be with child.'

Livia's knees gave way and she plumped down on the edge of the bath. 'With child?'

Mary Beatrice blushed. 'I think it was when His Majesty joined us at Bath,' she said. 'The waters. And I was so happy.'

'God be praised!' Livia was amazed.

'And the king prayed at St Winifred's well, and had a vision.'

'Of course!' Livia said delighted, hardly listening, counting on her fingers. 'So you will be brought to bed in July? This summer, at any rate.'

'Perhaps on the anniversary of my mother's death?' the queen whispered. 'Perhaps Duchess Laura has sent me an angel from heaven.'

The queen and Livia agreed that she should tell Father Petre, the king's confessor, and he should tell the Papal Nuncio who would in his turn tell the king so that he might formally announce the wonderful news to the court and country. Father Petre said there could be no delay. The recent progress had hardened feelings against the king; the pregnancy must be announced before Christmas to suppress the increasing ill-will of the country against the court.

'Once they know there is an heir to the throne they will object less to the changes,' Father Petre said. 'Once they know that there is no protestant descent through Princess Mary to Princess Anne, they will have to surrender. They will see the future royal succession of the true faith; and convert.'

'God has been good to us,' Ferdinand d'Adda observed. 'And Her Majesty is well?'

'There is no apparent danger,' Livia warned. 'But we are all, always, in God's hands.'

Count d'Adda smiled. 'The Holy Father himself prayed for this baby,' he said. 'This child is going to build the true faith in England, he will be the rock. I will go and tell His Majesty now.'

Livia watched him go and turned to Father Petre. 'It's true, we should pray. I don't think Her Majesty could bear the loss of a son. It would break her heart.'

He inclined his head to the angle of a priest listening to a confession.

'Of course, I will do everything in my power to keep her well.'

'As will we all,' he said softly prompting.

'But it might perhaps be wise . . .'

'Wise?'

'To ensure that there is indeed a boy, born to Her Majesty in July. There can be no stillbirth. There can be no girl.'

He was silent for a moment, taking in her whisper. 'That would be wise,' he said cautiously. 'But it would be hard to accomplish?'

'Not impossible,' Livia said.

'I could take no part in it. I would be the first suspect.'

'No,' Livia said, hiding her contempt. 'It would have to be one person, acting alone. Someone intimate with Her Majesty who could watch over her constantly and attend the birth.'

'Such a person would be richly rewarded. Most richly rewarded. Nothing would be too good for them, on earth and in heaven.'

'Amen,' Livia said, hearing the words of the Lord's Prayer and responding without thought. 'What exactly?'

He shrugged. 'Such a ministering angel could name her price.'

BRIDGETOWN, BARBADOS, WINTER 1687

The frigate *Assistance* came into Bridge harbour with the truncated boom of a seventeen-gun salute, as the fort was too short on ammunition to fire the full twenty-one guns. The half-drunk lieutenant governor of Jamaica Christopher Monck was welcomed ashore by the rattle of musket fire, as Ned took his bags from his cabin, and took his leave of the captain at sunset. He was directed to Johnnie's warehouse – now, everyone knew of the Stoney Exchange.

Ned hammered on the warehouse door; he saw a light, and in a moment, Johnnie had opened the door, a torch held high.

'Good Lord!' he said. 'Is that you, Uncle Ned? Did you come in on the frigate?'

'Aye. I told you I'd come,' Ned said, clapping Johnnie on the back. 'Didn't you believe me?'

'Of course. When d'you ever do the sensible thing, like stay home in safety?' Johnnie laughed, throwing open the door to lead Ned through to the back of the warehouse. 'Uncle Ned, it's good to see you! And up and walking and talking like nothing had ever happened.'

'Aye – it was your grandmother nursed me back to life, God bless her.'

'Amen. But didn't you get my letter? Rowan is lost, Ned. I'm so sorry. I wrote at once.'

'I got it. You know for sure she died?'

'Her master told me himself. I went out to his plantation.'

'You've seen the body, they've found it?'

'If she fell and died in the thick forest, they'll never find the body. I'm sorry, Uncle Ned, but her master had no hope. The pet dog ran off and Rowan was sent to find him and never came back.'

Ned's face was downturned; Johnnie could not see his hidden lopsided smile. 'She went after a pet dog and she didn't catch him? What sort of dog was it? Greyhound?'

'A little pug, I think,' Johnnie said. 'Why? What does it matter?'

'Just seeing it, in my mind's eye,' Ned said. 'Rowan outrun by a pug.'

'Such a waste!' Johnnie said. 'Such a waste of her life.'

Ned narrowed his eyes and looked at the younger man, at the lines around his mouth. 'You've taken it hard,' he observed.

Johnnie shrugged. 'It's been madness from the very beginning!' he exclaimed. 'Ma was dead against it, and my Ma's no fool. Rowan tricked me in Taunton and robbed me of my money. And then I thought I would chase out here and rescue her, like some kind of prince in a fairy tale, and I'm too late and now she's dead, and for all I know, she never even cared for me, but played me for a fool from first to last. Played us both. A pair of fools who chased halfway around the world for a woman who wouldn't even wait for us.'

'Wait to be rescued?' Ned cocked a crooked smile at his nephew. 'No, she'd not have done that either.'

The next night Johnnie took his uncle out to dinner at his old boarding house and on the way home they looked in at the fort where the governor was being welcomed by an enormous feast laid on by the wealthiest planters. Course after course came in, casks of rum were broached and tasted and dozens of bottles opened. Ned and Johnnie joined with the general goodwill, getting entry on the basis of their white faces. Ned was welcomed for news of England, which the planters called wistfully 'Old England', and Johnnie was highly regarded as a man who was bringing London fashion and London smartness to the town of Bridge.

Ned and Johnnie went back to the warehouse inspired by the international brotherhood of the very drunk. Johnnie went to his bed in the half-loft over the warehouse, and strung a hammock for Ned by the back door that faced the sea. Johnnie was asleep in moments, his snores echoing through the warehouse. Ned opened the door to hear the slap of the waves against the quay and smell the onshore wind, salty and warm.

He rubbed his face and his arms against the biting mosquitoes, and then went back in and closed the door. He shucked off his shoes, breeches and linen shirt, pinched out the flame of the candle, and lay back in his hammock in the darkness. He felt happy, as he had felt with Rowan on the voyage from Texel to Lyme Regis, as he had felt on the march with Monmouth, because he knew that she was near.

He heard something – some creature – stir in the rafters above him, and he pulled a scarf over his face for protection against some venomous insect dropping down on him. Then he heard another little noise, like a scratching rat at the shutter, and he pulled up the rough cotton cover over his chest. The noise came again, more insistently.

Ned sat up, one foot to the floor to steady the swinging hammock. The scratching sound came again, in a rhythm that no creature would make. Ned shook out his boots to ensure they were empty of any insects, pushed his feet into them and strode, naked but for his cotton bed sheet wound around his belly, to the shuttered window. Gently, he unbolted it and opened it a crack.

'Are you there?' he whispered into the darkness of the warehouse yard.

'*Nippe Sannup?*'

He was flooded with such emotion at the sound of her whisper that he clung to the windowsill as if a great wave from the ocean beyond the bar was breaking on his head.

'Rowan? Is that you? Rowan?'

'Can I come in?'

'Yes. Yes!' He flung the shutters wide and stepped back as she leapt up and heaved herself half in, and then swivelled her legs over the windowsill. Still he could see nothing, and he reached for his tinder box to make a spark to light the candle.

'Wait till I close the shutter,' she whispered.

He heard the creak and then the dropping of the metal bolt.

'Can I light now?'

'Yes, but be quiet.'

The shower of sparks from the flint was not enough to show her to him, nor the glowing charcloth, but the tiny flame on the splint guided him to the candle and it caught light and finally, he could see her.

His first thought was that she was just the same as the girl he had known, but when he held up the candle, oblivious to the hot wax on his fingers, and examined her carefully, he could see that she looked older, hardened in the two years they had been apart. She had a groove between her thick black eyebrows and her skin was darkened from living out of doors. Her hair was down to her shoulders, caught back by a twist of plaited vine. Her face was thinner, but her eyes, dark and smiling, fixed on his, were the same as ever.

She was wearing nothing but a skirt made from rags, and a string of shells at her throat. He thought she looked like a faerie child – a creature from beyond, that his sister Alinor would recognise her as one of her own. Her feet were bare and she had a large knife honed from a billhook in a leather sheath at her waist. She looked nothing like the manacled boy who had stumbled into the hold of the Barbados ship in Bristol, nothing like the frightened girl in the cabin of his ship at Boston. This was Rowan as she was born to be, as she was raised to be: half-naked, lean-muscled, armed.

'Have you been ill?' she asked, and he realised that she was examining him from head to foot as he stood before her, wrapped in his bed sheet, just as he had been observing her. She saw he had lost condition in the months of his unconsciousness, his muscles ropey under thin skin, his grey hair turned almost all white. She saw the twist of his lined face from the seizure and his lopsided shoulders. Her dark eyes were filled with pity. She knew that the loss of her had harmed him, while she, so much younger, had grown strong when she was alone.

'Nothing lasting,' he said. 'You look ...'

She laughed quietly as she realised he could not describe her.

'I came for you,' he said.

'I know. I knew you would come sooner or later. Did you get a passage with the new governor? I came as soon as I heard the guns.'

'Yes. It's Drunk Monck from Wellington. D'you remember?'

He watched her face light up with the memory. 'Yes! Of course. Is he sober now he's not frightened?'

'Not frightened: still drunk. You know this is Johnnie's warehouse? He came to free you. They told him you were dead. He ...' He could not bring himself to say: 'he loves you'. Johnnie would have to do his own courting.

She looked quite blank, as if she had forgotten all about Johnnie. 'Oh yes,' she said. 'I saw him ride away from the Peabodys'. But I don't need his help. I'm free.'

It was incredible to him that she stood before him, as light on her feet as she had always been, unharmed, in her own dress, as if the war in her own country and the rebellion in his had never happened. As if she were as free here, as she had been in her own forest, as if the white men had never come to the Americas at all.

'We're both here to free you,' he said, trying to be fair. 'Johnnie came at once. I followed as soon as I was fit to travel.'

The loud bell of St Michael's church tolled the half hour. 'What time is that?' she asked as if she was no longer ruled by the bells of the church and the clocks of the town.

'Half-past midnight,' he told her.

'I'll go,' she said. 'I just wanted to see you, and know you are safe. I wanted you to know that I'm safe. Will you go to Jamaica with Drunk Monck? Will you go back to England?'

'Not without seeing you again,' he protested. 'Rowan, I've come all this way to see you. I can't leave you after ten minutes.'

'You came to set me free?'

'Yes, and Johnnie did too.'

'I am free. You can tell him. There is nothing for either of you to do.'

'But I want—'

She was halfway to the window; he felt terror at the thought of losing her, but he would not lay a hand on her to make her stay. 'Rowan, let me see you tomorrow. Tell me where I can find you. I beg you. Tell me where to find you.'

She shook her head. 'I live in the forest. You can't find me. No-one can find me.'

'You're alone?'

She shook her head with a little smile and he had a pang of jealousy like a knife in his bowels. 'You're with a man?'

'Oh no, nothing like that.'

'Let me spend some time with you. I can get you some clothes and you can come and live here with me and Johnnie. He's bought this warehouse, this is his home. You could live here. We could work something out. He thought you might run this as your business until you have finished your sentence—'

'He wants me to run a shop for slave drivers? To serve them?'

'You'd be safe here. He'd pay you. And in eight years, when your sentence expired—'

Decisively, she shook her head. 'I'll not live in a house ever again,' she said. 'And I won't wear clothes. And I surely won't serve a man, not a white man, not a slave driver, not any man.'

'Then let me come to you.' He knew better than to catch her hand, but he was desperate that she should not just disappear into the darkness of the seashore. 'Tell me where I can meet you. I'll come alone, no-one will follow me.'

She looked thoughtful. 'All right. You can. Just you. You can visit the Peabody plantation. They will invite you. They invite everyone. When you're there, walk to the creek. Take a gun.

When you're in the forest and alone you can shoot your gun in the air. I will meet you in the forest.'

'You will meet me?' he asked her. 'You won't fail me? How will you know where to find me?'

She laughed. 'Of course I will find you in my own forest. But you must come alone, and tell no-one of me, don't even bring Johnnie.'

'I'll have to tell him I've seen you.'

She shook her head. 'He talks,' she said shortly. 'He drinks with them and he is their friend. He's one of them now.'

'One of them?'

'A master. A slave-master.' The contempt in her voice was unmistakable.

'But he came to free you!'

'He has slaves working here. He would have me work here. A slave, like them.'

Ned hesitated, saw her glance towards the shuttered window as if she wanted to go.

'All right! All right! I'll say nothing. I'll come to the Peabody plantation as soon as I can. As soon as I can get a horse, I'll come.'

She gave him a reassuring smile as if she knew he was afraid he would lose her. 'I will come to you,' she promised him. 'I will find you in the forest.'

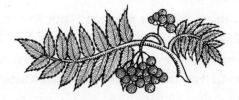

FAIRMERE PRIORY, SUSSEX, WINTER 1687

Alys thought that the family was riding high when their hired carriage turned in the new stone pillars that proclaimed 'Fairmere

Priory', carved in stone, a Christmas gift from the Nobildonna. Matthew, Mia, Gabrielle and Alys' husband Captain Shore were laughing and talking inside; a goose and a hamper of Christmas food was strapped on the roof, and following behind them was Rob's carriage bringing him and Julia and Hester. The carriage was hired with good money, all the bills were paid, and there was no debt outstanding on the wharf or at the re-named Priory. Even though Johnnie was trading on credit in Barbados, Alys understood this was the new way of business, the only way to do business over such long sea miles. Johnnie traded in private bills, signed promises to pay, drawn on the Barbados agents, passed from hand to hand and countersigned. Some of these he sent to England where Alys used them to buy goods to ship back to him in Barbados, or paid them in to Rob's father-in-law, Alderman Johnson the goldsmith, for safekeeping. After a lifetime of cautious accounting, keeping handfuls of coins in a strongbox in the warehouse, Alys had to trust pages of paper, signed by men whose fortune was so great that they could trade on their name alone.

The carriages drew up at the front door. Alys climbed down and led them all into the house. She glanced at Rob as they warmed themselves before the welcoming fire in the hall fireplace. 'Strange that she's not here,' she remarked, missing her mother.

'It's as if she were upstairs,' he said. 'Even now, months after her going, I never feel her absence, I always feel as if she's just in the next room.'

Gabrielle smiled. 'She would say that she was,' she said. 'Through a doorway that we can't see.'

Hester was excitedly greeting her cousins and showing them the gifts that were being unloaded from the trunk of the Reekie carriage.

'Hester!' Julia said quietly. 'My head!'

At once the girl fell silent and Alys invited Julia into the parlour for hot chocolate. Rob and Captain Shore went to the library for a glass of wine, and the girls and Matthew were left before the hall fire.

Mia unwound the scarf from her neck and tossed her muff on a chair. 'So nice to be here,' she said, smiling at Matthew.

The maid who had been serving in the parlour came and dropped a curtsey to Hester. 'Your Ma says you're to take her reticule.'

'Oh! I'll come at once.' Hester hurried to the parlour, limping slightly on her raised shoe.

'That woman!' Mia said. 'Christmas Eve but anyway she orders Hester around like—'

'I wanted to talk to you both,' Matthew said. He leaned on the mantelpiece and looked down into the fire. 'I have to say something.'

'What is it?' Gabrielle asked him. 'Is it the Nobildonna?'

'No!' He said it so quickly that she knew at once that his mother was interfering in his life. Mia waited hopefully, her dark eyes on his face.

'I have grown very fond of you both,' he said.

The dawning of Mia's smile showed that she thought this was to be a proposal of marriage. She rose from her chair and stood beside him, readying herself to respond. Gabrielle remained seated, watching the two of them.

'I had hoped to ask you, Mia, to be my wife.' Quickly, he glanced at her and then looked away again.

'Yes?' Mia said, encouraging him to ask.

Gabrielle found she was holding her hands tightly in her lap, knowing that something was very wrong. 'But you are not proposing?'

Mia threw an angry glance at her.

'He's not,' Gabrielle told her gently.

'I cannot do so,' Matthew said. 'It has come to my notice, I understand that . . . I may not. I cannot.'

'What?' Mia demanded.

He turned from the fire, scowling. 'I love you,' he declared to her. 'But I will have to love you – both – as sisters.' His glance took in Gabrielle. 'I hope that we will always be true friends.'

'Why?' Mia demanded. 'What's happened? Is it my grand-mother? Has she said something? Because I can tell her—'

Gabrielle rose to her feet and put her arm around her sister's waist. 'It's the Nobildonna,' she told Mia. Gravely, she regarded Matthew. 'Matthew, what has your mother said?'

He flushed that she knew it was his mother who had stopped him. 'She has an objection to your father's family. I cannot say what it is. From long ago, from Venice. She said that neither he nor she would accept a connection.'

'Like a feud?' Gabrielle asked.

He was grateful to her for quick understanding. 'Just like a feud.'

'But this is ridiculous!' Mia exclaimed. 'We don't have to be bound by their quarrels. Their old quarrels!'

Matthew wrenched himself away from the fireplace and headed to the stairs. 'I am afraid that we do,' he said, pausing at the foot of the stair. 'It is a question of honour. I have no choice. If there was any way that I could, in honour, propose, I would do so. But there was a grave injury, an unforgiveable injury, an unforgettable injury – and there can be no reparation.' His hand gripped the newel post, and he spoke to Gabrielle, who was watching him intently, and not to Mia, who stared at him, completely blank. 'There can be no explanation either. The injury was private. I am very very sorry,' he said to Gabrielle. 'You know that.'

'I know it,' Gabrielle said quietly.

'I am very very sorry, Mia.'

'Oh, what is the use of you being sorry?' she demanded furiously. 'And you a lawyer!'

Mia came to dinner with red eyes and ate little. When the ladies withdrew to the parlour, leaving the gentlemen to drink wine, Julia Reekie remarked to Alys that Mia was probably suffering from carriage sickness and that Rob could give her some laudanum to help her sleep.

'She'll be all right tomorrow,' Alys said comfortably. 'She's probably missing Ma. They'd grown very close.'

'I am sure that we all do,' Julia said frigidly. 'We all miss Mama Reekie.'

Alys, sewing fever tea bags, gritted her teeth at the correction to her speech. 'Will you come to church tomorrow?'

'Oh yes!' Julia was looking forward to the progression to the Peachey pew at the front of the church and the recessional when Matthew stood near the church gate, and his tenants came up to bid him good morning. 'So quaint,' she said. 'Do you expect the Nobildonna for Christmas Day?'

'Lord no!' Alys said gladly. 'She'll have to stay with the queen. Especially now she's breeding.'

A quiver of dismay went across Julia's face at the term. 'Did the Nobildonna tell you Her Majesty was so happy? I've heard only a rumour? Is it true?'

'We took an order for Venetian silk for a cradle,' Alys said. 'The court buys their best silks from us. This was an order for curtains for a cradle and silk sheets for a crib, lace for a gown and silks for a cap and gown. Sounds like they're hoping for a prince.'

'How wonderful for the queen and for the Nobildonna!'

'It'll be the saving of them if it's a boy,' Alys said, snipping off a thread. 'I quite thought to see parliament rise against them.'

'Surely not!' Julia hesitated for a moment. 'And I saw in the newspaper that the Nobildonna had been widowed?'

'Aye.' Alys put two pieces of muslin together and started on another bag.

'So sad!'

Alys said nothing, but she did not look sad.

'It said that the estate was entailed on a cousin.'

'Did it?'

'But that there were a number of bequests.'

Alys threaded her needle and started to hem. Julia regarded her in silence for a moment and then made one last try. 'Did Sir James remember his stepson in his will? Was there anything for our dear Matthew?'

'I don't know,' Alys said. 'Because it's not my business.'

'Avery House?' Julia whispered longingly.

Alys shook her head. 'Not my business,' she said staunchly.

Fairmere Priory,
Boxing Day.

I write to you from beautiful Fairmere. Your new gates
look very handsome! What a charming gift. We are
having a delightful time but were so sorry not to see you on
this occasion.

Matthew and Hester make a delightful couple together,
he gave her his arm into church on Christmas Day and
everyone remarked what a handsome pair they make. Her
foot is so much better that I will bring her to a drawing room
this spring, and she will be able to dance. I so hope to see
you there?

Matthew tells me that he has a pupillage and is going to set
out his plate as a lawyer. I am sure that should Doctor Reekie
have need of a lawyer he would go nowhere else. I will also
mention Matthew's name to my Papa, Alderman Johnson.

I send you the compliments of the season and, of course,
congratulations to our dear queen!

Julia Reekie

The Reekies – Rob and Julia – returned to London on Boxing
Day, taking Captain Shore in their carriage. The Captain
wanted to refit his ship for its next voyage, and Rob could not
be far away from his patients who expected him to be on call,
especially those ladies who were near their time.

'If only you could attend the queen!' Julia breathed.

Rob shook his head. 'To guarantee an heir for England is

beyond the skill of any physician, and you'd get no thanks for a girl.'

Hester was allowed to stay at the Priory with her cousins, her aunt Alys and Matthew until the end of the holidays; but she noticed a difference in her cousins. The sisters now walked side by side, and Hester and Matthew walked together. When they played cards in the evening Hester partnered Matthew. The four of them sometimes recaptured the old schoolroom camaraderie but Mia no longer sparkled in conversation. Alys, watching over them all, but distracted by rent day at the Priory and checking the linen cupboard, did not notice Matthew's reserve towards Mia nor her distance from him. Gabrielle was torn between pleasure at knowing that she would not lose her sister, sorrow for Mia's evident unhappiness, and a secret joy of her own that Matthew would not marry this year.

PEABODY PLANTATION, BARBADOS, WINTER 1687

'I think I'll take a visit inland,' Ned said to Johnnie at a breakfast of sugared coffee and sweet cakes in the warehouse galley. 'See if there are any trees left in the valleys that I don't know, see if I can find anything interesting.'

'You don't need a letter of introduction, you can walk up to any door and you'll be invited for a week,' Johnnie said. 'It's the friendliest place in the world.'

'Easy to be hospitable when you're rich from someone else's labour.'

'Everyone is rich from someone else's labour,' Johnnie declared. 'It's just here, that you see it.'

'I see labourers worked to death to save the cost of keeping them in old age.'

'Uncle, I'm no slave driver, though I've been offered the post of agent over and over. I only came here to rescue Rowan. I only stay here to recoup my costs. Don't blame me that the only way to make sugar is with slaves.'

'Imagine you've recouped your costs? And more than once?'

Johnnie ducked his head and grinned. 'All right! I'm making a profit. Like my Ma, like my family business, which you work for too.'

'Aye, you're right. And I eat sugar. Anyway, I'm hiring a horse and going up country. I'll go and see Rowan's plantation, since I've come so far.'

'They said they'd tell me if they ever found . . . remains.'

'I know.' Ned hated lying to Johnnie. 'I'll go anyway.'

'They'll be glad of a visit. You can take Mrs Peabody some ribbons from the store.'

Ned, on a hired horse with a bottle of rum and water in his pocket and a change of clothes in a saddlebag, rode for a few hours, northwards from the town of Bridge, through fields of unending sugar cane, following the wagon ruts of a road which had been ground down through the earth of the fields, until it hit the bedrock of the pale porous stone of the island. He thought the roads were like the land, like the working people, like this whole island: ground down until they were bleached with pain. He started his journey greeting the children with a smile and the women with 'Good day'; but nobody ever replied to him but the white man who sat high on his horse, a long hunter's whip curled in his hand. He had a servile smile and a tip of his hat for Ned – more slavish than any.

Sugar cane, like a wall of green, pressing against the road and extending for miles, made Ned feel enclosed, as if he too would never be free. When the crest of one of the rolling hills gave him a chance to look down on the land, all he could see was a plain green-leaved desert of waving fronds, and the ant-like gangs of weeders moving among them, a windmill on every hilltop, its sails stilled until the harvest. He could not see how Rowan could survive here, any more than among the hard streets of London in a land under the tyranny of one favoured crop and one favoured people.

Ned, borrowing Johnnie's surname of Stoney and explaining that he was Johnnie's uncle, come to Barbados to study the Sugar Islands for the new governor, was a welcome novelty on the Peabody plantation, and they recommended that he ride all around their lands and their neighbours but avoid the creeks that ran between the fields.

'You don't want to go too deep,' Samuel Peabody warned him. 'The ground falls away like a cliff under your feet. If you insist, I'll loan you a couple of men to go a little way in; but there are no paths, you can't get through it. Nobody's ever seen the bottom of the deep gullies. I've lost more than one man down there.'

'I'll borrow a gun if I may, and see if I can pot a dove for skinning.'

'You can borrow my hunting gear,' Samuel said with enthusiasm. 'I used to go out for game at one time. But my constitution doesn't suit the midday heat.'

Ned, forced into Sam Peabody's huntsman gear of gaiters, boots, breeches, waistcoat and heavy jacket, topped off with a hunter's hat, thought that he was not surprised that Samuel's constitution did not suit the heat. Ned himself thought he would die of it. He managed to rid himself of the two slaves that his host had assured him would find birds for him and beat the bushes to give him an easy shot. The two tall black men, dressed in nothing but cast-off baggy sailors' trousers hitched up to their naked chests, left him with silent indifference, without a backward glance. Ned was reminded of the deep loneliness of the slave-taker who lives among men and women; but thinking of them as beasts, loses his only chance of human companionship.

He did not dare go deep into the thick jungle of the river gully. The trails of aerial plants, the web of vines looked identical, every way that he turned. He knew that if he went too far in, he would never find his way out again. No white man would ever find him. He waited half an hour until he was sure the slaves were gone and then he discharged his musket into the air and slumped under one of the great trees, looking up at the strange flowers in its branches. He took off his jacket and wiped his face. The whine of mosquitoes and the constant prick of bites against his tender skin made him scratch, and swat at the air. If Rowan came now, he would look like a fool to her: red-faced and sweating, dressed for an English winter under a tropical sky. But he could not believe that she would come now. The forest was too thick for her to find him. He thought he would wait two hours for her to come and then pick some leaves and some of the ferns from the ground to show that he had been collecting, and struggle back to the plantation for dinner. He did not think she could possibly live nearby, or find him from the sound of one musket shot, and then he felt a gentle touch on his elbow, and she was there, beside him.

'*Nippe Sannup.*'

'I didn't hear you come.'

She nodded in agreement. He should not be able to hear her come through the forest.

'You live near here? So close to the plantation.'

'I have reason,' she said.

Again, she was wearing the ragged apron and a necklace of shells. Her nakedness did not disturb him: he had befriended her mother and her grandmother who never wore more, unless they were coming under the critical gaze of an English border town.

But the sight of her bare strong toes on the mulch of the forest floor turned his heart with tenderness for her.

'Can you follow me really quietly?' she asked him.

'I will.'

'And swear you will never tell them, any of them, that you met me and that I was here?'

'I'd never betray you.'

'Follow then,' she said. 'Give me that musket and that bag, and your jacket. And try to be quiet in those boots.'

She started at a steady trot, and within moments Ned was blown and struggling to keep up. She paid no attention to his increasingly hoarse panting but kept the same steady pace through the forest, ducking under branches and stepping over fallen boughs, dropping down and down through a gully. Ned could hear the drip of water falling beside them.

After a little while, she held up her hand and stopped; Ned stumbled to a halt behind her, his chest heaving. He had a pain in his labouring lungs, and a cramp in his leg.

She glanced back at him. 'Nearly home,' she said like a son to an ageing father. 'You've done well.'

Ned took a sobbing breath and looked around him. They were in a little clearing. Hot sunlight filtered through the thick canopy where a troop of monkeys moved and a parrot flew in a flash of green. They were beside a small cave formed from the white limestone rock, half-covered by the trailing roots of the bearded fig.

'We're here,' she said, and his heart sank at the thought of her living in this cleft in the rock like a beast without shelter.

'Rowan . . .' he started, as she ducked behind the roots of the fig and beckoned him to follow her.

Before he could protest, she had dropped to her hands and knees and crawled through a little hole. Ned followed her into the darkness.

Their route was downhill; he could feel the tumble of little stones shifting under his hands and knees as he went, following her, ever deeper into the cave system further and further downhill. It was dark at the entrance but it became pitch black; he was following her by sound, the rasp of his musket dragged behind her on the stones, the regular thrust of her hands and knees. The space became tighter around his shoulders until he thought that he might not get through. He felt the shoulders of the shirt rip on some rock and had a sudden panic of being stuck underground in the darkness – and then suddenly there was clean cool air, and a light ahead of him, and the sound of water falling, and she said: 'Here we are.'

The cave opened up and he blinked at the milky light. There was an opening in the vaulted roof far above him, and the bright sunlight was filtered through the falling water which poured down through the hole in the ceiling of the cave. Under the waterfall, there was a huge lake of luminously blue water; reflections danced on the ceiling, where long fingers of rock, sparkling with white crystals, extended downwards. Some of the rocks were folded like curtains of white silk, some of them pointed like cones of refined sugar. Ned looked around him in wonder: it was an extraordinary place like a fairy-tale palace. The quality of the light was enchanting and the cool air on his sweating face made him want to plunge into the turquoise water. Rowan smiled at his surprise.

'This is where I live,' she told him.

'You live here alone?'

'Others live here with me too.'

'What others?'

She took a breath of the cool damp air, as she trusted him with her secrets. 'Runaway slaves: a woman and her son.'

Ned slumped down to the floor. 'Rowan – if you're caught?'

'We won't be caught. These caves go back for miles. They may run through the whole island – we've found many entrances and many too narrow to enter. Everything that your people build is balanced on a hollow land.'

'Anyone could come in the way that we came in.'

'Yes, and that's why I brought you that way. The other, more secret ways, the narrow ways, hidden ways cannot be found. We can get in and out at a hundred places. This is a world your sister Alinor would understand. It is a world beneath the world, inside the world.'

'She has died,' he told her. 'Alinor died last summer.'

She nodded as if he were telling her something that she knew. 'Ah well,' she said. 'Did you bury her with her tools?'

He smiled, remembering the gardening basket on the coffin. 'Yes, I thought of your ways.'

'That was good.'

He gestured to the beach where the blue water lapped over the white sand. 'Any good dog could track you through that?'

She smiled. 'They don't have good dogs, and that's quicksand. It would swallow up a dog and all the men that followed it.'

'Then how do you get through?'

She gleamed in her pride. 'Watch this.' She set down his musket and went to the edge of the water, showed him how her brown foot sank the moment she came to the edge, and then she gave a little jump and a sidestep, and like a child playing hopscotch pattered from one hidden platform to another, reached the beach on the other side, and came back again, hopping and jumping from one sunken pillar of stones to another. She looked as if she were dancing on the water, reminding him of the hidden ways of the tidelands and how his sister could cross the harbour and never get her hem wet.

'Rowan, I see, I see! But you can't stay here forever!'

She nodded. 'I won't stay here forever. I will go home. *Sannup*, I need to know something: you came here on a ship and you saw the sky. Do I go to the setting sun to find the Dawnlands? Is it towards the setting sun?'

'It's a long way,' he warned her. 'Barbados is a little island, one of a string of islands.' He drew in the sand the map that he had seen in Christopher Monck's library. 'Your nearest land would be Spanish owned,' he said. 'Venezuela. About two days' sail from here, but these are dangerous waters, Rowan. They have tremendous storms and there are warships and pirates, and you'd be out of sight of land.'

'But the land there is a great land, not a little island?'

'Oh, you'll make landfall if you can go far enough.' He shook his head. 'I can't bear to think of you in a dinghy, making a journey like this.'

She smiled. '*Nippe Sannup*, you must think, you must dare to think of me. And I wouldn't be in a dinghy, I will be in a canoe. A sea-going canoe that can make a long journey in deep waters. Dream for me! Who could dream of freedom like you? Who would think we have come so far? That we could have done all that we have done? It is another adventure for me.'

He shook his head. 'Can't I smuggle you on a ship?'

'Me, maybe. But I am travelling with my sister and her son. You'd never get three of us on board.' She knelt beside him and took his hand. 'I brought you here to show you that I am safe. Don't be an old white man and tell me what you believe, when the opposite is true. I am safe here. This is not your Barbados, filled with loud men and women and their greed – their unending greed. This is our Barbados – beautiful, sacred, secret, hidden from the other one. Above ground is sugar and slavery. Down here is another world where the land is beautiful and the people are free.'

'We'll never meet again,' he foresaw. 'I belong in the world of sugar and slavery and cruelty. Even if I spend my life fighting against it: that's my world.'

'And this is mine. I knew you would understand. That's why I brought you here.'

'To say goodbye?'

She held the back of his hand to her warm cheek. 'To say goodbye. My debt to you is paid. You have no debt to me.'

'I wanted to rescue you,' he confessed.

'You rescued me once,' she assured him. 'But now I have rescued myself, and now I am free.'

He nodded; he felt himself get to his feet, as if the moment was so important that he had to move slowly and speak with great care. 'I never loved a woman before you.'

Her dark eyes were filled with tears but she was smiling. 'I know it.'

'And I am glad, more glad than words can say, that you are free, and with your people, where you should be, like a star in the night sky.

He got to his feet and shouldered his musket and picked up his game bag. 'So there is nothing more to say, because we never needed words?'

She nodded. 'I'll see you to the edge of the creek and sweep the ground of your footprints.'

'Aye.' Ned went ahead of her, through the tight hole of the cliff, wriggling out on the other side like a terrier out of a rat hole. She came out after him, in a swift easy dive, rising to her feet as she came into the forest. Again, she led the way, but this time she went slower on the harder uphill walk, back to the plantation and the world she had left. He watched the scarred leathery skin of her heels, the whipcord muscles of her calves; he followed with a new pain in his chest which was heartache.

At the clearing, where he could see the top of the cliff, and the green canes of the plantation, she halted.

'This is goodbye?' Ned confirmed.

He put his hand out as if he would shake her hand like a trader closing a deal. But as she put her hand in his, she drew him closer, and lifted her mouth to his.

'I love you, *Nippe Sannup*,' she said, and she kissed him on the mouth, and the next moment she was gone.

WHITEHALL PALACE, LONDON, WINTER 1687

Julia alighted with self-conscious pride from her new carriage, leaning with excessive weight on the arm of her own footman. At last Rob had been persuaded to set up a carriage for the use of his family, convinced by Julia that she could not visit a royal palace in a hired hack.

The enormous doors of the palace stood open, and Julia was greeted by Livia's footman in the royal livery who bowed to her and conducted her to Livia's private rooms.

A bright fire was burning in the grate and Livia, dressed in her usual magnificent style, had a fur stole thrown over her naked shoulders for warmth. She rose with a rustle of embroidered silk as Julia entered, and Julia – a goldsmith's daughter – priced to the nearest shilling the cost of the jewels draped in chains around her neck and in her ears.

'My dear.' One powdered cheek was pressed against another. 'My dear.'

The two ladies settled in the high-backed chairs either side of the fireplace and the footman brought in a silver tray with a silver teapot and two tiny porcelain cups and saucers for tea.

'You'll take tea? It is the queen's own blend.'

'Delicious,' Julia said, silently noting everything – the taffeta curtains at the window the match of those in the queen's drawing room, the extravagance of a carpet on the floor rather than on a table, the gilded portraits of Livia's aristocratic Italian ancestors on the walls. Dozens of wax candles competed with the weak winter sun that filtered through the Venetian glass of the windows.

'And how is dear Hester?'

'She is very well. So looking forward to coming to a drawing room! And how is dear Matthew? He brings his cousins to visit Hester sometimes. I don't see him – they like to walk so early in the morning before I am receiving! – but I know that Hester enjoys their company.'

'He is working hard at his pupillage. He will have his own briefs soon. I am so proud of him.'

'And shall he open a London house? I remember you saying . . .'

'Running a great house like Avery House is a burden for a young man, even with the best servants,' Livia declared. 'While he is a single man it is more convenient for him to keep his room at Lincoln's Inn. When he marries is time enough to move.'

'Of course, of course.' Julia sipped her tea. 'Hatton Garden is a much smaller establishment, but I have ensured that Hester knows how to run a big house.'

'I have no time for young ladies who think there is nothing to do in the world but read books.' Livia declared.

Julia caught the slighting reference to Mia and Gabrielle and smiled at her hostess. 'Hester has been raised to manage any household.'

'Of course, she and Matteo are both very young ...'

'Not so very young. Hester is nearly sixteen and Matthew must be ...'

'Nearly nineteen. I would have no objection to an early marriage for him. And in Venice, my home, we believe in girls marrying young.'

'I thought that Matthew was taken with Mia?'

Livia put down her tea cup. '*Allora!* I am looking for a better dowry for Matteo than that from a Venetian art dealer! And a better connection than a family in trade!'

'Oh quite! Quite!' Julia was torn between boasting of her father's wealth as a goldsmith and wanting to distance herself from vulgar work. 'I mean – Hester – for instance – has been raised as a lady! And she will have my fortune.'

Livia smiled. 'Matteo will inherit anything that Her Majesty chooses to give me,' she said. 'Fairmere Priory is just the beginning! I dare not tell you the value of the rents there, and it will be even more when the land is improved.'

Julia laughed lightly. 'And you are forgetting Matthew's inheritance from Sir James! Don't forget Avery House!'

Livia laughed too. 'I never forget Avery House!'

'I would wish for no other son-in-law,' Julia said, closing the deal as swiftly as her father would have done.

'It would be an excellent match,' Livia agreed. 'As his mother and guardian I have control over him until he is twenty-one. So better now than later. Is Doctor Reekie of the same opinion?'

Julia opened her fan and waved away Rob's opinion. 'Why should he not be as pleased as I? He thinks Hester is too young, and as a medical man, he has been anxious about her health. But now her foot is perfectly straight, and besides, it would have no effect on any children ... If you and I are agreed, dear Lady Avery, then I will inform him.'

The two ladies extended their silken-gloved fingers and shook hands, like a pair of old market hucksters, each thinking they had got the best of the bargain.

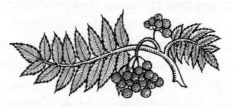

BRIDGETOWN, BARBADOS, WINTER 1687

Ned, packing seeds and leaves into barrels at the back of Johnnie's warehouse to send to London, heard a commotion from the front of the building and went through the doorway and into the shop.

One of the planters was brandishing a news-sheet, showing it to his wife and the other ladies who were gathering round. 'Had it straight off the ship,' he said. 'Brought it to you at once. Didn't even stop to see my carpenter's tools unloaded.'

'Oh, never mind the carpenter's tools! Tell me at once! Show me!'

'It's the queen, God bless her, they say she's with child. They're having a day of thanksgiving. January, so we missed that. But we can have our celebration now.'

There was cheering from the Exchange building on the other side of the street and the church bells of St Michael's started to toll.

Ned drew closer. 'May I see?'

The lady raised her eyebrows at a shop assistant interrupting her reading, but she handed over the news-sheet. 'I declare we shall give a party!' she said to her friends.

'The governor shall give a party,' her husband ruled. 'If it's a boy then the Stuarts are safe on the throne, and we have our royal charter forever.'

'Won't we all have to turn roman catholic?' his wife asked.

He shrugged. 'Who cares about that? If the country's papist, we'll have a parish priest for free, paid for by the church, rather than a vicar that we have to pay for ourselves. If the monasteries and convents come back then we won't have to keep the poor, the church'll do it for us. When we go home if the king's turned into a papist tyrant, there'll be no parliament, fewer taxes and no laws against us landlords. What have we lost?'

'The liberties of England?' Ned suggested quietly. 'The rights of free men to govern themselves, and to worship as they please?'

The man laughed and clapped him on the back. 'You go back to measuring your ells, my man. The king's going to have a son and that'll be the end to free men governing themselves, or shop-men speaking to their betters!'

'What's this?' Johnnie asked, who usually had a grand dinner sent round from the hotel, when he did not dine with one of the planters at an inn.

'English fare,' Ned said. 'To remind us who we are.'

Johnnie laughed. 'Am I allowed a rum punch?'

'I've got water,' Ned said. 'I'm not taking sugar anymore.'

Johnnie sat and ate, one eye on his uncle who moved quietly around their little galley kitchen, slicing fruits and bringing them to the table.

'You'll eat paw-paw,' he said.

'It was grown by a free man,' Ned said. 'And I bought it from him in the market at a fair price.'

Johnnie sighed. 'Uncle Ned – what's all this? Are you fasting because the king has finally got an heir? Surely, it was always possible?'

'It's that,' Ned conceded. 'I thought the country would rise against him or at the worst endure him till his death, and then there'd be a protestant princess who respects the liberties of the people. I thought the Stuart tyranny would die out.'

'And sugar?' Johnnie asked.

'I've seen how the slaves are worked, worse than the beasts. I can't abide it. It's got a bitter taste to me now.'

'I swear to God, Uncle Ned, if you talk like this in public, you will be hanged and I will be ruined.'

Ned nodded. 'I won't be talking like this. I'm going home,' he said simply.

'You've finished your collecting?'

'I've seen more than I can stand. I'm going home to fight for freedom in England.'

Johnnie pushed his plate away. 'Another defeat will kill you.'

'I'd rather die than be spoiled here,' Ned said. 'Mercy dries up here, like the sap in the cane. You said that you'd just open a store to get the cost of your passage and buy Rowan out. But it's you that have been sold. You were always for a profit but now you're trading in men and women, like a cannibal. You're part of it now. You're one of them. Like she said—'

'She said? Who said? If you've been talking to my shop girls—'

'They're not shop girls. They're slaves. You're driving slaves in your own shop. You're paid in slavery profits, you're sending slave goods back to England. You're part of it.'

'You can't be here and not be part of it!' Johnnie exclaimed. 'I said I'd never be a slave driver and I never will. But I have to work slaves in the shop! I can't be the only business in Bridge paying wages! I'd be a fool. I'd go out of business.'

'It was Rowan that said you are a part of it,' Ned said damningly.

There was an aghast silence.

'Rowan? You've seen her? She's alive?'

'She's gone,' Ned lied without a moment's hesitation. 'She's taken ship. Stowed away.'

'I can't believe it! Where was she hiding all this time?'

'I don't know.'

'When did you see her?'

'My second night here, on the quay. After the dinner for the new governor.'

'You didn't wake me?'

'The last trump wouldn't have woke you. You were drunk as a lord that night. She came to see us both. To say goodbye.'

'You never told me? And she went away without seeing me?' He had a sudden thought. 'She didn't see me like that, drunk and celebrating the governor, did she?'

'No. She wouldn't have minded the drink. It's how you live when you're sober that's worse. There are sides in this world, Johnnie. She's on the side of the imprisoned, the enslaved, the poor. And you're on the other. The slave masters, the slave drivers, those that profit from cruelty.'

'Everyone profits from it!' Johnnie raged. 'Me! The wharf! My Ma! You!'

Ned was stubborn. 'A lie – a vile lie. The slaves don't profit, the poor don't profit. I won't. It is possible to eat and not taste blood. To wear clothes that are not hemmed with some poor woman's sweat.'

'Well I won't,' Johnnie swore. 'I won't choose to be poor. Not for you. Not even for her. I can't choose to be poor. It matters to me more than life itself, Ned. I watched my Ma fight for every penny she earned and I swore that I wouldn't be poor like her, afraid of debt like her. I will do anything before I lose family money. And now I am making money, a fortune, day after day. I can't turn my back on it.'

'And I'll never side with the rich,' Ned said grimly. 'I'll never side with the rich and powerful against the poor and those struggling.'

There was a long silence between the two men.

'So, you'll go home?' Johnnie asked. 'There's no place for you here. You're either white and a slave driver; or black and a slave. There's no in-between place. There's no white man on the side of the slaves.'

'Not yet. But there will be. I know it. You'll stay here?'

'Until I am rich enough.'

'You'll never be rich enough.' Ned's prediction was like a sor-rowful curse. 'That's the thing about wealth and power. Once you've learned to want it – that's all you learn. You don't learn satisfaction, you just want more. There's never enough. You'll never be rich enough, Johnnie, and you'll die in dissatisfaction.'

'And you'll go home, and declare war against the Stuarts and tyranny? Get yourself half-killed again on a lost cause?'

Ned laughed in genuine amusement. 'Aye. If the call comes, I'll answer it. Every time. And one day enough of us will answer, and we will win.'

Johnnie sighed at his uncle's vision. 'The call?'

'Liberty! Like always. Liberty!'

WHITEHALL PALACE, LONDON, SPRING 1688

Livia sent a note to Matthew's new legal firm to ask him to call on her at the palace at his own convenience. In case he was so mistaken as to think she wanted him to consult his convenience, she added a post script: 'Six o'clock this evening.'

'*Signora Madre?*' He came into her private rooms and bowed over her hand. She rose up and drew his handsome face down and kissed him on the forehead and both cheeks.

'My Son. *Caro figlio!*'

'You sent for me?'

'I did indeed, but let me look at you before we sit down.'

She took him by the hand and looked him up and down. He was wearing a good suit of sober black as a lawyer should. The bulky cuffs had buttons of jet, rather than gold, and his linen shirt was plain but of good quality. In his hand he had one of the new tricorn hats with a modest black plume. She was struck by the kindness of his brown eyes and his square handsome face.

'Will I do?' he asked.

'You'll do very well,' she said. 'Sit down. I have been thinking about a marriage for you.'

He flinched. 'I have no plans for marriage.'

'No, why should you? As your guardian, it is I who make the plans.'

'*Signora Madre*, I don't wish to marry.'

'You did,' she said unkindly.

'Since then, I have no wish.'

'You know that you must marry, you have a country house and land, you have a good and respected name—'

'I have a name of your invention,' he said quietly.

Livia completely ignored him. 'You have an occupation that befits a gentleman. You have an income from your rents, you will have an inheritance from me, and you have already inherited a small sum from your stepfather Sir James. Obviously, you must have a wife, and a son to come after you.'

'I don't want to marry someone I don't know.'

She shook her head. 'I don't require it of you. I have made arrangements with Hester Reekie's mother.'

He hesitated. 'Miss Reekie?'

'You don't dislike her?'

'On the contrary.' He hesitated. 'She's a very ... of course, she's ... Nobildonna, it wouldn't be right. She would know that she's not my first choice. She knew that I loved Mia and I had to give her up.'

She smiled at him. 'Hester will inherit a considerable fortune from her parents and from her grandfather, the Alderman. She is an excellent choice. You can have no objection to her.'

'Of course, I have no objection to her! She is a friend, she is a dear—'

'Very well then.'

'But I have no desire to be married at all.'

'But given that you have to marry, as do we all, I hope you will agree that Hester is a young lady most likely to make an excellent wife.'

'Of course, I admire and respect her. But I don't want to marry anyone yet.'

'My son, as your guardian, it is for I to decide when you marry and who.'

'I know you are my guardian,' he said carefully. 'And I know this is your decision. But surely Miss Reekie is too young? Her parents would not order her.'

'My dear,' his mother said frankly, 'she is half in love with you already. Her mother tells me that you seek her out, that you are happy companions, that you are friends.'

He looked aghast. 'I have compromised her?'

'You have certainly shown a preference. And so has she. It would be awkward not to proceed.'

'Does she know of this?'

'Her mother will be telling her today. You and I will visit Hatton Garden tomorrow.'

He hesitated. 'I will ask her if she has any objection, I will not go further than that.'

'Very romantic,' she commended him. 'Toll-loll! Ask her yourself. And if either of you has the slightest of doubts, we, your parents and guardians will listen to you.' She smiled. 'Children used to obey their parents without question. But times have changed. No-one is being forced into anything.'

'She will not be ordered?'

'Not at all.'

'You will not order me?'

'My son, I think only of your happiness.'

'You are a rather surprising parent, you know,' he told her with a ghost of a smile. 'Last time I came to the palace I was saving the queen from a rebellion, now you tell me I am to propose marriage. Do you think we might discuss these matters before they are off at a gallop?'

She laughed. 'Sometimes, time is of the essence. And I am not a woman of patience.'

REEKIE WHARF, LONDON, SPRING 1688

The warehouse was closed and the wharf was quiet, the sun sinking low over the city. Alys had the new package of receipts from Johnnie's sales in Barbados spread over the parlour table. She always kept a running tally in her head of the stock she had sent out to him. But now, she saw the fortune that Johnnie was making from re-selling the goods. The most recent ship had brought in hogsheads of best sugar, and this package of notes of credit from Barbados planters to be redeemed at their London agents.

There was a knock at the kitchen door and Alys heard Tabs the cook open the top half and then exclaim. 'Well I never! God bless us! What a fine sight!'

She rose to her feet, knowing at once that it must be Ned. Only Ned always came to the yard, as if the front door were for gentry visitors. 'Is that you, Uncle Ned?' she asked, stepping over the parlour doorsill as he came into the hall with Tabs exclaiming behind him.

He was looking well, far stronger than when he had left, his face tanned and deeply grooved with lines, the pale scar of his wound puckered at his temple. He had gained weight in the months that he had been away, and he stood taller. His smile, still lopsided, was warm and untroubled. 'Well, here's the wharfinger, doing her business!' he exclaimed, taking in the account books spread on the table. 'You look just as you did when I left you.'

'God bless you, Uncle. You've not brought Johnnie with you?'

'No, I'm sorry to disappoint you, but he is well and happy there, and he sent you his love and a little gift for you, and – which you will want more – receipts and an order for goods which he made me swear to give you at once.' Ned plunged into the pocket of his sea jacket and brought out a crumpled roll of papers.

'He's not had the fever?'

'No, he's taking Alinor's tea.'

'And he's happy? I can tell from the receipts that he's doing well.'

'He's settled in, he has friends. He likes the life there.'

She saw the shadow that went across his face. 'So what's wrong? He didn't find Rowan, and neither did you?'

'She's escaped,' Ned said. 'I'm glad of it. She's taken her own freedom. I'd have been glad to free her; but she's a woman who can find her own path.'

'She wasn't dead?'

'Not her.'

'And Johnnie doesn't mind?'

'He did at first; but she'd never have worked in his shop. She'd never have commanded slaves, she'd never've married a man who was a slave driver.'

'Johnnie owns slaves now?' Alys could not keep the respect from her voice.

'He hires 'em. He tells me he'll not buy his own. But I think it unavoidable.'

She saw the weariness in his face. 'Here am I! Questioning you in the hall like a landlady. Take your bags upstairs to your old room, and come down and I'll have some small ale for you and I'll get dinner on. Or would you rather punch? Are you drinking rum now?'

'Nay,' he said. 'I don't take sugar. I won't take coffee, or tobacco. I've seen how its grown, and I won't benefit.'

She made a little gesture at the warehouse, at the parlour table and the account books. 'We can't help but benefit,' she said. 'It's how the world is. There is no profit in equality.'

He nodded. 'I know that all wealth flows from one to another, but I'll do what I can to keep my own hands clean.'

She waited until they had dined and were sitting on either side of the parlour fire. 'Are you back to stay, Uncle Ned?'

'Only for a while. I think there'll be a rising up against the king.'

'You don't want to be part of that. Not at your age.'

He showed his lopsided smile. 'Did St Olave's vicar read the king's declaration last Sunday?'

'He did not! He defied the royal order. He said that the king wants roman catholics to rule the great offices of state, and he could not say from the pulpit that it was righteous. The bishop of London himself has said he will not preach the sermon written by the king – even if it costs him his mitre.'

'It's against the law,' Ned told her. 'Never mind about not righteous.'

She shrugged. 'You know I don't take an interest in such things.'

'The bishops are supporting their clergy, and they've told the king that it's illegal to open the ruling of the kingdom to roman catholics. The law says clearly that only men in the Church of England can rule, from magistrates to Members of Parliament. The king's decree is against the law. But not even the king can change the English law by decree.'

'Uncle Ned . . .'

'It's tyranny,' he told her. 'If he moves openly against the bishops – the bishops of the Church of England – the people will take arms against him.'

'Then surely he won't do it?'

'Aye, we'll see,' Ned said with his old smile. 'Everything to play for.'

'It's not play for me,' she said crossly. 'It's bad for business.

London is in uproar. I can only open the wharf for half the day. There's trouble in the streets all the time, the lumpers run off and the apprentices break into the papist chapels and throw down the icons.'

'So it's starting,' Ned said in a voice almost of wonder. 'People are starting to resist. God bless us, it's starting again.' He smiled at his niece. 'It's extraordinary. Just when I think we have lost liberty for a generation ... it always starts again.'

HATTON GARDEN, LONDON, SPRING 1688

'I do hope you will be home this afternoon for tea,' Julia said to Rob as he rose from the breakfast table. She glanced down the table to Hester. 'Go to your room, Hester, I need to speak to your father.'

Hester got up as she was ordered, curtseyed to her mother and went to her father to kiss his cheek. 'See you later,' she whispered to him.

When the door had closed on her, Rob asked: 'I can come home at four o'clock but it will take me out of my way. I was visiting the Bridewell this afternoon. Do I need to be here?'

'You do!' she said smiling. 'Guess why?'

'Not for the pleasure of the Nobildonna's company,' he said. 'I don't mind Matthew, if he's coming with the girls.'

'What d'you mean you don't mind him?' she exclaimed. 'You've encouraged him to run in and out of this house with the Venice girls, and Hester has stayed with him every summer since he had Fairmere Priory.'

'It's called Foulmire.'

'That's not what it says on the gates.'

He sighed. 'No matter. My point is that I do not like the Nobildonna. I told you, Julia, that I did not want a friendship with her. As it happens, I do like Matthew. He was raised by my mother and my sister like a son, I have always thought of him as a child of our family.'

'I am glad you like him,' she said. 'He has become a most promising young man.'

'I agree. But why do I have to come home for tea?'

'He will be the heir of the Nobildonna, who stands very high in royal favour.'

'I don't know how much that will help him, if the king continues to quarrel with his parliament, his judges, and his church.'

'He has inherited considerable wealth from Sir James.'

'I thought much of it was entailed.'

'Avery House and an endowment! And he already has Fairmere Priory and all the lands.'

'He's done very well,' Rob nodded. 'I'm glad for him. My mother was very glad to go back there, in her last years. It was a great repayment for her kindness to him.'

'Lady Avery and I have agreed that Matthew would be a most suitable match for Hester,' she said, taking the plunge. 'I thought of it when we met her at the Priory, and I visited her at court and she proposed it. Or I did. I can't remember which of us spoke first – it's so obviously the right thing.' She stole a quick look at his stunned expression. 'You cannot be surprised! I thought you were encouraging him. Your sister did too!'

For a moment he was silent. 'Hester is far too young,' was all he could say.

'She's sixteen!' she exclaimed.

'Her foot . . .'

'You said yourself that it is almost straight. And besides, it makes no difference.'

'Julia, I can't consider it.'

She laughed at him. 'I have taken you by surprise, your little girl is fully grown, and she deserves the best settlement we can get for her. What good fortune that the most eligible young man is a friend of the family, and she is head over heels in love with him already. We are arranging a love match – the best of all possible worlds.'

'I don't believe it,' he said.

'She hangs on his every word. Whenever they have been at the Priory it is all "Matthew says . . ." and "Matthew thinks" – what did you intend when you threw a pretty girl and a handsome young man together for days at a time?'

'I thought they were, all four, children together.'

'Well, the children are grown up, and will have children of their own!'

As if those words unlocked something in him he stood and pushed back his chair. 'It's not possible,' he said flatly. 'They cannot marry.'

She blinked at his tone. 'My dear – you're too late – the lawyers are drawing up the contracts.'

'You cannot have instructed them without me!'

'I did not instruct them. Papa did so. They are his lawyers.'

'Does your father know that I have not been consulted?'

'It's his fortune that Hester inherits. It's his lawyers that draw up the contracts.'

'She's my daughter!'

'But of course. Which is why I want you here at tea-time!'

'It cannot be,' he said. 'Believe me, Julia, I am completely serious about this. It cannot be.'

'Then you can go and tell Papa,' she said easily.

'I shall go at once, and see your father, and tell him that this cannot happen.' He bit down his anger that she had gone so far, knowingly defying him, and went from the room without another word.

Hester was waiting for him on the turn of the stairs, where she used to wait for him when she was a little girl. As he ran up to his dressing room to get his jacket and his hat, he found her there.

'Papa, are you coming to tea? Did she tell you?'

'She told me. Hester, it's not possible. You're both far too young.'

'No we're not,' she said reasonably. 'And we will be betrothed for a year anyway.'

'There are obstacles, I can't discuss them with you, but there are insuperable obstacles to the two of you marrying.'

'You like him?'

'Yes, I do. I don't like his mother ...'

'That doesn't matter,' she smiled at him. 'You shall always come for Christmas to the Priory and she won't. She doesn't like to leave the queen. You'll see no more of her when I am married to her son, than you do now. And that was only once, Papa!'

Rob felt he was sinking into madness. 'I cannot tell you my objection,' he said slowly to her smiling face. 'But you must put this out of your mind. I am completely serious, Hester, it can't happen.'

She flushed and her eyes filled with tears. 'Papa! Don't say such a thing. I love him. I truly do. And he loves me. I won't marry anyone else but him. Papa, don't say such things to me!'

'My darling.' He took her hands, he could not bear to hurt her. 'You're young, you will—'

'Is Mama cancelling tea-time?' she interrupted him.

'No.'

'Does Mama say I shall not marry Matthew?'

'No, not yet. I have to see your grandfather.'

Her face lightened. 'Then I will see him this afternoon.'

'You can see him!' he exclaimed. 'But you can't marry him!'

'As soon as I see him, it will all be all right,' she said.

AMSTERDAM, HOLLAND, SPRING 1688

Once again Ned was walking the cobbled streets of Amsterdam, crossing the narrow bridges as he had done three years ago – three years to the very month. He could hardly believe that Rowan was not at his shoulder, hard on his heels. He remembered her dismay at the streets that stretched for miles, her contempt for the cosy little houses. He remembered laughing at her when she could not comprehend that people might choose to live indoors, build a house and stay in the same place all year round.

He had thought that he would miss her for the rest of his life, but increasingly, he felt at peace, with a deep gladness that they had been together on such a journey, in step together on a long march. He was glad that she had never left his side, not through voyage nor march nor battle, not even when he had ordered her to go.

Ned followed the directions he had been given to the English tavern in the city, limping a little on the slippery cobbles, but finding his way. He ducked through the low doorway, went down a short flight of wooden stairs. For a moment he paused, remembering the Duke of Monmouth looking up, illuminated by a shaft of light from a high window. He blinked his eyes against the smoke and the darkness of the room and an English voice said: 'God be praised! Is that you, Ned Ferryman?'

It was Robert Ferguson, Monmouth's preacher. Ned had last seen him praying with the troops for a righteous victory before the battle of Westonzoyland.

'That you, Padre?' he said, his lopsided smile warming his face. 'You here again?'

'You here again?' the man repeated, clapping Ned on the back. 'I thought you were transported? I thought they picked you up near dead?'

'I was,' Ned replied. 'Near dead and then transported. But it's a hard task to kill an old dog, and now I've come home.'

Ferguson drew him towards the table at the back of the room. Ned recognised a few faces from the Monmouth army. They gripped hands, they embraced each other, laughing at the fact that they had met again, naming quickly the men who had been lost.

'Nathaniel Wade was the last man I saw, as I went down,' Ned said, looking round.

Ferguson shook his head. 'Turned his coat,' he said shortly. 'D'you remember William Hewling? And his brother Benjamin?'

'I knew William,' Ned said. 'Met him at Lyme.'

'His sister was whipped off Jeffreys' coach door, begging for mercy. The two lads were hanged.'

'God send England better lords,' Ned exclaimed. 'Or no lords at all.'

'Amen!' Ferguson replied. 'Look. Here are some new comrades in place of the ones we have lost.'

'Glad to meet them.' Ned nodded at the handful of men. 'What's the plan?'

'We're waiting,' Ferguson said. 'When King James announces the birth of his son – that's our signal to rise.'

'We invade?'

Ferguson nodded. 'With William of Orange's army, and we make him swear to a constitution. We crown William and tie his hands, and stop his mouth.'

'We have an army? We have ships?'

Ferguson laughed. 'It's not like last time! We have his army and his ships, to fight our own battle. William of Orange knows he has to defend the English church or lose it to Rome forever. He's paying, mustering, shipping, and he'll lead us. He himself is invading England.'

'And what happens if James Stuart the king, doesn't have a son?'

'He's never going to admit to a girl or a stillbirth. They'll put some poor little bastard in the royal cradle.'

There was a rumble of assent around the table. Some man said that he knew for a fact that a midwife had already been hired to bring in a changeling.

'We wear the green sash again?' Ned asked.

Ferguson laughed out loud and raised his glass. 'We wear the green sash again. To liberty!'

WHITEHALL PALACE, LONDON, SPRING 1688

Matthew was announced to Livia's private rooms in the palace and found her tying the black silk bows of her hat under her chin before a large gilded mirror. He took her silk-gloved hand and bowed his head for her kiss.

'*Signora Madre*, I don't think we can go to Hatton Garden,' he said.

Livia did not take her eyes from the mirror and moved the bow a little more to one side. 'We have to go,' she said simply.

'It's not safe in the streets! I had to dodge two gangs of apprentices on the way here. There are people ringing the palace, shouting all sorts of things. The guards are closing the gates but they can't hold this palace against a full riot, there are too many entrances, they can't guard them all.'

'Rowdy apprentice lads,' she suggested.

'Not just young lads, it's the market people, women as well

as men. A lot of tradesmen by the looks of it, and watermen, chairmen, grooms. Everyone, really. People from the country, farmers and countrywomen. Everyone is up in arms about the king trying to destroy the church.'

She snapped her fingers with irritation. 'We know nothing in this palace, and everyone tells the king only what he wants to hear.'

'You don't know about the embassy?'

'*Allora!* What?'

'The Spanish ambassador has closed up his house and run away – no-one knows where. The mob threatened to burn the embassy to the ground. The new chapel has been closed. They broke in and robbed it of everything, they pissed on the walls.'

She was pale. 'Why doesn't the Lord Mayor stop this?'

'He's out every weekend, trying to control the streets. They won't listen to him.'

'I never get outside these walls, and all we talk about in here is the baby.'

'She's not safe here. She should go to somewhere that could be defended.'

'She wanted to go to Windsor, but they say the birth has to be here, witnessed by all the privy councillors ... what with everyone saying ...'

'What?'

'... all the things that they are saying,' she finished.

'She can't give birth here. What if they break in?'

'Surely we have the militia?'

'*Signora Madre*, the London militia is the very people who are running wild in the streets, shouting that they won't have a changeling foisted on them, that the Nuncio is the real father, and the Pope is invading! They are the same men and lads as the rioters.'

'Hush, hush, don't say such things! The king will have to bring in the army.'

'Won't that make everyone take up arms against him?'

'They would be massacred in France.'

'They'll think they're going to be massacred here, if he calls in the army.'

'When an heir is born, they will submit,' she said stubbornly.

He spread his hands. 'Maybe. Or maybe it will be the last straw.'

She was not in the least afraid. 'We'll have to go to St James' Palace. They can bar the gates there and we can defend her, and the baby prince. But anyway, we're going to tea.'

HAYCROFT AND JOHNSON GOLDSMITHS, LONDON, SPRING 1688

Alderman Jeremiah Johnson was a big man, dressed in a jacket of double-breasted dark navy wool with pairs of ostentatious gold buttons straining across his chest. He sat in a grand chair behind a broad desk covered with papers, freighted with silver pieces of equipment: a heavy paperknife, a set of goldsmith's scales as if he were taking in coin at his desk, a silver tinderbox and sealing wax, his own silver seal, a large silver tray for his letters, a substantial silver box for deeds.

'Now then, Doctor?' Jeremiah Johnson said with pleasure. 'Not often you find the time to visit me in the City. Did you get here without trouble? I have my lads on the front and back doors and even a few keeping watch in the streets. We close early every day now.'

'I came by the backways. Half of London is boarded up.'

'It'll go on like this until she gives birth,' the Alderman predicted. 'But the Lord Mayor himself said to me: soon as a boy is born and we put a roasted ox and free ale in every borough, they'll all be royalists again.'

'I suppose so,' Rob said. 'I came about a grave matter in my own family.'

'Aye, Julia sent me a message, that you weren't best pleased.'

'It's not a question of my pleasure, Sir.'

'She says that you like the lad?'

'It's not that. You remember that when I asked for Julia's hand in marriage I told you that I had been married . . . that is, I had gone through a ceremony . . . you remember?'

The Alderman steepled his fingers over his broad belly and regarded Rob as he might look at an unreliable debtor. 'I remember you told me that you had gone through a form of marriage with a strange woman overseas, in Venice, in the English church in Venice when she was neither English nor protestant, and there were no family witnesses.'

'You remember very well, then.'

'And she abandoned you on your wrongful arrest, came to England, stayed with your mother and sister under the pretext of being your wife, converted to the Church of England and had the good fortune to marry a gentleman of an old and highly regarded family.'

Again, Rob nodded in silence.

'Who accepted her?'

'Yes.'

'As your agreement with her was no marriage.'

'Yes.'

'He remembered her in his will? And named her as his widow?'

'Yes.'

'So what is your difficulty, with Hester's marriage, into that very same, highly regarded family?'

'Matthew is the stepson of Sir James Avery, not his son.'

'His stepfather acknowledged him with a considerable legacy.'

Rob leaned towards the desk, rested his hands on the deeply polished surface. 'Alderman Johnson, even if Matthew had been adopted by the Averys, we could not allow Hester to marry him, we have no idea who his father is . . .'

The Alderman shook with a silent laugh. 'It's a wise child who knows his father,' he quoted an old proverb. 'And, it behoves us to speak of a lady such as Dowager Lady Avery with utter respect.'

'Of course, I always do. And I would never say anything to Matthew. But Sir – you cannot want Hester to marry a young man whose father might be an Italian count or might be Felipe Russo, a Venetian master mason and dealer in antiquities, or might be . . . he could be . . . he could be of my fathering, Sir. What if he is my son? He was born during our . . . our time together, and when she came to England she brought him to my family, and told them he was my son.'

'Conceived during your connection?' the Alderman asked.

'Conceived before the ceremony,' Rob said wretchedly. 'She was my lover before she was my wife.'

'She was never your wife, at all,' the Alderman corrected him. 'The ceremony was invalid, so the question of his fathering does not come into it. My daughter tells me that Matthew is the son of Lady Avery's first husband the Prince Fiori, and the stepson of Sir James Avery. Anything else is slander.' He looked severely at Rob. 'Probably actionable.'

Rob dropped his face into his hands and rubbed his aching forehead. 'He wasn't even a prince!' he exclaimed. 'Look, Sir, I have no wish to bring this all up again. I am just anxious for Hester's health and happiness—'

'Julia says that she is halfway to being in love with him already?'

'I should never have allowed him to come to the house. I should never have allowed Hester to visit him.'

'Spilt milk,' the older man said shortly. 'And how could you have denied your mother's foster child? Look, Julia wants the connection, she's no fool when it comes to her advantage. The lawyer has drawn up the contract and the settlement is generous. We haven't heard from the Yorkshire executors yet – there's no post from the north while these damned riots are going on. Hester likes the young man, he likes her. She gets a great name, and an introduction to the royal court. She might even get a post as a royal lady-in-waiting. Think of that! The young man gets a good dowry just as he is starting out in life, and he has a handsome manor to spend it on. You need meet his mother only once, at the signing of the register. She's a lady, she'll make no mention of the past—' He broke off. 'You've told Julia nothing about Venice?'

'Nothing! As we agreed.'

The Alderman nodded his great head. 'As we agreed. Good. And the lady is not going to discuss it. I think we're all well and good.'

The grandfather clock behind him made a whirring noise and began to strike the hour. The Alderman became paternal. 'You're my son-in-law,' he told Rob. 'You don't have a father to advise you, so I'll tell you something ... What happened in Venice between a pretty widow and a young man was an affair, a secret affair, a sowing of wild oats. Whether you thought you were married, or she did, is neither here nor there. It's not the sort of thing you tell your wife, it's the sort of thing you forget about. The lady has put it behind her and gone on to rise very high in society. It's not for you, as a gentleman, to bring it up again. It was many, many years ago. Forget it.'

'They cannot marry if they are within the proscribed degrees of affinity,' Rob said tightly. 'They cannot marry if they are closely related in blood, even if not in law.'

'And that's where we leave it to the young man's mother, who is the only one of all of us who knows who his father is. She's not going to let something like that darken his life, spoil the line. She wouldn't have suggested it, if there was any doubt in her mind. Of course she would not. She's not going to risk having a misbegotten misconceived grandson! Obviously, she knows you're not his father. Who are we to raise the question? Such an indelicate question!'

'No,' Rob said half-convinced. 'Of course – it's against her own interest to marry Matthew to Hester if they are half-sister and brother.'

The Alderman laughed at his son-in-law. 'You were badly stung!' he said. 'You don't think much of her at all, do you?'

'She never does anything against her own interest,' Rob told him.

'The same as all of 'em,' the Alderman said fondly. 'God bless 'em. Selfish as weasels every one. But she won't be putting a foot wrong here, you can count on it.'

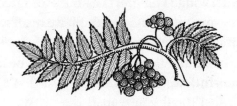

HATTON GARDEN, LONDON, SPRING 1688

Livia and Matthew left the barge at the Holborn water stairs and walked up the road to Hatton Garden. She took his hand to support her walking in her high-heeled shoes. When they reached the door she raked him with a glance from the top of his brown hair to his shining shoes. 'Good,' was all she said. 'You can knock.' She pinched his fingers. 'Don't call me "Dowager,"' she hissed.

The moment the knocker had sounded, the door was opened by a footman.

'Lady Livia Avery and Mr Matthew Peachey,' Matthew said, obeying the pressure of his mother's hand and giving her Christian name and title rather than the more usual title of 'Dowager'.

The footman bowed and opened the door to them, preceded them to the drawing room and opened the door. Hester was not in her usual place – looking out for him in the window-seat – but demure on a silk-covered sofa with a gilt chair placed at her side. Julia was on the other sofa. Both ladies rose, curtseyed, and Julia gestured that Livia should sit beside her to allow Hester and Matthew to sit together.

'So pleased you could come,' Julia said.

'Delighted,' Livia returned.

The two of them looked with pleasure at their two children, who sat in silence, both of them paralysed with embarrassment.

'And how do the wall hangings look in your new drawing room?' Livia turned to Julia. 'Did you choose the yellow silk?'

'Ah, I promised to show you, didn't I? Do come.' She turned to Hester who had risen from her seat. 'You stay, Hester, pour Mr Peachey a cup of tea when the tray comes. We're just going to look at the drawing room curtains for a moment.'

She led the way out of the room. Matthew and Hester were alone in an awkward silence.

'I'm sorry,' he said. 'My mother . . .'

'She's wonderful,' Hester said simply.

'You know what they've agreed?'

Hester blushed a deep red.

'I won't have you bullied,' he said shortly. 'I would be happy . . . that is to say I will propose to you, if you wish it. But I want you to know that if you don't want it, I won't even say. And I shall tell my mother that I decided against speaking. You don't have to refuse me. I know your mother is very . . . That is to say . . . they've cooked this up together . . . But you are not to be forced. I mean it. I won't say a word, unless you tell me to.'

She turned a smiling face towards him. 'Am I to propose to you?'

'No! No!' he said. Her laughter was infectious. 'No, that's not what I meant. I don't want you to be forced.'

'I'm not,' she said shyly. 'Mama would not force me, and anyway Papa thinks I'm too young.'

'He's probably right . . .'

'We could have a long engagement.'

'We could, if you would like that?'

'I would,' she nodded, her eyes on her hands in her lap.

'You would like me to propose, you would like to be my wife? It's not just them?'

Her colour rose again and she snatched a quick look at his warm face. 'Please,' she said, like a little girl.

The door opened and Livia and Julia came in; the footman

followed behind with the tea tray. Hester gave a tiny exclamation of impatience, and Matthew laughed.

'You seem very merry?' Livia asked charmingly.

The footman arranged the tray, bowed and went out.

'Are you agreed?' Julia asked.

'Did you propose?' Livia addressed her son.

'I did propose, and I have been honoured with an acceptance,' Matthew said, smiling at Hester and taking her hand. 'We want to be married in two years' time. When I am twenty.'

'Very good!' Livia clapped her hands together and crossed the room to kiss Hester on both cheeks. Julia followed her; but just as they were congratulating the young couple the door opened and Rob came in.

'Here you are, just in time to wish them happiness!' Julia cried. 'Papa said you would come.'

Rob looked from one smiling face to another and then he turned to Livia. He could see nothing in her luminous face but happiness for her son.

'I hope you give your blessing, Doctor Reekie?' Livia confirmed.

'Yes. Of course,' Rob said quietly, then he crossed the room, shook Matthew's hand and kissed Hester. 'I wish you may both be very happy.'

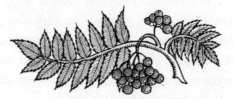

BRIDEWELL, CLERKENWELL, LONDON, SUMMER 1688

The grand front door of the workhouse stood open for the doctor to leave, and the matron exclaimed irritably at a young woman, collapsed on the broad stone steps. 'You can't wait here,' she said sharply. 'Go round the back.'

'Please, Ma'am . . . I'm very near my time.'

'They all say that! Come back when you have your pains. I'm not feeding you before then.'

Rob Reekie joined the matron on the doorstep, watched the girl limp off into the darkness, heard the noise of running feet and shouting from the rioters. 'You're very strict, Mrs Fadden. The streets aren't safe these days.'

She shrugged, indifferent. 'Thank you for coming, Sir. There was no need for you to trouble yourself . . .'

'I'm sorry I couldn't save the mother.'

'She's left us another mouth to feed.'

'There must be some way to get hold of the baby when it's stuck like that, high in the birth canal . . . Doctor Chamberlen has some sort of device, I know it. If he would only let me see . . .'

'Maybe he thinks there's enough pauper brats born in the world, without dragging out the unwilling ones.'

'Will you call me if you get another breech birth, or a woman labouring after her waters break?' A silver coin passed from his pocket to her waiting hand.

'Of course,' she amended. 'Of course, Sir.'

Rob bowed his thanks, put on his black beaver hat against the drizzle and turned into the darkness. He did not see the figure on the opposite side of the road, beneath the shelter of a tree, watching the doorway of the workhouse. He was so absorbed in his sense of his failure that he did not even hear the footsteps behind him. He was thinking of the woman, the young woman, her legs splayed, her belly straining, the stink of sweat and the reek of the spirits that they forced down her throat as she screamed and cried and begged to die.

'A nightmare,' he said to himself. 'A terrible death.'

'Sir?'

Rob turned. 'Matthew? What are you doing in the streets like this? It's not safe, there are gangs around everywhere. My carriage is picking me up.'

'I was waiting for you, Sir.'

'Is it about the betrothal?' He started walking again, his head bowed against the rain which was getting heavier.

'No, I wanted to see you, Sir. They said you were attending a lying-in.'

'Small good it did me. Or her.'

The young man fell into step beside him. 'Is it charitable work you do?'

'Little charity to them.' Rob was speaking to himself, in a monotone of frustration and anger. 'God knows, I did no good for the poor woman tonight. But there has to be a way. I keep thinking that I will find a way ...'

'A way of what, Sir?' Matthew quickened his pace to keep up.

'If a baby presents its haunches first, not its head, you understand, or even lying sideways, or God knows what it is doing, presenting an elbow or its foot, it can get stuck. Sometimes the midwife gets hold of it, like a farmer might rope the leg of a stuck calf and pull it out. My mother could do that. More, she could turn a baby from stroking the woman's belly. She had such a gift. But the Chamberlen family has a device, it must be some kind of loop to pull the baby out without cutting it or breaking its bones. They have something. Their babies live and the mothers live too.'

'Can't you ask them?'

'It's their secret. But they boast they can get a baby out, even a breech birth, even high.'

For the first time the young man's interest was genuine. 'And it's true?'

'Aye. I've seen the babies – live babies. And the mothers who lived through it.'

'What do the mothers say?'

'They blindfold them, so they can never tell. They get hold of a dying woman and they make her wear a blindfold before they will save her. God knows it's a wicked thing when doctors make a profit from medicine.'

'They charge women for the use of their device?'

'A fortune. That's why they won't tell anyone the secret but the physicians in their own family.'

'They won't tell you?'

'For me to save pauper babies? No. What's the profit in that?'

They came to Rob's waiting carriage, in the distance they could hear the crash of someone breaking a window and cheers.

'So what d'you want, Matthew?' Rob said. 'The streets aren't safe, you should be at home. Are you worried about the betrothal? I'll help you withdraw if it's against your will?'

'No, it's not that. Can we go to a coffee house? I need to talk to you.'

'I'm tired,' Rob said. 'I've been up all night and I stink. I've done no good but brought another orphan into this world where there are so many already. We'll get a drink and then I'll go home.'

Rob led the way into an inn. It was almost empty; no-one wanted to be out on the damp streets with gangs of men roaming around swearing that they would string up papists and lynch priests. Matthew seated himself beside the fire where they would not be overheard. Rob went into the yard to wash, and then came to the fireside, pulling down his sleeves, and dropped into the high-backed settle.

'Your best wine,' he said briefly to the landlord.

'I have an excellent Bordeaux . . .' the man started. 'Or a spiced sweet wine from Venice?'

'The Bordeaux,' he said as if he did not want to hear of Venice.

'Something to eat? I can send out for a hot dinner, anything you might like?'

'I'll take some soup and bread and cheese,' the older man said. 'Matthew, d'you want anything?'

'The same.'

The landlord produced a bottle of wine, poured the glasses. The doctor raised his glass to Matthew and drank deeply.

'I've been asked to speak with you. It's a delicate matter,' Matthew began.

Rob was guarded. 'Is it your delicate matter?'

'No, Sir. It's someone else.' He leaned forward. 'It's the queen,' he said.

'Then I doubt that I can help you,' Rob replied. 'I'm not a court physician.'

Matthew leaned closer. 'The queen is near her time,' he said quietly. 'She wants a boy, she wants to ensure a safe birth.'

'Every woman in England wants a boy and a safe birth.'

The landlord laid a cloth on the little side table and put down two bowls of soup, a trencher with a loaf cut into big pieces, and some yellow cheese, the sweat glistening on the side.

'Her Majesty requires my services, does she?' Rob inquired sarcastically. 'And sent you to the Clerkenwell Bridewell to find me, with my previous patient going out of the back door to a pauper grave in bloodstained rags?' Rob finished his bowl of soup and took another hunk of bread. 'What do you want, Matthew?' he asked.

'My mother sent me,' Matthew confessed. 'To ask you what she might do to make sure. The queen is near her time now – she has to have a boy to save the throne.'

'London's up in arms. Is the rest of the country rising?'

Matthew nodded. 'But if she has a boy, then the Stuart line of succession is guaranteed and the kingdom can be at peace. A live Stuart baby will bring the country back to the king and to God.'

'If he's going to do so much for God, then God had better provide him,' Rob said bluntly.

'My mother is asking you to provide him,' Matthew said so quietly that Rob had to lean forward to hear him. 'She's asking for you to give us a baby boy, a newborn boy that we can put in the bedchamber, in the royal cradle. You had one born this very evening. My mother wants one like that.'

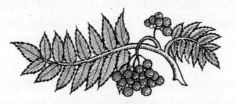

WHITEHALL PALACE, LONDON, SUMMER 1688

The danger from the rioters was so great that they did not dare to move the queen until midnight under a waning moon and a cloudy sky. The earlier rain had driven many from the streets and a mist coiled up like smoke from the river.

A closed sedan chair stood ready for the queen, a hot brick on the floor to warm her feet, thick blankets and pillows on the seat so that she should be cushioned from the roll of the chairmen's walk.

Livia and Mary Beatrice came down the stairs and found the chairmen and the chair drawn up under the arch of the privy gateway. Livia helped the queen into the chair, wrapped her up, pulled up her hood so that her face was hidden, and kissed her cheek.

'I'll meet you there,' she said. 'They say I cannot walk beside you for fear of attracting attention.'

'Are my other ladies already there?'

'Yes, and the king. And some of the gentlemen are here to escort you and a whole company of guards.'

Livia kissed her again, stepped back, closed the door and watched the chairmen take up the poles and step out into the darkness.

'There go the hopes of England, of Christendom itself,' Father Petre said quietly beside her. 'Are you going directly to St James'?'

She shook her head. 'I have to make another visit first.' She looked around for Matthew. 'Come with me,' she told him.

They went through the palace to the Whitehall Stairs down to the dark fast-moving river. Matthew hailed a wherry.

'By rights, I should have gone home,' the wherryman complained.

'Holborn Stairs,' Matthew said to him. 'Up New Canal.'

'It's double price in this weather,' the man said.

'Double,' Livia agreed.

Matthew took a seat beside her as the wherryman rowed, going quickly with the tide. 'I said all that you told me but nothing would convince him.'

'I will convince him,' she said simply.

They sat in silence until they reached the stairs and Matthew helped his mother up the Holborn Stairs, walked her to Hatton Garden, and tapped lightly on the front door.

'Is Doctor Reekie still up?' he asked the footman.

'Yes, Mr Peachey Sir,' the footman said. He bowed to Livia. 'Your ladyship.'

He showed them to Rob's library at the back of the house. Rob was seated at the fire, studying a book of anatomy. He looked up frowning when they came in and then he jumped to his feet as Livia put back the hood of her cape and came forward to the fire to warm her hands, as calmly as if she were a regular visitor and it was not past midnight.

'I am here to tell you why you have to do what Matteo asked,' she told him calmly. 'Are Mrs Reekie and dear Hester gone to bed?'

'Yes.' He glanced at the little clock on the mantelpiece. 'It's very late. I can't see you or speak with you.'

She nodded. 'Matteo, wait for me in the hall.'

Matthew bowed and left the room as the Nobildonna took a seat without invitation at the fireside. Rob stood at the mantelpiece and looked down at her. 'I gave my answer to Matthew,' he said. 'Of course I will not give you a pauper baby, for you to impose upon England. The idea is madness. Nothing could make me join in such a deceit. I am appalled that you ask it of me, against my oaths as a doctor and my loyalty to my king. And through Matthew as well! I think you must have run mad.'

She stripped off one long glove, pulling at the fingers one by one and then drawing off the glove, revealing the curve of her naked arm. Then she took off the other and laid them across her lap. He found he could not help but watch her.

'I know,' she said frankly. 'And I understand. But I have something to tell you.'

He waited.

'Matteo is your son, conceived when we were lovers.'

He was stunned. It was the very last thing he thought she would say, and the worst thing he could have heard. 'He is not.'

'I should think I would know,' she smiled.

'You assured my wife, your lawyers assured Alderman Johnson's lawyers . . .'

'Yes,' she said. 'And if I don't say differently to them, the marriage will go ahead.'

'It cannot go ahead if they are half-brother and sister!' he exclaimed. 'Livia – you cannot have thought! Any child they have could be horribly maimed, and the danger to Hester's health . . . besides the laws of the church . . . the law of the land . . . your own feelings as a mother . . . how could you?' He was lost for words. 'This betrothal must be stopped at once.'

'I will stop it tonight,' she said simply. 'Discreetly. Easily. Have no fear. I will stop it tonight.'

He was panting. 'You will?'

She nodded. 'In return for one favour: a newborn baby boy, brought to me the moment the queen goes into labour. By you.'

He was aghast. 'You would force me to do this, against my conscience? Against my doctor's oath?'

She gave a little laugh. 'I assure you, your conscience would trouble you far worse if you let your daughter marry her half-brother.'

'You said he was Felipe's child!'

'I never said so. Felipe thought he was the father, but so did you. I am the only one who knows for sure. But I am saying to you now, on the very day of your daughter's betrothal, that Matteo is her half-brother. Obviously, you cannot let them be married. Obviously, you will do anything to prevent it.'

She gave him a moment to think of it. 'But you have no power: you will not shame yourself and embarrass your wife – I should think it would kill her – and slander me. Your daughter will be heartbroken, your father-in-law will threaten you, it may be that Matteo will sue Hester for breach of promise, and the Alderman's lawyers for acting in bad faith.' She shrugged negligently. 'I really don't know. I have not thought of all the bad consequences. There is no need to think of them because they will not happen.'

He was watching her as if fascinated. 'Did you plan this from the beginning?'

She laughed at him. 'Don't be so ridiculous! How could I have known nearly twenty years ago that the one thing I need, a newborn baby, would be the one thing you can easily provide?'

'How will you stop the betrothal?'

'I will tell the Alderman that you are Matteo's father, and withdraw Matteo from the betrothal. And I will order Matteo to ask Hester that she release him.'

He flushed. 'Will you tell him I am his father?'

She shook her head. 'It's not necessary. He will do as I say without my confiding in him.' She looked thoughtful. 'I think it better – don't you? – that we don't trouble our children with old difficulties?'

'You swear you will not double-cross me?' he demanded.

She sighed. 'I? Swear? What guarantee would that be for you?'

'Then how can I trust you will separate them forever?'

'Because by putting a changeling in the royal cradle, I am taking the greatest risk in the world. I am putting my neck in your hands.'

'My neck too, if I provide the baby.'

She gleamed at him. 'And there you have your guarantee! Neither of us can cheat the other.'

He shook his head in bewilderment. 'I don't know how you can live with yourself,' he said quietly. 'You're not like a true woman, you're like the worst of men.'

She laughed out loud at that. 'How would you know a true woman? You, who went from being my slave, to marrying a woman with laudanum in her veins?'

She thought he would flare up in a rage, but he slouched as if he was beaten. 'I'll get the baby,' he said. 'God knows, there are enough unwanted babies. I'll bring him to St James' Palace and give him to you. We will agree that I don't know what you want him for, and we will never speak of this again. You will tell the Alderman that you have counted your courses and now you see that Matthew could be my son, and that you must withdraw him from the betrothal. And you will tell Matthew some lie – any lie that you like, as long as it does not name me. You will never again claim me as your husband nor as Matthew's father.'

She pulled on her gloves, like a woman whose business is done.

'Agreed,' she said simply. 'I will send a letter to the Alderman tonight, I will tell Matteo as we go to St James'. You will bring a baby the moment that I give you the word.'

'When is she due?' he asked. 'If it is to pass as a newborn ...'

'Next month,' she said. 'But I expect him to come early. So be a good doctor and watch carefully over your patients. We'll need a newborn very soon.'

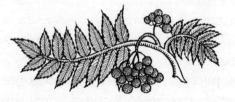

ST JAMES' PALACE, LONDON, SUMMER 1688

Mary Beatrice, sleeping fitfully from dawn, sent for Livia at six in the morning and when she came into the queen's bedchamber she found her friend alone, looking like a lonely child, in the huge royal bed.

'Are you well?' she asked. 'My dear? Where is your maid?'

'I feel strange,' the queen said, her voice a thread. 'It's too early, isn't it too early?'

'It's very early morning,' Livia said. 'Lie down and I'll send for a hot chocolate for you, or some mulled ale. Try to sleep.'

Obediently, the queen lay back on her pillows, but when Livia came back with a cup of hot chocolate she sat up again. 'I can't sleep,' she said. 'I feel strange.'

She pulled back the rich covers of the bed and slid to the ground. Livia saw how her belly was standing out taut under the nightgown.

'My back aches,' Mary Beatrice said.

'Then lie down, lie down, I will rub it . . .'

'I can't settle,' she said and took a few steps to the fireplace. 'Get someone to make the fire up,' she said. 'And open the window. It's so fusty in here.'

'I'll get someone to bring firewood,' Livia said. She went quickly from the room to her own apartments. Her page boy was there. She gave him a note for Doctor Reekie and told him not to wait for a reply. There would be no reply. Then she hurried back to the royal bedchamber.

The queen was prowling around the room. But suddenly, she stopped, put a hand on her belly and cried out.

'Was that a pain?'

'Lord! Yes. A great pain.'

Livia glanced at the clock, noted the time.

'Is it starting?' the queen asked her.

Livia spread her hands and gave a pretty laugh. 'My dear, I've only had one child and that so long ago, I can hardly remember. Shall I send for the midwife?'

'Yes, send for her, and I'd like something to eat.'

'Some pastries? Some little cakes?'

She shook her head. 'New-baked bread, hot from the oven,' she said. 'The kitchens should be baking bread for breakfast, get me some.' She thought for a moment. 'And cheeses,' she said. 'And some meats.'

'You are hungry?' Livia opened the door and sent the guard running for the maids.

'I am starving!' the queen exclaimed. She prowled about the room for a moment then she suddenly stopped and put a hand to her belly. 'Ohhhh,' she gave a great groan. 'That was like the world turned.'

Livia looked at the clock: it was less than an hour since the last pain. 'I think it may be starting,' she said.

'Send someone to tell the king. The king has to send for the witnesses.'

'And we must dress you.' Livia went to the cupboard and got out the queen's best nightgown, ruffled with white lace, and an embroidered robe and a fur stole. 'And I'll send for the girl to comb out your hair.'

The women of the bedchamber arrived, and Livia dropped into a curtsey as the king entered.

'Princess Anne is still at Bath,' he fretted.

'She should be here,' Mary Beatrice said, turning to him.

'I know. We all thought you had another month. I pray it's not coming too early.'

'Amen!' Mary Beatrice crossed herself.

'And the Archbishop of Canterbury? Is he here?' She stopped, and flushed at her mistake.

The Archbishop of Canterbury was in the Tower of London, imprisoned by the king, for refusing to order the king's speech to be read from every pulpit. Seven bishops were imprisoned with him; the king was openly at war with the church at the very moment that he needed their blessing on his son and heir.

'Oh, I suppose he doesn't matter,' she said. 'As long as our priests are here.'

Father Petre entered the room and stood beside the king, so close that their shoulders brushed. 'I have notified the rest of the privy council,' he whispered. 'Are we not too early?'

'Hold my hand,' Mary Beatrice demanded, as James stepped awkwardly closer to the bed. 'Hold me in your arms.'

'You keep back,' Livia hissed to Father Petre. 'You know what they're saying about you.'

As the morning wore on and more and more people arrived to serve as witnesses, it became clear to everyone that the queen was in labour; the pains came more and more frequently though the midwife said that it could still take days. The Lord Chancellor and Lady Sunderland arrived, and one by one, all of the Privy Council. The lady of the bedchamber and the midwife turned back the covers at the bottom of the bed so that everyone could see the queen's bare feet and knees under the expensive night-gown. The Dowager Queen, Catherine of Braganza, entered as if she were expecting a party and remarked that the room was overcrowded and the birth taking too long.

'He's so high,' Mary Beatrice said pitifully to the king. 'I can feel him so high!'

'He will come.' The king nodded towards Father Petre. 'We're all praying for him, my dear, and for you.'

She moaned as the pains came again, gasped when they stopped, and the king pulled off his wig and held it before her face to shield her from the staring faces of the official witnesses. She clutched his hand as the pain came again, and Livia edged towards the door, unnoticed by all the people, the senior nobility, the privy council and the ladies-in-waiting who were watching the bed. Livia got silently out of the room and ran downstairs to the queen's private kitchen two floors down, halfway between the cellars and the ground floor of the palace. Here the queen's private cooks made her hot chocolate or a light breakfast to eat before the meal served to the full court. Here they made little pastries which they served in her rooms with the tea that they blended and brewed for her.

Now, they were cooking tisanes and heating birthing ale, boiling up kettles of water for her to wash her face and hands. One cook was making a sustaining broth in case labour lasted for hours, another was making sweet jellies and pastries to tempt her appetite. Others were preparing glasses of wine and dishes of tea for the guests and witnesses in the bedchamber. Livia went through the kitchen without a word to anyone, took a cape from the back of the door and crossed an inner court at a gliding walk, and entered the gardens, heading towards the shelter of an overgrown arbour. Rob Reekie rose up from the hidden seat and Livia hid a sigh of relief. He was hunched with one arm held awkwardly inside his coat. She saw, with a leap of delight, that he had a tiny bundle tucked under his jacket.

'You've got him,' she breathed.

'I have him,' he said, opening the front of his jacket and transferring the tiny bundle into her arms.

'Why doesn't he cry?' she demanded. 'Don't tell me he's weakly?'

'No, he's just fallen asleep, he's a healthy baby.'

'Newborn?'

'Born this morning. His mother bled to death, God bless her. I couldn't save her. I've left the cord on him.'

Livia stood still before him and let him open her cape, press the baby into her arms, and close the cape over them both. She realised that he had no awareness of the intimacy of the gesture. He touched her waist, pressed the baby against her breast; but all he was thinking of was keeping the baby warm.

'We'll never speak of this again,' he told her. 'And you will write to the Alderman.'

'I will,' she promised. 'And I will tell Matteo something to make him release Hester from their betrothal.'

'You won't tell him the truth? And you will never use his fathering against me again?'

'How could I?' she said reasonably. 'It's a weapon that can only be used once.'

He ducked his head and turned to leave. 'God bless you and keep you safe,' he said tenderly.

Livia warmed for a moment and then realised, with a little jolt, that he was not blessing her, but speaking to the baby. 'He will be King of England!' she exclaimed. 'He doesn't need your prayers.'

'I don't want to know,' Rob said and disappeared.

Livia cleared the kitchen, saying that she needed privacy to make a special caudle for women in childbirth that only her family knew. Even in the kitchen, two floors below the bedchamber, Livia could hear the sound of people walking anxiously backwards and forwards. The whole palace, all of England, everyone was waiting for the news. There was an urgent clatter of wooden clogs on the stone stairs and the midwife came running into the room and looked around for the cooks. 'She wants small ale!' she exclaimed.

'In the jug,' Livia said. 'I'm bringing a warming pan.'

The midwife grabbed the jug and dashed up the stairs, taking them two at a time. As soon as she was gone, Livia lifted a warming pan down from the hook and opened it. It was dusty with ashes and blackened with soot. Livia swept a cloth around, and tucked the sleeping baby, nestled in his blankets, in the pan. She unwrapped the rags around the baby to see a long trail of the cord and smears of dried blood. Livia opened the door to the meat larder and put her hand into the butchered belly of a hanging buck. She scooped fresh blood and smeared some on the baby's head, and dripped some on his little belly. He stirred, but he did not wake as she closed the lid on the warming pan, and taking it by the handle with a cloth over her hand to protect her from imaginary heat, ran up the stairs after the midwife and pushed her way through the crowd of onlookers into the queen's bedroom.

Mrs Cellier, the queen's midwife, lifted a corner of the bedding and Livia thrust in the pan, so that it lay next to the queen's open thighs. The queen was writhing in her pain, crying out in a deep lowing voice like a tortured animal.

'Can you not give her brandy or something for the pain?' Livia demanded.

'The king says no,' a midwife replied, gesturing to the knot of men standing at the foot of the bed and half a dozen more behind them. The king himself was with his wife, at the head of the bed, bare-headed, his huge wig in his hand.

'Has he been here all this while and not thought to get her a screen?' Livia said to herself and went to the head of the bed on the opposite side to the king. Mary Beatrice was half raised on pillows, the veins standing out in her temples, her cheeks blown out, bellowing with pain. 'Not long now . . .' Livia promised.

'I die! Oh! You kill me!' the queen screamed.

'Now!' the midwife exclaimed. 'Now he is coming. Push, Your Majesty!'

Mary Beatrice screamed like a woman being stabbed. 'Now be still!' commanded the midwife. 'Gather your strength. Rest.'

The queen dropped back panting; they saw her look around the room at the staring faces, then her face contorted with pain and the midwife shouted: 'Now! Push again! Now!'

With another scream Mary Beatrice bore down in the bed and, as if to help, Livia plunged forward blocking the view of everyone as the baby slithered in a rush of blood and waters out of the queen's body. Livia hit the midwife's hand aside so that she could see the baby's legs emerging from his mother, and caught sight of a tiny little penis. Dizzy with relief, she stepped back and the midwife drew the baby out of the sheets and held him in her arms.

She made an odd gesture with her hand to her head, and Lady Sunderland immediately repeated the sign to the king. Livia, watching, realised that there was more than one conspiracy around the bed, but a baby boy had been truly birthed, none of the plots had been needed. The child was a boy, the midwife had signalled to Lady Sunderland, she had signalled to the king: they had a papist Prince of Wales.

The cord was still pulsing as the midwife cut it with a knife, and the second midwife drew the afterbirth from the queen's body, as the queen cried out with her last pain, and then there was a terrifying silence. 'I don't hear the child cry?' Mary Beatrice whispered.

The baby choked, and then cried: a strong wail that made the whole room exclaim.

'Did you hear?' Livia said exultantly to Mary Beatrice. 'Do you hear now?'

She bent and kissed her friend's sweating face and then stepped back, drawing the warming pan from the bed. Madame de Labadie took the baby from the midwife and went to sweep him away to his nursery, but the king stopped her. 'What is it?' he asked gruffly.

'What Your Majesty desires,' she replied.

Lord Feversham shouted: 'Room for the Prince of Wales!' and everyone was laughing and congratulating the king and following the baby from the room. The king called upon the privy councillors to confirm that they had seen the birth of his son and they each swore that they had. Gracefully, helpfully, Livia carried the warming pan down the stairs, through the hall and up to her private rooms.

Inside, with the door locked, she opened the pan. Amazingly, the baby was still asleep. He was dusty but seemed none the worse for his brief imprisonment. Livia felt a rush of exhaustion, that the great gamble was over, that her great crime was not needed. The baby opened his midnight blue eyes and opened his rosebud mouth. His perfect little face flushed red as his eyebrows compressed; with a little gurgle he passed a black sticky mess into the blanket that held him, and he started to cry.

'God,' said Livia with revulsion. 'And now I've got to get rid of you.'

HATTON GARDEN, LONDON, SUMMER 1688

Londoners learned that the queen had been delivered of a son by a blaze of fireworks and a roar of cannon from the king's army. The announcement did nothing to quell the riots but brought more people out on the streets in a volatile mix of protests and celebrations. Bonfires to celebrate were set up in the market places and whole carcasses of meat were roasted on spits but instead of joyous feasts, they became the rallying point of riot. The anti-papists ate the roast meat and then rampaged, drunk, down the high streets breaking windows where anyone showed a light to celebrate the birth of the prince.

Alderman Johnson made his way through the streets in his coach with two armed guards riding on the back, and found the Hatton Garden area was quiet. Julia had a glass of madeira and biscuits served to him in the parlour.

'Your friend Lady Avery must be riding sky-high,' Alderman Johnson remarked to his daughter. 'I had a letter from her lawyers this morning.'

'What does it say?' Julia asked her father, looking up from some handkerchiefs she was hemming for Hester's trousseau.

'Haven't had time to read it yet,' he said. 'It came with such a run of creditors' notes at the news of a prince, that I had no time to do anything but put up our rates, and stuff it in my pocket to bring to you. The prince is already good for business! The rioters will go home, the country will settle down, and we can concentrate on trade. We can out-trade the Dutch and – if we need to – fight them on the ground in the Indies and the Americas. With a prince in hand and perhaps more to come, I expect to see the king take on the Dutch closer to home as well. He'll support the French against them and while the two of them are fighting over the Netherlands, we can move in on their overseas markets.'

'What does the letter say, Papa?' Julia persisted more sweetly.

'Oh, aye.' Alderman Johnson broke the seal. 'I don't expect any surprises.'

She watched his face grow blank.

'What is it, Papa?'

'Nothing,' he said, a closed look coming over him. 'I shall read this in the library. Send your husband into me as soon as he comes in.'

Julia, too well-trained to question her father, sat by the fireside and waited for Rob to come home at midday, while her father re-read the letter from Livia Avery's lawyers.

> *Sir,*
>
> *Dowager Lady Avery has given us to understand that her son Matthew was fathered by Doctor Robert Reekie, during her marriage to Conte Alberto Fiori who was impotent. She has written evidence of this from her physician and prepared to swear an oath. This information is STRICTLY PRIVATE and CONFIDENTIAL and can go no further than yourself.*
>
> *Accordingly, the Dowager Lady Avery is (without prejudice) withdrawing her son Matthew Peachey from his betrothal with Miss Hester Reekie, and our negotiations are at an end.*
>
> *Yours faithfully &c*
> *Struther and Sanders*

Alderman Johnson sat in silence by the library fire until he heard the front door open and close, and the footsteps of his son-in-law in the hall.

'Sir?' Rob said as he came in. 'This is a welcome visit.'

'I'll take a glass of brandy,' Alderman Johnson said. 'You better had, too.'

He flicked the letter across the polished surface of the library table, waited for Rob to serve them both from the cut glass decanter that stood on the shelf beside the books, and took a large gulp.

He watched Rob as the younger man read the letter. Rob's face, already grave, became stony.

'As you feared,' the older man said.

'Yes, Sir. But better that we know now than later.'

'Agreed. But why is she so obliging as to inform us now?'

Rob did not flicker. 'I have no idea. I imagine that a better offer has come up.'

'And the young man himself?'

'Will have no say in the matter. She is a woman of extraordinary will power and no scruples at all.'

'Unnatural,' the Alderman said.

'Quite.'

The two men were silent. 'I am sorry,' Rob said. 'I apologise for my part in this, though it was so long ago.'

'You warned me. I was wrong not to listen. I didn't think your doubts were good enough reason to turn down Avery House and the entrée to court.'

Rob shrugged. 'I'm glad that we know before this abomination could go ahead.'

'Will Hester be grieved?'

Rob shrugged. 'Yes. Of course. But better that she should grieve now, than later over a misbegotten child.'

'You'll tell her?'

'I'll tell her this evening after dinner.'

The Alderman nodded. 'And what will you say? And to Julia? The lawyer's letter limits the information you can reveal.'

'I'd not want them to know, even if I were allowed to say!' Rob said with revulsion. 'Good God! What a picture to paint for a young woman! I'll just say that the lawyers could not agree, that Matthew's inheritance from Sir James Avery was not what we were led to believe. That they are asking for too much in a dowry. I don't have to explain myself to them, if you and I are in agreement.'

'We are,' the Alderman said heavily. 'We are. I shall tell my daughter, and you may tell yours. Neither of them will question their fathers.'

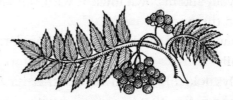

REEKIE WHARF, LONDON, SUMMER 1688

Alys was on the quayside as Captain Shore came from the house, his bag in one hand. She handed him the cargo manifest and he bent his head for her kiss.

'God speed,' she said, as she always did. 'Calm seas and steady winds bring you safe home, Abel Shore.'

'Amen,' he replied and strode up the gangplank and they ran it in behind him. 'You shut the wharf and keep yourself indoors,' he bellowed to her as they cast off and the water widened between them. 'Get the chest to Alderman Johnson's safekeeping and lock up the house till these troubles are over. Get yourself down to Foulmire if you need.'

She nodded and waved and watched until his ship was turned by the barges into the stream, caught the current, and started downriver. As soon as the ship was under way she had two strong lumpers escort her with the wharf strongbox in a hired carriage to the Alderman's bank at Cheapside. Alys feared a fire from a rioter's torch as much as she feared theft from them breaking in. Every night there were gangs roaming the streets and shouting for the exposure of the false prince, the tearing down of the throne and the freeing of the six bishops who had followed the Archbishop into the Tower for defending the protestant faith.

A group of lads halted the carriage and Alys lowered the window, while the lumpers inside grasped their cudgels.

'Free the bishops! Liberty!' they shouted.

'Aye,' Alys agreed pleasantly.

'You are with us? Or are you a papist?'

'I am with you, and my own uncle is with William of Orange's army,' she told them.

'He is?' a tow-headed freckled youth grabbed the edge of the window. 'Really?'

'Really,' Alys told him. 'And before that he marched with Monmouth, and before that he marched with Cromwell, so you can believe me when I say that I am for freeing the bishops. No tyrants! No papists!'

There was a great cheer and some of the men swore they would loose the horses from the carriage and drag their heroine wherever she wanted to go.

'No, no,' said Alys. 'I'm about my good uncle's business and I have to go to Cheapside for him.'

'Let the honourable lady pass!' someone yelled, and the cry was taken up down the road, past a temporary barricade where the men had entered a roman catholic house and were throwing religious paintings out of an upstairs window.

❧

Alys, controlling her fear, deposited her cash box safely with Alderman Johnson, received a receipt, and assured him she would go home for safety's sake by water.

'And then I'm closing the wharf till London is quieter,' she said. 'I'm going down to Sussex.'

'I would to God that I could go too,' the Alderman said. 'I thought it would quiet down with the birth of a prince. But it's never been this bad since the Oates riots.'

'And they were about a lie, and came to nothing in the end,' Alys said stoutly.

'They were bad enough to send those two – the king and his wife – into hiding in Scotland,' the Alderman said gloomily. 'I wish they'd go again. And I wish I could get Julia and Hester out of town.'

'They can come with us,' Alys said. 'Matthew would be pleased.'

'Would he?' the Alderman asked, wondering how much Alys knew of the failed betrothal. 'They were thinking of a match, you know?'

Alys shook her head. 'He's too young to be thinking of marriage,' she said. 'And if he had a preference at all, it was for Mia.'

'I'll send Mrs Reekie and Hester to you, if I may,' the Alderman decided. 'I don't want them in town with all this going on. Julia's nerves are so bad ... I can't risk it.'

'Of course they must come!' Alys said. 'We're leaving tomorrow or the next day. They must come at once.'

'I'll tell Doctor Reekie,' the Alderman decided. 'And he can send them in his carriage. Is there room for him too?'

'Yes,' Alys said. 'It's a very large house.' She flushed to think that she was boasting, and corrected herself. 'It's not ours, of course.'

'Yes, I know. I'll tell Julia to pack. It's good of you, Mrs Shore. And your strongbox will be safe in my cellar. It was safe all through the great fire, and nobody has ever got into my house.'

There was a sudden noise of cheering from outside, louder and louder, and the noise of many people running on the cobbled streets. The ragged shouts came closer.

'Stand to!' Alderman Johnson shouted at his clerks. At once, in a practised drill, they closed and bolted the shutters over the windows, bundled their papers into locked boxes, and took up heavy cudgels and waited at their posts, as the noise got louder as the mob got closer.

Alderman Johnson glanced back and saw Alys standing calmly beside his desk.

'Nothing to fear,' he said. But then he checked. 'Sounds like cheering ...'

It was an exultant yelling rather than a battle cry. Men and women's voices cheering wordlessly, filled with joy. Mr Johnson nodded for the front door to be opened a crack and he listened. Then he put the big man guarding the door to one side and stepped out.

'Not guilty! Not guilty!'

'Wait!' the Alderman, with his guard close behind him, grabbed a man running past, who was yelling at the top of his voice. 'What's the news?'

'The bishops are free! The bishops are free!'

'The judges freed them?'

'Declared them not guilty, defied the king. Not guilty! The jury would have none of it! That's told him!'

'The judges freed the bishops?'

'Holloah! God has saved the church!'

The man tore away, up to the corner of the street where people were building a bonfire to celebrate. Householders threw firewood into the street from their own stores, candles were lit at every window, cooks brought out food and wine and ale and the house owners were as wildly joyful as the people running through the streets. People were bellowing hymns to celebrate the victory of the English church over the English king, and then a fiddler struck up the mocking jig – 'Lillibullero'.

'A big loss for the king,' Alys said tightly once the Alderman himself had bawled the news to his counting house and everyone threw their hats in the air and were dismissed for the day.

He was exultant. 'It's the end for the king,' Jeremiah Johnson told her solemnly. 'If he'd been a king and not a tyrant he'd have allowed parliament to sit, and they would have voted him out, as they did his father. As it is, he closed parliament but he couldn't close down the people. If he can't pack a jury, if he can't control the judges, if he can't make the bishops preach his sermon, then he can't rule. Mark my words: the great lords will send for Princess Mary and her husband – and him the greatest soldier in Europe. You get yourself down to Sussex, Mrs Shore, and I'll send my daughter and my grand-daughter to you. This is the end for the king. There'll be another war to get rid of him. The baby was not his saviour but the final straw. William of Orange is coming with his army and he'll pull the last Stuart from his throne by brute force. And you and Julia had better not be in London when that happens!'

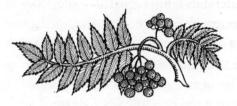

FAIRMERE PRIORY, SUSSEX, SUMMER 1688

Alys, safely at the Priory with Matthew, Mia and Gabrielle, welcomed Hester and Julia Reekie as if they were refugees from a city in flames.

'The city!' Julia exclaimed, stepping out of the Reekie coach. 'My heart!'

'Come in,' Alys said, guiding her through the front door and into the parlour.

Julia cast one scathing look at Matthew and beckoned Hester to come with her. 'My laudanum!' she demanded.

'Was the journey very bad?' Alys asked Hester quietly.

The girl was calm. 'No,' she said. 'We went west before we took the road south to Chichester so we were nowhere near the riots, and Papa sent outriders for the first hour. But Mama is easily frightened. And Papa would not come because he has patients. And then he said that if there was to be an invasion, doctors would be needed and that was when she had the vapours.'

'Well, you're both safe now,' Alys said warmly to her niece. 'Go and find the girls, they've been waiting for you. I can take care of your mother.'

Hester, Mia and Gabrielle turned the lock on Hester's bedroom door to ensure that they would not be disturbed and Hester, fighting her tears, told them of her brief betrothal to Matthew and the abrupt ending.

'I don't understand it,' Gabrielle said, looking out of the window of Hester's bedroom over the rose garden which was bobbing with a sea of blooms. 'I was certain that he was in love with Mia, and then he told us that it was a question of honour, a family feud.'

'He was clearing the way to marry Hester for her money,' Mia said spitefully.

Hester flushed red. 'I am sorry,' she said. 'My Mama and his arranged it, I would never have . . . and I truly think—'

'Of course we know!' Gabrielle said impulsively taking her hand. 'Mia, don't speak like that. Hester, of course we know you had no say in it, either a proposal or a refusal. Don't listen to Mia, she's still hurt . . .' She looked from one to another and declared: 'Now you see why women should always be true to each other! It all goes wrong when two women want the same man!'

'Only two?' Mia said pointedly, and when her sister flinched she burst out: 'Oh forgive me, Gabrielle. Forgive me, Hester! Let's be as we were when we all first met, and no-one was in love with anyone, and no-one was going to marry anyone, and we came for lessons at your house, and Matthew walked us there and back, and we were all such good friends!'

'Can you go back in time?' Hester asked. 'Because I can't just forget it. I told him I wanted his proposal, he said . . .' she broke off.

'Of course you can go back in time,' Gabrielle claimed. 'You can't live here and go to church past all those graves, and listen to the sea and not wander into the past. You can put the proposal behind you and know that it is just one shadow in a life that will have light and shade. The past is all around us: the priest and the mermaid, our Bisnonna and the man she loved. Even our grandmother and her crime that made them leave. It's all here, the tracks are still in the mud.'

'She's gone to the faeries,' Mia mock-whispered to Hester. 'It's in the blood. It's the full moon again.'

Hester managed a watery giggle. 'We three can be friends as we were,' she said. 'But how can we be friendly with Matthew? I can't look at him, I feel so ashamed. I'd never have come here again if my Papa had not insisted. He said London was too dangerous for us to stay.'

'Gabrielle can tell him that he has to apologise to you and make amends,' Mia ruled. 'She's the only one he hasn't insulted.'

'I wouldn't say I was insulted ...' Hester began. 'Papa said it was a problem from the lawyers, a question of settlements ...'

'He told me it was a question of honour,' Mia said. 'So Gabrielle is the only one who he hasn't been prevented from marrying by something that none of us understand. And that he won't explain. She has to tell him that we can be friends if he will say sorry to our faces and be as he was.'

'I really can't have a conversation like that,' Gabrielle demurred.

'No, you must,' Hester told her. 'The two of us can't say anything to him. And none of us will be happy unless we can all be friends again.'

'Tonight,' Mia insisted, 'we'll go to bed when Nonna does. You stay up with him and tell him then.'

Matthew was tongue-tied at dinner, and the girls talked among themselves. Alys looked from one young person to another and thought that it was inevitable that Livia would meddle with her son's happiness and hurt him in the process. There was no use warning him against his mother's influence, he would have to learn to not trust her. Alys felt bound by the agreement that she had made with Alinor, that they would raise Livia's child to respect his mother, and never reveal her secrets, just as they had never revealed their own.

She saw that Gabrielle hung back when the girls picked up their bedtime candles from the table in the hall, and she said goodnight to them all, only reminding Matthew to rake out the fire and put up the fire guard.

'Shall I draw the runes against wild fire in the ashes?' Gabrielle smiled, making Alys laugh.

'Ma would have liked it,' she said. 'You can do that. And don't be too late to bed.'

She went up the stairs with her firm tread and left the two young people alone in the parlour.

Gabrielle went down on her knees at the hearth, raked aside the logs, and drew the shapes in the ash that her great-grandmother had taught.

Matthew smiled. 'I'm glad she taught you,' he said.

She rose to her feet. 'And I wanted to speak to you,' she said shyly.

'Well, that's kind of you, because I have been feeling like a fool.'

Despite herself she nearly laughed. 'We're all in an odd position.'

'Hester has told you? About the proposal I very wrongly made to her?'

'Yes, she told us. And she and Mia asked me to speak to you.'

'This is all my fault,' he confessed. 'I apologised to Mia months ago, and in writing to Hester, but I can see they neither of them forgive me, and I've been such a miserable fool, Gabrielle. I have hurt the girls that I care for most in the world! And to propose to Hester so soon after speaking to Mia . . .'

'Was it the Nobildonna who made the proposal?' Gabrielle asked.

He hesitated. 'Yes,' he admitted. 'But I should have refused at the start of it all.'

'You should,' Gabrielle said gently. 'But I don't see how you could. She's your mother, she's bound to arrange the best match she can for you, and it's not as if you could defy her. You're still

483

a minor. And if you had to marry someone, I can see that you would prefer Hester to anyone else.'

'Exactly!' he said eagerly. 'So I sound like a man ruled by his mother as well as a fool. An obedient fool.'

'You have to be obedient,' Gabrielle said mildly. 'And now that your stepfather is dead, there is only your mother.'

'She terrifies me,' he said frankly.

'She is . . .' Words failed Gabrielle.

'She dares . . . it's as if she has no fear.'

'At court?' Gabrielle guessed.

He nodded. 'I dare not say – she has no fear even in the very greatest of events.'

'Well, you wouldn't have this house if she did.'

'I know, and I should be grateful. I am grateful – but what she dares!' He shook his head. 'And she employs me . . .'

'You haven't done anything . . .' Gabrielle was tentative. 'Matthew, you haven't done anything . . . bad?'

'I hardly know!' he burst out. 'I do a little part of the whole, but I don't know what the whole of it is. Just before the prince was born, she had me running errands around London, it was like a dream. There were riots in the streets, and fires burning at the crossroads, and lights in the protestant windows, and people tearing hangings out of the chapels, and I went from Lincoln's Inn to the palace to Hester's house and back again, and I had no idea what I was doing! I took her to Uncle Rob when it was past midnight and the house was dark and still she went in, and I have no idea what she said!'

'Doctor Reekie was part of it?'

'No!' he suddenly exclaimed. He knew that he should not speak of Rob. 'No, he had nothing to do with it. Don't think that. He refused to do . . . a favour. The Nobildonna sent me to ask something of him and he refused me. And later she told me he had refused permission for my marriage to Hester.'

'But why?'

'She said it was the lawyers. Then she said she could not say.'

Gabrielle rose up from her chair and put her hand on his

shoulder as he stood at the fireplace. 'Oh Matthew,' she said tenderly. 'Oh dear Matthew. This is too much for you.'

He turned and she stepped into his arms and he held her, his cheek resting against her smooth hair. 'Gabrielle, I was really afraid. I am afraid that she has done something . . .' he could not tell her what he feared.

Gabrielle felt his arms around her and made herself stand still, not pressing against him, nor looking up for a kiss. Matthew felt the rise of his own desire and released her at once; they stepped apart.

'We are friends,' Gabrielle told him. 'They both asked me to speak to you this evening to say that we all want to be friends as we were, as we have always been.'

'That's generous,' he said. He dropped onto a stool before the fire and pulled another over for her to sit beside him. 'I can't pin the blame on my mother,' he said. 'I don't hide behind her apron strings.'

'No. But none of this was of selfishness. You offered Mia your heart and the Nobildonna forbade it. You said sorry to Mia, and she forgave you. The proposal to Hester was an arranged marriage which both parents were making for you, without either of you having a say in it. Nobody can blame you if they changed their minds.'

'I am so sorry,' he said wretchedly.

'You must tell her, and then we can be friends again.' She rose up and offered him her hand. 'Agreed?'

He took her hand but, instead of shaking it, he drew her to him and he kissed her gently, just once, on the lips.

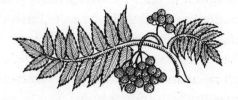

BRIDGETOWN, BARBADOS, SUMMER 1688

The cannons exploded from the fort and the bells of all the town's churches started to ring. Johnnie's customers put down the goods they were choosing and went to the shop door. They could hear the cheers from the Exchange and the rattle of people firing muskets into the air from the quay.

'What is it?' asked one of the ladies. 'Good news?'

'It must be the royal birth,' another said.

'Please God it is a prince, only a prince will keep Barbados safe from France.'

Johnnie stepped past them and grabbed a man who was running from the quay to the Exchange.

'What news?'

'It's a boy!' the man bawled. 'It's a prince! The king has an heir and confounded his enemies!'

'God bless the queen, God save the king!' Johnnie said quickly, wondering where Ned was and how this news would affect him. 'Is it news just in?'

'A ship from Plymouth, the baby was born in mid-June. Strong and well. They're serving rum out of the governor's house to drink his health.'

The women in Johnnie's doorway were hugging each other. 'Mr Stoney, what news!' they exclaimed.

'Hurrah!' Johnnie said politely. 'Let me pour you a glass of punch, we should toast the new prince. And I have had a bolt of silk – Prince of Wales purple. Now at last I can allow it to be seen.'

'New?'

'New in from London for this very occasion.'

'And you bought it in ready? How clever of you.'

Johnnie gestured to one of the slaves to fetch the bolt of silk from the back, and she spread it, in a ripple of colour, on the measuring table. It had been sitting for months on the shelves of the shop, overpriced and a hard colour to wear. But now it was 'Prince of Wales Purple', and Johnnie knew he would sell out.

REEKIE WHARF, LONDON, SUMMER 1688

London was gripped by riotous crowds, the people seemed ready to turn on the palaces and break into them as they had already raided roman catholic chapels and businesses and embassies of France and Spain and nobody, not the magistrates of the city, not the Aldermen or the heads of the guilds, not even the Lord Mayor of London could halt the rapturous progress of outraged crowds through the streets.

Alys made a flying visit overnight from Foulmire, unable to settle in the country without confirming that the wharf was safe and found her neighbours all but barricaded into their wharves, unloading ships at speed, and sometimes even refusing cargos from Rome and Italy for fear of triggering a protest among their own lumpers, who were refusing to touch 'papist goods'.

Alys went down the quayside to the boarded-up coffee house for news and was told by more than one person, with complete conviction, that the Lord Mayor had sent the keys of the City to William of Orange, that Rear Admiral Herbert, dismissed by the king for his protestant faith, had been replaced by a roman catholic commander of the navy. The sailors threatened mutiny when the new admiral brought priests on board his flagship and held a Mass in the face of his determinedly protestant crew. Everyone said that the dismissed Admiral Herbert had sailed for Holland to be appointed chief admiral of the Dutch navy.

'And that's a man who knows every inch of the coast,' Alys said to one of her regular captains. 'If he commands the Dutch navy in an invasion of England, he knows exactly where to come, he's got the charts of every port. He can sail right in.'

'He could sail right in anyway. No port in England'd turn their canons on the protestant Princess Mary and her husband William,' he replied. 'They're the true heirs, not some papist changeling. He can land where he likes.'

The whole country, even the royal forces, had turned against the king and queen. The army, at camp on Hounslow Heath were ordered and paid to celebrate the birth of the prince; but they cheered and set off cannon when the protesting bishops were freed. Oxford University, openly defied the king's threats, refused his nominee for the new chancellor and elected their own choice.

'Mrs Shore, this here says that the king is bringing over troops from Ireland,' Captain Walter said, pushing a news-sheet over the common table to Alys.

'We won't stand for an Irish army,' she predicted. 'Everyone would take arms against papist Irish. Lord, you'd think he was bent on destroying himself. And not one man in ten believes that he fathered that baby. The things they are saying are scandalous.'

'But they said, from the moment he was conceived, that they knew it was a boy, how can anyone trust that it was their child? How could they know unless they always planned to bring in a boy?'

'What's it going to do to business?' Alys demanded. 'There's Captain Shore at sea right now, and I daren't even open the warehouse. I can't keep the lumpers at work and, to be honest, I don't want to show lights at the window.'

'It'll end well,' Captain Walter claimed. 'You mark my words, Mrs Shore. The Princess Mary will come in and we'll have the Dutch as partners, not as rivals, and together we'll have the biggest navy in the world. Then we'll divide up the world between the two of us, just like the Pope did for the papists. You mark my words.'

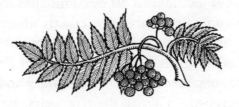

HELLEVOETSLUIS, HOLLAND, SUMMER 1688

In the magnificent dockyard of Hellevoetsluis the hundreds of warships of the huge Dutch fleet was finally ready to sail. Cannons and armaments were loaded, supplies stowed. The fleet was under the command of the English Admiral Herbert, newly arrived from England. Ned was attached to the regiment of English volunteers in William of Orange's army. Their status was uneasy: as treasonous rebels against their king, they had to prove their loyalty to his daughter Princess Mary and his son-in-law William, and their presence was an open secret, as was William's intentions to invade. Everyone knew the English volunteers were there, arming and ready, everyone knew the fleet was preparing to invade, but William declared nothing.

'I mean, this is going to happen, isn't it?' Ned asked while drawing weapons and uniforms for his regiment from the Dutch stores. The commissioner shrugged. 'Whatever the Elector orders,' he said, taciturn. 'For sure, the Dutch people have no wish to invade England.'

The English recruits learned that William had written to his father-in-law, James, King of England, assuring him of his continuing loyalty and friendship.

'Double dealing,' Robert Ferguson remarked.

'Lord, I hope so,' Ned said with grim humour. 'Because if he is a loyal son-in-law and hopes for nothing but good for his Papa then I have come all this way for nothing. And at my age – I begrudge it.'

'He must invade! What are all the ships for?'

Ned smiled. 'I wager it will be like the last time, we'll have to wait for the wind. But at least we won't have the Dutch authorities chasing us out of the port.'

'Aye. Now that was a gamble. It was your little lad went for the Duke wasn't it?'

Ned smiled, remembering Rowan going down the mooring rope like an acrobat.

'Aye. That was a greater gamble than this,' Ned said. 'How many men does William have?'

'Fifteen thousand,' Ferguson told him.

Ned gave a low whistle. 'He'll need them,' he agreed. 'The king has a standing army of twenty thousand, and when I left England they were talking about bringing in troops from Ireland.'

'But can he count on their loyalty?'

'He pays them. Once he got parliament to agree that he should have his own army and the funds to pay them, we lost the greatest liberty we ever had. We shouldn't have given that away. I wouldn't give a standing army to any ruler, not even to Cromwell.'

'Maybe we'll win it back,' Ferguson said. 'Have you seen the offer from the Whig lords? It doesn't give Princess Mary the throne in the old way, it sets conditions on her. We'll maybe have a king and queen; but we'll never have a tyrant again. This is a new world we're making, Ned, and this time we have the church and the lords, the parliament and the people on our side.'

WINDSOR CASTLE, AUTUMN 1688

Livia, admiring the queen's gown for her birthday ball, allowed herself to be persuaded into borrowing a waterfall necklace of diamonds and a pair of diamond earrings from the collection that the treasury had sent to the queen.

'It's hard to be merry,' Mary Beatrice said as she picked out a tiara for her hair and seated herself before her mirror.

Livia stood behind her and adjusted her curls of dark hair. 'So many faces missing,' she complained. 'So disloyal to stay away from your birthday ball. But with London so unsafe you know that it's not a slight on you. They don't dare to come in from the country.' She smiled at their reflection. 'I would never fail you.'

'I know you wouldn't.'

'And you have to show yourself, dearest, even if half the court has stayed away. And you are looking so beautiful.' She paused, dropped a kiss on Mary Beatrice's naked shoulder. 'With a prince in the cradle, it's only a matter of time before people realise that the succession is certain, and they settle down.'

'Father Petre says we must grind heresy out of their hearts,' Mary Beatrice said.

'I'm sure he's right. But not tonight!' Livia said cheerfully. 'Tonight you must dance and be happy—'

She broke off as the door was flung open and a lady-in-waiting curtseyed low. 'The king!' she said.

Both Livia and the queen curtseyed deeply, but the king

hardly saw them; he brandished a paper in his hand. 'Look at this!' he demanded. 'Proof that your son-in-law is lying to me! Certain proof! They are loading cavalry horses at Rotterdam. So he cannot be preparing a blockade for the French at sea as he said. Why would he want horses at sea? He has to be planning to invade?'

Mary Beatrice had nothing to say. Her hand crept into Livia's.

'He has played me for a fool! He has lied to me! And my own daughter has lied too!'

'Mary might not know?'

'Not know that her own husband is to make war against her own father? And she has not sent me a word. Not one single word of warning!'

'Mary wouldn't be disloyal,' Mary Beatrice protested. 'No daughter would.'

Livia, who had a higher opinion of the female dishonesty, said only: 'But if they're loading horses they must be coming at once?'

'I'll have to put the lord lieutenants and the magistrates back in post,' James said almost to himself. 'I'll have to apologise and reinstate them. No leave for the army and I'll turn out the militia. We defeated Monmouth, didn't we? What is this, but another bastard claim from a heretic poor relation against his father, his king, and against God Himself?'

'William is coming?' Mary Beatrice whispered as if she could not believe it.

'But when?' Livia asked.

Mary Beatrice leapt to her feet. 'The prince must go to safety,' she announced. 'We have to get him safe. Far from London!'

'Portsmouth,' the king assured her. 'I have Irish troops in Portsmouth who will never fail me.'

'And what about the ball? Shall we say . . . ?'

'We hold the ball as if we feared nothing,' he proclaimed, his face grey with fear.

'But when will they come?' Livia asked again.

'It should be never,' the king told her grimly. 'When the wind lets them out of port. When they have the wind with them.'

'They wait only for a wind?' Livia asked incredulously. 'We watch for the wind to change?'

'We wait for the wind,' the king told her grimly.

TORBAY, DEVON, AUTUMN 1688

The month of the king's fifty-fifth birthday saw an eclipse: the sun, the symbol of royalty itself, went dark, and then finally, the wind swung to the east. A protestant wind, and a few days later the invading fleet anchored off Brixham in Devon, and landed the horses and men at Torbay.

Ned, riding in the munitions wagon under a banner that read 'The Liberties of England', picked a branch of holly for lack of anything else green and put it in his hatband. The army marched east, as Monmouth had done before, and declared at Exeter in front of a crowd who remembered Monmouth and the deaths that had followed that uprising, and were quiet and sullen.

'Come on!' Ned recruited men from his wagon. 'I was here before with the duke, I was here before that with Cromwell. It's the same cause: the rights of the men and women of England. And this time we'll win.'

A few men came forward but it was cold, and in the night the army camped in the fields, without any visits from cheering townspeople. There was less confidence and little camaraderie on this march. Ned was not disheartened, he remembered that Monmouth's men had been volunteers, serving him for a belief in his cause and in freedom, Cromwell's army driven by a sense of injustice and their own mission. William's army were a mixture:

493

some professional soldiers of the Dutch states, mercenaries of all nationalities and many faiths, a few believers marching in a holy war, and a few staunch old Cromwellians. Ned judged that everything would depend on whether the king's army would rally to him to defend their homes against an invasion by a foreign power, or whether he had made himself so hated that they now found him even stranger than his Dutch son-in-law. It was a gamble – as it always was – between people's greed for the old ways, or their courage to dare for new.

Ned was in his element. On the cold frosty mornings he looked at the sun rising and thought of Rowan's dawn prayers. In the evenings when he took a bowl of stew from the field kitchens, he thought of her poaching game and making him soup. Every step of the march through the west country he remembered her at his side and felt that this march was a tribute to the one they had done together, and that when he was marching for freedom, he was most truly himself.

WHITEHALL PALACE, LONDON, AUTUMN 1688

James was closeted every day with his advisors, and they all recommended different courses of action. But every day another of them was missing from his place at court. James would turn for an opinion, strongly expressed the day before, and see an empty chair as one lord after another slipped away to his country seat, or to France or even – in the greatest secrecy – to the disinherited heir: Princess Mary and her husband William of Orange.

They hardly saw the king in the queen's rooms, and the queen and her ladies depended on Father Petre for news. It was him, not the king who told them that William had landed with a force strong enough to face the English army in battle.

'You must persuade the king not to march out himself,' the queen declared. 'What if he were to fall in battle?'

'But where are we to go for our safety?' Livia asked her. 'If the king leaves with his army, who is going to defend London?'

'Portsmouth,' the queen replied. 'Baby James is to go to Portsmouth now, this very day with his nursemaid, and I am to meet him there. The fleet is in Portsmouth, they will guard him until we arrive.'

'But why can't we go with him now? Why can't we all go together?'

'Father Petre says we must not look as if we are running away. When the king marches out of London, we have to stay here.'

'But when is he going?' Livia took a breath and tried to sound calm. 'Surely every day that he delays, more people join William? William gets closer?'

'I think he's going tomorrow,' she said wretchedly. 'But nobody tells me anything. Anyway, Prince James is to go tomorrow, and we will follow later.' She was struck by a sudden fear. 'You will come with me, won't you?'

'Yes,' Livia said. 'Of course. Dearest, of course.'

'The king called all his officers to him and said that if they were going to desert him, they should do it now, and not on the field of battle. Isn't it unbelievable? He asked them to leave him now, if they are not faithful.'

'And Princess Anne?' Livia asked, naming the younger daughter. 'Did she know all about it, like her sister? Is she faithless?'

'Oh, Anne would never betray her father,' the queen assured her. 'And now she thinks she is with child again. She'll stay safely in her rooms here. And her bosom bow Sarah Churchill's husband is one of the king's best officers, he swore that he would never leave the king. They'll all face danger together.'

'We'll be facing danger here,' Livia said, unmoved at the

thought of the king and his faithful adherents marching out to Salisbury and leaving them in riotous London with a bonfire at every corner and the queen's effigy burning before the palace. 'Probably worse for us. And we don't have an army.'

The king said a mournful farewell to Mary Beatrice and took his coach to the west country with his cavalry in full support and his infantry following. He stayed the night at the bishop's palace in Salisbury and collapsed with a nosebleed that nothing could stop. The next day he was even worse, constantly haemorrhaging, and in the night, the entire royal cavalry, led by his other faithless son-in-law: Princess Anne's husband George, and the king's false friend General John Churchill, slipped away from camp and went over to William's army.

Blood poured from the king's nose, he could not ride, and did not dare be seen by his troops, bleeding without a wound. William and his forces were said to be at Exeter; but the royal army did not march on them. Instead, the army of England camped unmoving, as if frozen in the snow at Salisbury; and in the wintry stillness, not believing their luck, the Orange army started to march, with more and more confidence, up the old road to London.

WHITEHALL PALACE, LONDON, AUTUMN 1688

'The Princess has been kidnapped!'

Livia was shaken awake by her maid. 'What?'

'Princess Anne has been kidnapped and stolen away in the night. Some say the queen has had her murdered! Or that William has had her seized out of her bed!'

Livia threw a robe over her nightgown, crammed her feet into slippers and ran through the palace to the queen's rooms. The queen was sitting up in bed, looking like a lost girl, a cap of lace on her head, her hair in her night-time plait.

Livia climbed on the bed and the two women clung to each other.

'Did you know?'

Mutely the queen nodded.

'Leave us!' Livia snapped at the maid. To the queen she said: 'Has she run away?'

'She came to see me last night,' Mary Beatrice whispered. 'She said she dared not face the king because her husband, George was in league with William. I promised that we would forgive her and George too. She thought he would treat them like Monmouth: make them beg forgiveness and then behead them anyway. She was mad with fear.'

'And where's her husband George now, and Sarah Churchill's husband?'

'What? With the king at Salisbury of course. D'you think William would dare to steal Princess Anne out of her own bed?'

'No,' Livia said grimly. 'I bet that all four of them – Princess Anne and her precious favourite and their two husbands – have gone over to William. It's nothing to do with not daring to face her father, they'll have planned this from the beginning. She's probably plotted with Mary from the moment you conceived.'

'No!' Mary Beatrice was horrified. 'She wept in my arms, she said she was sorry for ever being unkind. She said she was torn between her husband and her father.'

'That was goodbye,' Livia said bluntly. 'I bet she's halfway to Exeter.'

'It will break His Majesty's heart if Princess Anne has betrayed him like her sister.'

'It'll give William the keys to the kingdom, if George and Churchill have taken their regiments to him.'

'What do we do?'

'What can we do but wait till we hear of the battle?' Livia bit her lip. 'You have a carriage ready to take us to Portsmouth?'

'Yes, yes, the king ordered it before he left, and guards. In case ... in case ...'

'We wait,' Livia told her. 'They might be fighting the battle right now. And we don't know where.'

That night the king returned to Whitehall, without leading his troops in battle, without even ordering them out of camp, a bloodstained handkerchief pressed to his nose, unable to believe that both his sons-in-law had turned against him, and his daughter Anne had run away from home.

'It's over,' he said heavily to Mary Beatrice. 'I can't fight my own daughters, my heirs.'

'Our son is your heir,' she told him. 'You have to fight for him. You have to defend me.'

'Look at me!' he exclaimed. He showed her the bloodstained linen at his face, the constant flow of blood. 'I'm bleeding to death and no-one can stop it. It's heartbreak! All I can do is try to save you and him. I've ordered him to be brought back to London. The navy in Portsmouth has turned against me as well. He wasn't safe there. None of us are safe in England.'

'What?' The queen was horrified. 'Where is my son?'

'In a coach, I just said, coming from Portsmouth,' the king said thickly. 'The sailors scuttled their own ships when they were ordered to sea to intercept William's fleet. After all I'd done for them! After holy Mass on my flagship!'

'Where is my son?' she nearly screamed.

'On his way, I said! His nursemaid's bringing him. As soon as he gets here, you must go to Dover. Our yacht is waiting for you there. And we have one loyal friend: King Louis of France has sent the Comte de Lauzun to assist you. He warned me – I should have—' He took up a clean handkerchief and held it to his nose. It immediately darkened with fresh blood. 'The Comte de Lauzun will take you to France, take you to the king. I'll join you in there – unless I can make a last stand, unless I can turn it around.'

The queen looked at him in disbelief.

'But where is William's army now?' Livia interrupted. 'Forgive me, Your Majesty, but where is the army? Might they inter-cept the prince in the royal coach? Or capture us on the way to Dover?'

He made a gurgling noise. 'I cannot speak!' he exclaimed. 'Everyone betrays me and I am bleeding . . . bleeding—'

'I won't run away!' the queen swore. 'I'll stay here with you. Our baby will stay too. We are the King and Queen of England. My own son-in-law can face me on my throne if he dares.'

The king gave an exhausted sigh and slumped to a chair, throwing one bloodstained handkerchief on the ground and taking a napkin from the table. Livia looked in despair from the queen's determined face, to the king who looked as if he were weeping blood into the priceless table linen.

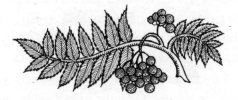

ON THE ROAD TO LONDON, WINTER 1688

William's army were in no hurry to reach London, cheerfully aware that the royal army was not stirring from their camp at Salisbury, leaving the road wide open. Ned, riding on the wagon with cannonballs still packed in their boxes, thought that it was more like an exercise in neutral territory than an invasion or a liberation; there was neither opposition nor an enthusiastic greeting.

'Not like it was before,' he remarked to Robert Ferguson.

'And I thank God for that,' the chaplain replied. 'This time we're winning.'

'The people aren't with us as they were with Monmouth, as they were with Cromwell.'

The other veteran nodded. 'Aye. This is for a change in the law, and perhaps a change in the king, but it's not for common people. It's for freedom for the lords, not for the working man.'

'We'll bring down a tyrant and a papist king,' Ned observed. 'And I've spent my life working for that.'

'Aye,' Robert Ferguson told him. 'But the new tyrant will be the merchant traders and the rich lords, and the new god will be money. And you'll find their reign will last for longer than the Stuarts.'

'A new tyranny,' Ned said grimly, thinking of sugar money, and slavery profits, and the seeping of power towards the rich. 'I'll have brought down one, while seeing the birth of another.'

FAIRMERE PRIORY, SUSSEX, WINTER 1688

'I'm going to have to go back to London,' Alys told Matthew, Hester, Mia and Gabrielle, at the breakfast table. 'Will you be all right here without me for a week or so? Captain Shore is due home at the end of the month, and I can't have him coming home to a dark wharf. Besides, he'll be bringing cargo and I have to get it safely stored.'

'Of course, Nonna,' Gabrielle said easily. 'We can manage here without you.'

Alys was only slightly reassured. She had timed her announcement to her grand-daughters at breakfast, so that she could tell Julia Reekie later, when she emerged from her bedroom at mid-morning. Julia would not welcome the news that she was to be in the Priory with the four young people. So far, she had used a string of imaginary ailments to avoid seeing them, and when forced to dine with them or sit in the same room with them she had been openly frosty. Hester was in disgrace with her mother for the failure of her betrothal, which Julia put down to the inefficiency of the lawyers. Matthew was despised as she blamed him for exaggerating his Avery inheritance.

'It's bound to be a bit awkward for you,' Alys said tentatively.

Matthew dipped his head so he did not meet anyone's eye, and the girls made sure not to giggle. 'A bit,' he said quietly.

'But it can't be helped,' Alys said. 'It's business.'

'And we won't be alone with Mama,' Hester volunteered. 'For my Papa will come down today or tomorrow. Mama was supposed to tell you ...'

'I hardly saw her yesterday,' Alys said grimly. 'It was yesterday she turned her ankle when she stepped on the grass, and had to rest it.'

'Well, he said he would come in his carriage. So you can take it back to London, if you like.'

'You're very free with your father's carriage?' Alys smiled at her niece.

'Of course, he would want you to use it, when you have taken us in, and you have looked after Mama so well, and it's not been easy . . .'

'No trouble at all!' Matthew remarked, one eye on Gabrielle who was fighting the giggles.

Hester flushed. 'I do know,' she told him.

'Don't tease Hester,' Alys reproved them. 'Her Mama has always been delicate. And the worry has very been bad for her. She'll be better when she has her husband at her side, and better again when she can go back to her home. Did your father say when he would come?'

'He said he'd leave first thing, he should be here by midday.'

'Then I'll take his carriage back to London tomorrow,' Alys decided.

'Should you travel alone?' Matthew said. 'We don't know where the armies are nor the state of London. Hadn't I better come with you? And shouldn't I be with you at the wharf?'

Alys had a bright smile for her foster son's concern. 'God bless you, Matthew. I'd be glad of your company. Yes, you come with me and Rob can hold the fort here.'

'That's good of you, Matthew,' Hester said, getting a little revenge. 'But what a pity that you will miss my Papa!'

'And that's you told, Matthew,' Mia said smiling. 'We all know you'd rather face William of Orange's army than Hester's papa!'

WHITEHALL PALACE,
LONDON, WINTER 1688

Livia was wakened at midnight by a knock on the door.

'It's the Comte de Lauzun,' her maid whispered, scandalised that the French adventurer should be making calls in the middle of the night. 'He says he must see you. What is it, Madam? Has William of Orange come?'

'Go and fetch me some mulled ale from the kitchen,' Livia said to get her out of the way. 'Make sure that it boils well.'

She got up from her bed and stripped off her nightgown. Beneath it, she was dressed. She picked up her bag and seized her cape. The count, waiting outside, was relieved to see that she was ready. 'Wake the queen,' he told her. 'Tell her it's time.'

Livia went into the queen's rooms and found her Italian nurse and her lady-in-waiting frantically packing her bags. 'Aren't you done yet?' she said furiously. 'Only take her jewels and her furs. She can buy everything else new.' She strode in to wake the queen.

'Is my baby here?' were her first words.

'Yes, he's here, God bless him. Now quick – the count gave me this for you.' It was a plain black silk dress, with a thick cape and scarf.

'I am to dress as a servant?' the queen asked in horror.

'Lord Sunderland went disguised as a woman,' Livia said bluntly.

'Where's Father Petre? I won't leave him here.'

'He's gone.'

For a moment she did not understand the betrayal. 'What do you mean?'

'Run away. Abandoned you. They're all saving their own skins. The palace is almost empty.'

The queen was stunned into silence as Livia threw the gown over her head, tied the cape around her and pulled up the concealing hood. Livia ransacked the boxes in the bedroom and slipped jewels in her own pockets and tied a heavy purse of priceless rubies around her neck. 'Come on,' she said.

Quietly, the two women crept out of the room. The count bowed low when he saw the queen and led the way down the stairs to the nursery. The prince was fast asleep tucked in his nurse's arms; Lady Powis his lady governess, dressed like a scullery maid, exchanged one resentful look at Livia who had a better cape. Beckoning them to follow, Livia went after the count into the palace gardens.

It was bitterly cold, the frost white on the formal paths, the towering plant pots showing dark shadows of black ice. There was a shout of 'Halt!' and four guards raised their muskets.

'My family and servants,' the count said quickly.

Livia slid her hand in his arm and dropped her hood to smile at the guards. 'Please let us through,' she said. 'My services are no longer needed here, and we want to go home.'

The guard stood to one side. 'Take care,' he warned the count. 'The apprentices are tearing London apart and there are blockades at every crossroads to catch papists.'

'What do they do when they've caught them?' Lady Powis quavered.

The guardsman shrugged. 'They cut off a priest's arm to get the crucifix he was holding.'

'Let's go,' Livia whispered to the count, and he led the way. Glancing back, Livia saw the queen nearly fainting with fear, supported by Lady Powis. The nursemaid, carrying the baby in her arms, was behind them.

'There's our carriage,' the Comte de Lauzun whispered, as

they came through the garden gates, and saw a plain coach without arms on the door, drawn up for them, the blinds down in the windows.

'The king has come for me?' the queen exclaimed.

As soon as they opened the door, they saw it was empty. 'No, he sent it for you, Your Majesty,' the count said, helping her into a seat.

'Is he coming?'

'I don't know. He wouldn't say.'

'Will they kill him?' she whispered to Livia.

'No, no, he'll go back to the army,' Livia assured her. 'He'll lead them into battle.'

'Will the citizens kill us?'

'No, for we will take the road to Dover and our yacht is waiting for us there. The *Isabella*, your own yacht. Then we'll be safe.'

'Quickly!' the queen said. 'Quickly!' for the count was talking quietly to the driver. He stepped into the carriage and closed the door. Livia saw his face was grave. She clutched the queen's cold hand.

'I have bad news,' he told them. 'Dover Castle has been taken by the rebels. We can't sail from there.'

'William's army is at Dover?' Livia demanded incredulously.

'No. It's the townspeople. They've risen up and taken the castle and the town for William. Just like Portsmouth. I don't know about any other towns, but we should assume that nowhere is safe.'

The queen gave a little moan. 'What can we do?'

'Perhaps Rye?' The count turned to Livia. 'What ports are there on the east coast?' he demanded. 'Where might be loyal? This is not my country.'

'Nor mine,' she snapped.

Lady Powis let out a little moan of fear. 'Where can we go? We must go!'

Livia looked from one frightened face to another. No-one knew what they should do now that the coastal ports were turning against them. 'Southwark,' Livia said. 'I know a wharf there, and the captain of a ship.'

The count, nodded put his head out of the window and yelled: 'The stairs!' at the driver and the dark coach with the blinds down rocked over the cobbles through the darkness of Tothill Fields towards the Horseferry Stairs.

The count's boat, a low-lying punt, was moored at the stairs.

The river was high, the wind whipping the dark water into waves; rain came in scuds out of the darkness, and the queen flinched from the wet stairs and the little boat.

'Go on,' Livia said. 'Courage.'

Still the queen hesitated, but then there was a sound of many running feet and bobbing torches coming down Market Street behind them. They could hear the shouts and the smashing glass of windows. Mary Beatrice plunged down the stairs and stepped into the rocking boat and everyone followed. Dangerously over-loaded, the boat bobbed low in the water as the count took up the oars and rowed into the middle of the dark river. The water swirled around them; Livia saw torchlight on the north side and was glad to be away from capture; but they were still very far from the south bank. She felt the purse of jewels around her neck and thought it would be a cruel irony if they capsized and the weight of the queen's treasure pulled her down. The nursemaid shrank in fear and made the little craft tip. 'Sit still!' Livia snapped.

The count leaned forward and hauled on the oars, grunting with effort. Livia found she was gritting her teeth as they seemed to make no progress against the wind and the tide. Slowly, the south bank came closer, the steps, the ramp where they led the horses, and then the nose of the little boat juddered against the stone steps and Livia grabbed the iron ring set into the wall. She held it while the queen, the nursemaid with the royal baby, and Lady Powis climbed out, then the count tied off the boat and helped her up the stairs and jumped ashore himself. The rain suddenly swept down on them in an icy wind.

'I have a coach waiting at the Swan Inn,' the Comte de Lauzun said in Livia's ear. 'Wait here, I'll get them to bring it round.'

'She can't wait outside in this weather,' Livia objected.

'She can't be seen,' he replied and ducked under the archway into the yard.

The queen looked at Livia.

'Stay here,' she whispered.

They huddled in the lee of the church tower; the baby tucked under the nursemaid's cloak started to cry.

'He's got to be quiet,' Livia swore.

The nursemaid glared at her. 'How?'

A man came out of the inn, hat pulled down over his head to shelter him from the rain, and checked when he saw the four of them, hiding against the church wall. He turned and came towards them. The queen gave a little moan, certain that they would be discovered. Livia put her head down and started to run, like a servant getting out of the rain, dashed across the road, fell to the ground at his feet and brought him down as well. 'Oh!' she cried. 'I'm so sorry. I was running to get out of the rain, and I slipped. Did I hurt you? So clumsy of me!'

'No, no,' he said. 'But who's that over there —'

'My mistress waiting for her coach. Look! Your cloak's filthy. You must get it cleaned at once before it dries, I shall wash it for you myself!' she assured him. 'Go into the inn at once and I'll get it clean.'

He glanced towards the little party in the rain.

'Oh Lord!' Livia exclaimed. 'You can't see it. Quite dreadful. It looks as if you have soiled yourself. I'll come and wash it for you. Come. Come and get it off quickly.'

She pushed him before her and made as if she were following him, but as the coach came out from under the archway, she doubled back to open the door and bundle the nursemaid and Lady Powis into the coach and help the queen inside. Lauzun stepped in after them and told the driver to drive along the south bank to Southwark.

The coach jolted along the road, the queen rigid in one corner, her eyes fixed on the road ahead. She said quietly: 'There are men blocking the road.'

A wagon was drawn across the narrow road as a makeshift

barricade, the driver seated on the box, his horse with its head bent low against the driving rain. The coachman pulled up. 'Give way!' he bawled.

'Not to you!' the wagonner shouted back. 'Not to a coachload of papists!'

'Tell him you're an English lady going to Southwark.' Livia pushed Lady Powis towards the door and dropped the window for her to lean out.

'Why me?'

'All the rest of us sound foreign. You tell him!'

'I'm no papist,' Lady Powis quavered to the wagonner.

'Spit on the Pope!' came the yell.

'This is a betrayal!' the queen said, her eyes dark with horror. 'We are denying our faith and running from our kingdom. We are like Peter, denying Christ!'

'No we're not!' Livia desperately. 'We're staying alive for the next battle!'

'I will die rather than deny my faith.' She went to rise up, pushed Lady Powis from the window and went to declare herself.

Livia grabbed her by the waist and pulled her back into her seat. 'Sit down!' she hissed furiously.

The wagonner shouted at Lady Powis: 'Say cheers for William and Liberty!'

Livia laid hold of Lady Powis' wrist with a two-handed grip, and twisted it so the skin burned. 'Cheers for William and Liberty!' Lady Powis cried out in pain.

He laughed good-naturedly and pulled the wagon to one side to let them pass.

'Close the window, draw up the blind,' Livia hissed. 'Don't let him see her.'

The count hauled on the window strap and pulled down the blind on the queen's side, the carriage rocked and moved forward, past the flickering torch and the laughing dark face.

'There's a back yard,' Livia said to the count. 'A back yard to the wharf where they load the wagons. It's the last yard before Savoury Dock.'

The coach went slowly along Shad Thames Street, between the rows of wharves on the riverside and the poor houses behind them.

'Get out and lead the way,' the count said.

Livia hesitated.

'We can't make a wrong turn and get stuck,' he said shortly. 'If we get trapped in one of these alleys they could block the doors and burn us in the carriage.'

Just as she was about to argue, the bells of St Olave's began to toll, sounding an alarm, calling out the militia. Livia opened the door of the slowly moving coach and jumped down, ran before the horses and shouted: 'Follow me!' at the coachman on the box.

Ahead of her, at the quayside, she could see a ship but she could not tell if it was Captain Shore's *Sweet Hope*. She led the way right down the alleyway between the old Reekie warehouse and their new building. The gate to their yard was barred from the inside. Livia went through the lantern door and struggled with the heavy beam. Crying with rage she flung herself at it and levered it up to swing the big double gates open. The coach turned into the yard and the coachman pulled up the horses. Livia pushed the gates closed behind them, and dropped the beam into place with a sob of relief, as the light at the kitchen window showed that someone was home.

REEKIE WHARF, SOUTHWARK, LONDON, WINTER 1688

Alys and Captain Shore, together for the first time in many months, were in the warehouse, going through the accounts of the ship that they had unloaded together earlier in the day when they heard the tolling of the St Olave's bell calling out the militia.

'Trouble?' Captain Shore raised his sandy eyebrows to his wife.

She lifted her head to listen. 'Was that the yard gate?'

He got up from the table. 'Are the lumpers gone home?'

'Not yet, and your crew are eating their dinner on board before they go.'

'I'll check on the ship,' he said, going out to the quay as Alys took a lantern from the hook, went through to the kitchen, lit it from the fire and opened the kitchen door. Her gaze took in the carriage, the hooded women, the count letting down the stairs of the coach and putting out his hand to the lady getting out. He bowed as low as for a queen. The baby let out a cry as Livia came towards the door from barring the gate.

'What have you done now?' Alys demanded of Livia. 'What trouble have you brought to my door?'

'I can explain.' Livia surged towards Alys, holding out her hands. 'You are the only one who can save us,' she said in a quick undertone. 'I truly believe the mob will kill her, and the baby. We have to get them away.'

The lantern was steady in Alys' hands. 'You mean that my husband, Captain Shore, has to get them away.'

'Yes, yes, is he here?'

'He has just this day docked, and in this weather!'

'Then tell him not to dismiss the sailors and that he is to set sail again! At once! To France.'

'No,' Alys said steadily.

'Alys, I beg of you . . .'

'No.'

'You would have done it before! I could tell everyone that you would have sailed for her before. I could tell them that you are a papist yourself!'

Alys raised the lantern so that it swept the empty yard. 'No-one here but us,' she said simply. 'And I doubt you'd want to raise a mob, with her in my yard.'

The queen, white-faced, leaned on the count's arm.

'Please, Alys,' urged Livia. 'There's nowhere else for her to go.'

'And whose fault is that?' Alys demanded, goaded into anger. 'Who chose to camp a private army on Hounslow Heath? Who chose to attack the church? Who chose to close parliament? Who chose to hang half of the west country for following Monmouth? Fired a cannon into my own uncle's face? Ruined business?'

'Her husband! Not her! She's a woman, like you and I are women. We have to go where our husbands command; not where our heart is.' Livia came a little closer. 'I have only once lived free and followed my heart.' She pulled off her glove and put her cold hand on Alys' warm one. 'Once,' she said. 'With you.'

'You betrayed me, and took the man who loved my mother.'

'I made the worst mistake of my life,' Livia swore. 'But I missed you, Alys, every single day. I dreamed of you every night. You're the one person I ever truly loved. I will kneel at your feet, here in the rain, if you will only forgive me.'

'You can come out of the rain at any rate,' Alys said impatiently. 'But they have to stay outside. I'm not having them in the house.'

'Not in the house,' Livia repeated eagerly, following Alys into the kitchen and putting back her hood, her face alight with hope. 'Let's get them get straight on board, and Captain Shore can take them away.'

'You cause nothing but trouble!' Alys exclaimed.

Livia threw back her cloak and stepped very close to Alys, as if to whisper. Their lips were so close that if Alys had turned her head they would have kissed. 'Forgive me,' Livia breathed. 'Help me. And then I will be free to come to you.'

The kitchen door opened and Captain Shore came in and recoiled when he saw Alys and Livia, as close as lovers. 'Mrs Shore?' he said uncertainly.

Alys turned to him. 'You remember the Nobildonna,' she said coldly. 'She's here with the queen and the baby in the yard. They want you to sail them to France.'

'We'll die if you don't take us,' Livia said simply, stepping towards him, her beautiful face imploring his help. 'If William of Orange's army, or the mob gets hold of her, they'll hang her from a roof beam. We have to get her away.'

'What's wrong with the royal navy?' Abel Shore demanded.

'Traitors,' she said shortly. 'Scuppered their ships rather than sail for her. She has no friends. I don't speak for the king, but for her, and her innocent child.'

'If it is her innocent child?' Captain Shore said unhappily. 'I take no interest in it myself. I don't rightly know what should be done.' He looked at his wife. 'It's a bad business,' he said. 'I don't see why we should stick our finger in such a pudding.'

There was a scud of icy rain on the window. Livia took hold of Alys' hand. 'There's something I've not told you,' she said urgently.

To Captain Shore she said, 'Forgive me.' and drew Alys a little away from him and bent her head to whisper in her ear. Alys could smell the perfume on Livia's hair, a hint of roses that conjured the memory of nights in Livia's bed: her desire, her joy.

'It's Rob,' Livia said simply. 'Your brother. I'm so sorry, Alys, but he gave us the baby. I asked him to do it, and he gave us the prince.'

'It really is a changeling?'

Livia nodded. 'Yes. It's Rob's changeling. If we are captured, everyone will know that Rob gave us the baby. He'll be tried for treason if the mob don't get him first. He'll be hanged and drawn and quartered.'

Alys was white. 'Why would he do such a thing?'

'He loved me once,' Livia said. Her gaze on Alys' face was steady, irresistible. 'He did it for me. For love. You loved me once. Just save me, Alys. It's the last thing I'll ever ask of you. Let me get to France with the queen and the baby that Rob gave her, and I will never trouble you again.'

She could see Alys was weakening. 'You can't endanger Rob,' Livia pleaded. 'It would be a death sentence. And can you tell Matteo that I came to you for help and you let me, his own mother, be torn apart on your doorstep?'

Alys shook her head. Suddenly the tolling bell of St Olave's stopped ringing. The silence was more terrifying than the noise had been.

'What does that mean?' Alys turned to her husband.

But it was Livia who answered: 'Perhaps they are searching for us.'

'Take her,' Alys said, turning to her husband. 'To France if you can, anywhere. Please, Abel.'

He clapped his hat on his head. 'I'll get the ship readied,' he said. 'Tide's still high. Get them aboard and get rid of that carriage.'

Livia was out of the back door without another word, to command the coachman to back out and go home, to pull the travellers into the kitchen. 'We're not staying,' she said breathlessly to the queen. 'We're boarding at once.'

The queen, white-faced, turned to Alys. 'Thank you,' she said simply.

Alys nodded grimly. She took a loaf of bread from the larder and a round of cheese, a stone jug of small ale. 'You can take this,' she said to Livia and put it in a basket and pushed it into her hands. She threw a shawl over her head and went out of the room, down the hall and they heard the front door slammed by the wind as she stepped over the sill to the quay.

No-one said anything in the kitchen, the baby snuffled at the nursemaid's cape. They heard the front door open and Alys came in again. 'You can go aboard,' she said shortly. 'They've got a barge putting lines on.'

'Praise God,' said the count. He took Alys' hands and kissed both of them. 'I can never thank you enough,' he said.

The queen put out her hand. 'God bless you,' she said gently.

Alys did not curtsey as she should have done. She shook hands as if to an equal, and then she led the way to the quay, head down against the wind and the rain, and guided them up the gangplank. Livia turned to her when she was on the deck. 'Alys ...'

'I did love you,' Alys admitted. 'But I don't want to ever see you again.'

Livia kissed Alys gently on the mouth. 'I never deserved your love,' she said. 'I hope you will forgive me.' She went below as Alys turned to her husband who was shouting over the noise of the wind and the rain, to stand by the lines on the barge, and prepare to cast off.

'God speed. Calm seas and steady winds bring you safe home, Abel Shore.' she said, as she always did, as if nothing had changed and nothing could change between them.

'God bless you, Alys.' He stepped close to her and gave her a firm kiss on her mouth.

Alys went down the gangplank and stepped back as they ran it on board. The rain was easing off and the wind picking up; as the *Sweet Hope* got into midstream and Livia and her mistress, the Queen of England, and the royal baby set sail for France. Alys watched them go, expressionless.

BARBADOS, WINTER 1688

Rowan, Caskwadadas and young Wómpatuck sat with their feet in the creek, sweating and exhausted beside a massive fallen branch of a cedar tree. It had been sheered off the trunk by lightning. Rowan had found it further inland and the three of them had rolled and dragged it to the brink of a cliff where the creek poured in a waterfall to the sea below. Hidden by the thick forest the three of them had worked on the branch, trimming off the side branches and scraping off the thick bark. Next, they would shape it, giving it a bow and a stern, and then burn it out and carve out a rough scoop from the centre, deep and long enough for the three of them to sit, one behind each other, to paddle, one on each side.

Caskwadadas, from the north of the Dawnlands, had travelled far out to sea in the ocean-going dugout canoes all her life, and knew that it would take weeks, even months of work for the three of them to get the branch into seaworthy shape for a two-day journey. But she knew it could be done. They would wait for high tide, a high tide with a full moon and an onshore wind, when the sea at the foot of the cliff was at its deepest, to launch the canoe down the waterfall and into the sea.

'Men's work,' Rowan said, nudging the boy who laughed at her.

'I shall do it all on my own,' he told her. He showed her his callused palms, where the sharp stones they used for shaping the tree had blistered his hands.

'I shall sit in the canoe and you shall paddle me,' Rowan told him.

'Straight into the setting sun,' he promised gravely. 'Until we reach land.'

She nodded.

'Do you really think we will find our people?' he asked. 'My sisters that were sold as servants?'

'We may find them,' she said cautiously. 'I hope we do. We're not allowed to live together as a People, and we have no land of our own any more. But some of us have been enslaved on our old lands. We might be able to find your sisters and free them.' She looked at his troubled face. 'And I know of three Pokanoket who have survived; and will live on their lands again, and one of them will grow to be a man.'

'Me?' he said with his shy smile.

'You,' she confirmed. 'So the People of the Dawnlands will be home once more.'

They worked for a moment in silence.

'And we know that we will reach land?' he asked. 'We are sure?'

Rowan heard the anxiety in his voice and took up a twig and drew in the sandy earth beneath their feet, as Ned had drawn it for her. She showed Barbados as a teardrop shape, and the other islands as little dots in a semi-circle to the west, beyond that a sickle shape of land like a great bay. It was the map that Christopher Monck had shown Ned in faraway London. 'It looks like this,' she told him. 'If you were a frigate bird, up very high, looking down, you would see it like this.'

'Was it a frigate bird that told you?' he asked, completely seriously.

'One like a frigate bird,' she replied. 'One that sees a long way, and flies very true, and keeps faith. He has never told me a lie. I trust him. He told me that if we paddle west, we will make landfall. We will find our way home.'

REEKIE WHARF, LONDON, WINTER 1688

Ned, released from William's army, since it was clear that there would be no fighting, tapped on the back door of the warehouse. Tabs swung open the top half and saw him, with his pack on his shoulder, in the yard. 'God be praised!' she said. 'I was afraid it was papists.'

'No, just me.'

'God bless you, safe and sound again,' Tabs exclaimed. 'I'll tell Mrs Shore.'

She bustled to the warehouse and Alys came into the kitchen. 'Uncle Ned!' she hugged him and then stepped back to scrutinise his face, the weary slope of his shoulders, the dust from the road on his clothes. 'Are you safe? Were you with William of Orange's army?'

'Yes. We're disbanding, except for the regular troops who are going to control the city.'

'Thank God they're here at last. They put out a fire in Savoury Dock that could have ripped all through here. Is William come without a shot being fired?'

'Invited by the lords, and welcomed by the people,' Ned said. 'It's done. God be praised. It's done again. We have a leader who is here by consent, not by birth. One that will consult with the people and not tyrannise over us.'

She shook her head. 'I never thought I'd see it come all around again.'

'Me neither. I never thought I'd outlive the Stuarts.'

'You always kept the faith,' she conceded. 'You never faltered. Has the king really gone? William did not take him?'

'He made sure he did not! Last thing he wanted was to keep James Stuart in England. Besides, the old king had no stomach for it. He's fled to France after his wife. They'll get help there, but I doubt they'll ever get back.'

'She was here,' Alys told him quietly. 'The Nobildonna brought her again. Through the city, past all the riots. Captain Shore got her away, God bless him, he's not yet back. But we would've heard if they'd been caught at sea, wouldn't we? Abel will be safe?'

'They won't be caught at sea,' he said smiling. 'William of Orange is no fool. He doesn't want her or the king hanging around the palaces, arguing that they should still be on the throne, and people feeling regret, the baby in her arms and a royal christening. William wants them wasting their time and money in France, safely out of the way. If anyone met with the *Sweet Hope* they'll have turned a blind eye.'

'And no-one will accuse Captain Shore? It's my fault she came here, and it was me that begged him to take them away.'

Ned sat down heavily on one of the kitchen chairs. 'No lass. Never fear. No-one is going to accuse Captain Shore,' he said. 'He's done us all a favour. William is not looking for enemies, he's made a parliament from the old royalists and the new men, he marched under a banner of liberty, he didn't claim the throne until James ran away and left it empty. He didn't even claim it by conquest, it was the English lords who offered it to him. He's not going to persecute a loyal sea captain from a little wharf. He's blind to his enemies these first months, he won't see such as us.'

'So you've won,' she said wonderingly. 'In the end you won, without a shot being fired.'

'It's been a long battle,' he agreed. 'But at last we've got a fair man on the throne. We've got a king who will rule with parliament, according to the law of the land. A man can't be arrested on another's say-so, a woman cannot be snatched from her own field. We've not won against slavery, nor against greed, the rich are still more powerful than the poor. Not all men and women are equal before the law. It's not yet time to beat our swords into plough shares, and our spears into pruning hooks; sit every man under his vine and under his fig tree; and be not afraid. There is still injustice and cruelty. There's still greed. The struggle goes on.'

'Will it ever end?' she asked him. 'The struggle against the over-mighty?'

'Only when we choose it,' he told her. 'That's what I believe now. I've seen my country choose a godly Commonwealth, and I've seen us choose a king, and now I've seen us choose a king to rule alongside parliament. We can think right, we can do right. And when we choose liberty, and justice for all, we will have it.'

FAIRMERE PRIORY, SUSSEX, SUMMER 1689

The three girls, Hester, Mia and Gabrielle, were in the rose garden with a dish of flour, laughing at the preparations for seeing their future husbands on Midsummer Eve. Gabrielle alone was taking the ritual seriously: she had Alinor's receipt book and she was reading instructions to the others who were capering in the eerie light of the longest day, as Matthew came out of the house with the flour all over his face making him ghostlike and a kitchen broom in his hand making whooping noises.

'Shush! Shush!' Hester begged them. 'If my Mama looks out of her bedroom window and sees us up this late, she'll come down and send us to bed and we'll never know who we are to marry.'

'We'll never know anyway,' Mia said reasonably. 'You don't seriously think that this is going to work? That you're going to see the name of the man you will marry written in a plate of wheat flour?'

'Grandmother Alinor said . . .'

'She said that it was for fun not foretelling.'

'What's that noise?' Gabrielle asked.

'Did you hear a ghostly scream?' Mia laughed. 'I did! I'm sure I did!'

Matthew listened. 'Is that horses?'

'The headless horseman!' Mia cried out.

Hester gasped. 'I know there's no such thing.'

'Listen,' Matthew said. 'I can hear real horses. Coming up the drive.'

Gabrielle was still holding the bowl of flour and the plate for the fortune telling, Matthew still carrying the broom, as they made their way to the front of the house. A hired carriage was before the door, the roof piled with luggage.

'Wipe your face,' Gabrielle warned Matthew and he fell back and rubbed the flour from his face onto his sleeve.

'Is it Aunt Alys come back so soon?' Hester asked.

The footmen jumped down from the back, opened the door and let down the carriage steps. Matthew, still scrubbing flour from his forehead, recoiled when he saw his mother, the Nobildonna, step down from the carriage, shake the creases out of her rich silk skirts, push back the hood from her beautiful face and smile at their aghast faces. '*Allora!*' she remarked. 'You look as if you had seen a ghost.'

'*Signora Madre*,' Matthew stammered. '*Signora Madre*. I thought you went with the queen? Where have you come from?'

'From the royal court of King James, in exile at Paris,' she said, as if it were completely reasonable. 'I was with the queen, of course.'

'But Nobildonna, why have you come back?'

She turned to wave the footman to take the many bags into the house. 'My dear friend the queen does not need me at her side all the time,' she declared. 'In exile, you understand, without a court, on the goodwill of the French ... And no money ...'

The girls exchanged a hidden look. 'You tore yourself away?' Mia prompted.

'From the losing side,' Gabrielle whispered.

Livia turned her confident smile on them. 'Of course, I have long admired Princess Mary, the new queen. She will need to know how to go on, she has been away from England for so long! But more than anything, I could not leave my home here! My England! I could never be parted from my only child: my son.'

'Your home?' Matthew queried. 'Your England?'

'My Son,' she said fondly. '*Caro figlio!* Where else should I go? I have come home, to live here forever. I shall make a home for you, as your loving mother. I have returned to my beloved home: Fairmile.'

'It's Foulmire,' Gabrielle challenged her.

'Isn't it Fairmere?' Hester suggested. 'On the gates it says: "Fairmere".'

'Dear Hester!' she smiled. 'I should think I know the name of my own home! It is Fairmile.' She smiled at them, quite indifferent to the horror on their faces. 'It has always been Fairmile. I will put up new stone gates. Heavens! How happy we shall be!'

AUTHOR'S NOTE

Once again, a novel teaches me both history and emotional truth in the three years of its writing.

I could not have understood the twists and turns of English radical history without the help of authors, historians and museums. The book list which follows shows the writers who have taught me the most about the tragic history of English radicals including Monmouth and his followers, and I am indebted also to the Lyme Regis Museum, to the several TV programmes about the march, and especially to the Battle of Sedgemoor Visitor Centre at Westonzoyland and Bronwyn Fraley. The historians Elizabeth Bawdon and Richard Martin not only explained the battle to me on the ground, but they also alerted me to the continuing awareness of the Somerset exiles in Barbados.

The Barbados scenes were inspired by a visit to that most beautiful island, and especially a visit to Barbados Wildlife Reserve, Harrison's Cave, and to the museums in Bridgetown and St Nicholas Abbey plantation. The invaluable histories, journals and geographies are listed in the bibliography.

I could not have written this without the support and encouragement of the Pokanoket People, especially Po Wauipi Neimpaug, William Winds of Thunder Guy, Sagamore of the Pokanoket Nation; Po Pummukoank Anogqs, Tracey Dancing Star Brown, Sachem of the Pokanoket Tribe and her son Po Menuhkesu Mekenok, Don Strong Turtle Brown, Pokanoket Tribal Historian. And Quogqueii Qunnegk, Deborah Running

Deer Afdasta, First Council Person; Po Kehteihtukqut Woweaushin, William Winding River Brown, *Pinese*; and Po Popon Quanunon, Ryan Winter Hawk Brown, *Pinese* who greeted me at Montaup when I visited their historic homeland. Their desire to have some aspects of their story told, and their deep connection with their past was especially inspiring.

Dunstan Speight, librarian at Lincoln's Inn was so kind to show me around the library and historic grounds, and Malcolm Gaskill and Anne Murphy were both generous with their time, discussing the mechanics of early transfers of money.

Finally, I should like to thank my colleagues at Simon & Schuster in the UK and the US, and Victoria Atkins and Zahra Glibbery for their continuing and invaluable support.

BIBLIOGRAPHY

ENGLAND

Amussen, Susan Dwyer. *Caribbean Exchanges: Slavery and the Transformation of English Society, 1640–1700*. Chapel Hill: University of North Carolina Press, 2007.

Baer, William C. "Early Retailing: London's Shopping Exchanges, 1550–1700." *Business History* 49, no. 1 (2007): 29–51.

Brennan, Laura. *The Duke of Monmouth: Life and Rebellion*. Barnsley, UK: Pen & Sword History, 2018.

Brook, Timothy. *Vermeer's Hat: The Seventeenth Century and the Dawn of the Global World*. London: Profile Books, 2010. First published 2008 by Bloomsbury (New York).

Burgis, Simon. *A Full Answer to the Depositions; And to all other the Pretences and Arguments whatsoever, Concerning the Birth of the Prince of Wales. The Intreague thereof detect'd, the whole design being set forth, with the way and manner of doing it. Whereunto is annexed, A Map or Survey Engraven of St. James's Palace, and the Convent There: Describing the Place wherein it is supposed the true Mother was delivered: With the particular Doors and Passages through which the Child was convey'd to the Queen's Bed-Chamber*. First published London, 1689.

Carrel, Armand. *History of the Counter-revolution in England, for the Re-establishment of Popery, Under Charles II. And James II*. Miami, FL: HardPress, 2018. First published London, 1846.

Clarke, Nigel J. *Monmouth's West Country Rebellion of 1685*. Charmouth, UK: Nigel J. Clarke Publications, 2011. Kindle.

Coad, John. *A Memorandum of the Wonderful Providences of God to a Poor Unworthy Creature: During the Time of the Duke of Monmouth's Rebellion and to the Revolution in 1688*. Miami, FL: HardPress, 2013. First published London, 1849.

Douglas, Hugh. *Jacobite Spy Wars: Moles, Rogues and Treachery*. Stroud, UK: Sutton, 1999.

Field, Ophelia. *The Favourite: Sarah, Duchess of Marlborough*. London: Sceptre, 2003. First published 2001 by Hodder and Stoughton (London).

Frankopan, Peter. *The Silk Roads: A New History of the World*. London: Bloomsbury, 2015.

Gregg, Edward. *Queen Anne*. Yale English Monarchs. New Haven, CT: Yale University Press, 2014. First published 1980 by Routledge & Kegan Paul (London).

Grey, Ford. *The Secret History of the Rye-House Plot: and of Monmouth's Rebellion: Written by Ford Lord Grey, in MDCLXXXV.* Miami, FL: HardPress, 2018. First published London, 1754.

Haile, Martin. *Queen Mary of Modena: Her Life and Letters.* London: J. M. Dent, 1905.

Hibbert, Christopher. *The Marlboroughs: John and Sarah Churchill 1650–1744.* London: Penguin Books, 2001.

Holdsworth, Angela, ed. *A Portrait of Lincoln's Inn.* London: Third Millennium, 2007.

Hopkirk, Mary. *Queen over the Water: Mary Beatrice of Modena, Queen of James II.* London: John Murray, 1953.

Jordan, Don. *The King's City: London under Charles II: A City that Transformed a Nation – and Created Modern Britain.* London: Little, Brown, 2017.

Keates, Jonathan. *William III & Mary II: Partners in Revolution.* Penguin Monarchs. London: Penguin, 2015.

Keay, Anna. *The Last Royal Rebel: The Life and Death of James, Duke of Monmouth.* London: Bloomsbury, 2016.

Keay, John. *The Honourable Company: A History of the English East India Company.* London: HarperCollins, 1991.

Lemmings, David. *Gentlemen and Barristers: The Inns of Court and the English Bar 1680–1730.* Oxford: Clarendon Press, 1990.

Lincoln, Margarette. *London and the Seventeenth Century: The Making of the World's Greatest City.* New Haven, CT: Yale University Press, 2021.

Lindsay, Alexander. *A Memoir of Lady Anna Mackenzie: Countess of Balcarres and Afterwards of Argyll, 1621–1706.* Miami, FL: HardPress, 2019. First published Edinburgh, 1868.

Mackintosh, James. *History of the Revolution in England in 1688: Comprising a View of the Reign of James II. From His Accession, to the Enterprise of the Prince of Orange.* Miami, FL: Hardpress, 2018. First published London, 1834.

McNally, David. *Blood and Money: War, Slavery, Finance, and Empire.* Chicago: Haymarket Books, 2020.

Miller, John. *James II.* The English Monarchs Series. New Haven, CT: Yale University Press, 2000.

Morgan, Gwenda, and Peter Rushton. *Banishment in the Early Atlantic World: Convicts, Rebels and Slaves.* London: Bloomsbury Academic, 2013.

Oman, Carola. *Mary of Modena.* London: Hodder and Stoughton, 1962.

Paul, Herbert W. *Queen Anne.* Independently published, 2019. First published 1906 by W. Brown (London).

Peck, Linda Levy. *Court Patronage and Corruption in Early Stuart England.* London: Routledge, 2003. First published 1993 by Unwin Hyman (London).

Pepys, Samuel. *Diary of Samuel Pepys.* First published London, 1669.

Postrel, Virginia. *The Fabric of Civilization: How Textiles Made the World.* New York: Basic Books, 2020.

Roberts, George. *The Life, Progresses and Rebellion of James Duke of Monmouth & to His Capture and Execution: in Two Volumes.* Vol. 1. Miami, FL: HardPress, 2019. First published London, 1844.

Smith, Pamela H., and Paula Findlen, eds. *Merchants and Marvels: Commerce, Science, and Art in Early Modern Europe.* London: Routledge, 2013. First published 2002 by Routledge (London).

Stone, Peter. *The History of the Port of London: A Vast Emporium of All Nations.* Barnsley, UK: Pen & Sword History, 2017.

Trevor-Roper, Hugh. *The Crisis of the Seventeenth Century: Religion, the Reformation, and Social Change.* Indianapolis: Liberty Fund, 1967.

Van der Kiste, John. *William and Mary: Heroes of the Glorious Revolution.* Stroud, UK: Sutton, 2003.

Whitehead, Julian. *Rebellion in the Reign of Charles II.* Barnsley, UK: Pen & Sword History, 2017.

Woolrych, Humphry William. *The Life of Judge Jeffreys: Chief Justice of the King's Bench Under Charles II, and Lord High Chancellor of England During the Reign of James II.* Miami, FL: HardPress, 2018. First published 1827 as *Memoirs of the Life of Judge Jeffreys, Sometime Lord High Chancellor of England* by Henry Colburn (London).

NEW ENGLAND

Breslaw, Elaine G. *Tituba, Reluctant Witch of Salem: Devilish Indians and Puritan Fantasies.* New York: New York University Press, 1996.

Brooks, Lisa. *Our Beloved Kin: A New History of King Philip's War.* New Haven, CT: Yale University Press, 2018.

Calloway, Colin G., ed. *After King Philip's War: Presence and Persistence in Indian New England.* Reencounters with Colonialism: New Perspectives on the Americas. Lebanon, NH: Dartmouth College Press, 2000. First published 1997 by University Press of New England (Hanover, NH).

DeLucia, Christine M. *Memory Lands: King Philip's War and the Place of Violence in the Northeast.* New Haven, CT: Yale University Press, 2018.

Dunbar-Ortiz, Roxanne, and Dina Gilio-Whitaker. *"All the Real Indians Died Off" and 20 Other Myths about Native Americans.* Boston, MA: Beacon Press, 2016.

Fisher, Linford D. "'Why shall wee have peace to bee made slaves': Indian Surrenderers During and After King Philip's War." *Ethnohistory* 64, no. 1 (2017): 91–114. Accessed October 20, 2020. https://www.ncbi.nlm.nih.gov/pmc/articles/PMC5654607/.

Gaskill, Malcolm. *Between Two Worlds: How the English Became Americans.* Oxford: Oxford University Press, 2014.

Gookin, Daniel. "An Historical Account of the Doings and Sufferings of the Christian Indians in New England, in the Years 1675, 1676, 1677." Chap. II in *Transactions and Collections of the American Antiquarian Society.* Vol. II. Cambridge, MA: American Antiquarian Society, 1836.

Jordan, Don, and Michael Walsh. *White Cargo: The Forgotten History of Britain's White Slaves in America.* Edinburgh: Mainstream Publishing, 2011. First published 2007 by New York University Press (New York).

Kupperman, Karen Ordahl. *Indians and English: Facing Off in Early America.* Ithaca, NY: Cornell University Press, 2000.

Leach, Douglas Edward. *Flintlock & Tomahawk: New England in King Philip's War.* New York: Macmillan, 1958.

Lepore, Jill. *The Name of War: King Philip's War and the Origins of American Identity.* New York: Vintage, 1999. First published 1998 by Alfred A. Knopf (New York).

Moore, Jay, and Charles Rivers Editors. *King Philip's War: The History and Legacy of the 17th Century Conflict Between Puritan New England and the Native Americans*. Brookfield, WI: Charles Rivers Editors, 2016.

Newell, Margaret Ellen. *Brethren by Nature: New England Indians, Colonists, and the Origins of American Slavery*. Ithaca, NY: Cornell University Press, 2015.

Olexer, Barbara J. *The Enslavement of the American Indian in Colonial Times*. Milwaukie, OR: Joyous Publishing, 2005.

Schultz, Eric B., and Michael J. Tougias. *King Philip's War: The History and Legacy of America's Forgotten Conflict*. Woodstock, VT: Countryman Press, 1999.

Silverman, David J. *This Land Is Their Land: The Wampanoag Indians, Plymouth Colony, and the Troubled History of Thanksgiving*. London: Bloomsbury, 2020. First published 2019 by Bloomsbury (London).

Weatherford, Jack. *Indian Givers: How the Indians of the Americas Transformed the World*. New York: Crown, 1988.

———. *Native Roots: How the Indians Enriched America*. New York: Fawcett Books, 1992. First published 1991 by Crown (New York).

Wilbur, C. Keith. *The New England Indians: An Illustrated Sourcebook of Authentic Details of Everyday Indian Life*. Illustrated Living History. Guilford, CT: Globe Pequot Press, 1978.

BARBADOS

Armstrong, Eric. *A History of Money and Banking in Barbados, 1627–1973*. Kingston, Jamaica: University of the West Indies Press, 2010.

Beckles, Hilary McD. *The First Black Slave Society: Britain's "Barbarity Time" in Barbados, 1636–1876*. Kingston, Jamaica: University of the West Indies Press, 2016.

[Frere, George]. *A Short History of Barbados, from Its First Discovery and Settlement, to the End of the Year 1767*. Miami, FL: HardPress, 2018. Kindle. First published London, 1768.

Gragg, Larry. *Englishmen Transplanted: The English Colonization of Barbados 1627–1660*. Oxford: Oxford University Press, 2003.

Handler, Jerome S. "Escaping Slavery in a Caribbean Plantation Society: Marronage in Barbados, 1650s–1830s." *NWIG: New West Indian Guide / Nieuwe West-Indische Gids* 71, no. 3/4 (1997): 183–225.

Ligon, Richard. *A True and Exact History of the Island of Barbados*. Edited by Karen Ordahl Kupperman. Indianapolis, IN: Hackett, 2011. First published London, 1657.

Parker, Matthew. *The Sugar Barons: Family, Corruption, Empire and War*. London: Cornerstone Digital, 2011. Kindle. First published 2011 by Hutchinson (London).

Sloane, Hans. *A Voyage to the Islands Madera, Barbados, Nieves, S. Christophers, and Jamaica*. Legare Street Press, 2021. First published London, 1707.

Stuart, Andrea. *Sugar in the Blood: A Family's Story of Slavery and Empire*. London: Granta Books, 2012.

If you enjoyed *Dawnlands*,
discover more from bestselling
author Philippa Gregory

TIDELANDS

The first book in the *Fairmile* series

It is 1648 and the country is in the grip of a bloody civil war. The king is in exile and the people have learnt to keep their allegiances secret. In the tidelands of Sussex, where land and sea join together, the villagers are focused on survival and those who are different are regarded with suspicion.

Without a husband, Alinor is struggling to make ends meet. The villagers suspect her of possessing dark secrets and they watch her every move. When she meets James, a man of status who needs a place of refuge for the night, she risks everything to show him the hidden ways across the treacherous marsh, not knowing if she is leading a spy and an enemy into her life.

This is a time of witch mania, and with Alinor's fate inextricably linked to James, soon both their lives will be at stake . . .

AVAILABLE NOW IN PAPERBACK, EBOOK AND EAUDIO

SIMON &
SCHUSTER

DARK TIDES

The second book in the *Fairmile* series

**Midsummer Eve, 1670.
A turbulent time to seek the truth ...**

A wealthy man waits outside a poor London warehouse
to meet with Alinor, the woman he failed twenty-one years
before. He has everything to offer: money, land, status. He believes she has the only thing he cannot buy: his son and heir.

Meanwhile in New England, Alinor's brother
Ned cannot find justice in the New World, as the King's
revenge stretches across the Atlantic and turns the pioneers
against each other and against the American Indians.

Then, a beautiful widow, Livia, arrives from Venice. She claims
Alinor as her mother-in-law and has come with the news that
Alinor's son Rob has drowned in the dark tides of the lagoon.
But is this true or could this woman be an imposter ...?

**From London to New England and Venice, the dark tides
always rise, and with them come secrets and enemies ...**

AVAILABLE NOW IN PAPERBACK, EBOOK AND EAUDIO

**SIMON &
SCHUSTER**

THE
LADY OF THE
RIVERS

Cousins' War #3

Jacquetta, daughter of the Count of Luxembourg and kinswoman to half the royalty of Europe, was married to the great Englishman John, Duke of Bedford, uncle to Henry VI. Widowed at the age of nineteen, she took the extraordinary risk of marrying a gentleman of her household for love, and then carved out a life for herself as Queen Margaret of Anjou's close friend and a Lancaster supporter – until the day that her daughter Elizabeth Woodville fell in love and married the rival king Edward IV.

Of all the little-known but important women of the period, her dramatic story is the most neglected. With her links to Melusina, and to the founder of the house of Luxembourg, together with her reputation for making magic, she is the most haunting of heroines.

AVAILABLE NOW IN PAPERBACK, EBOOK AND EAUDIO

**SIMON &
SCHUSTER**

THE
WHITE
QUEEN

Cousins' War #1

Elizabeth Woodville, of the House of Lancaster, is widowed when her husband is killed in battle. Aided and abetted by the raw ambition and witchcraft skills of her mother Jacquetta, Elizabeth seduces and marries, in secret, reigning king, Edward IV of the family of the white rose, the House of York.

As long as there are other claimants to Edward's throne, the profound rivalries between the two families will never be laid to rest. Violent conflict, shocking betrayal and murder dominate Elizabeth's life as Queen of England, passionate wife of Edward and devoted mother of their children.

AVAILABLE NOW IN PAPERBACK, EBOOK AND EAUDIO

SIMON &
SCHUSTER

THE RED QUEEN

Cousins' War #2

Heiress to the red rose of Lancaster, Margaret Beaufort is sent to a loveless marriage in remote Wales. There, she gives birth to a son whom she names for the king, her cousin, Henry VI of England, fast sinking into madness.

Devoted in her belief that her House is the true ruler of England, Margaret feigns loyalty to the usurper King Richard III and masterminds one of the greatest rebellions of all time.

AVAILABLE NOW IN PAPERBACK, EBOOK AND EAUDIO

SIMON &
SCHUSTER

THE KINGMAKER'S DAUGHTER

Cousins' War #4

Anne Neville and her sister Isabel are daughters of the most powerful magnate in 15th century England. But Anne's life is overturned when her father turns on his former allies, escapes England and invades with an enemy army.

Widowed at fourteen, fatherless, with her mother locked in sanctuary and her sister a vengeful enemy, Anne faces the world alone. She plots her escape from her sister's house and finds herself a husband in the handsome young Duke of Gloucester, who she marries in secret. But danger still follows her.

AVAILABLE NOW IN PAPERBACK, EBOOK AND EAUDIO

SIMON &
SCHUSTER

THE
WHITE
PRINCESS

Cousins' War #5

Beautiful eldest daughter of Edward IV and
Elizabeth Woodville – the White Queen – the
young princess Elizabeth faces a conflict of loyalties
between the red rose and the white. Forced into
marriage with Henry VII, she must reconcile her
slowly growing love for him with her loyalty to the
House of York, and choose between her mother's
rebellion and her husband's tyranny.

Then she has to meet the Pretender, whose claim
denies the House of Tudor itself . . .

AVAILABLE NOW IN PAPERBACK, EBOOK AND EAUDIO

**SIMON &
SCHUSTER**

THE
KING'S CURSE

Cousins' War #6

As an heir to the Plantagenets, Margaret is seen by the king's mother as a powerful threat to the Tudor claim to the throne. She is buried in marriage to a Tudor supporter – Sir Richard Pole, governor of Wales – and becomes guardian to Arthur, the young Prince of Wales, and his beautiful bride, Katherine of Aragon.

Amid the rapid deterioration of the Tudor court, Margaret must choose whether her allegiance is to the increasingly tyrannical Henry VIII or to her beloved queen. Caught between the old and the new, Margaret must find her own way, concealing deep within her the knowledge that an old curse cast upon all the Tudors is slowly coming true . . .

AVAILABLE NOW IN PAPERBACK, EBOOK AND EAUDIO

**SIMON &
SCHUSTER**